Dear God in heaven. With a sob, she raced into his arms and they tightened protectively around her.

"Thank God you're all right," Brendan breathed against her tangled dark hair.

"Hold me, Brendan. Please don't let me go."

"I won't," he promised. "I won't let you go." He wouldn't let her go. He wasn't sure he could. He held her and let her cry and thanked Almighty God for giving him the strength to save her. He stroked her hair and whispered soothing words and felt her clutching the back of his neck. When she lifted her face to look up at him, he gently kissed her forehead. There were tears on her cheeks, so he kissed them, too.

Her bottom lip trembled. Brendan lowered his mouth in the briefest of touches. His hands came up to cradle her face. He kissed her eyes, her nose, then settled his mouth on her lips. It seemed so right he should kiss her, so achingly right.

"Silla," he whispered, his fingers delving into her thick mane of hair, his mouth tasting hers, seeking, coaxing. His hands stroked her skin, slid the strap of her chemise off her shoulder. "So lovely," he said, looking down at an upturned breast. "It fits my hand just perfectly."

Priscilla moaned softly, her body trembling with the last of her fear and the blaze of fiery sensations. *Dear God, what is happening to me?*

Kat Martin

Natchez Flame

BANTAM BOOKS

NATCHEZ FLAME
A Bantam Book

PUBLISHING HISTORY
Dell mass market edition published February 1994
Bantam reissue edition / December 2005

Published by Bantam Dell
A Division of Random House, Inc.
New York, New York

This is a work of fiction. Names, characters, places, and incidents
either are the product of the author's imagination or are used fictitiously.
Any resemblance to actual persons, living or dead, events,
or locales is entirely coincidental.

Bantam Books and the rooster colophon are trademarks
of Random House, Inc.

ISBN-13: 978-0-440-20805-1
ISBN-10: 0-440-20805-X

Printed in the United States of America
Published simultaneously in Canada

For the men in my life: the fabulous Martin boys, Mike, Mitch, Matt, and Monty. May you all find your dreams. For my husband, Larry, and my brother, Michael.

I love you guys. Life wouldn't be nearly as much fun without you.

CREOLE FIRES

"Martin dishes up a tasty dish of sizzling passion and true love, then serves it with savoir faire."
—*Daily News* (Los Angeles)

"Kat Martin's finest romance to date. This is a warm, emotional love story that will enchant readers."
—*Romantic Times*

"The heat of passion between Nicki and Alex is skillfully alluded to and pulsates throughout this exciting story. Another tumultuous story from Ms. Martin."
—*Rendezvous*

"Kat Martin consistently entertains the reader . . . *Creole Fires* is rich in its content and characters . . . Kat Martin has a way with characters that leaves me feeling like I've made new friends."
—*Inside Romance*

"Fast-paced adventure and lively romance. . . . Moves along quickly—a good page-turner."
—*The Time Machine*

Bantam Dell Books by Kat Martin

CREOLE FIRES

SAVANNAH HEAT

NATCHEZ FLAME

Chapter 1

Galveston, Texas
July 20, 1846

Lord in heaven, what have I gotten myself into this time? Priscilla Mae Wills stood at the rail of the steamship *Orleans* surveying the scattered wooden buildings, weathered and unpainted, and the unkempt, seedy-looking men who lined the dock of the strand.

In the distance, the dirt streets of Galveston bustled with activity, wagons heavy with bales of cotton rumbling toward the wharf, men and animals clattering along in confusion. Puddles of mud still dotted the road from a recent summer rain.

Though the rest of the passengers had already departed, Priscilla searched the long wooden dock for the hundredth time, hoping against hope that Barker Hennessey, the man sent to meet her, had discovered the *Orlean's* early arrival and might yet appear.

You're a grown woman, Priscilla. You can do this on your own. But in all her twenty-four years she'd never traveled by herself, and even with her Aunt Madeline had never gone far from home. And she'd certainly never expected the newly formed state of Texas to be this untamed.

Bedraggled and wind-chafed and tired clear to her bones, Priscilla scanned the dock in search of anyone who might be Barker Hennessey. Several brown-skinned Mexican men singing in Spanish strolled past, but no one that her fiancé could possibly have sent to meet her.

Forcing a stiffness into her spine, she stepped off the wharf onto the wide dirt streets. A hot, muggy breeze whipped the dark brown skirts of her service-able cotton day dress, and with every weary step the stiff white ruffle around the neck scratched the soft white skin beneath her chin. Strands of dark brown hair had come loose from the tight chignon hidden at the back of her bonnet and whipped tauntingly in the wind.

Priscilla glanced up the street. The sign for the Galveston Hotel and Saloon gleamed red and white in the hot July sunshine beside another large painted sign advertising Samuel Levinson's Bath House. Barker Hennessey, the man her fiancé, Stuart Egan, had sent to escort her on the final leg of her journey, would look for her at the hotel once he discovered her ship had come in.

And someone from the hotel could fetch the heavy steamer trunks that contained her trousseau: the finely crafted dresses she had carefully sewn over the past few weeks, as well as the doilies and linens and dainty embroidered tablecloths she had stitched and laid in her hope chest throughout the years.

Determined to ignore the heat and the tightly laced stays of her steel-ribbed corset, Priscilla walked the bustling dirt streets. Weathered batten-board struc-tures crouched beside a few sturdy establishments built of pinkish-white stone.

The hotel was by far the best-looking building in

town, she thought as she drew near. At least the paint wasn't peeling and the walk in front had been swept clean. It was a far cry from Cincinnati, with its sophisticated brownstones, elegant restaurants, and lavish opera houses. Still the thought of being inside, out of the blistering sunshine, made her quicken her pace.

That's when she noticed the commotion out front. A crowd had gathered, grumbling among itself, then seemed to be backing away.

"Look, Jacob—ain't that Barker Hennessey?" a slender man in a red-checkered shirt asked the small man beside him. The name registered immediately, and Priscilla glanced toward the big-boned man at the opposite end of the porch.

"That's him, all right," Jacob said. "Barker's madder'n a wet hen 'cause he lost his poke to some gambler."

Gambling, Priscilla thought, feeling sorry for the big strapping man in the black felt hat who stood in front of the swinging double doors to the saloon, *the devil's own sport*. But hearing his name, she also felt a wave of relief that she had found him so easily.

"Excuse me, please." Nudging her way through the crowd, she headed for the porch, intent on catching Mr. Hennessey before he got away. With her mind on the coming introduction, it took a moment for her to realize he was speaking.

"You're a cheat and a liar!" Hennessey called out just as she stepped on the boardwalk. "I want my money back, Trask, and I aim to get it!"

At the angry tone of his words, Priscilla swung her

gaze toward the object of his wrath, the tall, broad-shouldered man standing right beside her.

"I won that money fair, and you know it," Trask said.

"Mr. Hennessey!" Priscilla called out, waving a white-gloved hand and starting in his direction.

"Goddamn it!"

Priscilla felt the tall man's hand on her arm, his grip so hard it made her flinch. His free hand slapped against the leather holster tied to one long leg. She saw the bluish flash of metal, heard the deafening roar of gunfire. Whipping her head toward Barker, Priscilla breathed the acrid smell of burnt powder and stared in horror at the opposite end of the porch.

Barker Hennessey's eyes remained open, his mouth gaping wide in an expression of astonishment. He swayed on his feet while his sausage-sized fingers clutched the still-smoking pistol in his hand. Only a trickle of blood ran from the small round circle that marked the entrance of the tall man's bullet—centered squarely between his eyes.

Watching Hennessey crumple to the porch, Priscilla wet her suddenly dry lips. Her mouth moved as she tried to say the words that hovered at the corners of her mind, but no sound would come. Her ears buzzed and her knees felt weak. The images on the porch suddenly blurred and jumbled.

Heart hammering, she swayed toward the man named Trask whose painful grip seemed the only thing holding her up. His angry blue eyes fastened on her face just seconds before her lids flickered closed, the world tumbled sideways, and Priscilla sank into darkness.

"Jesus Christ, what next?" Brendan Trask swung the slender young woman up into his arms and stepped off the boardwalk onto the street.

"Nice shootin'!" Jacob Barnes called out to him as he strode toward the shade of an oak tree that grew beside the watering trough just half a block away.

"You'd better get the sheriff," Brendan called back without breaking his long-legged stride.

"She all right?" the little man asked, catching up and trying to keep pace without running.

"Just fainted. She's lucky she didn't stop a bullet." Brendan recalled all too clearly the moment she'd started to step in front of him. He glanced down at the small round hole in the full white sleeve of his shirt.

The man followed his gaze. "Lucky ain't the half of it."

"Get the sheriff," Trask reminded him.

"Sheriff got hisse'f kilt last week. I'll see if'n his deputy's down at Gilroy's Saloon." The man scurried off to find the law, though Brendan figured what little there was had probably already been summoned. Galveston might be the wildest port on the Gulf, but a shooting was a shooting, and Barker Hennessey worked for one of the most powerful men in the country.

"Damn." Brendan said the word beneath his breath, wishing he could have avoided the killing, but Hennessey had left him no choice. He just hoped to hell there wouldn't be trouble.

He'd had enough of that already.

Brendan propped the lady against the trunk of the oak tree, noting her somber brown dress, high-necked and long-sleeved, and the tiny waist pulled tight by her corset. Clothes like that in this heat—no wonder she'd fainted. Sometimes women didn't have the sense God gave a mule.

Shaking his head at life's little absurdities, Brendan walked to the old stone trough where a young boy watered several horses. The animals nickered and blew, sucking in great gulps of the cool reviving liquid.

"Guess I missed all the fun," the youth said, a boy of about fourteen. He looked down at the gun riding low on Trask's hip, unlike the pistols of most men, who wore theirs at the waist, and noted the flap that had been cut away from the heavy leather holster for easier access.

He puffed out his chest. "Been savin' my money for a gun of my own. Someday I'll be able to shoot like that. Man don't have to clean stalls and tend horses, he kin shoot like that."

Brendan flashed him a look that made him take a step backwards and melted his cocky half-smile. "Better to be cleaning stalls than lying out there in the street. That dead man could just as well have been me—someday it probably will be. You'd best think on that, son."

Turning away from the boy, Brendan dipped his handkerchief into the water, wrung out the excess, and returned to the base of the oak tree. He untied the woman's bonnet strings and pressed the wet cloth against her forehead.

At the sound of a soft moan, he wet her dry lips. They were full, he noticed, and a delicate shade of pink. Her features held a trace of that same fragility:

slim, straight nose, fine chestnut eyebrows, thick dark lashes. She wasn't really a beauty, but she was definitely attractive.

He thought of Patsy Jackson, the woman he'd spent the night with. He remembered her full ripe curves, red-painted mouth, and fun-loving warmth in bed. There was nothing frail about Patsy, nothing prim or proper. She was the kind of woman who could pleasure a man, have a rollicking good time in bed, but didn't give you trouble in the morning.

Not like this one. This little miss would probably pass out again just thinking about what he had done to Patsy last night. Pretty as she was, she held little appeal for him. Brendan liked his women lusty.

Still, in a town where men outnumbered women a dozen to one, she'd undoubtedly be considered quite a catch. He wondered which man she belonged to— and why that man hadn't the good sense to keep her out of trouble.

She moaned a second time, and her lids fluttered open. Warm-brown, gold-flecked eyes looked up at him in confusion. Brendan shoved his broad-brimmed hat back on his head and assessed her pale oval face. If he hadn't spotted her from the corner of his eye, she'd probably be dead right now. The thought sent a shudder down his spine, and a bit of his anger returned.

"Lady, you are some piece of goods." The words came out a little harsher than he had intended. "What the hell did you think you were doing? Don't you know any better than to stroll into the middle of a gunfight?"

"Gunfight?" she repeated, looking more confused

than ever. Her pretty face paled even more. "Mr. Hennessey," she said, sitting up straighter, "is he . . . is he . . . ?"

"Barker picked that fight, not me. I won his money fair and square, and I shot him in self-defense."

"Oh, dear," she said, looking ready to faint again. Her dainty pink tongue wet her lips. "I don't feel very good. I think I'm going to be sick."

"Oh, no, you don't—" Brendan pressed the cool wet cloth against her brow. "Just lean your head back and try not to think about it."

The woman swallowed hard and closed her eyes. Eventually the color returned to her cheeks, and he noticed again how pretty she was. Catching the glitter of the sun on wisps of shiny dark hair beside her cheeks, he wondered what the heavy mass would look like freed from her wide-brimmed, coal-scuttle bonnet.

"Thank you," she said softly, taking the cloth from his hand. "I'm feeling a little better now."

Brendan felt a wave of relief, until an unpleasant thought occurred. "Barker wasn't your husband, was he?" Until that moment it hadn't crossed his mind that a man like Hennessey could have a wife. Especially such a young and tender one.

She shook her head. "No. He's the man my fiancé sent to escort me on to his ranch." Her bottom lip trembled. "I never met him before, but he looked like a nice enough man."

Brendan's face went taut. "There wasn't a nice bone in Barker Hennessey's body. He'd have killed me without a second thought if I hadn't shot him first."

Priscilla chewed on that for a while and took a long assessing look at the man who squatted with easy grace on the stiff salt grass beside her. His hair was as dark as hers, but a richer, warmer shade of brown, and he wore it longer than he should have. Several day's growth of beard roughened a rugged jawline, but his mouth curved nicely and his eyes, a light shade of blue, watched her with a look of concern that melted away the fear she should have felt.

How could that be? she wondered. He'd just killed a man—a man whose help she desperately needed. He was a gambler and a gunman, yet there was an honesty about him, a sense of compassion—and something else she couldn't quite name. Something that told her the words he spoke were true.

"Does that mean the sheriff won't arrest you?"

"Not as long as he learns the truth," he said with sincerity.

Priscilla had always had a knack for judging people. Since she was a girl, she could size a person up in only a meeting or two. On making a new acquaintance, Aunt Maddie often asked her opinion, though she never admitted Priscilla's assessment actually mattered.

And this man *had* saved her life—probably at considerable risk to his own.

He took her hand and helped her climb shakily to her feet. Priscilla clutched his arm to steady herself and felt the flex of muscle beneath his shirt. Though she stood taller than the average woman, Trask towered above her, his wide shoulders blocking the hot yellow rays of the sun. Hard-edged, unkempt, and rugged though he appeared, even in his worn homespun shirt and frayed blue twill breeches he was handsome.

When he discovered her watching him, Priscilla flushed and glanced away. "I . . . I can't believe Stuart would have sent the kind of man you describe here to meet me. We would be traveling together and I don't think—"

"This is rough country, Miss . . . ?"

She swung her gaze to his. "Wills. Priscilla Mae Wills, and I believe your name is Trask."

He nodded. "Where did you say you were headed?"

"Rancho Reina del Robles—the Triple R. Stuart Egan is my fiancé."

Trask's hard features closed up. There was an edge to his voice that hadn't been there before. "That explains Hennessey—he's Egan's right-hand man."

"Then you know Stuart?"

He shook his head. "No, but I've heard of him. Most folks 'round these parts know who he is. Why didn't Egan come for you himself?"

"Apparently he was short-handed. The ranch is quite large, you know."

"So I've heard." Something flickered in his light blue eyes. "I'll have someone get word to him and he can fetch you home."

Priscilla's dark brows shot up. "But that would take weeks! I can't stay here—"

She felt his hand on her arm, halting her protest and urging her back toward the hotel.

Priscilla let him lead her, trying to gather her thoughts. From what Stuart had written, the ranch was still quite some distance away. It would take weeks for a letter to reach it and just as much time for Stuart to come, or send someone to get her. In the meantime she'd be alone in this wild Texas town. A place where people got shot in the streets! She had only enough money for a few days lodging and food —what would she do after that?

As they approached the hotel, Priscilla surveyed the porch in dread, expecting to see Barker Hennessey's lifeless body sprawled on the boardwalk among a crowd of onlookers. Instead only a handful of men lounged beside the door of the saloon. The plinkity plink of a cheap piano and the high-pitched sound of women's laughter seemed almost sacrilegious in light of what had just happened.

The scraping of a chair drew her attention.

"Where'd you get the new gal, Trask?" one of the rough-looking men called out. "Looks like a real little lady—you always did have a way with the women." The other two men guffawed, obviously well into their cups though the day was still quite early.

Trask ignored them, but his grip on her arm grew tighter.

Another man stepped through the swinging double doors. "Didn't think ya liked your women so proper, Brendan." The red-haired man swept her with a glance so raw it left no doubt as to what he was thinking. "This little gal's so gussied up it'll take half the day just to get her clothes off." Priscilla's face grew hot and her feet refused to move another step.

"Leave her be, Jennings," Trask warned. "And that goes for the rest of you men, too." He urged her on, and Priscilla forced her feet to move ahead.

She'd come by steamboat down the Ohio, down the Mississippi all the way to New Orleans. She'd traveled to Galveston by steamship, her stomach tied in knots and hating every moment on the sea. She'd sold everything she owned to come west, to marry a man she had never even seen. But nowhere had she encountered men like these.

"Deputy's expectin' you in his office," the one called Jennings said. He grinned and cocked his head toward the hotel. "Better not take too long."

As his meaning hit home, Priscilla's step faltered once more. She fought to keep her eyes straight ahead, but lost the battle and glanced again at the men. *They probably eat boiled harness for breakfast,* she thought, noting the greasy canvas breeches, shaggy unkempt hair, and the scraggly growth of beard on one. How would she survive the next few weeks alone in a place like this?

Trask tugged her forward, his grip a little harder than it should have been. "Town's full of men like these," he said roughly. "What the hell was Egan thinking, letting you come out here alone?"

"He didn't know I was coming alone," Priscilla defended, beginning to get angry herself. "My aunt died rather suddenly and . . . well . . . there were expenses I hadn't planned on. I couldn't afford to bring a lady's maid, not that it's any of your business."

"Where you from, Miss Wills?" Trask shoved open the door to the lobby, ringing the bell, and held it so she could walk past.

"I was born in Natchez, but I was raised in Cincinnati. As I told you, I was on my way to join my fiancé, which, thanks to you, has just become an exceedingly difficult task." Priscilla felt like crying. *Difficult* was hardly the word.

"I suppose you'd prefer I let him shoot me."

"Maybe. Maybe I would at that." Shoulders thrown back, Priscilla marched up to the desk where a green-visored clerk leaned over a huge leather-bound guest book.

"I'd like a room, please, and I need someone to obtain my trunks from aboard the steamship *Orleans*."

The gray-haired clerk eyed her from top to bottom. "You ain't by yourself, are you?"

"Well, yes . . . I . . ." Priscilla lifted her chin. "My traveling companion fell ill some ways back. I was forced to continue alone." She glanced at Trask, daring him to contradict, and found his mouth curved up in amusement.

"This is a respectable hotel, miss. You look proper enough, but . . . well, let's just say if you're plannin' anything different, you'd best be headin' next door."

Priscilla flushed crimson. *Dear God, what kind of people are these?* "Surely you aren't implying—"

"Get the lady a room," Trask ordered, stepping closer to the desk, "and be quick about it." The little man swallowed and shoved the guest book in her direction.

"Yes, sir, Mr. Trask. Sign here, ma'am." Dipping the quill pen in the inkwell near her elbow, he handed it to Priscilla, and she signed her name in graceful blue letters.

"How long will you be stayin'?" the clerk asked.

She studied the sign on the wall behind him and

chewed her bottom lip. Even at the modest rate posted, she couldn't stay more than four days.

"I . . . I'm not really certain." She'd expected Barker Hennessey to see to her needs until she reached the Egan ranch. She clutched her reticule tighter, wondering what in heaven she would do when her four days had ended.

"She'll be here at least three weeks," Brendan told the desk clerk. "It'll take that long to get word to her people and for them to come get her."

Priscilla swallowed hard. "That . . . that isn't exactly correct," she said. "As I said before, I'm not quite sure how long I'll be here." If only she could find someone to take Mr. Hennessey's place. She could reach the Triple R as they had planned and Stuart wouldn't have to be burdened.

Priscilla glanced at Trask, who appeared ready to argue, and felt a jolt of inspiration that seemed almost divine.

Trask! Trask could do it! He was obviously well suited for the arduous journey. He had shot Hennessey, the tough man sent to protect her, he could take Hennessey's place. In fact, it was only fitting—Trask should be the one to take her. He owed her that much.

She flashed him the brightest smile she could muster, which under the circumstances, wasn't all that much. "Do you think Mr. Hennessey booked passage in advance for our journey to Corpus Christi?"

"Probably. But I'm sure they'll be happy to refund the money."

"How far is it from there to the Triple R?"

"From what I know of it—and I've never been

there—I'd say a good four-day ride over some very rough country. Why?" he asked warily.

"Surely you can see, Mr. Trask, the obvious solution is for you to escort me. It could take weeks for word to reach Stuart. It would take time for him to make travel preparations and time to make the trip here. I, on the other hand, am packed and ready to leave."

"No," he said simply.

"Why not? Since you're the man who . . . who . . . posed this particular problem, you are obviously the man who should solve it."

Trask shook his head. "Not a chance, Miss Wills. You're Egan's problem, not mine. Besides, I'll be leaving Galveston at dawn. I've got a job waiting for me on the Brazos."

Priscilla clutched the folds of her skirt, determined he would not see her cry. "What kind of a job, Mr. Trask? Some sort of hired gun—or do you plan to make your money gambling—foxing weaker people out of theirs?"

Trask's look turned hard, his lips becoming a thin grim line. "As a matter of fact, I plan to do a little bit of both."

"You owe me, Mr. Trask. Barker Hennessey was here to protect me. Who's going to protect me now?"

Good question, Brendan thought, for she had just voiced the problem that had been plaguing him since the moment he'd discovered she was alone. Who the hell would look after her? Egan had chosen well with Hennessey. For all his faults, Barker was loyal to Egan and tougher than a cob. Now, thanks to Hennessey's too-quick temper, the woman was left with no one.

He glanced in her direction, saw the worry she tried to conceal—and a surprising amount of determination. She wasn't as young as she'd first appeared, but she was still damned well naive, determination or no. She'd nearly gotten killed her first five minutes on the street. With the sheriff out of the way, and considering the kind of women they were used to, those bastards next door wouldn't think twice about dragging her off for a little fun and games.

"Goddamn it," Brendan swore, feeling his resolve begin to weaken, "this isn't my problem."

Priscilla spun on him in outrage. "Don't you dare blaspheme! If you hadn't been gambling in the first place, none of this would have happened. Mr. Hennessey would still be alive, and I'd be safely on the way to my fiancé."

"There's not a damn thing safe about the country you'll be crossing on the way to the Triple R. And I'll damn well swear if I want to!"

"I believe you have an appointment with the law, Mr. Trask," she said with a haughty little tilt of her chin. "Surely the sheriff will have something to say about what happened to poor Mr. Hennessey. Thank you for your assistance, and good day." She whirled toward the man behind the counter, but Brendan caught her arm.

"I told you I shot him in self-defense."

"You shouldn't have been gambling. It's a sin, just like swearing. Now Mr. Hennessey is dead, and I'm stranded in the middle of nowhere with no money and no way to get to my fiancé.''

"No money? What do you mean 'no money'? Surely Egan gave you the money to get here.''

Her cheeks turned pink and she looked as if she wanted to cut out her tongue. "Mr. Egan offered, I refused. I've never even met the man, I wasn't about to accept his money.''

"You've never met him?''

"We've been corresponding, of course, and my Aunt Maddie had met him.''

Brendan turned toward the man at the counter, dug into his pocket, and tossed the man a coin. "Have someone fetch the lady's trunks up to her room.'' He turned back to Priscilla. "I'll pay for your stay. Egan will come for you, and everything will be just fine.''

"Not on your life. I wouldn't accept Stuart's money; I certainly won't take yours.''

"This is Hennessey's money. He would have used it to get you to Egan so in a way it belongs to you.''

She chewed her bottom lip and Brendan thought how soft and pink it looked, how delicate she looked all over.

"If I do take the money, I'll just use it to hire someone else to take me.''

"The hell you will. You're staying here. I'll pay for the room in advance if I have to.''

"I'm not your prisoner, Mr. Trask. Somehow I'll find a way to get to Stuart—with or without your help.''

Brendan eyed her from top to bottom. She was a fiery little thing when she got riled up—she just might try it. "You saw those men out there. Where you gonna find somebody you can trust?"

"There's got to be someone. If Stuart's as well known as you say, there's bound to be someone who'll take me to him. Stuart can pay him when we get there."

"You're bluffing. You'd probably faint again if one of those men came near you." *But what if she wasn't?* What if she was crazy enough to try it? The likes of Conway Jennings would chew her into little bitty pieces—after he and his cronies pleasured themselves with her soft little body.

Damn her! "This is blackmail, Miss Wills, and I don't like it one damned bit." Grabbing her arm, he tugged her toward the door.

Priscilla let him lead her. "Where are you taking me?"

"I've got an appointment with the law, remember? You happen to be a witness. You can tell the deputy what happened—how I shot Hennessey in self-defense—and on the way we can discuss our trip."

"I didn't see that much." Just a blur of images, a flash of crimson, then darkness. Priscilla stopped short. "Does this mean you're taking me?"

"It's beginning to look like I've got no choice."

She still didn't budge. "Why?" she asked warily.

Brendan almost smiled. "Probably because I'm crazy. But you're right about one thing. Hennessey's dead and I'm the man who killed him. In a way that makes me responsible for you. Egan might not get your letter for weeks. In the meantime anything could happen." *And probably would.*

"I'm sure Stuart will reimburse you for your trouble."

"Word reaches him about Hennessey's death before we get there, he'll probably shoot me on sight." Brendan tipped her chin up. "You realize you'll be traveling with a stranger—a man who just killed another man right in front of you."

Priscilla searched his face. "I trust you, Mr. Trask."

"You don't even know me. Why the hell would you trust me?"

"I have my reasons."

"Such as?"

Priscilla flushed but didn't look away. "You've got kind eyes."

"Kind eyes?" he repeated, incredulous. "You trust me because of my eyes?"

"That's right."

Brendan shoved his hat back on his head and looked at her with a mixture of amazement and frustration. "Then, Miss Wills, I guess I'd better take you. Any woman who's that big a fool hasn't got a chance in a town like this."

Chapter 2

 The trip to the sheriff's office resulted in a few heated words when Priscilla refused to confirm Trask's story. Of course, she didn't deny it either.

"I told you before, I saw very little of what happened."

"How could you have missed it?" Trask glowered down at her, long fingers clamped on a pair of narrow hips. "You were standing damned near between us!"

"You can relax, Trask," the deputy put in. "We don't need your lady-friend's word. We've had half a dozen people in here telling us Barker drew first."

Though Trask stood a few feet away, Priscilla could feel the tension ebb from his body.

"Then I guess we'll be leavin'." He settled his hat on his head and pulled it low on his brow.

"I don't like your kind, Trask," Deputy Grigson warned. "Why don't you do us all a favor and clear outta town?"

Trask turned a hard look on Priscilla. "Miss Wills has seen to that. We'll be leaving on the first ship headed for Corpus Christi."

"That'd be the *Windham*. She steams outta port in the morning."

"Good-bye, Deputy Grigson," Priscilla said, extending a white-gloved hand.

"You take care, little lady." The lanky older man accepted her handshake, but didn't offer to help her, and he didn't say anything more to Trask. In truth, it appeared the deputy was a good bit afraid of him.

"It seems your reputation precedes you, Mr. Trask," Priscilla said, once they were back on the street.

"What's the matter, Miss Wills, your 'kind eyes' theory beginning to fall a little flat?"

As Priscilla stepped off the boardwalk, her foot hit a stone and she stumbled. Trask's sure grip stayed her fall. One hand circled her waist to steady her and she felt the same strength and gentleness she had noticed before.

"I've no doubt you're a man to be reckoned with," she told him. "I wouldn't trust you to get me there if you weren't. But trust you I do, and unless you do something to change that, I'll expect you to call for me in time to make our morning departure."

Trask worked a muscle in his beard-roughened jaw and opened his mouth to speak.

"And don't you dare blaspheme!"

Trask just grinned. "I wouldn't dream of it, ma'am," he drawled. Some of the hardness left his face, and for a moment he looked almost boyish.

She wondered how handsome he'd be clean-shaven, his tanned skin and sensuous mouth more clearly revealed. At the wayward thought, Priscilla's heart began to pound. When they reached the lobby of the hotel and he turned to walk away, Priscilla's eyes drifted down to a pair of hard-muscled hips in snug blue twill breeches. She watched the movement of his long sinewy legs, caught herself in horror, and started praying he'd stay just as rough-looking as he was.

Priscilla paced the hotel lobby, a large, homey room with a big rock fireplace at one end. Hand-hewn chairs with overstuffed needlepoint cushions sat in friendly clusters, and several guests, all of them men, sat quietly talking and smoking. The sun had been up for the past half hour, and still Brendan Trask had not arrived.

Had she been that wrong about him? He'd said he had a job waiting for him on the Brazos. Maybe he'd changed his mind and headed in that direction. *Lord in heaven, what will I do if he's gone?* She'd paid her hotel bill, but had little money to spare. If he didn't show up, she would have to get word to Stuart and find some sort of work to do in the meantime.

She could always take in mending; she was a very good seamstress. Surely with all the men in town and so few women there would be something she could do to earn her board and keep.

Priscilla looked down at her hands. They were slender and graceful, but work-roughened and a little bit calloused. Taking care of her aunt had certainly not been easy. Not with money a problem and no one to help with the cooking or cleaning. Her invalid aunt had been a handful and then some.

"This floor needs polishing," Aunt Maddie would say, though Priscilla had completed the task only a few days before. "And when you get through you can darn that hole in my slipper."

What hole? Priscilla wanted to ask, having knit the slippers only two weeks before.

Still, Priscilla hadn't really minded. Madeline Wills had raised her from the time she was six years old. She was the only family Priscilla could remember— she owed Aunt Maddie—something Aunt Maddie never failed to remind her of.

The bell above the lobby door rang as it opened, and Priscilla sagged in relief when she spotted the tall dark-haired man who entered. She started to chide Trask for his tardy arrival, but when her eyes reached his face, she forgot her reproof and her breath caught somewhere in her throat.

"G-good morning," she stammered, forcing the words past her suddenly numb lips.

"You look surprised to see me, Miss Wills. With your unfailing sense of judgment, surely you didn't believe I wouldn't show up?"

"Of course not," she lied. "I . . . I just didn't recognize you without . . . without all those whiskers." He had shaved and trimmed his hair, though it still curled well below his collar. Soft doeskin breeches clung to his thighs, and a clean white chambray shirt stood open at the throat, framing a patch of curly brown chest hair.

Priscilla forced her gaze away. She had never seen a more handsome man. *You always did have a way with the women*, the man named Jennings had said. Priscilla didn't doubt it, not for a moment.

"We'd better be going," Trask said. "Your trunks still upstairs?" Priscilla just nodded. "I'll send someone back for them once we get to the ship."

"All right."

Trask eyed her strangely, noting, she was sure, the

color that had risen in her cheeks. "You haven't changed your mind, have you?" He looked hopeful.

"Certainly not." Priscilla lifted her chin.

"Then I guess we'd better be going." With a sigh of resignation, he walked to the door, opened it, and held it while she passed. "If I had a lick of sense I'd turn around and head the other way. But I guess if you're fool enough to go, I'm fool enough to take you." Once outside, he offered his arm and Priscilla accepted it. "Just remember when the going gets tough, this was your idea not mine."

Trask led her down the boardwalk, out from under the overhanging porch, and into the wide dirt street.

"Yoo hoo, Bren, honey! Up here!"

Priscilla turned at the sound of the woman's voice. A buxom blonde dressed in a see-through nightgown leaned over the balcony above the saloon, waving a man's white handkerchief.

"Excuse me, ma'am," Trask said with a grin, "I believe I'm being summoned." He left Priscilla standing in the street and walked in the direction of the woman leaning over the rail, her bosom all but exposed in the see-through nightgown.

"You forgot your hanky, Bren, honey. I put some of my perfume on it, so you wouldn't forget me while you're gone." She dropped the big white square and it drifted toward the earth. Brendan caught it before it touched the ground.

"Thanks, Patsy." He held the cloth to his nose and inhaled, then almost gagged at the too-sweet smell.

"Thank *you*, lover," Patsy said. She tossed a glance at the lady standing in the street. "You'll behave yourself, won't you?'' She watched him through golden lashes.

"I like my women with a little more meat on their bones—or hadn't you noticed?''

"I noticed, darlin'. Believe me, I noticed.'' She laughed then, throaty and rich, her red-rouged mouth generous and smiling. He remembered the things she had done with that mouth the night before.

Unwillingly, he glanced at Priscilla Wills. In her modest high-necked dress, she stood ramrod straight, staring down the road in the opposite direction. *Christ, what a priss she was.* Still, she had the smoothest skin he had ever seen, and the prettiest pale pink mouth. Her waist was so tiny he could span it with his hands, and her fingers were graceful and feminine.

So what if her breasts were too small and her hips most likely the shape of a slender young boy's?

"What are you lookin' at?'' Patsy demanded, following the line of his gaze and snapping him out of his thoughts.

Brendan turned back to Patsy, winked at her and grinned. "Just thinkin' how much woman you are, Sugar. You keep it warm for me till I get back.''

"You got it, honey.''

Brendan left her then and returned to the lady in the street, whose face had flushed a shade far pinker than her lips. When he offered her his arm, this time she ignored it.

"I find your taste in women and your vulgar street talk as appalling as the rest of your bad habits. I hope you'll try to restrain yourself at least until your return." Stiff-backed, she started marching down the street.

"I'll do my best," he assured her, "not that it's any of your business."

The lady didn't comment, just held her head high and kept on walking. Brendan watched the movement of her hips beneath the full dimity skirts of her prim dove-gray traveling dress. With a practiced eye he assessed the thickness of her petticoats over the curve of her behind and found himself smiling. Slender yes. But boyish—he was beginning to wonder.

The smile slid from his face. Wondering about Stuart Egan's intended was the last thing he needed. He'd better keep his breeches buttoned up and his thoughts as far from that subject as he could get them.

And he intended to do just that.

Trask held open the low wooden door, and two men carried Priscilla's trunks into the tiny inside cabin. Mr. Hennessey had indeed booked her passage, as well as that of the traveling companion Stuart assumed would accompany her. But even if he hadn't, Priscilla believed Trask would have seen to it. Once he'd made up his mind to help her, the man took charge as if born to command. She wasn't quite sure she liked it. Then again, she *had* asked for his assistance.

"I'll check on you later," he said as the crewmen set down her trunks and walked back outside, "after you get settled in."

"I'll be fine."

With a grunt that summed up his feelings on that

subject, Trask walked down the narrow passage toward the ladder that led to the deck.

Sometime later Priscilla climbed that same ladder and went to stand at the rail. The sea looked frothy as it swept beneath the gray-painted hull, the water an odd shade of green. With the help of a harbor tug, the small ship steamed from the dock right on schedule, but the minute they reached the open seas, Priscilla's stomach began to churn. She had always hated boats of any kind. Aboard the *Orleans*, she had been sick off and on though the sea had been flatter than one of Aunt Maddie's doilies.

Feeling the wind against her cheeks, watching the seabirds and listening to the muted roar of the engines, Priscilla thought of her late aunt with a surprising jolt of sadness. She could still see Aunt Maddie's bloodless face as she lay in her coffin, serene in death as she never had been in life. It was one of the few times Priscilla could remember that she had been in the same room with her aunt without receiving one of her lectures.

The scoldings were so commonplace, Priscilla had learned to listen without really hearing. She would smile and nod and say "Yes, Aunt Maddie," while her mind drifted a million miles away.

She'd be thinking about the black-and-white puppy who had followed her home from the market —though her aunt had strictly forbidden her to let it into the house—or the little girl with the long blond curls who had smiled at her so sweetly down at the bookstore. She had always loved children. One day, she had vowed, she would have a child of her own.

Several drops of water landed lightly on her cheek

and Priscilla looked up at the sky. The fluffy white clouds she had spotted sometime earlier had thickened and turned as gray as the hull. Her stomach rolled in warning.

Merciful heaven, please don't let me get seasick. She could just imagine Trask's look of disdain if he knew how close she had come to disaster aboard the *Orleans*. She'd been barely able to eat, her skin pallid and her stomach queasy. If the seas grew rough, she was certain to disgrace herself.

Fortunately, for the time being, Trask had gone down to the main salon with some of the men to play poker. Though his gambling galled her no end, Priscilla had remained silent. What Trask did with his time aboard ship was really none of her business. Besides, she needed his help to reach Stuart, and she didn't want to chance his anger. So far he'd been a perfect gentlemen—much to her surprise—but she didn't doubt his capacity for violence; she'd seen that first-hand. Priscilla didn't want to find herself on the receiving end.

Several more raindrops fell, and Priscilla faced the inevitable need to go below. Though her stomach already protested, she'd have the steward bring her a tray and force herself to eat supper. After a good night's sleep she'd feel better, she was sure. In just five days she'd be on dry land again. Surely she could survive until then.

"Three aces beats my three jacks. You win again, Trask, you lucky bastard."

It's hardly a matter of luck, Brendan thought, raking in his winnings, big Texas currency not yet exchanged for U.S. dollars, Spanish *reales*, and shiny gold eagles. The three men sitting across from him through the tobacco smoke were obviously city gents, as easy to read as the naive little lady tucked away below decks.

"I'm out." Nehemiah Saxon, a thin-faced, balding man in a rumpled brown sack coat slid back his chair. The ship dropped into a trough, and the man stumbled a little before he could get to his feet.

"Too rich for my blood," said the rotund merchant named Sharp, who chomped noisily on his fat black cigar. "Think I'll go topside afore this storm gets any worse and get a little fresh air."

"I will stay in," said the big German farmer lounging against the back of his squat oak chair. Walter Goetting was by far the shrewdest of the lot. If he hadn't played poker much before, he was certainly catching on quickly.

Brendan silently saluted his growing expertise and vowed to watch him a little more closely. Accepting a slim cheroot that the big German offered, Brendan cupped his hand against the flame and lit up. Though tobacco was the one bad habit he had yet to acquire, he relaxed with an occasional cigar.

"Mind if I sit in?" The gruff male voice cracked across the sparsely furnished room; and Brendan swung his eyes toward a beefy man in a sweat-stained red-checkered shirt and fringed buckskin breeches.

"There's two seats open." Brendan blew out a plume of smoke. "Trask's the name." he extended his hand, and the beefy man shook it.

"Badger Wallace." His grip was solid, just like the man himself.

Brendan kept the smile carefully fixed on his face. "Badger Wallace. I've heard the name. Texas Ranger, if I'm not mistaken."

"That's right." Wallace turned his chair around backwards and settled himself astride it. The other men introduced themselves and the game started up again.

"Trask," Wallace repeated, rolling the name around his mouth, which was barely visible beneath his thick black handlebar mustache. "Wouldn't be Brendan Trask, would it?"

"Might be," Brendan evaded, drawing on the cigar to give himself some time. "How do you know Trask?"

"Never met the fella, but I heard tell he's a real good man with a gun. Friend of mine fought with him against the rebels down on the Yucatán."

"What friend is that?" Brendan asked, feeling a little less wary.

"Fella named Camden. Tom Camden. He'll be joinin' us sooner or later. Never could resist a good game of cards."

Brendan grinned and leaned back in his chair. "Tom Camden. How the hell is he? Figured he'd be dead and buried by now, crazy as he is with that pistol he totes."

"Did take a bullet in the shoulder a ways back," Badger drawled, "didn't slow him down much."

"Nothing slows Tom Camden down."

Badger spit out a wad of tobacco, missing the brass cuspidor on the floor near the wall by a good two feet. He wiped his mouth on the back of his sleeve. "Same as he says about you." He tossed his floppy-brimmed hat at the line of oak pegs mounted near the door, missed, and it slid to the floor. "Pleased to meet ya, Trask," he said. "Now let's play cards."

Brendan relaxed and picked up the hand he'd been dealt. The rangers hadn't yet heard about the shooting in the Indian Territory. If his luck held out, maybe they never would. He wondered what Priscilla would say about his "kind eyes" if she knew Barker Hennessey wasn't the first man he'd killed—or even the second. But then, she didn't look like a fool, just far too trusting, and way too naive.

He felt the ship lurch sideways as the fury of the storm increased, and crushed out his cheroot. The *Windham* wasn't really a passenger steamer—there weren't that many passengers traveling to Corpus Christi these days. Not since General Taylor and his troops had pulled out five months ago.

Brendan had heard the place looked like a ghost town with all the buildings empty. They had sprung up nearly overnight to house the hangers-on, gamblers, and scoundrels who chased after the gold in the soldiers' pockets.

Now Taylor had headed south to fight the Mexicans.

Unconsciously Brendan rubbed the scar on his upper left arm. He'd done his share of fighting back in forty-one. After a two-year stint in the Texas Marines, he'd taken a musket ball in a battle on the Yucatán. The wound had been bad and he'd damn near died—

would have if one of his comrades in the Mexican prison outside Campeche hadn't helped him.

Brendan thought of Alejandro Mendéz and, as always, something painful constricted inside his chest.

"It is your turn to bet, *Herr* Trask," the German reminded him.

Damn. He'd better start paying attention or he'd lose his winnings and then some. He made his wager, a conservative bet this time, and glanced at the round brass ship's clock screwed to the bulkhead across from the table. Nearly time for supper. He'd check on Priscilla, take her in to dinner if he had to, then, as much as possible over the next five days, he'd leave her alone.

Against his will, he thought of her slender curves and luscious pink mouth. He remembered her dainty waist, and found himself speculating on the size of her breasts. He wondered what her hair looked like, freed from her bonnet.

"You lose, Trask." Badger Wallace chuckled as Brendan flipped over his cards. "Maybe Tom'll do all right, after all."

"Tom Camden never won a hand of cards in his life," Brendan grumbled. He'd been traveling with the lady below decks for less than eight hours and already she was causing him trouble. He'd damn well see to it she didn't get a chance to cause him more.

"Time for supper, Miss Wills," Trask called through the door to her cabin, rapping his knuckles lightly against the heavy wood.

Priscilla clamped a hand over her mouth to keep from throwing up. "I . . . I'm not hungry just yet."

"Whatever you say." Relief rang in his voice. "I'll have someone bring you down a tray."

"Thank you." Just the thought of food sent Priscilla running for the chamber pot again. Forehead beaded with perspiration, she forced herself to hold on until Trask's footfalls receded, then she bent over and emptied the contents of her stomach for the sixth time in the past three hours.

Dear God in heaven, don't let Trask find out. She prayed that the seas would calm and that she would start feeling better. Lying down on her narrow berth, Priscilla closed her eyes and tried to sleep, but a fresh bout of nausea forced her back to the chamber pot. How would she survive five days of this torture?

With shaky fingers, she wiped her face with a damp linen towel, then worked the buttons at the front of her dress, thankful they weren't out of reach. Once she'd removed her horsehair petticoats, she freed the laces of her corset, no small task, took off her chemise and pantalets, and pulled on a clean cotton nightshirt. Then the ship lurched into a trough, and Priscilla felt her stomach lurch right along with it. After another harsh round of vomiting, she climbed wearily back into her narrow bunk.

Priscilla heard the knocking at her door and roused herself from her heavy-lidded slumber.

"Steward, Miss Wills," a now familiar voice said. "I've got tonight's supper tray."

Priscilla swallowed the bile that instantly rose in

her throat. "I . . . I'm not hungry yet," she called through the door. "But I thank you for your trouble."

"You sure you're feeling all right?" His voice sounded garbled through the thick plank boards of the door.

"I . . . I'm fine," she lied. "I'll go down to the salon and get something later." She'd been telling him that for the past three days. Telling the same thing to Trask, whenever he came to her door, which wasn't that often. She guessed he believed her, because he always seemed relieved.

In truth, she'd been lying on her berth, barely able to move, so weak she did little besides vomit and drift back to sleep. The room smelled so foul she wouldn't even let the steward in—she'd clean it herself, she vowed, just as soon as she felt able.

Lulled by the vibrations of the steamship's engines, Priscilla shifted on the berth, and her hand brushed the book of Robert Burns's poems she had tried unsuccessfully to read. She lifted the small leather-bound volume, but her hand shook so hard she dropped it on the floor. It was stifling in the airless little cabin, and the smell of her own sickness nearly overwhelmed her.

Just two more days to Corpus Christi—or was it three? She felt so dizzy it was sometimes hard to remember. Surely the seas would soon calm and she'd be able to get back on her feet. She'd scrub the offensive odors from the cabin before anyone discovered her secret. No one ever need know how terribly sick she had been.

Least of all the tall, handsome man who acted as her escort. The thought of Brendan Trask seeing her limp and disheveled caused another round of light-headedness. She would do anything to keep that from happening—anything.

Priscilla refused to ask herself why Brendan Trask's approval had become so important.

"Excuse me, sir," the little steward said. "Aren't you Trask, the man who's traveling with the lady downstairs?"

"I'm Trask." Brendan rested on a deck box, his feet propped up, watching the rising moon against the backdrop of the sea. "Why?"

"I'm worried about her, sir." Black-haired and sporting a tiny mustache, the steward stood facing him, a cloth-covered tray in his hands. "Every time I take her a tray, she says she'll get something to eat in the salon. She never lets me in—won't even open her door."

"So she's eating in the salon," Brendan said absently, but he felt a little guilty for abandoning her so completely.

"Nobody's seen her down there. Cook hasn't made anything special—I think she's . . . well, just saying that, sir, to keep me away. I don't think she's had a bite of food for the last three days."

"What?" Brendan swung his long booted legs to the deck and stood up. "Surely you're mistaken." But she'd said those same words to him each day, just as she had the steward.

"Sea's been pretty rough, sir. If the lady wasn't used to it—"

"Goddamn it!" Instinctively, Brendan knew the steward's guess was right. Prim and proper Priscilla

Mae Wills wouldn't want anyone seeing her seasick. He brushed past the little man and strode toward the ladder that led to the passengers' quarters below decks, the steward hurrying behind.

When he reached her cabin door, he pounded on it hard. "It's Trask, Miss Wills, I want to talk to you."

"I . . . I'm not dressed," she replied. "I . . . I'll talk to you later."

"You'll talk to me now. Open the door."

"I told you, I'm not dressed. It wouldn't be seemly—"

"Open this goddamned door, Priscilla. Open it, or I swear I'll break it down!"

Even through the planking, he could hear her gasp of horror. "Give me a little time. I . . . I'll come upstairs—I promise."

"You've got three minutes, Miss Wills. Then I'm coming in."

"No!" she shrieked, raising up on her berth then fighting the dizzying swirls in front of her eyes. "You can't come in here. This is my room. I absolutely forbid it!"

Brendan cursed roundly. "Time's up, Miss Wills." Wedging one broad shoulder against the wooden planks, he slammed hard against the door. With the second hard effort, the lock gave way and the door burst open to crash against the wall. Brendan forced himself not to recoil at the smell of sickness that permeated the tiny airless cabin.

In the flickering light of a small whale-oil lantern, Priscilla lay on her berth, her brown eyes huge and sunken, her skin so pale it looked translucent. Her hair hung loose around her shoulders, dark against her thin white cotton nightgown. He noticed the rise and fall of her breasts where they peaked beneath the gown, much fuller than he had imagined.

"I don't want anyone to see me," she said dully. "Please, go away."

Brendan looked at her sallow complexion, saw the trembling in her hands, and anger seared through his veins.

"Forget it, lady. You're my responsibility—as you so cleverly pointed out. You're wasting away to nothing and I won't have it. Why didn't you tell me you were sick?"

He lifted her into his arms as gently as he could, considering the temper he found himself in. Why hadn't he watched her more closely? He knew when he'd agreed to this job, it wouldn't be easy. The lady was as helpless as a newborn babe. How the hell would a woman like this survive on the Texas frontier?

"M-my clothes . . . ," she said, glancing down at her thin cotton nightgown. "I'm not properly dressed. Th-this is indecent."

"I don't give a damn about decency."

"*That*," she said, in a show of spirit he welcomed, "goes without saying."

Brendan muttered an oath and kept on walking. As he strode the narrow passage, the little steward approached.

"I'll take care of the cabin, Mr. Trask. You just take care of the lady."

Brendan nodded. "Before you start working in there, bring me a cup of beef broth and some soda crackers."

"Yes, sir, Mr. Trask." He scurried past them both and headed up the ladder.

Priscilla sniffled, trying to fight back tears. "I can't go up there—please don't make me. I'm only wearing my nightgown. What will people think?"

Brendan's hold tightened. "It's late and it's dark— and I don't give a tinker's damn what people think. I promised to take you to the Triple R. I mean to get you there in one piece. I'm not about to let your modesty get in the way of your health. Christ, lady. How could you do this to yourself?"

Priscilla steadied herself against his shoulder. "I thought I'd start feeling better."

Brendan crossed the deck and seated himself on the deck box, cradling Priscilla on his lap. The breeze blew strands of her thick dark hair against his cheek and plastered her damp nightgown to the curves of her body.

"You're too thin," he said gruffly, guilt and worry combining to prod his temper. "You were slender before; now you're downright skinny."

Priscilla flushed crimson. In the silvery glow of the moon, he could see the rosy hue that tinged her cheeks. The points of her breasts pushed into his chest and her bottom felt warm and feminine where it pressed against his thighs. *Skinny? Like hell*, he thought. She'd lost a little weight, all right, but she sure wasn't skinny.

The steward arrived with the soda crackers and broth, and Brendan held the mug to her lips. "Just a little at first. If you keep this down, you can have some more a little later."

Seeing no one on deck, just as he had said, Priscilla relaxed a little and began to nibble a cracker. "I can't remember when anything tasted this good."

Brendan smiled at that. "The seas are beginning to calm. A little fresh air, and you'll be fine."

Priscilla looked down at herself, saw the matted strands of hair on her shoulder and her perspiration-soaked nightgown. She wanted to crawl in a hole. "I don't suppose there's a chance of my getting a bath," she said softly.

Brendan's hand touched her cheek. "Captain Donohue is a very creative man. He's figured out how to heat water with the steam engines. After this much rain, the stores will be full. I imagine I could manage to get the only woman on board this tub a nice hot bath." He smiled. "Especially if it makes her feel well enough to join him for a little conversation."

Priscilla leaned into his shoulder and looked up at him. "I wasn't wrong to trust you, Brendan Trask," she said, meeting a pair of worried blue eyes, "but I'll never forgive you for what you've done to my modesty."

Brendan looked down at the scant covering her nightgown provided and wondered what she'd say if she knew he'd already imagined her naked.

Chapter 3

Priscilla shoved the last pin into her dark brown hair, fastening the heavy coils behind each ear, and tried to see her reflection in the tiny metal mirror above the chipped porcelain water pitcher on the bureau. A single chair, a scarred wooden table, the bureau, and her berth were the only pieces of furniture in the little inside cabin.

Before her return from the deck two nights ago, the steward had scrubbed the cabin spotless, and, as Brendan had promised, Captain Donohue had provided a steaming copper tub filled with heated rainwater in which she was able to bathe.

The captain had sent lengthy apologies for her uncomfortable quarters, the only thing available to passengers on the small merchant steamer, and the first mate had offered her his, which Priscilla immediately declined. She wanted no special treatment, she just wanted to feel good again—which at last she did —and she wanted to reach Corpus Christi—which they would in the morning.

It had taken her two full days to recover her health, but her appetite had returned with a vengence, and the weight she had lost reappeared on her slender frame. Trask had been solicitous, bringing her food, walking with her on deck. They hadn't really talked much, Priscilla hadn't felt much like talking.

Not until tonight.

Glancing once more in the mirror, she reached behind an ear and screwed in a small pearl earbob, an inheritance from a mother she couldn't remember. It being her last night at sea—praise the Lord—the captain had announced a dinner party of sorts. Priscilla had bathed again, the one great luxury the captain could provide, and dressed in one of the gowns she had sewn for her trousseau.

She wished she could see how she looked in it, but the lantern was too dim, and the mirror no more than a shiny piece of metal. The gown she had chosen was one of several she had made after her aunt died. Ella Simpkins, one of Aunt Maddie's few friends, had given her the fabric as a wedding present, a lovely pink crepe more beautiful than anything she had owned before.

In a moment of daring, Priscilla had fashioned the gown in the latest vogue, the waist cut in a deep vee to accent her slender torso, the bodice sweeping lower than any she had ever owned. The dress was still conservative, by society's standards, barely displaying the tops of her breasts, but Priscilla felt perfectly wicked. She couldn't wait to see Trask's handsome face when he saw her—skinny, indeed!

Priscilla's light mood faded. Why should she care what Brendan Trask thought of her? She was betrothed to a very fine man. Soon to become his bride. She would have everything she'd ever dreamed of. The last thing she needed was the approval of a worthless gunman, a tumbleweed of a man without a home of his own or any thought of the future.

Stuart Egan would look after her, take care of her

needs, and she would be sensitive to his. They would have children, raise them together, grow old together.

One day they might even find love.

Brendan knocked on the cabin door and heard the light patter of footsteps. "It's Trask," he said, though the lady was expecting him.

"I'm almost ready." He heard the rustle of her skirts a few moments later, then the door swung open and Priscilla stepped into the corridor.

Brendan stopped breathing. Even in the dim yellow light of the passage, he could see she looked lovely. *Pretty*, he had thought, *not beautiful, but attractive*. God, he must have been blind! Then again, it wasn't really his fault—not after the effort she had made to disguise it.

"Pink is definitely your color, Miss Wills," he said when he finally found his voice. "Stuart Egan is a very lucky man."

Priscilla smiled softly. "Thank you."

Taking in the simple but expertly fashioned gown, the tempting yet modest display of bosom, Brendan felt his body stir. Damn! Every time he thought of the woman lately, his blood began to boil. What the hell was the matter with him? He wasn't some randy youth. Nor a man who let his mind be ruled by his loins.

Forcing his thoughts in a safer direction, Brendan offered his arm and Priscilla accepted it, assessing his appearance without the censure he'd half expected. Maybe her eyes even held a hint of approval.

"Black breeches and a clean white shirt aren't exactly evening clothes," he apologized, "but these days it's the best I can do."

"There's nothing wrong with your clothes, Mr. Trask." *And nothing wrong with the way you look in them.* Broad shoulders and narrow hips encased in the masculine garments he wore with an easy grace any man would envy. He stood so tall he had to duck to keep from bumping his head on the beams above them.

"Why don't you call me Brendan?" he said with a lazy smile. "Surely we know each other well enough." There was something in his expression that said he was remembering her near-naked state on the deck, and Priscilla fought to keep from blushing.

"That would hardly be proper, *Mr. Trask*," she said pointedly, but her mind repeated his first name over and over, and it was all she could do to keep it off her tongue.

Trask's smile faded. "Whatever you say." As he helped her climb the ladder, one long-fingered hand at her waist, Priscilla's pulse began an unsteady rhythm. *Surely it's just anticipation of the evening ahead,* she told herself, and worked to calm the trembling in her limbs.

Brendan led her across the deck and opened the door to the main salon to find all five male passengers and Captain Donohue awaiting them. One look at their suddenly flushed faces gaping at Priscilla with awe told him they weren't disappointed.

"So glad you're feeling better, Miss Wills," the captain said, stepping forward to greet them. He accepted her smile along with her white-gloved hand.

"May I present Nehemiah Saxon, Arnold Sharp, Walter Goetting, Badger Wallace, and Thomas Camden."

"How do you do, ma'am?" the men said nearly in unison.

"Brendan told us you're traveling to Rancho Reina del Robles," Tom Camden said as they all took their seats. "That's a pretty far piece, ma'am."

"So Mr. Trask has warned me. You wouldn't be heading that way, would you?"

Brendan had told Priscilla that Tom was a Texas Ranger. He looked at his longtime friend, trail-toughened, and gun-wise. It would have been damned comforting to have him along.

"Sorry," Tom said. "Me and Badger got business down in Brownsville." Tom glanced in his direction with what was clearly meant as a warning. Tom knew only too well his reputation with the ladies. Brendan fought the pull of a smile.

"You got a good man there," Tom told her. "He'll see you get to your man safely."

Brendan frowned. He'd get her there, all right, but it galled him to do it. From what he knew of Stuart Egan, the man was a ruthless, power-hungry, arrogant son of a bitch. If the rumors he'd heard proved true, Egan might be a damned sight worse than that. At the least, he'd grind Miss Priscilla Mae Wills under the heel of his expensive handmade boots.

"I'm sure we'll be fine," Priscilla was saying. "Mr. Trask appears to be a very capable man."

"Where'd you meet Egan?" Badger Wallace asked.

"In truth, Mr. Wallace, I haven't. We've been corresponding, you see—"

Badger spit rudely into the brass spittoon. "Correspondin'?" he grumbled. "You mean to tell me you ain't never seen 'im?"

"Well, my aunt knew him, you see, and I—that is—we wrote to each other quite often."

"You was my daughter, I'd be wantin' you to know more about the fella than what he says in his letters. Man can write 'round his faults with the scratch of a quill."

"As I was saying, Mr. Egan was a friend of my late aunt," Priscilla defended, but Brendan noticed her hand shook when she accepted the sherry the captain gave her. Donohue poured a whiskey for each of the men, and Priscilla seemed relieved at the chance to change the subject.

"I understand you and Mr. Trask have been friends for some time," she said to Tom.

"We served together in the military, fightin' for the Republic." Tom flashed a grin. "Damn near got ourselves kilt, we did."

"Trask saved your bacon, from what I heerd." Badger lifted his whiskey glass in salute, then emptied it with a single swallow. The ends of his thick mustache glistened with traces of the liquid when he finished. "Damned lucky for you he were there."

"Lucky for a bunch of us," Tom agreed.

"What happened?" Priscilla asked.

"Nothing much," Brendan cut in, not liking the path of the conversation. "Tom and some of the others got pinned down on a ridge. Mexican cannon fire was hitting them pretty hard. I put a stop to it."

"Damn cannon was rippin' us to pieces," Tom amended. "Brendan had to cross the open, scale the side of a rocky ravine, and take on six Mexes to reach it. He went hand to hand with the last of 'em—kilt one fella with his own knife." Tom chuckled, but Priscilla turned pale.

"I think that's enough, Tom," Brendan warned, but Camden didn't even slow.

"Bren jammed a rock down the barrel a' that artillery piece. Wedged it in real tight, and blew the damned thing to kingdom come—that's when they took him."

"It's all in the past, Tom." Brendan's face had gone taut.

"They captured you?" Priscilla asked with a look of concern.

"Tossed him in a Mexican prison," Tom answered for him. "Place was a real hellhole. I was one of the lucky ones."

"How did you get out?" Priscilla asked.

"Look, Miss Wills," Brendan snapped, "this isn't exactly dinner conversation. I'd appreciate it if we could change the subject."

The table fell silent. Priscilla busied herself with her napkin, and the captain poured another round of whiskey for the men. Finally Walter Goetting launched a discussion of raising vegetables in the thriving German settlement of New Braunsfel, and Brendan felt a wave of relief.

When he glanced at Priscilla, he found her watching him with a slightly different look in her eyes. He wondered what she was thinking.

Priscilla enjoyed the meal and the men's conversation—the other men, that is, since Brendan said very little and excused himself early. The captain escorted

her on a stroll of the deck, explaining different parts
of the ship, then walked her down to her cabin. She
turned in early, and slept more soundly than she had
in days.

They reached Corpus Christi the following morning, a few hours after sunup. Aside from herself and
her escort, only the big German farmer, Walter Goetting, left the ship to go ashore. The day was hot and
muggy, and even the breeze from the ocean felt
warm. Priscilla wore her beige muslin day dress. The
material was lighter than some of her others, but the
sleeves were long and the neck high, increasing her
discomfort.

"It has been a pleasure, *Fräulein* Wills," the German said, once they'd left the shore boat. "Godspeed
on your journey to your bridegroom."

"Thank you. I hope you enjoy your visit." He had
relatives on a nearby German farm, he had told
them.

"I am certain I will." He turned to Brendan. "Godspeed, *Herr* Trask."

Trask accepted his handshake. "Maybe we'll meet
again some time. You keep playing poker the way you
were on the ship, next time I could be in a whole lotta
trouble."

Goetting smiled at that. "I do not think so." He
waved good-bye over one thick shoulder and moved
off toward town.

Priscilla's trunks were brought ashore and carried
to a flatbed wagon pulled by two mules that sat at the
edge of the sand. Trask carried just his saddlebags.

"Howdy folks, I'm Red Ding," said the wagon
driver, a stocky auburn-haired man in his middle

thirties. He gave them a welcoming smile. "I been hired to meet each ship till a man name of Hennessey gets in. Guess he ain't gonna show aboard this 'un."

Priscilla started to speak, but Trask interrupted. "Mr. Hennessey met with an unfortunate accident. I'm afraid he's dead. This is Miss Wills, Stuart Egan's intended, and my name is Trask."

Red touched the brim of his slouch hat. "Pleased to make your acquaintance." He surveyed Priscilla, then turned back. "You takin' her to him?"

"Somebody had to."

Priscilla glowered, but Trask ignored her. He helped her climb up on the wagon seat, his hand warm and strong at her waist, then he climbed into the back. He was wearing his blue twill breeches and a clean white homespun shirt. He hadn't worn his gun since they'd boarded the ship.

"We'll need provisions," he said, leaning back against the sideboard. Beneath the wide, flat brim of his hat, his light eyes looked different, almost eager, as if this untamed land stirred feelings of home. "Take us to Old Man Latimer's."

"Ain't there no more," Red Ding called over his shoulder. "Took off with Taylor and his men. I'm to take you to Colonel Kinney's Tradin' Post up on Live Oak Point—I mean Lamar's—that's what they're callin' it these days. You can get what you need and charge it to Egan. I'm to leave you the wagon and team."

"I'll also need a saddle horse—one I can count on."

"Mr. Hennessey left a fine-looking black in the livery out behind the tradin' post. I'll fetch him while you get supplies."

"Thanks."

"What happened to everyone?" Priscilla asked, glancing at the scores of empty buildings, most of them little more than shacks.

"There were less than two hundred people in Corpus," Trask explained, "until General Taylor set up a base of operations here last summer. Some three thousand men, ready and able to fight the Mexicans."

"Town sprang up overnight," Red Ding added. "Looks like a goddamn ghost town now." Priscilla's eyebrows shot up, but she forced herself to silence. She was out of her element here; she had better remember that.

As the wagon rumbled down the nearly empty dirt streets, Priscilla surveyed her surroundings: boarded-up saloons and gambling halls, empty mercantile buildings, hotels, even the tattered remnants of several tents, one of which appeared to have served as a livery.

"Two thousand civilians or thereabouts," Red told them, "all come to town just itchin' for a taste of the soldiers' pay."

"Looks like they left in a hurry," Trask said.

"Wasn't much reason to stick around. Soldiers was what brought 'em here in the first place. Once they was gone, the most of 'em hightailed it outta here."

A group of men leaned against the porch of a still-open saloon. Several touched their hat brims as the wagon rolled past. Priscilla could have sworn they were leering.

"Bunch a cutthroats moved in after," Red continued. "I was kinda hopin' some a' them Rangers might show up to clean the place out for us."

"Most of them are fighting the Mexicans, in one way or another."

"Doin' a damn fine job of it, too, from what I hear."

Priscilla looked at the seedy-looking men who rode their tough little horses past them in the street or strolled with a brash air along the wooden boardwalks.

"Are there many women in town?" she asked hopefully. They'd reached the corner of Mesquite and People—according to the broken street sign dangling in the hot, damp wind.

"Handful of women. No ladies—'ceptin' you, ma'am, a'course. I'd stay close to Mr. Trask here, if'n I was you."

Priscilla swallowed hard. "Of course."

The wagon reached the trading post and rumbled to a halt beneath a nearby oak tree. "Too bad Colonel Kinney ain't around. He always enjoys meetin' new folks."

Red set the brake, jumped down from the wagon, and started around the stone building toward the livery some distance away.

Brendan jumped down and helped Priscilla alight. He started toward the trading post and that's when he saw them. A group of five horses, hard-ridden and lathered, tied at the side of the building. They nickered softly and pawed at the hard black earth.

"You wait here," he said, setting her away from him and scanning the outbuildings for signs of possible danger. In a town where women were as scarce as starched white shirts, this one would surely be a prize. "I want to see what's going on in there."

"All right."

Brendan pulled his holster from his saddlebag, strapped the heavy belt around his waist, and tied the leather thong to his thigh. He checked the shot and wad, and made sure the Patterson—a .36 caliber belt model—rode easy in its holster.

"If things don't look right, I'll get what we need and meet you right here." Without awaiting her reply, he walked to the heavy plank door, pulled it open, and stepped into the cool interior.

Coarse men's laughter and the sound of a whiskey bottle clinking against glasses drew his attention toward the back of the room. The smell of meat and chili filled the air, and four men sat around a rough-hewn table immersed in the business of eating. From their unkempt hair and several weeks' growth of beard—and the array of rifles and pistols they carried—it was obvious they weren't the sort of men he wanted to tangle with.

They glanced up at his entrance, but seemed more interested in eating.

"May I help you, sir?" said a tiny, bespectacled man behind the counter near the door.

Brendan glanced once more at his surroundings. Colonel Kinney's Trading Post was a solidly built stone structure with open-beamed ceilings and a tall rock fireplace at one end. Indian blankets hung from the rafters beside cougar pelts and deerskins, furs of badger and skunk. Bolts of calico and gingham stacked in two-foot columns, sacks of coffee, twists of tobacco, cones of sugar—all of it made the place a jumble of colors and smells.

"I need some provisions," Brendan said, "sugar, flour, coffee, beans, a few potatoes, some jerked beef, a slab of bacon. There'll be two of us—enough for about five days." That would be more than enough supplies, but he could always use the extra. It was the least Stuart Egan could do.

"Yes, sir. I've got some Indian corn, some melon, some sweet potatoes and black-eyed peas, if you've got the room."

Brendan nodded. "What about bedding? We'll need a tarpaulin and blankets, a few pots and pans— and a rifle and ammunition, the best you've got."

"I'll get it all together in a jiffy." The little man eyed the others warily and began to scurry around the cluttered room collecting first one thing and then another.

Brendan watched the four men sitting at the table —and worried where the fifth man was.

Red brought the big black horse, saddled and ready to ride, and tied it to the rear of the wagon. "Take care, Miss Wills."

"Shouldn't we pay you or something?"

"Mr. Egan's took care a' that. You be careful now." Tipping his hat, he headed off down the hill.

Standing beside the wagon in the shade, Priscilla shifted from one foot to the other, wondering what was going on in the trading post and why Trask hadn't come back out to get her.

Probably forgotten he'd left her there. He was inside where it was cool, he couldn't know how hot she was, how badly she needed a drink of water. Even the shade and the brim of her bonnet couldn't block the sun's harsh rays. She licked her lips, drier by the minute, and glanced around for some water. Seeing nothing, she walked around the building toward the rear and spotted a low rock structure, roofed but not enclosed, that looked to be a well. She walked in that direction.

As she had hoped, the structure was indeed a well, and on reaching it, Priscilla turned the crank to haul up a moss-covered bucket of water. It tasted brackish and warm, but wet, liquid, and soothing. Priscilla breathed a sigh of relief.

"Thirsty, *señora?*"

Priscilla spun toward the man's gravelly voice and found him standing just a few feet behind her. He was a tall man, dressed in tight black breeches that flared at the bottom and a full-sleeved white linen shirt.

"Yes . . . yes, I was. Thank you for the water."

"Do not thank me." The tall dark Mexican chuckled. "It is not my water you are drinking."

She smiled a little nervously. "I have to go," she said and started past him.

"Why do you not come inside and meet *mis amigos?* They have not seen a true lady for many months. It would give them great pleasure to see one such as you."

"I'm afraid I can't do that." She kept on walking. "I'm waiting for a friend."

The man started walking beside her, the silver circles on the side of his trousers flashing in the afternoon sun. "Your husband?"

She shook her head. "I . . . I'm not married."

"That is good." He grabbed her arm and turned her toward him. "Then I will not have to kill him." He made a grating sound of laughter at Priscilla's look of horror, then grabbed her wrist and jerked her against him.

"Let me go!" she cried out, but he silenced her words with his wet sticky lips. Terror welled up inside her. Priscilla squirmed against his hold as his beard rasped her cheeks and his mustache prickled her skin.

When he tried to force his tongue into her mouth, she tore free and started running. She'd gone only a few feet when he caught her, laughing, enjoying her fear, making her cry out in terror. Ignoring her struggles, he shifted both her wrists into one wide hand and jerked the bonnet from her head with the other. His thick fingers raked through her hair, painfully tearing the pins free, and the heavy dark mass slid loose around her shoulders.

"Let me go!" she wailed, trying to kick him, fighting to hold back her tears. "Somebody help me!"

"You want help, *señorita? Bien*, we will go and find my friends." He laughed again, the sound more chilling than any she had heard. He dragged her toward the rear of the trading post, but stopped just outside the back door.

Priscilla's heart beat so hard she feared it would tear through her ribs. The only thing controlling her terror was the knowledge that Brendan was inside the building. If the Mexican took her in, surely he could help her.

"Y-your friends are inside?" Priscilla whispered.

"*Sí, señorita.* But first I wish to see for myself the prize that I bring them."

Priscilla felt his thick fingers at the neck of her dress, heard the rending of fabric, and screamed as he ripped the gown to her waist. Circles of darkness whirled at the edge of her mind. *God in heaven, please don't let me faint.* Willing her legs to hold up, she tried to fight him, her breasts heaving, and all but exposed above the top of her steel-ribbed corset.

The Mexican just laughed. Wrenching her arm up behind her back, he ripped at the bodice of her dress until it hung in tatters around her waist. Her hair appeared a jumble of dark glistening brown against her pale skin.

"Now we will meet my friends," the Mexican said.

Priscilla whimpered as he wrenched her arm higher, and salty tears rolled down her cheeks. What if something had happened to Brendan? What if the man's friends had captured him? Dear Lord, what would she do if he wasn't there to help her?

Brendan paid the clerk and picked up a box of supplies. He had just pulled open the door when he heard a scuffling at the back of the room. A woman's high-pitched scream whipped him around, but at first he didn't see her.

Not until he realized she stood in the center of the circle of men, the fifth of whom, a tall olive-skinned Mexican, had an arm around her waist and a hand clamped over her mouth to keep her quiet.

Brendan's blood ran cold. Priscilla! With her hair unbound and her bosom nearly exposed, he almost hadn't recognized her. Now that he had, it took all

·his control to keep from storming across the room and tearing the man's dirty hands off her.

"*Silencio!*" the Mexican warned her, tightening his hold till she pried at his fingers, gasping for air. "Be quiet, *señorita*, and I will remove my hand."

Priscilla nodded, trembling all over. The man uncovered her mouth, but kept her pinned against him, his forearm wedged beneath her chin.

Brendan set the box back down on the counter, picked up the rifle lying beside it, and quietly checked the breech. When Priscilla finally spotted him, he flashed her a look of warning, and she dragged her eyes away.

The Mexican grinned at his companions. "I have brought you a present, *amigos. Muy hermosa, no?*"

Damned right she's beautiful, you bastard. Brendan forced himself to stay calm, to look at her terrified face with an air of detachment. He scrutinized the rifle in his hands.

"Eight-shot revolving breech Colt," whispered the little clerk, his green eyes huge behind the thick lenses of his glasses. "She's loaded and ready." That said, he slipped quietly down behind the counter.

Brendan turned back toward Priscilla. Her eyes looked bigger than the clerk's as she fought to stay calm in the grip of the rough-looking men.

"You done real good, Ruiz," said a man the others called Shorty.

With a raspy chuckle, the Mexican turned Priscilla into his arms, slid his thick brown fingers around the back of her neck, and forced her mouth to meet his, grinding her soft pink lips against his teeth.

Priscilla whimpered.

Clamping his jaw against the rage he suddenly felt, Brendan thumbed back the hammer of his rifle, propped it against his hip, and leveled it toward the men in the back of the room.

"Let the lady go," he warned with soft menace. Five men turned in his direction—and the smiles slid from their faces.

"You would do well to stay out of this, *señor*." The Mexican motioned, and the men began to spread out, making themselves more difficult targets.

"The next man who moves, dies," Brendan warned. From the corner of his eye he caught a flesh-colored blur, just the flicker of Shorty's hand toward his pistol. Brendan swung the rifle, fired, and the stocky man's chest blossomed red with blood. His eyes rolled back in his head, and he slid with a moan to the floor.

The rifle fixed on the Mexican. "I said let her go—unless you want to be next."

The Mexican released her, and Priscilla stumbled away. For a moment she swayed on her feet, her eyes looking vacant and glassy, then she drew herself up. Brendan heard a tiny whimper as she raced across the room to his side, clutching her tattered dress, tears streaming down her pale cheeks.

He wanted to hold her, to comfort her. "Get those supplies out to the wagon," he said instead, afraid a sympathetic word might end the last of her control.

Priscilla gazed at him numbly. "Go on," he commanded. "Get the clerk to help you."

The little man popped up from behind the counter. "Whatever you say, mister. I don't want no trouble."

He grabbed a box of supplies and headed out the door. Priscilla still didn't move.

"You too," Brendan said to her harshly. "If you'd damned well stayed where I told you in the first place, none of this would have happened."

Priscilla gaped at him. Her bottom lip trembled. "But I . . . I . . . only wanted—"

"Go!"

Priscilla faltered a moment more, then stiffened her spine and picked up one of the boxes.

Brendan steadied his look on the men. "You boys reach for those guns real slow and let them drop to the floor. Easy now. We don't want another . . . accident."

Cursing, the four men did as he said. Brendan held them at gunpoint until the rest of the gear had been loaded, then he started to back toward the door.

In a single lightning-quick motion, Ruiz leapt for his pistol, grabbed it and fired, the muzzle spitting flame. Brendan fired back, rolled behind some boxes, and fired again. He heard the whistle of a blade, saw it thud into the crate near his head, and pulled the trigger again. Ruiz cried out and plunged headfirst over a flour barrel, spilling the contents as he crashed to the floor, his dead eyes staring into space.

Brendan's own heavy breathing matched that of the other three men.

None of them moved, just crouched where they were, unwilling to reach for a weapon. The fight had gone out of them the minute their leader had died.

"You men better listen and listen good. That little lady you assaulted is Stuart Egan's intended."

"Egan," one of them whispered, almost with reverence. "I don't want no part a' him."

"Very wise. The rest of you better heed your friend's words. You come after us, and if I don't kill you, Egan will."

The men said no more, just rose slowly to their feet and nervously stared at the floor.

"Get their weapons and toss them outside in the bushes," Brendan instructed the clerk, who did exactly what he was told.

When he had finished, Brendan pulled open the door, stepped outside, and closed it behind him. Beneath the oak, Priscilla sat atop the wagon seat, clutching the front of her dress in a death grip. Hennessey's big black gelding stood tied to the rear.

Knowing he should stay behind to cover their back trail but unsure how much more Priscilla could take, Brendan climbed up on the wagon seat beside her.

He released the brake, slapped the reins on the rumps of the mules, urging them into a quick-paced trot, and headed off down the road that led out of town to the north.

"Keep an eye out behind us," he ordered, careful to keep his tone firm. Priscilla said nothing, just stared over her shoulder, holding onto the remnants of her dress.

"Christ," he swore and kept on driving.

He knew she was hurting when she didn't protest his swearing. Still, he kept on. Not far out of town, the road became a wagon-rutted lane. An hour after that, he pulled off the path up onto a knoll into some shade where he could get a good, clear view of his back trail.

Seeing no one behind them, for the first time since they'd left the trading post he felt his tension ease. Climbing down from the seat, he walked around the wagon and reached up to help Priscilla, holding her around the waist and lifting her gently to the ground.

Her hair fell over his arm, dark yet sparkling with golden highlights, brushing against him as soft as silk. Tears had dried on her cheeks, and her eyes looked bleak and forlorn.

"Are you all right?" he asked gently.

Her stiff fingers moved over the ragged fabric of her dress. "I . . . I'm not properly clothed."

He looked down at her soft white breasts, nearly exposed above her corset. They rose and fell softly, the strands of her dark hair curling against their whiteness.

"No," he said, touching her cheek, "you hardly look proper at all."

Priscilla stared up at him, and fresh tears gathered in her eyes. "I . . . I didn't go far," she said. "I was just so thirsty."

Brendan laced his fingers in her hair, cradling the back of her head, and pulled her against his chest. "It wasn't your fault." His voice sounded odd, rough with worry and something he couldn't quite name. "I was hard on you because I needed you to be strong."

Tears slipped down her cheeks and trickled across his fingers. She turned her face into his shoulder and started crying harder, deep, wracking sobs that touched him in some dark, secret place he had closed up long ago. Her fingers clutched his shirt and her tears dampened the fabric.

"Odds are they won't come after us," he soothed.

"Not without a leader. You'll be safe once you get to the ranch. Egan's got an army of men to protect you. Nothing can hurt you there."

She only clutched him tighter.

"You would have been safer with Hennessey. He's known around these parts. Once they knew you were traveling with him, they probably wouldn't have touched you."

He lifted silky tear-damp hair from her cheeks, noting the smoothness of her skin and the graceful arch of her neck. His body stirred, hardened, and he hated himself for his wanting. "You did good back there. You never let on you knew me. I was proud of you."

Priscilla drew back to look at him. "You were proud of me?"

"Yes."

She leaned back into his chest, but her crying had slowed.

"God, you're beautiful," he said, his voice husky. "Why do you work so hard to hide it?" When Priscilla looked up, he handed her his handkerchief. She blew her nose and dried her eyes.

"You think I'm beautiful? Really?"

He smiled at that. "Really."

"Not just sort of pretty?"

"More than pretty."

"No one's ever said that before." Over the gently sloping land thick with salt grass, Priscilla looked back toward the trading post, no longer visible in the distance. "You killed another man."

Maybe two. "It didn't appear I had much choice."

A hawk circled above them, soaring and diving

with the currents of hot summer air. "I don't suppose you did."

"I told you, Priscilla, this is rough country. A man does what he has to. If he doesn't, he doesn't survive."

"What about a woman?" She turned to face him. "How does a woman survive?"

"Some of them don't," he said bluntly.

"And those who do?"

"Learn to adapt. They change what they can, accept what they can't, and find a good strong man to protect them."

"A man like Stuart Egan?"

Brendan looked away. "Egan's a survivor, that's for sure."

"Then the rest is up to me." She spoke the words more to herself than to him, her eyes staring off in the distance. When she came back from wherever she had been, she was the very proper woman he had first met in the street.

Chin held high, she started toward the rear of the wagon. "I'll need something else to wear."

Knowing it was necessary, Brendan climbed up into the rear and opened her trunks. Though he willed himself not to, he couldn't resist just one last glance at the tempting curves of her body. Prim and proper she might be, but underneath her prissy clothes she was a woman. He wished he'd be the man to find out just how much woman she was.

Chapter 4

 "Is money the reason?" Brendan's eyes remained fixed on the team as they rumbled along the dusty trail that served as a road. "For marrying Egan, I mean."

Priscilla glanced at the tall man beside her, reassured by his imposing presence as she had been since that very first day. She had changed into a dark green calico dress with a matching wide-brimmed bonnet. Properly dressed once more and now that they'd left the trading post somewhere in the distance, she had begun to feel better.

"I suppose in one way it is, but not in the way you mean. I'm marrying Stuart because when my aunt died I had no one else to turn to. He's promised to take care of me, and I believe he will. Stuart's money will supply a home—which is important to me since I've never really had one of my own—and a great deal of security. But it's his companionship and the children we'll share that mean the most to me."

"But you don't even know him. What makes you think the two of you will get along?"

The wagon hit a bump, jolting Priscilla against Brendan's side. With an apologetic smile, she moved away. "The letters he wrote me, of course. Stuart's a very sensitive man. He wants a family as much as I do. He'll provide for me, see that our children want for nothing—I'm a very lucky woman, Mr. Trask."

He just grunted. "That remains to be seen, Miss Wills."

They were back to being formal, and Priscilla felt relieved.

"You haven't reached the Triple R yet," he said. "There's a lot of Texas between here and there. You've discovered already how hostile this land can be."

Priscilla flushed. She didn't want to think about the terrible men they had left behind, the way they had touched her, abused her. She didn't want to remember the mind-numbing horror that had crept over her when Brendan had shot them, the rising tide of terror that had threatened to overwhelm her.

She wanted to pretend Texas was the land of abundance and beauty she had dreamed. She wanted to believe in the happiness she would share with Stuart.

Instead she glanced at Brendan—when had she started to think of him as Brendan instead of just Trask? It was dangerous to think of him in this more intimate manner, but she couldn't seem to help herself.

She watched the way he held the reins, the way he scanned the landscape around them, his light blue eyes missing nothing. Beneath the broad, flat brim of his brown felt hat, shadows outlined the curve of his jaw, his straight nose, and well-formed lips. The hot Texas wind tossed strands of his hair against the corded muscles of his neck, the dark-tanned surface of his skin.

Watching him sitting there, so straight and tall, something warm and liquid moved through Priscilla's veins. She thought of the feel of his hands on her waist, the gentle arms that had held her when she cried.

He was waiting for a response. It was a hostile land, he had said.

"I'll get used to it. I really have no other choice."

"You've got a choice, Miss Wills. This is America. Everyone here has a choice."

Priscilla wanted to argue, to tell him that she wasn't prepared for any other kind of life than the one Stuart Egan offered. That she really didn't want anything different. Ever since she was a child, she had dreamed of being a wife and mother. She wanted children so much she ached with it.

"Things will work out, Mr. Trask. I'm sure of it. Stuart wants the same things I do."

He looked at her hard, his eyes fixed on her face as if there were something he wanted to say but couldn't. "It's getting late. I think we'd better find a place to camp. We've got a long day ahead of us tomorrow."

Priscilla just nodded, and the wagon rumbled along.

They camped on a knoll some distance from the road. A small creek trickled nearby, and Brendan saw Priscilla heading toward it, meaning to wash some of the dust away.

"Don't go far," he warned her, "and watch where you're walking. There are—" *rattlesnakes and scorpions, deadly centipedes six inches long, and spiders as big as my hand* "—things out there you need to watch out for." With all she'd been through, it wasn't time for that lecture now.

"I'll be careful."

"I'll get supper. You just take it easy."

And so he did. Roasted rabbit he had shot and skinned just a few minutes after he'd staked out the horse and mules, served with sweet potatoes, and melon. They washed the meal down with cups of steaming hot coffee. Priscilla thought it truly a feast.

When they had finished eating, Brendan rolled out his bedroll, the saddle serving as his pillow, and carried hers toward the wagon. "You can sleep in the back."

It seemed so very far away, and after the men at the trading post. . . . Priscilla shivered, though the sun still beat down fiercely. "I don't suppose . . . ?".

Brendan stopped and turned in her direction. "You don't suppose what?"

"I know it's highly improper . . . but I was wondering if you would mind—just for tonight, I mean—letting me sleep closer to you."

Brendan's hand tightened on her bedroll. "Christ, Miss Wills."

"Don't blaspheme, Mr. Trask."

Grumbling, he headed toward his pallet beside the dying fire. "You must think I'm some sort of saint," he muttered.

"Hardly that, Mr. Trask."

He unrolled her bedding a foot or so away from his, sprawled on his pallet, his head resting on the saddle, and settled his hat down over his eyes.

"Would you mind unbuttoning my dress?" He'd been the one who had buttoned it. You'd think he would remember how difficult it was for her to reach it.

Brendan sat up and clamped his hat back down on his head. Grumbling something unpleasant about women, he climbed to his feet. He unhooked the fastenings at the back of her dress with an ease she didn't want to think about, then he turned away.

"I suppose the corset would be too much to ask." She could loosen it without him; she'd done it by herself ever since she'd left home—she was just so unbelievably tired.

Brendan swore an oath she didn't quite catch, thank heaven. With a hand that shook a little, he untied her corset and tugged on the strings until Priscilla sighed with relief.

"Now can I get some sleep?" he asked gruffly.

"Of course." While Brendan stretched out on his bedroll, Priscilla rummaged through her trunks.

Out of sight on the far side of the wagon, she removed her garments and pulled on her long white cotton nightgown. Unrolling the makeshift knot of hair she had fashioned at the back of her head, she plaited it into a single long, thick braid, then padded back to her bedroll and lay down to sleep, pulling the blanket up to cover her though the night was far too warm.

Knowing he rested there beside her, that she could reach out and touch him if she wanted, the night sounds didn't seem quite so frightening. Still, she strained to hear them, wondering what each one was, until the howl of something not nearly far enough away bolted her upright.

Brendan didn't move. "Coyote," he said from beneath his hat brim. "He's more afraid of you than you are of him."

"You're sure of that, are you?"

Brendan set his hat aside and looked over at her. She could see the hard planes of his face outlined in the reddish glow from the embers of the fire.

"I've told you how hard this land is, Priscilla. What I haven't told you is how rich it is, how wonderfully abundant. Once you learn its ways, the land can keep you safe. It can provide food and water, shelter you when it's cold." He glanced up at the bright mat of stars. "There's no ceiling more beautiful than the one over your head right now, no landscape more compelling. The sounds of the night are music to those who know them; they can ease your way to sleep."

"You love it here," Priscilla said with some wonder. "I saw it in your eyes when we first arrived."

He shoved his hands behind his head. "I fought it some at first, just like you. Believe it or not, I was born in England. My father was a minister to King George the Fourth."

"Now you're teasing me."

Brendan chuckled softly. "Hard to believe, isn't it? He died when I was eight, but I remember him well. My mother didn't live long after. My brother Morgan raised me." He sighed. "It was pretty tough on us for a while after they were gone, but they left us with some great memories. I'll never forget them."

"I wish I could remember my parents. They died when I was six. I don't remember them at all."

"Surely you remember something. I can recall lots of things—trips to the country, sailing with my father across the channel to France. I couldn't have been more than four at the time."

Priscilla felt a prickling down her spine. It happened whenever she thought of her parents. Her heart set up an uncomfortable rhythm, and her palms felt damp. "You must have a far better memory than I," she snapped, not really meaning to. "I don't remember a thing."

He looked at her oddly. "Sorry I mentioned it." He rested the hat back over his face and in minutes his breathing leveled out and sleep settled in. It took Priscilla far longer, her mind searching the emptiness where the memories of her family should have been. Was it unnatural not to remember? Brendan wasn't the first to suggest it.

Whenever she had mentioned her parents to her aunt, Aunt Maddie had quickly changed the subject. They'd been killed in a boating accident. That was all she knew. She carried a locket with tiny porcelain miniatures of them, but even the pictures couldn't bring their images to mind.

Then again, what did it matter? They were gone now, had been for years.

Setting the problem aside as she always did, Priscilla turned on her side, trying to get comfortable and listening to the buzz of cicadas, the distant chirp of crickets. When the coyote set up his mournful howl this time, Priscilla only smiled. Eventually she fell asleep.

Brendan stirred on his bedroll, dimly aware of the ache in his loins, the sheen of perspiration that covered his forehead. With gentle insistence, he kneaded the soft warm breast beneath his fingers, teasing the nipple at its peak into a pebble-hard bud.

He was dreaming, he was sure, noting the strength

of his arousal. Dreaming of a woman with slender curves and gently rounded hips. Her breasts weren't large, but the one he held filled his hand and pointed deliciously upward. He wanted to slide his fingers beneath the barrier of the nightgown she wore, wanted to stroke her smooth skin, and make her writhe with passion. He wanted to kiss her soft pink lips until they ripened with desire.

Priscilla's scream shattered his illusion, and Brendan bolted upright, jerking his gun from its holster in the same quick motion. "What is it? What's the matter?"

She scrambled from her bedroll, so close to his, to a place some distance away and stood staring at him as if he were a stranger, her gold-flecked brown eyes huge in the oval of her face.

"You . . . you were sleeping?" she asked, with a hint of accusation.

"Of course I was sleeping. What the hell did you think I was doing?"

"I thought you were awake."

"What difference does it make?" He shoved the gun back into its holster and raked a hand through his hair.

The sun wasn't up yet, but the moon shone brightly, backlighting Priscilla's body through her white cotton nightgown. He could see her slender curves, the rise and fall of her breasts. Against the buttons of his breeches, his shaft remained hard and throbbing. His hand tingled with the memory of the upturned breast he had held.

"Jesus Christ, that was you."

Priscilla swallowed hard. "Please don't blaspheme."

When she took another step backward, Brendan felt a surge of guilt. He wanted to swear again, but didn't.

"Look, Priscilla, I tried to warn you. I'm a man, just like any other. I didn't mean for that to happen, but maybe it's good that it did. We've got three more days of travel before we reach Rancho Reina. If I didn't feel so damned responsible for you, I'd probably try to bed you. With that in mind, I suggest you keep your distance. Now go back to sleep."

Priscilla just stared at him.

"I was asleep, for Christ's sake. I thought I was dreaming."

I thought so, too. Sometime during the night, she must have snuggled up to him and he'd pulled her into his arms.

Bending down, Priscilla dragged her bedroll several feet away from him. She lay back down, but she didn't fall asleep. All she could think of were the strange sensations Brendan had stirred in her body. Her breast still felt heavy and achy, and the place between her legs throbbed and burned.

Was this desire? She hadn't believed she could feel such a thing; her aunt surely hadn't. Aunt Maddie had been a spinster, a virgin till the day she died. The notion of a man's organ penetrating her body had repelled her. Priscilla often wondered if that hadn't been one of the reasons her aunt had never married.

Priscilla had long ago resigned herself to that particular fate. She wanted children and she knew what it took to get them—not in detail, of course—a woman wasn't allowed to know that until she married. She only knew that submitting to a man's lust was essential to making a baby. But did a woman feel lust, too? She had certainly felt something.

From beneath her lashes, Priscilla watched the rise and fall of Brendan's muscular chest. As long as she'd been half asleep, sure the hot sensations were nothing more than an odd sort of fantasy, Priscilla had to admit she'd enjoyed them. She'd found herself moaning softly, and pressing her bosom into the warmth she'd discovered was Brendan's palm.

Merciful heaven, what a shock that had been!

Priscilla shifted restlessly and fought to block the hot sensations that coursed through her veins every time she remembered the way he had touched her, molded her breast to his hand and made her ache for . . . What? she wondered.

She looked again at the tall broad-shouldered man who had touched her so intimately. Could Stuart Egan make her feel that way? Part of her hoped so. The other part prayed he could not. Even as innocent as she was, instinctively she sensed there was some sort of power in what Brendan had done to her.

Already it was difficult to keep her mind off him. Dear Lord, she didn't want to give him any more hold on her than he already had.

Priscilla awoke to the delicious aroma of steaming hot coffee. Brendan bent over her, extending a speckled blue tin cup.

"Time to get up," he said, handing her the coffee. "We've got a lot of ground to cover."

Priscilla gratefully accepted the mug. "You should

have awakened me sooner. I could have made breakfast."

"I thought . . . after what happened—at the trading post, I mean—you could use a little extra sleep."

Priscilla blushed. It was the other "what happened" that worried her more.

"About last night . . . ," he said, reading her
thoughts.

"It wasn't really your fault. I'd rather we just forgot it."

Easier said than done, Brendan thought. He recalled the painful hours he had spent before dawn,
trying not to think of her slender curves, her ripe
little bottom, the feel of her small upturned breasts.
As she sat there sipping her coffee, his eyes traced the
line of her thick dark braid, saw where it nestled
against her bosom, and he had to turn away.

"You'd better get dressed," he said a little more
gruffly than he meant to. One look at her in that
damned cotton nightgown and his breeches fit way
too snug. Three more days of this torture and even
Patsy Jackson would be hard-pressed to give him the
ease he'd need.

"There's some bacon over near the fire," he said.
"I didn't take time to make biscuits. Mine aren't
worth a damn, anyway."

"Mine are," Priscilla said proudly. "I'm a very
good cook, you know."

Brendan's face lit up. "God, I'd give six months'
pay for some real home cooking. Think you could
bake a pie if I found some wild berries?"

"Pies are my specialty."

While Brendan cared for the livestock, Priscilla

dressed in the dark green calico she had worn the day before. She ate the bacon he had fried, along with a slice of melon, and cleaned the skillet in the creek, using the clean sand in the bottom to scour away the grease.

When they finished breaking camp, Brendan helped her up on the wagon seat. "You drive the team," he said from the ground at her side. "I want to do a little scouting, see what's up ahead."

"Me? B-but I—"

"Just stay on the road—such as it is. I won't be far away." He gathered the big black horse's reins and swung effortlessly into the saddle. The animal snorted and pranced, but Brendan spoke to him with quiet authority and the animal settled right down. "Ready?"

Priscilla swallowed hard. "What do I do first?"

Saddle leather creaked as Brendan shifted his weight to look at her, his light blue eyes accusing. "Son of a bitch, I should have known." With a scowl that told her exactly what a priss he thought she was, he swung down from his horse.

"I didn't say I couldn't do it, I just need you to tell me how."

Brendan grinned at that, the hard lines easing, his blue eyes twinkling. "Well, Priscilla my girl, you might find it just a tad more difficult than it looks." He tied the horse to the back of the wagon and climbed up on the seat beside her. Unwinding the reins from around the brake, he released the lever and slapped the mules lightly on the rump.

"Well?" Priscilla pressed when he made no move to give her the reins.

"Something might happen. I don't want to take any chances."

"As you pointed out last night, we've got a good three days' journey ahead of us. Teaching me to drive the team will help pass the time."

He shook his head. "No."

"If I'm going to live on a ranch, I'll have to learn sooner or later."

For a moment he didn't answer, then with a sigh, he pulled the team to a halt. "All right. I guess you can't get in too much trouble as long as I'm sitting beside you." *Like hell*, he thought, his eyes skimming over her body.

He'd decided to scout ahead more to cool his blood than because he really needed to. There'd been no sign of the men from the trading post. Odds were they wouldn't see another soul until they reached the Triple R.

"Hold out your hands." Priscilla did as he said, and Brendan laced the leather lines through her fingers. "Slap the reins against their flanks and talk to them."

"Talk to them? What do I say?"

He smiled at that. "Since we don't know their names you can call them whatever you like. Just keep your voice quiet but firm and tell them to get going."

She set her gaze on the animals in determined concentration. "All right, mules, let's go," she said, lightly slapping the reins. To her relief, they brayed and started right off.

"They like you," he teased.

"They are kind of cute, in a lop-eared sort of way."

"They're cute, all right, as long as they're doing what you want them to."

"How do I turn them?"

"It's just the opposite of riding a horse—instead of using the pressure of the rein on the animal's neck, you pull. Pull on the right rein, you go right, the left rein, you go left, and ease up on the other side."

"Since I never learned how to ride, I shouldn't get too confused."

Brendan released a long, slow breath. "What in blazes are you doing out here, Miss Wills? You've got about as much business on the Texas frontier as a prairie dog does in a parlor."

"I'm not out here to ride horses, Mr. Trask. I'm here to provide a comfortable home for my husband and the family we will raise. *That,* I assure you, is something I'm more than capable of doing."

Brendan's eyes moved from the fullness of her breasts to the curve of her waist, then drifted lower. "If Egan has his way, he'll probably keep you barefoot and pregnant—and chained to the foot of his bed."

Priscilla flushed crimson. She didn't say another word.

They rode along in silence, lulled by the whir of the wheels over the hard-packed earth, the occasional caw of a blackbird. The landscape had changed from mostly flat land covered with salt grass to gently rolling hills dotted with live oaks and clusters of bushy mesquite. The land climbed steadily, though the angle was slight and the animals didn't seem to mind.

Priscilla did well with them until the trail disappeared into a recent wash, and they had to leave the path and cross a dry ravine.

"You'd better let me take them through." Brendan reached for the reins, but Priscilla wouldn't let go.

"How will I ever learn to handle them if all I do is drive straight ahead?"

"We can't risk the wagon."

"I can do it, I know I can."

Brendan eyed her a moment, gauging her it seemed. "All right, you stubborn little minx, give it a try, but you damned well better not break a wheel or we'll really be up a creek."

Priscilla grinned. She pulled on the right rein, and the mules turned off the dirt trail. She pulled on the left, and they straightened out and headed down into the gulley. She might have made it if it weren't for the long-necked, long-legged bird who raced out of a clump of mesquite in front of them, a small snake wriggling in its beak.

The mules reared up in their traces, braying wildly, and then bolted forward.

"Damn!" Brendan made a grab for the reins just as the wagon hit a chuckhole. Priscilla flew up from the seat and would have gone out of the wagon if Brendan's arm hadn't clamped around her waist. Her hold on the reins loosened for only a moment, but it was long enough to send the team through the ravine at a breakneck pace and up the other side, dumping most of their gear out the back, including Priscilla's trunks.

"For God's sake, don't let go!" Brendan shouted, holding Priscilla on his lap with one arm while reaching around her with the other to grab the reins.

Seizing a handful of leather, he hauled backward. "Whoa, mules! Easy now. Be gentle." At the firm tone of his voice, the animals slowed and finally came to a stop.

Priscilla sat on Brendan's lap, trembling all over. Two strong arms held her in place, and his warm breath next to her ear moved tendrils of hair beside her cheek.

Priscilla's heart, already thumping with excitement, started to pound even harder.

"You all right?" he asked, his face just inches away.

"Yes," she said, the word coming out in a soft breath of air. Priscilla licked her lips, and the arm around her waist grew tighter.

"Priscilla," he whispered, his voice suddenly husky.

She just stared at him, lost in the blueness of his eyes, the smooth bronzed hue of his skin. There were tiny creases across his forehead, she noticed for the first time, but they only made him more attractive.

"I know I shouldn't do this," he was saying, "but I have to—just this once." Before she could think what he meant, Brendan's long brown fingers moved to her throat. He lifted her chin, tipped it up, and settled his mouth over hers. Priscilla gasped in shock as his tongue invaded her mouth, silky smooth and so very warm. His free hand cradled her face, giving him control, but it wouldn't have mattered. She couldn't have moved away from him for all the cattle in Texas.

Brendan held her a moment more, kissing her thoroughly, expertly, she imagined. Then the kiss ended as abruptly as it had begun—thankfully—before she had really embarrassed herself. At a loss as to what she should do, pink from her neck to her hairline, Priscilla started to speak, thought better of it, and instead hauled off and slapped him, the loud crack making them both start.

"H-how dare you take such liberties," she stammered, as upset with herself as she was with him. "I-I'm engaged to be married, as you know only too well."

Brendan just rubbed his cheek and grinned. "My foremost apologies, Miss Wills. But finding such a lovely lady sitting on my lap, well . . . I just couldn't help myself."

Priscilla glanced down in horror. Hard thighs— and something distinctly masculine—pressed against her bottom.

"Dear God in heaven," she whispered, realizing just how long she'd been sitting there. She slid off his lap and onto the seat, her eyes carefully fixed on the horizon.

"I suppose you think this was my fault, too," she said, remembering how she had snuggled up to him in his bedroll with even more embarrassing results. "I certainly didn't mean to . . . that is . . . surely you don't think I—"

Brendan sobered, the easy grin gone from his face. "Not in the least, Miss Wills." He set the brake and wrapped the reins around it, securing them tightly. "I haven't doubted your virtue for a moment." One last grin. "Your wisdom, yes, but your virtue—never."

He jumped down from the wagon. "I'll reload the supplies. You stay put—and whatever you do, don't touch those reins."

Chapter 5

"I almost made it," Priscilla said, "next time I will."

"You almost fell out on your pretty little bottom." Brendan squatted on his haunches to set the last stone in the circle around the dry wood and branches he had readied for the fire. Neither of them had said much since his return to the wagon. He'd just settled himself on the seat beside her and clucked the team into a trot.

"I shouldn't have let you try it," he added, pulling a box of wooden matches from his pocket. "You almost got hurt."

Priscilla stiffened. "There are risks involved in everything. That doesn't mean I should sit around and do nothing. Before we reach the Triple R, I'm going to learn to drive that team."

"Sorry. You'll have to get Egan to teach you." Brendan struck the match against a rock and held it to the dry grass and kindling. Soft yellow flames licked the air and began to blacken and curl the wood.

"Surely you didn't expect me to be perfect the very first time," Priscilla argued. "I'll do better, I just need a little more practice."

"No."

"Why not?"

"Because you're my responsibility. I mean to see you get to Egan safe and sound."

"You won't teach me because of Stuart? You certainly weren't worried about Stuart when you kissed me." *What had possessed her to say that?* Just thinking about that kiss sent a flood of warmth to her cheeks—and several other places as well.

"If you're looking for another apology, forget it. I warned you about getting too close. You were *definitely* too close." Brendan got up from the fire, stretching with an easy grace to his full height, a good eight inches taller than Priscilla.

"I need to rub down the livestock." He gave her a last fleeting glance. "I guess . . . after the kiss and all . . . that pie would be out of the question."

Priscilla couldn't help but laugh. "You are truly a rogue, Mr. Trask. If you can find the berries, I'll bake the pie."

Brendan smiled, the hard lines easing, his light eyes almost playful. "Truth is, I spotted some just a little ways back." The smile turned cocky. "Why do you think I picked this particular place to camp?"

Priscilla laughed again as Brendan grabbed a metal pot and retreated toward the woods. She watched the movement of his powerful shoulders and narrow hips, and found it hard to look away. He was the boldest, most arrogant man she had ever met. So unbelievably cocksure of himself, at times so utterly charming. She had never known anyone like him.

Priscilla's bright mood faded. Brendan Trask was a gambler and a gunman. A hard-edged man who could kill with the blink of an eye. She mustn't let his charming manner blind her to the kind of man he really was.

Digging through the pots and pans he had stacked beside the campfire, Priscilla found the items she needed and set them aside. She would bake him a cobbler, the closest she could come to a pie out here in the wilderness.

She lifted the heavy cast-iron Dutch oven. Though she could cook—wonderfully, in fact—she had never used one of the heavy iron kettles to bake in. On the old black cookstove in their town house back in Cincinnati, she had cooked mouth-watering meals that had the neighbors clamoring just for the leftovers.

What she hadn't told Brendan was that she had never cooked a bite of food over an open fire.

Brendan found the berry patch they had passed on the trail, filled the pot with the succulent fruit, washed them in a nearby stream, and brought them back to Priscilla. Entering the camp on silent feet as he had learned to do, he spotted her bent over a rock, busily making a crust, her hands white with flour up to her slender wrists.

As she added a drop or two of water, working to get the consistency of the dough just right, he watched her backside shift gracefully, and his body began to harden. Damn! The woman had the strangest effect on him. Every time he thought of her, his loins grew hot and throbbing.

He thought of Patsy Jackson, of robust hips, heavy breasts, and a red-rouged mouth. There was nothing wrong with Patsy, yet she seemed almost a caricature of a woman to him now.

He cleared his throat, and Priscilla turned and smiled. "I've already washed them," he told her, extending the bucket of berries and moving in her direction.

"Just set them here beside the rock. I'll get to them in a minute."

"Anything else I can do?"

She glanced at the fire, seeming a bit hesitant. "No, thank you. Supper will be ready within the hour."

"What are we having?"

"Hoecakes and molasses, and a version of Hopping John. Of course, I don't have quite the right ingredients."

Brendan licked his lips. "Hopping John. I haven't had that since the last New Year's Day I spent in Savannah. That was at least six years ago."

"What were you doing in Savannah?"

"I was raised there. My brother and I headed for the South after we left England. I only came to Texas seven years ago."

"Why here?" she asked over her shoulder, continuing to knead the dough.

"Adventure, I guess. I joined the Texas Marines not long after I got here. Tom Camden told you how that turned out."

"Yes. . . ." She turned around to look at him. "You were thrown into a Mexican prison. How did you—"

"I've got to take care of the livestock. I'll be back in time to eat." He started to walk away, but halted. "By the way. You've been walking pretty far from camp to . . . take care of your needs. I warned you about that before." He looked at her hard. "I don't mean to scare you, but there are snakes out there, to say nothing of scorpions, tarantulas, and centipedes."

"I don't intend to compromise my modesty, Mr. Trask." Her chin went up and tilted at a firm little angle. "But I certainly will be careful."

Brendan shook his head. "Women," he muttered.

Priscilla found a grate among the cooking gear and balanced it atop the fire on the circle of rocks. She set the kettle of Hopping John—a stew made with slab bacon and black-eyed peas, minus the usual coconut, which they obviously didn't have—on top of the grate, and flames licked the bottom of the pot. The Dutch oven she placed at the edge of the fire and silently prayed it wouldn't burn. The hoecakes she would do in the skillet, once the stew neared completion.

It didn't take long for Priscilla to realize that cooking on a blazing campfire was hardly the same as cooking above the fire that roared in the cookstove. In minutes, the stew spewed bubbles of red-hot broth, and the heavy Dutch oven hissed some sort of warning about the pie.

Priscilla reached for the handle of the pot with a dishcloth so as not to burn her fingers, lifted the kettle, then dropped it as flames caught the edge of her towel and burned the underside of her wrist. "Ouch," she said aloud, though the burn was minor. More importantly, the pot hadn't spilled.

"Priscilla!" The urgency in Brendan's voice spun her around.

She saw him racing across the clearing at the same instant she realized the hem of her skirt had burst into flame. Priscilla screamed at the feel of white-hot fabric searing into her skin, the sight of wicked red-orange fire eating its way upward toward her face.

As she slapped frantically at the flames, fighting down her terror, Brendan barreled into her, knocking her into the dirt. He rolled her one way and then the other, then turned and batted the remaining fire from her petticoats with the flat of his hand.

"Sweet Jesus!" he said into her terrified face. She could feel his heavy weight pressing into her, then he shifted and came to his feet. "Don't move," he commanded, "I'll be right back."

Priscilla nodded and sat there shaking. In minutes he returned carrying a chunk of spiny cactus wrapped in one of the handkerchiefs he always carried. Snapping the cactus in two, he knelt beside her and reached for the hem of her skirt. Unconsciously, Priscilla's hand shot out to stop him.

"There's something in the cactus," Brendan said gently. "The Indians use it for burns. It'll take away the pain."

"It's really not that bad." It wasn't proper for a man to see a woman's legs, and she had already been improper enough. "I only burned my ankle. I think I can do it myself."

All trace of gentleness fled. "I assure you, Miss Wills, yours won't be the first woman's ankle I've seen. I'll hardly be overcome with lust and ravish you."

While Priscilla's face turned as red as the flames they'd just put out, Brendan lifted the blackened remains of the bottom of her skirt and several inches of fire-chewed petticoat. He started to apply the salve, but his eyes picked up a flash of color and his hand stilled in mid-air.

He lifted the skirt a little higher and glanced down at her petticoat. One corner of his mouth curved up. "You sew this?"

Priscilla blushed more than she had before. "Yes." In a burst of color across her lap, bright red flowers bloomed in profusion, covering the entire white circle of fabric. Somber colors pleased her aunt; the vibrant colors Priscilla so loved were forbidden. Her petticoat, and several others like it, were a secret show of defiance—as Trask seemed to guess.

"So prim and proper on the outside," he drawled in that sensual way of his, "I wonder what you're like underneath."

Ignoring the retort she started to make, Brendan rolled down her scorched and burned stocking and applied some of the clear, sticky salve he scraped from the inside of the cactus.

At the soothing feel of the mixture, Priscilla breathed a sigh of relief. "Whatever it is, it's wonderful." It did indeed relieve the pain, which had grown considerably in the last few moments. "I could use a little on my wrist, too."

Brendan grumbled something she couldn't hear and finished applying the salve. "What the hell were you—"

"The stew!" Priscilla wailed at the distinct odor of burnt meat. She tried to get up, but Brendan pressed her back down.

"Son of a bitch," he growled, lifting the kettle of

burnt Hopping John off the grate. "Why didn't you wait for the fire to die down?" He reached for the heavy Dutch oven, set the cobbler aside, lifted the lid, and groaned.

"I suppose it's ruined, too," Priscilla said morosely.

"I thought you said you could cook."

"I can."

"You sure couldn't prove it by me."

"Under normal conditions, I'm a very good cook. I . . . I just never tried it on a campfire."

Brendan swore softly. "Why didn't you tell me?"

"Because I thought I could do it." *And I wanted to prove myself.*

"Well, obviously you can't."

Oh, yes I can. "We'll see, Mr. Trask."

Brendan didn't answer. The set of his shoulders told her he wasn't about to let her try it again.

At least the hoecakes were good. Brendan cooked the batter and they ate them with hunks of beef jerky. It wasn't exactly what either of them had in mind, but it was filling, and darkness had settled around them.

After supper Brendan checked her ankle, grunted in satisfaction that the burn really wasn't that bad, and they both curled up in their bedrolls—Priscilla's some distance from Brendan's.

She heard him stir sometime before dawn, watched him pull on his boots and start the fire. Pretending to be asleep, Priscilla watched from her bedroll while Brendan made coffee, then quietly left to check on the livestock. Afterward he would probably go down to the creek to shave, as he had each morn-

ing since their departure, which would give her the
time she would need.

Priscilla dressed hurriedly in a clean brown gingham dress, took care of her morning ablutions in the
opposite direction from where Brendan had gone,
then went over to the fire. This time she spread out
the coals, as she had seen him do, and carefully kept
her skirts a goodly distance away.

She had bacon frying and pan biscuits warm and
ready to eat when he arrived. The bottom of the cobbler had burned, but some of the berries were still
good, making a fine rich jam.

Brendan strolled into camp, wearing his doeskin
breeches and a clean white shirt, his hair still damp
and curling against his collar. Seeing Priscilla bent
over the fire, his expression turned hard. "I thought
you understood—from now on, I'll do the cooking."

Priscilla just smiled. "Homemade biscuits, warm
berry jam, and crisp fried bacon. There's even a bit of
gravy made from the drippings."

"Biscuits?" he repeated, unconsciously running a
tongue over his lips.

"With warm berry jam—or gravy, if you prefer."

Brendan's mouth curved up in a lazy grin. "I'll
have both." They sat down to eat, and Priscilla
watched him through dark, lowered lashes. The look
on his face was worth all the effort—and maybe even
the burns.

"This is delicious." Closing his eyes, he savored the
bite of biscuit he chewed with incredible relish. "I've
never tasted any better. And that gravy—God, Priscilla, you do have a knack."

She should have stopped such informality long

ago, had made a half-hearted try or two, but now it was too late. Instead she beamed at the compliment. "I'm glad you like it."

"Like it? I love it. Now I feel twice as bad about the Hopping John."

Priscilla laughed. "I'll make another batch tonight. We've still got two more days before we reach the Triple R."

Brendan stopped chewing. His eyes fixed on her face until she had to look away.

He set his tin plate down beside him. "You'd better finish eating. It's time we hit the trail."

Two days, she thought, and suddenly the food seemed to lodge in her throat. Setting her half-finished plate aside, she rose numbly and started cleaning up the dishes.

Neither of them said much for the rest of the morning.

The trail paralleled the stream for most of the day, heading north into drier country. Patches of cactus and stands of oak and pecan trees dotted the landscape; wild grapes in stifling green curtains hung from the branches, blotting the sun and nearly touching the earth.

"Lots of wild turkey hereabouts," Brendan told her. "A little fresh game would sure be good in that stew you're planning to make."

"I'm not quite sure how to pluck one, but if you'll show me—"

"I'll get it ready," he said with a smile. "You just cook it." He gazed at the landscape ahead of them, wearing a look of pleasure. "Pretty country, isn't it?"

She studied the raw red dirt, the rocks and the cactus. "You think this is pretty?"

"It is if you know what to look for." He pulled the wagon to a halt and pointed toward a pecan tree near the narrow streambed. "There's a doe and fawn over there, but their coloring blends so well you can barely see them."

Priscilla looked hard, but couldn't seem to spot them.

"Just a few feet to the left of the tree. The mother is starting to walk away."

"Yes, I see them now." She felt a rush of warmth as she watched the tiny fawn, its protective white-speckled coat blending into its surroundings. "They're beautiful. I've always loved animals."

"My brother and I always kept a menagerie around the house. I had a big red retriever named Dillon I was crazy about. Funny, I haven't thought about that dog in years."

"What happened to him?"

"He just got old. He had a helluva good life, though. Aren't many people get as much love and affection as Dillon got from the two of us."

It didn't seem hard to believe.

"I like the freedom of this land," he went on, saying more than he usually did. "It brings out the best in a man."

Not always, she thought, remembering the men at the trading post.

"At night the sunsets can be spectacular. Almost worth suffering the heat of the day. In the spring the grass comes up soft and green, and there are wildflowers of every size and color."

"I've always wanted a flower garden. It's hard to imagine whole fields of them."

Brendan smiled at that. When Priscilla smiled back, he cleared his throat and looked away. Urging the mules a little faster, he fixed his eyes on the horizon as if he wished he could make it move closer.

Priscilla straightened on the hard wooden seat and settled her eyes on the same distant line. To her amazement, she found herself wishing she could move it farther away.

Two more days, her mind repeated. In two more days she would reach the Triple R and the man she would marry.

What would he look like? Aunt Maddie had described him as handsome. Her aunt had met Stuart Egan on a trip back to Natchez to see Deder Wills, Maddie's dying brother, the last of Priscilla's family in Natchez. At Aunt Maddie's insistence, Priscilla had stayed in Cincinnati with Ella Simpkins so she could finish her schooling. That had been two years ago.

Stuart had been in mourning, still grieving over the death of his first wife when Aunt Maddie had met him through Uncle Deder. They had struck up an unlikely friendship—Priscilla still could not fathom why. Whatever the reason, they'd begun corresponding. Then Maddie had taken sick, and Priscilla had answered Stuart's letters in her stead. Their friendship had grown, and a long-distance courtship had begun.

When Aunt Maddie died, Stuart had proposed, solving her financial problems and promising to fulfill her dreams of having a husband and family. If Priscilla hadn't known better, she would have be-

lieved Aunt Maddie had planned the whole thing—
controlling her even from the grave.

She glanced across at Brendan. How would Stuart's good looks compare to Brendan's ruggedly
handsome profile? Her eyes traced the line of his
nicely arched eyebrows, the straight nose, and firm,
strong lips. Priscilla remembered the kiss they had
shared, and a warmth curled in the pit of her stomach.

"We'll rest the mules up ahead on that knoll—get
out of the sun for a while and cool off a bit."

Priscilla nodded. "It feels a lot hotter today."

"I've got a hunch it's gonna be worse tomorrow."

Priscilla groaned.

"Better get used to it, Miss Wills. This is Texas. You
don't like hot weather, you shouldn't be here."

Priscilla stiffened her spine. "As you pointed out,
Mr. Trask, there are good things and bad things
about this land. If I want to share in the good things,
I'll learn to put up with the bad."

Brendan studied her a moment more, but made no
further comment. They pulled up on the knoll into
the shade of a live oak tree, and Brendan climbed
down. His hands went around her waist and he
swung her to the ground beside him.

While he unhitched the team and led them to water, Priscilla headed down the slope to relieve herself. The landscape was a bit more barren, mostly
cactus and mesquite, but Priscilla determinedly
scanned the area looking for a large clump of brush
or a cluster of rocks to give her some privacy.

The best place lay a goodly distance away, but after

jouncing all morning on the hard wooden seat, the walk would give her a chance to stretch her legs.

Crossing the dusty open space, she skirted the rocks and discovered a secluded place behind them. As she started her return to the wagon, she spotted Brendan in the distance, leading the mules back into their traces.

Priscilla lifted her skirts and started to hurry, knowing he'd be angry if he saw her this far away. Spying what appeared to be a shorter return route, she hurried in that direction. Once she cleared the rotting fallen log that blocked her path, she'd be home free.

Raising her skirt even higher, Priscilla set one sturdy brown shoe on the top of the log. A bone-chilling buzz erupted from a rock beneath her leg, raising the hair at the back of her neck. With a scream of terror, she tried to avoid the piercing fangs of the coiled up, brown-speckled rattlesnake, but they tore into her tender flesh as she leapt over the log.

Pain shot up her leg, but she kept on running, her heart thundering wildly against her ribs. Her leg throbbed and her body shook with the remnants of fright, but all she could think of was the tempest that awaited her back in camp. Brendan would be furious! He'd rail at her for being so careless and tell her again what a fool she was for coming to Texas at all.

She saw him racing toward her and ran straight into his arms.

"Priscilla, what is it?"

"R-rattlesnake," she stammered. "Over by that

log." She pointed with a shaky finger, fighting to hold back her tears.

Brendan grabbed her shoulders and set her away from him. "I told you not to go that far from the wagon."

"Please don't be mad."

He felt her trembling and pulled her against his chest. "It's all right. Just don't do it again."

Her arms tightened around him. "It isn't all right," she whispered. "My leg—" Priscilla's knees gave way and only Brendan's hold kept her from falling.

"Sweet Jesus!" He settled her down on the ground and hurriedly lifted the hem of her brown gingham skirt. "Where?" he asked, searching her pale flesh, finding no fang marks on her ankle or calf.

"Higher," she whispered. Brendan pushed her onto her back and hoisted her skirts even farther. "I still don't see anything. Are you sure he struck you?"

"Higher," she repeated, blushing from head to foot. "On the inside."

Brendan swore softly, jerked her skirts up to her waist and spread her legs apart. He spotted the hole in her soft cotton drawers high on the inside of her right thigh.

With a great ripping tear, he parted the fabric, exposing her skin and most of her thigh. Priscilla's face flamed hotter, and she twisted and tried to sit up.

"You stay right where you are." He pressed her back down. "Your damnable modesty will just have to wait." Pulling his knife from the scabbard at his waist, he shoved it into the burning sand beneath them and worked to cleanse the blade as best he could. "Saw this done down in Mexico. I hope to God it works."

"W-what are you going to do?"

"Lance the wound and suck out the poison." Before she could protest, he cut an x on her thigh with two swift clean strokes.

Priscilla stifled the terror she felt and began to tremble even more. Brendan ignored her, just spread her legs wider and settled himself between them.

"Dear God in heaven," Priscilla softly intoned, feeling his hands on the inside of her thigh.

"Damned puritan," he grumbled, easing her embarrassment apparent in every rigid muscle and joint. "I'd enjoy this, if it wasn't so damned serious." With that he set his mouth against her leg and began to suck out the venom.

Even as scared as she was, Priscilla felt a jolt of heat slide through her body. Brendan's hands gripped her thigh and his mouth moved over her flesh, sucking hard again and again. In the eye of her mind, she could see his lips moving over her skin, see his long dark fingers touching the flesh of her upper thigh.

Unconsciously, Priscilla moaned.

"It's all right, Silla," he soothed, "I'm just about done." A few moments later, he pressed his handkerchief against the wound and grabbed the ruffle at the bottom of her petticoat. Tearing off a length of it, he wrapped the material around her thigh and tied the handkerchief in place with several sure tugs.

When he had finished he lowered her skirts, lifted her in his arms, and started back toward the camp.

Priscilla clutched his neck to steady herself, and corded muscles bunched beneath her hands.

"What happens now?" she asked, forcing herself not to notice how solid he felt.

"That depends mostly on you. How your body reacts to the poison." His eyes narrowed with worry and seemed a slightly darker shade of blue. "You shouldn't have run, Priscilla. It speeds up your heartbeat, makes the poison move faster—damn it, Sill, it's the worst thing you could have done."

"I didn't know."

"That's the problem—you don't know a damned thing about this country. Egan ought to have his head examined for bringing you out here. One way or another, you're bound and determined to get yourself killed." He set her down in the shade of an oak tree.

"Brendan?"

"What?" he snapped.

"I'm starting to feel kind of . . . dizzy."

The harshness went out of his manner. "Just take it easy. I'm going to make a poultice out of some tobacco. I'll be right back."

"Brendan?"

He stopped and turned to face her.

"If anything . . . happens . . . I want you to know I appreciate how hard you've worked to take care of me."

"Nothing's going to happen," he said gruffly, deep lines etching his forehead. "I'm not going to let it." With that he strode off toward the wagon.

While he rummaged through their supplies, looking for God knows what, Priscilla leaned back against the oak, thinking about his words.

She'd been right, of course. His "I told you so"s were even worse than she'd expected. Still, it felt good to hear the protective note in his voice when he'd said them. It felt good to know he cared, and that he was there to help her.

Brendan returned a few moments later. While Priscilla fought her embarrassment, he pulled up her skirts, reached between her thighs, and applied the tobacco poultice, securing it again with the length of petticoat.

"We'll make camp here," he said, "until you're out of danger . . . speaking of which, I want you out of those clothes."

"What?"

"You're bound to run a fever," he patiently explained. "It's hotter than Hades out here already." He turned her around and started to unbutton the back of her dress.

Priscilla pulled away. "I refuse to sit here half naked in front of a stranger."

Brendan bent over her. "If I'm not mistaken—and I know I'm not—you're wearing that damnable corset of yours. I want you out of it and that's the way it's gonna be. And I'm hardly a stranger."

Priscilla started to argue, but a wave of nausea swept over her and beads of perspiration popped out on her forehead. She wet her suddenly dry lips. "All right. I'll take off my corset and petticoats, but I'm leaving on my dress."

Brendan put a hand to her forehead. It felt clammy

and warm. "All right, have it your way." *For now*, he thought. The way things were going, it wouldn't be long before she got too sick to care. He unbuttoned the back of her dress and started to pull it off her shoulders.

"Just loosen the corset," she said, "I can do the rest." But she didn't look like she could. "Turn around," she ordered.

"Christ, Priscilla."

"Please don't blaspheme." It was little more than a whisper.

Brendan turned his back to her. "Finished?" he asked. When Priscilla didn't reply, Brendan turned to find her slumped forward, her dress half on, half off.

"Damn you, lady." But his hand shook as he took in her sallow complexion, the ragged sound of her breathing.

As gently as he could, he undressed her, removing first her dress, then her flashy red-embroidered petticoats—which still coaxed a smile—and the most god-awful steel-sided corset he'd ever seen. In a burst of fury at her maddening sense of propriety, he bunched it up and threw it as far as he could. Nothing but a damned nuisance. And it wasn't as though she needed it.

Determined to strip her naked and put on her nightgown, he pulled the string to her white cotton drawers, but wavered. Damned woman would probably rather be dead than have him see her naked.

Cursing her again for her infuriating modesty, he left her in her soft cotton drawers and chemise. He tried not to notice the gentle curve of her hips, how small her waist was even without the corset, the peaks of her upthrusting breasts.

Mostly he tried not to notice how deathly pale she looked—or how much it hurt him to see her so sick.

Chapter 6

Stuart Egan swung down from his palomino stallion to join the broad-faced, thick-chested Indian who crouched a few feet away, carefully studying the earth.

"What do you make of them?" Stuart asked, trying to read the wide swath of hoof marks.

"Comanche," Tall Wind replied. "Ten, maybe more. They head north. Go back home." Once a great Kiowa warrior, Tall Wind had succumbed to the lure of the white man's whiskey. He'd wound up drunk and half starved wandering the desert like a nomad until he stumbled onto the Triple R.

"They shouldn't have been around here in the first place," Stuart said. "They've agreed to a peace—shaky as it is—besides, they know damn well what will happen if they raid the Triple R."

Tall Wind stood, the hot breeze ruffling his breechcloth as well as his coarse black hair. "Some afraid. Others not care. They fight for their land. They die for the ways of their people." Something in his hard black eyes said he admired them for it, though Tall Wind had pledged his loyalty to the man standing near him—the man who had come to his aid when no one else would have. Stuart Egan. The man who had saved his life.

"They'll die, all right," Stuart said, "make no mistake about that."

Tall Wind didn't answer. Stuart knew the Indian didn't doubt his word, or his power to make it happen. Though a part of the warrior would remain with his heritage, Stuart trusted him, as he did most of the men who worked for him. He demanded loyalty from those around him. He knew how to get it, and he would tolerate no less.

"You don't think they'll double back, do you?" Noble Egan, Stuart's only son, swung down from his saddle. "Barker could be crossing the trail south of here. We've got no way of knowing which ship he'll be taking to Corpus, or when it might arrive."

"Comanche ride north," the Indian repeated, pointing in that direction.

"That's good enough for me," Stuart said. "With that latest shipment of cattle, we're damned shorthanded. We can't afford to lose a single hand."

"What about Miss Wills?" Noble pressed. He stood nearly as tall as his father, with Stuart's same light complexion, sandy hair, and hazel eyes. At eighteen, he was mature for a boy of his age, and he blindly worshipped his father. "If there's any chance of a run-in with the Comanche—"

"Tall Wind says they're returning to their homeland. Barker is plenty tough enough to take care of Miss Wills and her traveling companion." When Noble still looked doubtful, Stuart added, "If I thought there'd be any trouble, I'd go after her myself." This last was true enough, though he couldn't afford the time.

Besides, the rough trip with Barker would do the woman good. She'd have to toughen up if she intended to live on the frontier. There'd be no frills with Barker. He'd get her here in one piece, see that she came to no harm, then Stuart could step in and play the hero. It was a tactic he had used again and again to inspire the kind of allegiance he demanded.

"We'd better get a move on," he said to Tall Wind. "I want to check the upper mesa."

The Indian just grunted and returned to his wiry white mustang. He swung onto the horse's back and nudged the animal forward with his knees.

Stuart surveyed the parched landscape a moment more, the forty thousand acres that had once been Rancho Reina del Robles—Queen of the Oaks—and was now the Triple R. He had bought Don Pedro's land grant for a song—after the old Mexican's disastrous string of unfortunate "accidents." The land was his now, and this wide-open tract was just the beginning. Eventually Stuart intended to own a hundred thousand acres and tens of thousands of head of cattle. He'd be the wealthiest landowner in Texas.

To say nothing of his lofty political ambitions.

What he needed was a wife to give him an appearance of stability, and, most importantly, more sons. A man needed sons to run a ranch the size of the Triple R. Noble was a good boy, but if anything happened to him—and in this rough country there was always that chance—Stuart would be left without an heir. He intended to remedy that possibility with all haste.

He just hoped the woman was as comely—and as docile—as her crotchety old aunt had said.

"No, Mama. No, Mama! Mama, I'm scared."

"It's all right, Silla. Everything is going to be all right." Brendan wiped the perspiration from her brow with a damp cloth, appreciating as he had a dozen times before the delicate planes and valleys of her face, her clear skin, and long dark lashes.

She muttered something else and shoved the blanket down to her waist. Her breasts rose softly beneath her thin chemise, the dark circles at each peak making his body stir.

With the fever still raging, she shouldn't be covered at all, he admitted, but he'd grown so damned uncomfortable looking at her slender body, speculating —however unwillingly—how tempting she'd look in nothing at all, that he'd finally tossed a blanket over her.

"No, Mama," she repeated, drawing his attention to the slender hands she fisted like a child. She had mumbled in her sleep several times before, but said nothing he could make sense of until now. He wondered at the ominous words and tried to imagine the childhood memory she suppressed. He wondered if not being able to remember was a curse—or a blessing.

With a businesslike movement of his hand, Brendan checked the poultice he had placed on her thigh, forcing himself not to notice how smooth and white her skin was, how long and supple her legs. Though she still tossed and turned, the wound hadn't festered, and some of her color had returned.

He moved to the campfire and fixed some broth from the slab of bacon he had brought, hoping that when she awakened she would be able to eat, then he settled down beside her. He must have dozed because he awoke with a jolt to find her awake and watching him.

"Silla," he said without thinking, feeling a rush of relief. "Thank God." He sat up tiredly and raked a hand through his wavy dark brown hair.

For a moment she seemed uncertain, then she wet her lips and smiled. "I'm going to be all right," she said staunchly, and Brendan smiled, too.

"So it seems."

He fetched the broth and fed her some, and afterward she drifted back to sleep. Since the fever had broken and there was no more tossing and turning, his worry eased, but still he only rested.

He kept thinking about his lovely charge, wondering what would happen to her once they reached the Triple R. Egan would marry her—he had no doubt about that—but would she be happy? And why did he care?

The debt he owed her would end the moment they reached the ranch. Egan could take over, use his power and money to keep her safe. She'd have expensive clothes, servants. If Egan had his way, they might even wind up in Washington. Surely she would be happy—what woman wouldn't?

Unfortunately, she'd be Egan's possession, forced to live under his rule just as his men did. Still, lots of women lived that way. If he were her husband, he'd be pretty damned demanding himself.

Brendan started, wondering where such an odd thought had come from, then doggedly his thoughts returned to Egan and Priscilla. Eventually the sun came up, putting an end to his musing, and Priscilla awoke with it.

"Good morning," she said with a much brighter

tone than he had expected. When she tried to sit up, he gently urged her back down.

"I gather you're feeling better, but there's no need to rush things."

She yawned behind her hand and smiled. "I gather I wasn't feeling too well last night."

"For a while there, no. I was damned worried about you."

Priscilla spotted the blanket that covered only her feet, blushed prettily at the parts she exposed, and pulled the light red wool up to her chin. "My leg hurts some, but other than that I feel pretty good. I hope I wasn't too much trouble."

Brendan's mood turned dark as he thought of how close she had come to serious injury. "Trouble, Miss Wills, is your middle name. I'm just glad you're all right."

If she noticed his frown, she didn't acknowledge it. "If I am all right, I imagine it's because of you."

"Maybe," he admitted. "Mostly it's how much venom you took, or any number of things. Since I've been out here, I've seen plenty of snakebit horses and men. For the most part, a centipede bite seems more often fatal." He looked at her hard. "You'll damn well be more careful from now on, or I swear, Priscilla, you won't leave my side, modesty or no."

"I'll be careful," she promised with an odd look of pleasure at his words.

Priscilla couldn't help herself. No one had ever watched out for her the way Brendan did. He looked bone-tired, his face lined with worry and roughened by a day's growth of beard.

"We'll stay here another day," he was saying. "If

you feel well enough to travel in the morning, we'll head out."

"I'm sure I'll be fine," she assured him. "And thank you."

Brendan just scowled. What was he thinking? she wondered, watching him move toward the fire with his usual catlike grace. He returned with a steaming cup of coffee, which she gratefully accepted, and she began to feel even better.

At Brendan's insistence, she ate lightly and rested through most of the day, but by late afternoon she felt restless and ready to move about.

"It's time I got dressed," she pronounced. "I don't suppose there's a stream nearby—someplace I might bathe?"

"There's a creek at the bottom of the rise. If you're bound and determined to go, I'll carry you."

She paused at that. "You don't intend to stay, do you?"

Trask just grinned. "I'd love to, ma'am," he drawled, but I don't suppose you'd ever get into the water."

"You're right." Priscilla wrapped the blanket around her and reached for her brown gingham dress. She felt a warmth in her cheeks as Brendan gathered up shoes, stockings, and petticoats, rummaged through her trunk for clean pantalets and chemise, then scooped her into his arms.

"I don't want you putting too much weight on that leg," he said.

Priscilla started to protest, but it felt so good to be nestled against his chest, she decided not to. She had never been held by a man until she met Brendan.

She'd already determined that she liked it, unseemly or no. She just hoped Stuart could make her feel the same warm, cared-for sensations.

True to his word, after checking the banks of the stream, Brendan left her to bathe. Though the water wasn't deep, it was cool and cleansing, erasing the stickiness left from her fever. After washing her hair and body, she checked to be sure he wasn't looking, eased herself out of the water, dried a moment in the sun, then began to pull on her clothes.

All went well till she reached for her corset. A search of the garments on the rock beside her turned up no sign of it. Priscilla finished dressing, a little surprised she could fit in her clothing without it, then climbed the hill in search of Trask.

She found him tending the mules, rubbing their sleek dark gray coats with a flour sack while they munched contentedly from a bag of grain.

"I'm sorry to bother you," she said, walking up beside him. "But I can't seem to find—"

"What the hell do you think you're doing? Why didn't you call me? I told you I didn't want you putting too much weight on that leg."

"My leg feels fine. It's just a little bit sore."

His brows drew together in a scowl.

"As I was saying, I hate to bother you, but I couldn't seem to find my . . . ah . . . corset." It felt awkward discussing such a subject with a man, no matter how much of her he had seen.

He returned to rubbing down the mule. "I threw the damned thing away. This is not the place for such a god-awful contraption. You ought to have sense enough to know that without being told."

Priscilla's temper heated. "My undergarments are hardly your concern, Mr. Trask. You ought to have sense enough to know *that* without being told! I want my corset back and I'm not budging from this camp until I get it."

Brendan turned to face her. "You are without a doubt the stubbornest, most irritating—" He tossed the flour sack away. "Christ."

"Don't you dare blaspheme!"

He took what appeared to be a deep, calming breath. "Look, Miss Wills. I don't have the slightest intention of spending the night searching the wilderness for your damnable corset." Priscilla stubbornly set her jaw. "Nor do I intend to delay our departure so you can look for it—and probably get into more trouble. We'll be leaving at dawn. If we push hard, we can make up some lost time. The sooner I get you to Egan, the better off we'll both be."

Silently seething, Priscilla whirled away from him and headed back to camp. Cursing Brendan Trask for the bounder he was, she dug through the pots and pans, pulling out several and slamming them down on the top of a rock by the fire. The man was impossible! He was domineering, infuriating—

And the thought of never seeing him again almost made her weep.

Once you reach the Triple R, everything will be all right, she told herself firmly. Stuart would make her forget Brendan Trask. She'd have a home of her own, the family she dreamed of—Trask could just go hang!

* * *

In spite of her anger, Priscilla cooked the wild turkey Brendan had shot and cleaned, and made another batch of hoecakes. Trask was enthralled. He ate with such obvious pleasure, it was hard to stay mad at him.

"I don't believe I've ever known anyone who enjoyed a woman's cooking as much as you do," she finally said.

"I don't believe I've known a better cook," he countered with a grin.

"Did you always have such a big appetite?"

He shook his dark-haired head. "Guess it must have been the time I spent in that Mexican prison. We ate anything that walked, crawled, or moved, just to stay alive."

"It must have been awful. How did you escape?"

Brendan stopped chewing. There was a guarded look on his face that hadn't been there before. He seemed to be carefully choosing his words. "I wouldn't have if it hadn't been for my brother. Morgan and a handful of Texas Marines broke in through an old abandoned tunnel in the ruins where they kept us. He got all of us out . . . at least those of us who were still alive."

Priscilla could almost feel his pain. It was there in the slump of his shoulders, usually so broad and straight, and the darkness that had crept into his eyes. "You must have lost some very good men," she said softly. "Maybe even some friends."

Brendan set his plate aside, leaving several bites unfinished. "It's all in the past, Miss Wills. I've spent the last five years trying to forget it. I'd prefer we changed the topic."

"All right." It was easy to see how much the discussion had bothered him. "What shall we talk about instead?"

"Anything but the war."

She smiled. "Then tell me what kind of a bird was that back at the ravine—the one that spooked the mules?"

"Chaparral cock. Some people call it a roadrunner, some a *paisano*."

She pointed to a tall spiny cactus. "What about that?"

"Spanish bayonet—I thought we weren't going to talk about the war—"

Priscilla laughed softly. "All right, you pick a subject."

"How about your fiancé?" he said with what seemed a trace of bitterness. "Why don't we discuss the fact that you'll be marrying a man you've never even met, someone you don't know a damned thing about. Why don't we talk about living on the Texas frontier when you can barely tie your own shoelaces."

Priscilla jumped up from the log where they'd been sitting. "All right, why don't we? While we're at it, why don't we discuss the fact that I haven't a penny to my name, I have no skills other than those of a wife and mother, and that up until Stuart came along, no other man had ever shown the slightest interest in me."

"You probably never gave one a chance."

She didn't deny it. "I had my aunt to look after—I owed her that for taking me in—and believe me, Aunt Maddie was a full-time job."

"Egan might be way more than you can handle."

"I'll manage."

"Like you've managed everything else so far?"

"I'm marrying Stuart, whether you approve or not. You just get me there."

"Oh, I'll get you there, all right. And damned good riddance." With that he stormed out of camp and into the darkness.

Priscilla felt the sting of tears, though from anger or despair she couldn't quite say. Determined not to let them fall, she busied herself cleaning up, but her thoughts remained on Brendan. Why had he said those things? Couldn't he see how frightened she was already?

I have no choice, she wanted to scream, wishing he would try to understand. Except by reputation, he didn't even know Stuart Egan. Trask most certainly wasn't contemplating marriage. She wasn't sure he even liked her.

Damning him to hell in the most ladylike terms she could, Priscilla shoved back the last traces of sadness. Just a little longer and she would be safely where she belonged. Stuart would take care of her, and Brendan Trask would be gone from her life forever. He'd be nothing but a memory that would fade with the course of time. Just a little longer, she repeated, and she would finally be home.

She ignored the voice inside her head that whispered, *Maybe you're already there.*

As dawn grayed the sky to the east, Priscilla stood beside the wagon, waiting for Brendan. He had read-

ied the team and then disappeared. She wondered
where he had gone.

His steps almost silent, he approached from behind her, clearing his throat to draw her attention.
Priscilla turned to face him and found him watching
her with an uncomfortable look on his face. When he
held out his hand, her steel-ribbed corset dangled
from his long brown fingers. Priscilla flushed crimson and grabbed for the garment, but Brendan
jerked it away.

"You can have it on one condition."

"Which is?" Bright heat burned her cheeks.

"That you don't wear it until we reach the Triple R.
If Egan wants his woman all gussied up, that's his
business. My business is to get you there. Do we have
a deal?"

She smiled at that, imagining the trouble he had
gone to to find it. "We have a deal." She reached for
the corset, but Brendan pulled it away.

"I'll stow it in your trunk." Climbing into the back
of the wagon, he unbuckled the leather straps of her
steamer trunk, and laid the corset away.

Priscilla watched his movements, appreciating the
muscle and sinew that bunched beneath his shirt,
then he helped her climb up in the wagon.

Wordlessly, he took the seat beside her and handed
her the reins. With a rush of pleasure, Priscilla urged
the team forward, and they headed back toward the
trail serving as road. Several hours later they passed
a flat rock lying at the side of the trail, and Brendan
told her to pull up.

"Way stone," he said, jumping down from the seat
to read the words chiseled into the rock. "Triple R

Ranch. Stuart Egan, owner." Beneath it an arrow pointed west down an even rougher looking path.

"We must be getting close," Priscilla said, feeling an unpleasant tightening in her stomach.

"Not that close. Egan owns the old Dominguez land grant—right at forty thousand acres. Once we reach his boundary, which is still some distance away, we'll be crossing his land for some time."

Priscilla only nodded. They rode along in silence for a while.

"There's something I've been meaning to tell you," Trask finally said. "I figured you might want to know."

She turned to look at him and found his blue eyes resting on her face. "What is it?"

"The night you were sick . . . after the snake bite. You were mumbling in your sleep. Most of it I couldn't understand, but once you said something about your mother. 'No, Mama.' Then you said, 'Mama, I'm scared.' I figured you ought to know. Maybe something happened you don't want to recall."

Priscilla felt a chill that swept her like a wave. "I-I don't remember."

"Part of you does. You seemed pretty upset."

Unconsciously, Priscilla's fingers tightened on the reins. "Thank you for telling me. I'll give it some thought." *No you won't*, a voice said. *You don't want to know*. What did it matter? She had been just a child. Her parents were gone—Stuart Egan would be her family now.

"Maybe you're better off letting it rest," Trask said.

And Priscilla silently agreed.

The wagon bumped along the rutted, dusty road, Priscilla driving rather competently, she suspected, for Brendan had paid her a rare compliment in suggesting he take the horse up ahead for a look while she kept the wagon moving along the trail.

"I'll be fine," she assured him as he regarded her from his seat on the big black gelding, looking tall and handsome—and a little bit worried. "I'll just take it easy."

He reached into his saddlebags, resting behind the cantle, pulled out his spare pistol, a little smaller than the one he usually carried, and handed it to her. "If anything happens, cock it and fire off a round. I won't be far away."

"I'm sure I won't need to." But it did feel good to know she could reach him. She eyed the frightening, heavy-looking weapon. "I guess you don't need both of them."

"I've got my rifle, too." He gave her a last brief glance, then nudged the big black forward. "Be careful," he called over one wide shoulder.

In minutes he had ridden atop a knoll and dropped out of sight. She wondered if he had noticed something that made him wary—or if he was just bored with her company. Either way, she found herself missing his imposing presence already.

Chapter 7

Tochoway, a chief of the Kwahadi Comanche, looked down from his vantage point beneath a cluster of live oaks on the top of a shallow rise. Down the dusty trail in the distance, a heavy wagon rumbled along, pulled by a sturdy pair of mules.

As the team drew near, Tochoway saw the full skirts and wide-brimmed bonnet of a woman, as well as several trunks and other supplies. Goods his people could use—and a chance to rain havoc on the man called Egan.

Tochoway's heavy jaw tightened. The others were afraid of the sandy-haired white man, but he wasn't. Egan might kill him, but death for Tochoway would be welcome—as long as he got his revenge. The Comanche chief smiled, creasing his weathered face beneath his blue war paint, deepening the tiny wrinkles at the corners of his hard dark eyes.

How clever he had been to leave tracks leading north for Egan to find. How carefully his small band of men had circled around, removing all trace of their presence, before riding south, to the trail that crossed Egan's land. Sooner or later, Tochoway knew, men would come with supplies.

The Ranch of the Oaks was large, the people who lived there many. Sooner or later, he would find the chance to pay Egan back for the raid he had made on the Kwahadi—the bloody attack that had killed his family and left him alone.

What did it matter that Tochoway had attacked Egan first? He was a white man, just like the Spanish who came before him. He didn't belong here—the Comanche knew that, and so did their brother warriors to the west, the mighty Kiowa.

Tochoway watched the lone wagon rumble along and wondered why a woman traveled the dangerous road alone. Perhaps her man had been injured or killed. Perhaps she hurried to Egan for help. What did it matter? She was his now, along with the treasures she carried.

Tochoway smiled. He would take his fill of the woman, capture the goods, and send her lifeless body as a message to Egan. Except for this small band bent on raiding and war, his Comanche brothers had all moved safely to the north, out of the white man's grasp. Tochoway would teach Egan a lesson. He would flee this land to safety, then return in the spring for more of the white man's bounty.

Priscilla's fingers ached from gripping the reins for so long. Yet there was a feeling of pride in accomplishing her first real frontier task. The mules heeded her firm touch, responded to the authority in her voice, and Priscilla felt renewed hope that she would indeed be able to find a place in this new land she meant to call home.

Unconsciously her gaze shifted down to the pistol on the wooden seat beside her. She had never even held a gun—it had felt heavy and uncomfortable in her hands. Still, using a weapon was just one more skill she must master. Tonight she would cook something special, then convince Trask to give her a lesson on the use of the gun.

Priscilla scanned the horizon, taking in the gently rolling hills covered with chaparral, mesquite, and the inevitable prickly cactus. Along several tiny streams, live oaks grew, as well as dark-green-leafed pecans. Her eyes searched for the tall, broad-shouldered man on horseback, but he was nowhere to be seen. Instead, beneath the blazing Texas sun, the wagon rumbled steadily along in solitude, throwing a cloud of dust in the air, the only sound in the hot summer air the screech of a hawk overhead, and the creak and sway of the wheels.

The road grew rougher for a distance, evidence of another washout, this one not so deep but enough to jolt the wagon and knock the pistol onto the floor of the wagon boot at her feet. Priscilla knew a moment of alarm that the gun might go off, but it didn't. She breathed a sigh of relief.

That's when she heard it—at first a sort of high-pitched keening, then several short barks that knifed through the air, then an onslaught of blood-curdling screams and the thunder of horses' hooves. Priscilla whirled toward the sounds and saw the cluster of hard-riding men astride their lathered mustangs, and her heart slammed hard against her chest.

Indians! Dear God in heaven! Naked to the waist, their bodies greased and painted, they looked more fearsome than she could have imagined in her vilest nightmare. Shrieking and shouting, they raced across the plain, guiding their horses with their knees, bows and arrows held aloft, one with a knife blade clamped between his teeth.

Stifling a shriek of terror, Priscilla slapped the reins hard on the two mules' rumps.

"Hurry!" she cried, and the animals tore off at a gallop that swelled to an all-out breakneck run. Behind her the Indians whooped and hollered, and their horses' hooves pounded across the earth. Trembling all over, Priscilla fought the reins with one hand and tried to keep her balance while she reached for the pistol with the other.

Groping the floor of the wagon boot with no success, she lengthened her hold on the reins and bent to search the floor again. The butt of the pistol slid into her palm, but the right rein slipped free with the effort. It sailed into the air, floated precariously for a moment, then landed on the ground behind the mules, dragging in the dirt that rushed beneath the wagon.

"Dear God," she whispered, the other rein useless by itself. It took all of her control to fight down her panic and keep her seat as the wagon raced over the rocky earth. With an iron resolve and a trembling hand, she raised the heavy pistol, aimed it into the air, and tried to squeeze the trigger. It wouldn't even budge.

Lord in heaven! Had the gun been damaged when it fell on the floor of the wagon? Or, as with everything else she had tried, was she simply too unschooled to know how to use it?

Brendan, where are you? She gripped the wagon seat, afraid to look behind her, afraid not to. She finally swiveled her neck just in time to see a half-naked brave leap into the back of the wagon.

She screamed as the melee of neighing horses and savages in war paint and feathers rushed the wagon, engulfing the bolting team, turning the mules off the road, and slowing their headlong flight. The brave in the back moved forward, his face painted black and red, smelling so foul Priscilla almost swooned.

Instead she raised the useless pistol, realized with sudden insight that she had forgotten to cock it, pulled back the hammer, and fired. With a shriek of agony, the Indian's face erupted in a mass of bloody gore, and he disappeared from sight out the back of the wagon.

Merciful God, what have I done? Darkness swirled at the edges of her mind. She tried to fight it down, tried to stay in control, but all she could see was the Indian's bloody face—or what was left of it. Then the image began to change, twisting and swelling, holding her captive, hauling her backward into the past.

Blood and death.

Terror and mind-numbing loss.

The feelings expanded with crushing force until all else faded away.

Hard, dark-skinned arms gripping her waist jolted Priscilla from her terrors of the past. She heard the wicked whoop of triumph, felt rough hands groping her breast, and the rending of fabric. Then darkness swirled in once more.

Priscilla closed her eyes, and gave herself up to merciful blackness.

*   *   *

Brendan heard the pistol shot, turned with dread from the shoeless-hoof prints he had been studying, and knew in an instant what the ominous gunshot meant.

His chest tight with worry, he swung into the saddle without using the stirrup and pulled his rifle from the scabbard behind the cantle. He checked the breech, assuring himself the gun was ready to fire, then whirled the black horse and dug his boot heels into the animal's powerful sides.

Damn! He'd been afraid this might happen. Only his belief that Egan would have been waiting in Corpus with an armed escort if there'd been any sign of Indian trouble had kept him from worrying. The man might be ruthless, but he protected what belonged to him—or very soon would.

Brendan swore bitterly at the unexpected presence of the Indians—probably Comanche. Pulling his hat brim lower across his brow, he thought of Priscilla, prayed she could somehow get to safety, and urged the black into a flat-eared run.

As he had promised, he wasn't far away, just over a low-lying ridge and down at the end of a valley. It didn't take long to reach the place where the shot had been fired, and when he did, his stomach balled into a harder knot than it was already.

Pulling his horse to a sliding halt in the cover of a cluster of oaks, Brendan swung down from the saddle, tied the horse out of sight, and crept closer. Below the ridge where he crouched, the wagon lay on its side, two wheels still spinning, the mules freed from their traces and being loaded with goods. Priscilla's trunks had been opened, their contents scattered across the prairie, some stomped into the dirt by the Indians' ponies. Several braves wore pieces of her clothing; one paraded wickedly in her beautiful pink crepe gown.

Already they had ransacked the supplies, found the jug of whiskey he carried for emergencies, and had been passing the bottle around. From the look of it, the stout brew had begun to induce a bit of drunkenness—one small advantage against overwhelming odds.

Brendan's grip tightened on his rifle as he worriedly scanned the wreckage for Priscilla, his heart thudding painfully in his chest. He spotted her some distance away, sprawled on the ground, stripped to her chemise and petticoats, her hair a dark tangle around her shoulders. She lay pinned beneath a flat-faced, thick-chested Indian wearing bright blue war paint.

Even from a distance, Brendan could feel her terror, and it stirred such a deep-seated anger in him that it took all his control to battle it down. The Indian nestled between her legs, groping her breasts while Priscilla tried futilely to fight him off.

"Easy, baby," Brendan whispered as if she could hear him, "I'll get there as fast as I can." Creeping even closer, he settled himself behind a low-lying cluster of rocks and wedged his revolving-breech Colt's rifle into a crevice. As his finger curled around the trigger, his mouth curved up in the grimmest trace of a smile. Texas Navy issue—eight shots—something else to even the odds.

Priscilla screamed, and Brendan steadied his aim on the thick-chested Indian atop her, a brave who growled orders and appeared to be the chief. With cold determination, he leveled the rifle and pulled the trigger. A shot rang out and a mushroom of bright red blood erupted on the man's broad back. Priscilla screamed again, the sound muffled by the Indian's body slumping forward onto her breast. Brendan worked the ring on the rifle, revolving the breech for another shot, and fired at a second brave, causing him to reel backward into the dirt.

Pandemonium broke loose. The rest of the braves took cover and began to return fire, some with muskets, others with arrows that sliced the air just inches away from his head. He worked the ring again, fired, and picked off another brave. One of them fired a pistol in return—probably the one he had given to Priscilla—shouted something in Comanche, and the remaining braves raced toward their horses.

By now they'd discovered their attacker was a lone gunman and wildly raced toward him, their horses' hooves thudding against the earth. Shouting for blood, they divided their forces to surround the rocks and close in. Brendan picked off two more braves, but three of them bore down on him. Using his rifle as a club, he knocked one man from his horse, drew his pistol and fired at a second, then dodged a lance and dragged the third man down to the ground.

Fighting hand to hand, his pistol knocked aside, Brendan felt the warrior's blade slash into his upper arm, but ignored the jolt of pain and caught the Indian's wrist. A muscular man of Brendan's same height, the brave pressed his knife toward Brendan's heart with every ounce of his strength. A shadow emerged from somewhere behind them. Brendan swung the brave around to intercept the thrust of a lance meant for him, and the warrior took the blade between the shoulders.

As the Indian sagged into the dirt, Brendan wrenched the knife from the dead man's hands, picked up his pistol, and whirled to face the still-mounted men. Instead of rushing him as he had expected, they rode screeching and shouting back toward camp.

Son of a bitch! Sick with dread, searching desperately for his rifle, Brendan saw the lead Indian ride toward Priscilla, who raced toward the safety of the hill. Leaning down, the muscular brave slid an arm around her waist and lifted her into the air. Though she fought and screamed, he carried her easily, forcing her face down across his horse's withers. The others grabbed mules, horses, and supplies. With a whoop of victory, they rode north, away from the white man's bullets to safety.

Damn. Ignoring the pain in his arm and the blood that soaked his shirt, Brendan found his rifle and raced toward the black. A jerk of the reins untied him, and Brendan swung up in the saddle.

He could see them in the distance, the dust blowing up in their wake. Leading the mules slowed their flight, and the big black's size and speed gave him the edge he needed.

In minutes Brendan rode within firing range. Running the big horse hard, positioning himself so as not to hit Priscilla, he slammed the butt of the rifle against his thigh and fired at the brave who had taken her.

The bullet struck and the Indian jerked rein, caus-

ing his horse to rear, then he tumbled backward onto
the ground and slid into a small ravine. When Priscilla fell off a moment later, Brendan's chest tightened and he prayed she hadn't been hurt. The last
remaining braves kept on riding with barely a backward glance.

Brendan rode hard for Priscilla, who stumbled to
her feet on unsteady legs. As the horse slid to a halt,
he leapt from the saddle and in long, determined
strides ran toward her.

Priscilla started running, too. Trembling all over,
tears soaking her cheeks, she took in Brendan's torn
and bloody shirt, heard his urgent footsteps, and saw
his handsome face darkened with such concern that
something expanded inside her heart. She had
watched the Indians attack him, seen him fighting
for his life, but had been unable to help him.

Dear God in heaven. With a sob, she finally reached
him and threw herself into his arms. Crying against
his shoulder, clutching him and whispering his
name, she felt his hard arms around her, holding her
so close she could scarcely breathe.

"Thank God you're all right," he breathed against
the tangle of long dark hair around her shoulders.

"Hold me," she pleaded. "Please don't me let go."

"I won't," he promised. "I won't let you go." He
wouldn't let her go. He wasn't sure he could. He
held her and let her cry and thanked Almighty
God for giving him the strength to save her. He
stroked her hair, and whispered soothing words,
and felt her clutching the back of his neck. When she
lifted her face to look at him, he gently kissed her

forehead. There were tears on her cheeks, so he kissed them, too.

Her bottom lip trembled. Brendan lowered his mouth in the briefest of touches. His hands came up to cradle her face, he kissed her eyes, her nose, then settled his mouth on her lips. It seemed so right he should kiss her, so achingly right.

Priscilla must have felt the same, for she tilted her head back and her arms slid farther around his neck. She was kissing him back now, at first with uncertainty, then with such urgency he groaned.

He deepened the kiss and Priscilla responded, touching her tongue to his, opening her mouth to him, begging him for more. She felt so soft and yielding, so fragile, and yet so fiery. Her breath tasted warm in his mouth and her fingers teased his hair. His breathing grew ragged, and his shaft grew thick and throbbing as he molded her against him. He had to have her—he would die if he didn't.

Kissing her all the while, he lifted her into his arms and carried her beneath an oak tree, where he lowered her gently to the earth. Priscilla moaned softly when his tongue moved deeper into her mouth. Her response was innocent, but so fierce it amazed him. How could he ever have believed her cold?

Priscilla couldn't think where she was or what she was doing. She felt alive as she never had before, alive with passion and wonder and desire for this man who had saved her, who had nearly given his life for hers, who held her and protected her, who was brave and strong and unlike any man she had ever known.

"Silla," he whispered, his hand delving into her

thick mane of hair, cradling the back of her head in his palm, his mouth tasting hers, seeking, coaxing, setting her aflame.

His tongue felt silken, sending warm shivers down her spine, making her ache for him. She felt every movement of his hand, the heat of his flesh against hers, the fiery sensations that hardened the peaks of her breasts.

She felt his fingers skimming over her throat, touching, teasing, while his mouth burned hers, and his tongue felt like warm satin flame. He moved to her ear, nibbled the tender lobe, then returned to her lips. His hands stroked her skin, slid the strap of her chemise off her shoulder.

When he deepened the kiss, her fingers dug into his back. Corded muscle bunched beneath her hand, and Priscilla's desire flamed brighter. His palm felt rough on her breast, kneading it, pebbling the already hard peak into a tight, throbbing bud.

"So lovely," he said, looking down at the upturned mound, a husky note to his voice. "It fits my hand just perfectly."

Priscilla moaned at his words and the hungry way he said them. She lowered her eyes to the breast he had bared and now caressed so boldly. At the sight of his long brown fingers stroking her pale skin, damp heat surged to the place between her legs.

Dear God, what is happening to me? Priscilla swallowed hard, dimly aware for the very first time of the sinful things he was doing. It occurred to her that she must stop him, end this madness that threatened her very soul.

That tomorrow she would meet the man she would marry.

Then his mouth claimed hers, his tongue silken and conquering, and Priscilla no longer cared. She felt powerless and wanton. Compelled to serve his wishes. How could that be so?

Brendan lowered the second strap to her chemise, leaving her naked to the waist, and Priscilla arched upward, begging for his touch. Her hands slid into the open front of his shirt, skimmed across the muscles of his chest, felt the stiff brown hairs that arrowed down to his hard flat stomach, and her body seemed to burn. What weapon did he wield to render her so helpless? What spell had he cast?

"Brendan," she whispered with a gentle sob, "what's happening?"

Brendan's hand stilled its movement. Beneath his calloused palm, Priscilla's soft flesh quivered, her lovely cone-shaped breast with its dusky-rose nipple silently begging for more. He looked into her gold-flecked eyes, saw them glazed with passion, knew that she wanted him, and that he could take her.

There, too, he saw uncertainty, her fear and disbelief that this could be happening.

Brendan swallowed hard, his hand beginning to shake as he fought to control his need. His shaft tightened and throbbed until he clenched his fist against the bittersweet pain. Christ, he wanted her. In all his life, he had never desired a woman so much.

She's Egan's, a voice said. *She's mine,* said another.

But even if he claimed her, what good would it do?

He was a wanted man, a gunman, and a gambler. He enjoyed women, but not for more than a night or two. He certainly didn't want marriage.

He looked again at Priscilla, saw her mounting hesitation, knew where this was leading, and how she would hate him when they were through. She wasn't the type of woman to bed and discard, for all her fiery passions.

Too many years without a man, he told himself. She would respond like this to any man with the patience to arouse her. She would respond like this to Egan.

Brendan's stomach clenched at the thought, but at least he'd had time to regain some control. In the noblest gesture he could remember, he adjusted the straps of Priscilla's chemise, once more covering her lovely milk-white breasts, and eased himself away from her.

"Oh, no," Priscilla whispered, watching him withdraw and feeling his loss like a splash of cold water. At the masklike expression on his face, her passion suddenly died, and her dark eyes clouded with shame. "Lord in heaven, what have I done?"

Priscilla turned away, but Brendan reached out for her, catching her shoulders and forcing her to look at him. "This isn't your fault, Priscilla. You were overwrought—I took advantage."

Unconsciously, her hands came up to cover her breasts, though the thin chemise already sat firmly in place. "I . . . I should have stopped you." Tears burned her eyes, but she wouldn't let them fall.

"You're inexperienced, I'm not. This isn't your fault."

"It *is* my fault," she said, breaking free and climb-

ing to her feet. "I'm engaged to be married. Instead I
. . . I acted like a harlot. I'll never forgive myself."

Brendan stood up beside her. "You're a lady, Priscilla. You have been since the moment I met you.
Today you saw death and destruction unlike anything
you could have imagined. You let your guard down
and I took advantage. I've wanted you almost from
the start—and I was so damned scared you'd been
hurt. . . ." He picked up his wide-brimmed hat,
dusted it against a sinewy thigh, and settled it back
on his head. "If you'll accept my apology, I promise
it won't happen again."

That was the moment she knew. Standing there
listening to him profess her virtue, trying to take the
blame for the passion they had shared and to ease
her sense of shame—that's when she knew the kind
of man he was.

And that she could never forget him.

That's when she knew she was falling in love with
him.

She looked at his dear, worried face, memorizing
each feature, her eyes moving down to his powerful
shoulders and muscular chest.

"Your arm!" she cried, unable to believe that she
could have forgotten. Hurriedly she reached for him,
grabbed his sleeve, and tore the fabric away.

"It isn't as bad as it looks. The bleeding will
cleanse it a bit." He smiled at her wearily. "If you
can spare another strip of petticoat, we'll find some
water and wash it, then you can bind it up for me."

"All right," she agreed, forcing a lightness into her
tone she didn't feel. When they had completed the

task, Brendan settled her aboard the big black and swung himself up behind her.

"We'll go back to the wagon and see what we can salvage. We'll have to ride double the rest of the way, but we'll make it. That much I promise you."

Priscilla glanced away. "I know we will," she said, trusting him completely.

It occurred to her that reaching the Triple R had suddenly become far more important to him than it was to her.

"I killed a man today." Sitting beside the dying campfire, Priscilla twirled a leafy branch in the dust at her feet.

"Yes," Brendan said gently. "I saw his body from the knoll."

"I blew his face away. There was nothing left but a bloody—"

"Don't, Priscilla. Don't do that to yourself." He sat cross-legged on the ground beside her, a careful distance away, smoking a thin cigar he had found among the scattered debris left by the Comanche.

While Priscilla had waited, Brendan had gone back to the grisly scene of the attack to retrieve his lost pistols and salvage what was left of her clothing and their supplies, which wasn't much, but something for her to wear and all they could carry.

Afterward, they'd camped near the closest water, eaten the rabbit he had shot—though Priscilla didn't have much appetite—and now sat quietly watching the fire.

"You pulled that trigger because you had no

choice," he was saying. "You were only trying to protect yourself."

"I'll never forget it, not as long as I live." She picked up another dead leaf and studied the dry brown veins. "It made me feel sick inside, like I'd killed a part of myself. No matter the reason, I'll never do it again, even to save my own life." She tossed the leaf into the flames and watched it wither and blacken. It crackled harshly in the still night air.

Priscilla glanced across at him. "And something else happened out there. It was something I can't explain. Something . . . I don't know . . . it was like I was lost in some terrible abyss. All I could see was blood and death. All I could feel was terror and pain."

She shook her head. "I don't know if I can live like this, Brendan, if I can face this kind of life day after day. After all that's happened . . . I just don't know."

An ember hissed in the fire, filling the uneasy silence. Brendan's long sigh nearly matched the sound. "Killing a man is never easy," he said. "No matter how right you are, no matter how necessary it is."

She raised her eyes to his face. "Would you stop if you could?"

A muscle bunched in his jaw. "As much as you may think so, I don't kill people unless I have to—not for money or any other reason. Texas is a lawless country. It's young and wild—but it's also growing. That's the reason I came here in the first place. Parts of it are more settled than others, all of it will be someday. In the meantime, it takes a hard man to hold on to what's his."

He met her searching look squarely. "Some men go a lot further. They take more than their share, even if they have to lie, cheat, and steal to get it." He started to say something more, but in the end just clamped the cheroot between his even white teeth and stared into the flickering red-orange flames.

"How's your arm?" she asked gently, though it was the other one he unconsciously rubbed. It was a habit she had noticed before, whenever he was upset or uncertain.

"Not bad," he replied. One corner of his mouth curved upward. "I needed a scar on my right arm to match the one on my left."

She smiled softly. "I'll check it again before we set off for the ranch."

The lightness in his eyes seemed to fade. He tossed his cheroot into the flames. "Way I've got it figured, we'll arrive sometime before noon . . . not exactly in fine fiddle, the way I intended, but alive." His face looked taut. He seemed remote, more distant than he'd been before.

"Once you're there," he continued, in that strange distant fashion, "Egan and his men will look after you. I'm sure he'll be generous, see you get new clothes, anything at all you might need. You won't have to be afraid, Priscilla." *At least not of Indians.*

"What about you? What will you do?"

He took the branch she held and poked it into the flames, sending a shower of sparks into the black Texas sky. Above them, a veil of stars lit the heavens, and Priscilla felt the vastness, saw some of the untamed beauty that Brendan so loved.

"I'll do what I always do. Move on. Find someplace to light for a while. Then move on again."

"Why?"

"What do you mean 'why'? Why not?"

"You're a good man, Brendan. Surely you want more out of life than what you've got now."

"Maybe I did once. Times change. Things happen. After the war, it didn't seem to matter anymore."

"What could have been so terrible that it could keep you running?"

"Who says I'm running?"

"Aren't you?"

Brendan didn't answer, just stared into the darkness beyond the fire. A cricket sang in the shadows, a melodic lament she had never really noticed before.

"It's time we got some sleep," he finally said. "Things always look brighter in the morning."

Wishing he could take the advice about sleeping he had earlier given to Priscilla, Brendan listened to the hoot of an owl, decided it really was a bird and not an Indian, and relaxed once more against the saddle serving as his pillow.

He'd been trying to fall asleep for the past three hours, but his mind had steadily refused. Instead he kept seeing Priscilla's fragile body pinned beneath the Indian, kept feeling the awful, searing pain he had felt in knowing she was in danger.

When he wasn't remembering that, he was thinking about her lovely cone-shaped breasts, the luscious way they pointed upward, the way they fit so neatly into his hand. That memory made him hard and aching, so he fought the image down.

Lastly, he mulled over her words. Was he really running from his past? In truth, he knew he was. He was wanted in the Indian Territory, but the odds were good they wouldn't hunt him in the wide-open spaces of Texas. He had money put away—quite a tidy sum, in fact. He was well-educated, far beyond most of the men he knew. He could change his life if he wanted.

But did he really want to?

Before he met Priscilla, the thought of settling down had never even crossed his mind. Oh, he'd had plans for the future, goals and dreams that every young man had. He'd thought about a career in the military—gotten as far as lieutenant before discovering that road didn't suit him. Land and cattle appealed to him, and he'd pursued that goal for a while after the war, even gone as far as buying some property, but he'd never really felt like making a go of it.

Assuming Priscilla would even consider marrying him—which with what Egan could offer seemed highly unlikely—would marriage make a difference? And did he want it to?

Hell, he liked his independence, his carefree, no-strings existence. A woman was nothing but a millstone, a burden that tied a man down. Marriage would put an end to his freedom, saddle him with family and unwanted responsibilities.

He thought of the way Priscilla depended and looked up to him. In a way it felt good to be needed. In another way it scared him to death.

Brendan listened to the sounds of the night, let

them lull him as they usually did, and felt his weariness beginning to overtake him.

Egan was the man for Priscilla. He had money and power—and stability. Priscilla wanted children, so did Egan. She wanted a home—from what he'd heard, Egan lived in a damnable mansion. So she'd have to bend to her husband's wishes—so did a thousand other wives.

Brendan inwardly scoffed, finding it hard to imagine Priscilla taking orders. He thought of her grit and intelligence, her gentleness, and determination. He thought of her shapely body, and a vision of another man's hands roaming over her smooth pale flesh rose up to taunt him.

That he desired her, he didn't deny. *A man always wants what he can't have.* He'd get over her. He'd get on with his life as he had before. The last thing he needed was a rope around his neck—the hanging kind, or the kind that came with marriage. Free and easy, that's the way he wanted it. Hard drinkin', fast women, and easy money. Tomorrow he'd get Priscilla off his hands once and for all, and things would return to normal.

He'd travel north, see some places he hadn't seen before. It wouldn't take long to forget a too-fragile female who was nothing but trouble.

Brendan settled deeper into his bedroll, refusing to remember the loneliness that traveled that same road.

Chapter 8

"Riders coming in!" The cry went up from the guard at the gate, a wide wooden structure that stood open unless there was trouble. A low stone wall extended from each side, forming a huge enclosure that surrounded the compound. It was a subtle means of defense, but protection just the same.

"They'll be passin' through the gate any minute!" Jaimie Walker, a red-haired man of twenty-six, galloped to the house on his small paint horse and slid to a stop in a whirl of dust and barking dogs.

"Can you tell who it is?" Stuart asked, standing in front of the heavy oak door leading into the marble-floored entry. Built of pinkish-white limestone, the thick-walled house stood two stories high, with balconies off the upstairs bedrooms and a wide, covered verandah out front.

It had been built twenty years ago by Don Pedro Dominguez in the grand Spanish manner. Stuart had remodeled the house, refined it, and added on. It was a magnificent structure he was excessively proud of.

"Just one horse," Jaimie said. "Looks like two riders. At first I thought it was Hennessey, but I don't think so. Maybe it's Harding. He's already a week overdue."

Stuart had sent one of his best men to Natchez to investigate rumors of a problem he might be facing down there. He wished to hell it *was* Harding. He needed to know exactly what the situation was with his ex-partner, Caleb McLeary—and he needed to make it end.

Stuart took a last draw on his expensive Havana cigar and flipped it into the shrubbery beside the porch just as the big black gelding he recognized immediately as Barker Hennessey's made its way through the gate. A slender, dark-haired woman sat forward in the saddle; a tall, broad-shouldered man rode behind.

Wearing his gray brocade waistcoat and a pair of black broadcloth trousers but no jacket, Stuart waited in the doorway for their approach, then stepped out on the wide, covered verandah to meet them.

Several dogs yapped at the horse's heels, and the Juárez children, offspring of his Mexican overseer, tagged along behind.

"You Egan?" the tall man asked. He wore snug blue twill breeches and a homespun shirt, a pair of worn leather boots, and a wide-brimmed brown felt hat. The pistol at his hip looked to be a .36 Patterson belt model. It rode lower than any man's he had ever seen.

"I'm Stuart Egan."

The man swung down from the horse and reached up for the woman. She was slenderly built, with delicate features, a smooth complexion, and heavy-lashed wide brown eyes.

"Trask's my name," the rugged man said. "This is Priscilla Wills, your fiancée."

Stuart allowed his surprise to show—but not his

irritation. "Priscilla," he said, stepping down from the porch and across the dirt courtyard to grasp both her slender hands. "What in the world has happened? Where's your traveling companion? And why aren't you with Barker?"

"I'm afraid Mr. Hennessey is dead," Trask replied for her. "He met with an accident in Galveston. Miss Wills persuaded me to bring her in his stead. As to her companion . . . the woman took sick a ways out of Cincinnati."

Trask's mouth looked grim. "On top of that, we've faced outlaws, snakes, and Indians. You're lucky the lady got here at all." There was censure in his voice, and it rankled Egan more than a little.

He turned his attention to Priscilla. "You have no idea how much this grieves me. If I'd had any idea there'd be trouble, I would have come for you myself."

"I'm sure you would have," she said softly. "As it is, Mr. Trask did the best he could. I believe he saved my life."

"Is that so?" He glanced at Trask, whose expression remained inscrutable. "I'll see Mr. Trask is well compensated for his trouble."

Stuart's gaze returned to Priscilla, taking in her torn blue muslin dress with its prim white collar, the thick braid of shiny dark hair that hung to the middle of her back, her narrow waist, and the subtle swell of her breasts. He noted her proud carriage, and an expression of uncertainty tinged with determination. She looked ragged and weary, but she had survived. It boded well for the sons she would bear.

"I apologize for my appearance," she said, as if

she had read his thoughts. "The Indians destroyed my clothing, as well as my trousseau—what little they didn't steal." There was a subtle straightening of her spine. "We were both nearly killed."

Stuart put his arm around her shoulders and gently drew her against him. "I'd give anything if this hadn't happened. But now that you're here, you'll be safe. I promise you, Priscilla, you'll have ten new dresses for every one you've lost. I'll have the finest seamstress in Texas brought in."

"I lost the things in my hope chest," she said sadly. "Personal mementos, items I'd sewn for our wedding. Mr. Trask found only my locket."

"Your locket?"

Her bottom lip trembled, the first show of weakness he had seen. "It's very special to me. It contains my parents' portraits."

"It's all right, my dear," Stuart soothed. "Mr. Trask has brought you to my care, and from now on everything's going to be fine."

Priscilla glanced at Trask and something flickered in her eyes. She really was quite lovely, Stuart thought. Far more so than he had expected. Her figure looked tempting, as well.

He followed her gaze to the rough-looking stranger, noted his lean but powerful build and self-assured, catlike stance. Beneath the brim of his brown felt hat, light blue eyes watched cautiously from a beard-roughened face even a fool could recognize as handsome.

Stuart fought a stab of anger that they had traveled the prairie alone.

"Why don't I take you inside?" he said to Priscilla,

not really expecting an answer. "Jaimie," he called
to the red-haired cowhand, a hard-working employee of the last five years. A shame the man was too
damned soft to take Barker's place as foreman. "See
that Mr. Trask is fed and taken to the bunkhouse. He
can rest there as long as he likes."

"I'll be leaving as soon as I eat," Trask said.

Stuart didn't argue. For a moment, Priscilla looked
as though she might, but in the end didn't. "I'll bring
the money you've earned out to the cookhouse."

"I'll take the horse and saddle as payment, if that's
all right with you. I'll need a few provisions, some
bedding, and some fresh ammunition."

"I'll see you get it—along with a full month's pay."

Trask tensed for a moment, then shrugged his wide
shoulders. "Money's the reason I took the job in the
first place. That's more than fair."

Stuart recognized the lie for what it was, and his
irritation grew stronger.

Trask turned and walked to his saddlebags.
"There's a couple of dresses in here, Miss Wills, and
a few other things I managed to find back at the
wagon."

"Jaimie can fetch them," Stuart said, "and see that
the animal is cared for."

Priscilla glanced up at her fiancé, then left his side
and walked woodenly to the place beside Brendan.
All morning she had prepared herself for this moment, but now that it had come, she wasn't sure how
she'd get through it. She watched his long fingers
work the buckle on one side of the saddlebag, lift the
flap, and pull out a length of ivory silk. Frothy ivory
lace fell softly across his dark hand.

"My wedding gown," Priscilla whispered. "I thought the Indians had taken it."

Wetting her suddenly dry lips, she turned toward Brendan's dear handsome face. He hadn't shaved today, as if the stubble of beard he wore was the first step in returning to the hard-edged man he'd been before. In his journey back to solitude, how long would it take him to forget her?

Brendan extended the gown and Priscilla reached for it. Their hands touched. His skin felt rough and warm, a contrast to the smooth cool feel of the silk. Her throat closed up and she blinked against a sudden well of tears.

"Thank you," she said softly.

"Sorry it's so wrinkled."

"It was kind of you to bring it." Her hand shook as she draped it across her arm. She fingered the wedding gown, the beads and lace she had stitched so carefully, so lovingly. It seemed inconceivable she would wear this dress for a man she didn't know, not the caring, passionate man who stood so tall and proud before her.

"Good luck, Miss Wills," he said. She didn't miss the huskiness in his voice, or the warm way his eyes ran over her, then lifted to settle on her face.

"Take care of yourself," she said.

His hand touched her cheek, but only for a moment, then it dropped back down to his side. "You'll be all right, you know. You can conquer this land if you want to."

I could if I had you. "I'll do my best to remember the things you taught me. To look for the beauty and not just the harshness." *I'll look at the color of the sky, enjoy the animals, listen for the sounds of the insects. Mostly I'll remember what I felt when you touched me.* "Where will you go from here?"

"I always wanted to see San Antone."

I don't want you to go. "What about the Indians? That's the way they were headed, wasn't it?"

He flashed a sad, weary smile. "They got what they were after. All except you."

And I got what I was after—all except you. She thought of the time they'd spent together, of the gentleness that always appeared whenever she needed it, of the passion he fought to control.

He'd been more of a man than any she had ever met, more giving, more caring—willing even to risk his life to protect her.

"I'll never forget what you've done for me."

Brendan cleared his throat and glanced away. She noticed the slight inflection of the muscle in his jaw and thought of the way his skin had felt beneath her fingers, the warmth of his mouth over hers.

When he spoke, the words sounded raw, husky. "I'll have a hard time forgetting you, too."

Priscilla closed her eyes. If he didn't leave this minute she would surely disgrace herself. "I'd better go," she whispered, her throat so tight she could hardly speak. "Stuart is waiting."

Brendan's eyes grew distant. "He doesn't deserve you," he said, so softly that only she could hear. "I've yet to meet the man who does."

She wouldn't cry, she wouldn't. Trask didn't want her—and she certainly didn't want him.

Liar. You're in love with him. "Thank you again. For everything."

When Stuart started walking in their direction, Brendan's face closed up even more. He touched the brim of his hat in farewell. "Good-bye, Miss Wills."

"Good-bye . . . Brendan." She shouldn't have used his first name, but she couldn't let him leave without knowing how special he was, how much she cared. He flashed her a last brief glance she couldn't quite read, turned, and silently walked away.

Priscilla watched him go, her hands clenched tightly in the folds of her dusty blue skirt. God in heaven, why must this be?

Priscilla felt Stuart's hand at her waist, his fingers firm and possessive.

"I'm sorry this had to happen. If you're feeling up to it, why don't we go inside and you can tell me the whole story. It'll give us a chance to get to know each other."

Priscilla nodded, relieved he should care. Forcing her eyes not to search for Brendan one last time, she let Stuart guide her toward the house. As they walked along the stone path, she told him about the rattlesnake and the way Brendan had looked after her. She told him about the men at the trading post and how he had saved her, then explained how he had fought off the Indians.

"He took very good care of me," she said with a sad little smile.

"I'm sure he did, my dear." Stuart listened with careful attention, seething inside all the while.

As his housekeeper, Consuela, showed Priscilla to her upstairs room, he sent for Jaimie, who should have been tending the brood mares in the stable, but instead loitered near the porch for a better look at Priscilla.

"Pick a couple of men you think can get the information I need. Send one to Corpus Christi, one to San Antonio. I want to know everything you can find out about Brendan Trask. And I want to know what happened to Barker—go all the way to Galveston, if that's what it takes."

"Yes, sir, boss." Jaimie lifted his sweaty gray hat and blotted his forehead in the crook of one wiry arm. "Anything else?"

"That's all for now. We know where he's headed. We can find him if we need to."

Jaimie nodded and, as always, did as he was told.

"You have everything you need, *Señorita* Wills?"

"Yes, Consuela, thank you. You've been very kind." Priscilla stood at the window of her elegant bedchamber surveying the courtyard below. She had bathed, washed and dried her hair and pulled it back from her face, then changed into borrowed clothing.

"I will take care of your dresses," Consuela promised. "I hope you do not mind wearing Dolores's things until yours are ready."

"They're fine." A bright red skirt and simple peasant blouse, her own sturdy shoes and a pair of white stockings Brendan had managed to salvage. "Tell your daughter I appreciate her kindness."

Consuela nodded her black-haired head, stepped out into the hallway, her plump figure filling it, and quietly closed the door.

The room was furnished in grand style—pink damask draperies, a four-poster bed with matching pink counterpane, marble-topped dressers and rosewood armoire, a fancy French desk in the corner, and Oriental rugs on the wide-planked oak floors. Watching for Brendan as she had been for the past half hour, Priscilla turned back to the wide, shuttered window that overlooked a small covered porch off the master bedchamber next door.

It wasn't long before she saw him riding across the courtyard, sitting tall and proud, the big black horse beneath him as imposing as its master. He looked neither right nor left, just kept his eyes fixed ahead until he had passed through the gate. Then he settled his hat a little lower across his brow, and urged the big horse into a gallop.

Priscilla's throat closed up as she watched him ride away. Even with his back turned to her, she noticed the supple grace with which he rode, the easy command he had of the powerful animal. She watched without moving, her throat aching and hot tears rolling down her cheeks. All too soon he became just a speck on the horizon, then he disappeared from her vision.

Priscilla swallowed past the painful lump but couldn't make it go away. How lonely she felt. How desperately, achingly lonely.

How could that be when the man she would marry waited in the elegant rooms downstairs?

Priscilla took a last brief look at the horizon, saw only a flat brown line broken by chaparral, and moved away from the window with an iron resolve. There was nothing left for it now but to make the best of things. She had pledged to marry Stuart Egan—

come heaven or high water, that was what she would do.

She thought of Stuart's concern and reassurance. He was everything she had imagined—and more. He had described himself perfectly—sandy hair, hazel eyes, and a fair complexion—all in a pleasantly masculine face. Handsome, Aunt Maddie had said, and he was.

Not in the same disconcerting way as Brendan, she thought with a twinge of pain. Not rugged and chiseled, not tanned and lean and hard. Stuart looked to be some years older, somewhere nearing forty, but he stood almost as tall, was solidly built and obviously intelligent.

Though Priscilla prided herself on being a quick judge of character, she found Stuart a difficult man to read. There was an aura of power about him, and something protective in his nature she found appealing. And yet . . . In the brief discussion they had had, she'd found nothing of the sensitive man he'd revealed in his letters.

She hoped that whatever kind feelings she held for him would nurture and grow. And that they would deal together well as man and wife.

Priscilla ran her fingers over the lovely pink counterpane covering the four-poster bed and tried to imagine Stuart as her husband. Instead, it was Brendan's face she saw, Brendan who smiled back at her, Brendan who held her and kissed her, and set her body aflame.

Against her will, she imagined her wedding night, imagined lying beneath an expensive satin canopy instead of a veil of twinkling stars. She imagined Stuart's mouth over hers, not full and warm like Brendan's, but cooler, his cool lips hard and unyielding. She thought of blunt pale fingers instead of slender brown ones, thought of them skimming over her flesh, teasing her nipples, lifting and molding her breasts.

Priscilla felt her stomach lurch and the bile rise up in her throat. *Dear Lord, why must it be this way?* For a moment she hated Brendan Trask for what he had done, for what he had made her feel. Then the dear lines of his face came back to her, and she had to blink away tears.

She'd get over him, she vowed. She'd make Stuart a fine wife and his children a good mother. She'd forget Brendan Trask and the sinful things he had made her feel.

She'd forget the passion she shouldn't have discovered—and somehow she would go on.

Supper was an elegant affair, taken on gold-trimmed porcelain plates in the huge formal dining room. Standing in the entry, Priscilla apologized for her lack of appropriate attire, and Stuart was solicitous.

"Don't be foolish, darling. Everyone understands what has happened. As soon as it's feasible, we'll send to San Antonio for a seamstress and bolts and bolts of fabric. You'll be amazed at the quality of goods that make their way into the interior."

Dressed in an expensive black frock coat, burgundy waistcoat, light gray trousers, and wide white stock, Stuart put an arm around her shoulders and led her in to supper. Priscilla felt even more self-conscious when she saw the table, a long Hepplewhite mahogany surrounded by twelve beautifully carved, high-backed chairs; bayberry tapers glowing softly atop a crystal chandelier; and the two well-dressed gentlemen who stood at her approach.

"Judge Dodd, I'd like you to meet my fiancée, Miss Wills."

"Charmed, Miss Wills," the white-haired man said with a cordial inclination of his head. He was dressed in black, his coat a little rumpled and not nearly as expensively cut as Stuart's.

"And this is my son, Noble. Noble, your future stepmother, Miss Wills."

"Hello, Miss Wills," he said. "I'm glad you arrived safely. We've all been very worried."

Thinking of her perilous journey, Priscilla's smile faltered. "I'm afraid the trip was not without some trouble. I thank you for your concern."

Stuart had spoken of his son in his letters, describing him as sincere and warmhearted. A boy who worked hard and respected his elders. As she regarded him standing there now, a miniature of his powerful father, Priscilla wondered what it felt like to walk in such a man's shadow.

It occurred to her that she would soon find out.

"Why don't we be seated?" Stuart said, guiding her to a place at one end of the table.

Stuart took a seat at the opposite end and waved his hand toward a tall Negro servant who stood by the door to the kitchen. The man quietly exited and in minutes the door swung open to admit a flurry of servants carrying platters of steaming corn, butter beans, and melon, heaping trays of chicken and beef, as well as baskets of fresh baked bread.

"Bread is a real luxury out here," Stuart said. "Flour is difficult to come by. Most of the time we make do with cornmeal. We've our own grinding mill out in the rear of the compound."

Servants poured wine into crystal goblets, and brought in slabs of fresh-churned butter.

"This all looks delicious," Priscilla said, but when her plate had been filled, she found she could barely eat.

"We're nearly self-sufficient here at the ranch," Stuart told her. "We've a small dairy, which provides milk and butter, a blacksmith, a cooper, a smokehouse, the grinding mill I spoke of, and of course the soil is rich for vegetables."

"The huntin' is good here, too, Miss Wills," the judge put in. "Cain't hardly go a mile or two without seeing venison on the hoof. There's rabbits big as dogs, partridge, and prairie hen—man can pret-near live off the land."

"That's right, Miss Wills," Noble chimed in with enthusiasm. "Texas is the richest land on earth. My father intends to claim a goodly portion of it—me along with him. I'm sure you'll come to love it, too."

"I'm sure I will," Priscilla said softly, recalling Brendan's love of the land.

"If it weren't for the Indians," Noble continued, "the Mexicans, and some of that wild Texas scum—"

"That's enough, Noble," Stuart cut in. "Miss Wills has seen enough of that side of the country. From now on she'll be nurtured and protected. She won't have to worry about those sorts of things anymore."

Noble looked properly chastised. In fact, he looked

mortified. *Is pleasing his father all that important?* she wondered.

"I'm sure Noble meant no harm," she found herself defending. "In a way, maybe it's good I've experienced some of the harsher side of this land. When I'm away from the ranch, I'll be more careful."

"Nonsense," Stuart scoffed. "You'll remain within the compound at all times from now on. Should you wish to ride or see some of the country, you'll do so with an armed escort. Tomorrow you'll become my wife. I won't have you putting yourself in danger."

Priscilla's fork hit the table with a resounding clatter. "Tomorrow?"

He smiled at her indulgently. "Judge Dodd generously agreed to stay here until your arrival. He's been at the Triple R for quite some time already. Aside from that, there's your reputation to consider. We're a bachelor household here."

An odd look crossed his features, then it was gone. "Considering your somewhat unorthodox arrival, the sooner the wedding takes place the better. There's been quite enough gossip already."

Priscilla's mouth felt so dry she could barely speak. "But I assumed we'd spend some time getting to know each other."

"And I assumed you'd be well chaperoned." There was a lengthy pause, and then he smiled. "I know you're exhausted, my dear, and barely recovered from all that has happened. But believe me, I know what's best. Trust me, Priscilla. From now on I'll take care of everything."

"I . . . I had hoped we'd be married in a church. Or at least by a man of the cloth."

"There's a service performed here on the ranch every Sunday by one of the hands. The priest stops by whenever he can, but that's all there is this far from a city." Stuart smiled again. "I'm afraid Judge Dodd is the best we can do for now. If you like, we'll remarry in church a little later."

Priscilla said no more. With trembling fingers, she reached for her long-stemmed wine glass and took a steadying sip. How could he expect her to marry him tomorrow? By a judge, no less?

Then again, what difference did it make?

Sooner or later she'd have to face the inevitable and become Mrs. Stuart Egan. There was really no other choice.

"The meal was delicious," she finally said to the men. "I hope you'll all understand if I excuse myself and retire a little early. As Stuart pointed out, I really am quite tired."

"Of course, my dear." Stuart slid back his chair, rounded the table and pulled out hers. The other two men stood up.

"What time is the wedding?" she asked woodenly.

"Eight o'clock tomorrow evening." Stuart flashed a smile that could only be called triumphant. "After the workday is finished, we'll all be able to enjoy the celebration."

Priscilla's smile felt wan. "It's bad luck for the groom to see the bride before the wedding, so I suppose this is good-bye until then."

"Nonsense, my dear. You can sleep late, gather

your strength, and then I'll show you around your new home. Surely you're eager to see it."

Priscilla forced herself to answer. "Of course." She started to leave, but Stuart caught her arm.

"I'll walk you up." Taking her hand and placing it on the sleeve of his expensively tailored coat, he guided her up the wide staircase to her second-story bedchamber and stopped outside the door.

"I'm sorry I can't give you more time, Priscilla, but after we're married, you'll see it's for the best."

Priscilla just nodded. She started to move away, but Stuart turned her gently into his arms. "A kiss for your future husband shouldn't be too much to ask."

Before she could answer, he lowered his mouth and kissed her. His lips felt as cold and unyielding as she had imagined. With a jolt of desperation, Priscilla slid her arms around his neck and kissed him back, willing herself to feel some of the passion she had felt with Brendan. Instead she felt nothing.

Stuart pulled away, an assessing look on his face. "I'll mince no words about this, Priscilla—you are in fact a virgin?"

She blushed, the warm heat spreading all the way to her toes. "Of course."

"With our wedding night approaching, I felt it important to know."

Where was the gentleness she had expected? The tenderness she had read in his letters?

"I wouldn't have accepted your proposal if I weren't," she said a bit defensively.

Stuart seemed pleased. "Of course not, my dear." He bent and kissed her cheek. "Good-night, Priscilla.

Sleep well." While Stuart held open her door, Priscilla stepped inside.

"Good-night, Stuart." When the door closed solidly behind her, Priscilla started to cry.

Chapter 9

 "Buenos días, Señorita Wills." Consuela drew back the heavy pink draperies to admit the late morning sunshine. "I have brought your breakfast. *Señor* Egan is expecting you to join him downstairs in one hour."

Feeling more exhausted than she had last night, Priscilla shoved back the covers. "I didn't mean to sleep so late. I hope I didn't inconvenience anyone."

Consuela's wide girth swayed rhythmically as she walked to Priscilla's marble-topped bedside table to set the breakfast tray down. Beneath the white linen napkin she drew off, a cup of coffee steamed beside a plate holding a slab of fried ham, scrambled eggs, and deep-fried corn dodgers. After the night Priscilla had spent tossing and turning, they only made her stomach churn.

"I'm really not very hungry. I think I'll just have coffee."

"Today is your wedding. You must eat. Everyone eat good on Rancho Reina."

Priscilla smiled at that. Wearing a borrowed cotton nightshirt, she swung her legs to the edge of the bed, her long thick braid falling over one shoulder. "It's good to know Stuart takes care of the people who work for him."

"*Sí, señorita,* that is so." A light knock sounded at the door, and Consuela rumbled over to open it. A

pretty dark-haired girl stood in the hallway, holding
Priscilla's few salvaged dresses, cleaned and freshly
pressed.

"This is my daughter, Dolores," Consuela said
with a touch of pride. The dark-skinned girl, no older
than seventeen, with a pretty face, shapely figure,
and shiny black hair, peeked around her mother's
broad girth.

"Hello, Dolores. I'm happy to meet you."

"*Buenos días, señorita.*" Looking shy and a little
embarrassed, she handed her mother the dresses and
slipped quietly back out of sight.

"She worries you will not like her." Consuela's
black eyes searched Priscilla's face. Since the first
time they'd met, Priscilla felt as if the woman were
sizing her up.

"Why in the world would your daughter think
that?"

Consuela shrugged her beefy shoulders in a gesture of nonchalance, but the expression on her face
seemed wary. "Dolores is young and pretty; you will
soon be *el patrón*'s wife. Wives often worry about
such things."

"But surely you don't think I would be jealous?"

Another beefy shrug.

"Consuela . . . is there something I should know
that you aren't telling me?"

For a moment Consuela seemed uncertain. Another appraising glance went from the top of Priscilla's dark head to the bare feet peeping from
beneath her nightshirt, then Consuela squared her
shoulders.

"Whether I tell you now or someone tells you later,

sooner or later you will know. I pray my judgment of you is correct."

"Please, Consuela, tell me what it is."

"Dolores was *el patrón*'s woman."

Priscilla's hand trembled against the folds of her nightgown.

"Several weeks ago," Consuela continued, "when he learned you would be his wife, he stopped seeing her. Dolores's life became as it was before and she is happy. But now that you are here, she is afraid you will send her away." There was challenge in the cool black eyes.

"Your daughter was Stuart's . . . mistress?"

Consuela glanced toward the window, her gaze somewhere in the distance. "There are few women out here . . . *el patrón* is a man of strong appetites."

Priscilla swallowed hard, her fingers unconsciously twisting the nightgown. "Was . . . Dolores . . . in love with him?"

"No, *señorita*. That was not the way of it. My husband was killed some time ago—in the days when Don Pedro owned Rancho Reina del Robles. There were many problems. . . . Don Pedro was forced to sell, and *el patrón* was kind enough to take us in. When Dolores grew older, *Señor* Egan began to desire her. After the kindness he had shown us, my daughter had no choice but to go to him."

She looked at Priscilla with the eyes of a mother whose child might be in danger. "Now that he takes a wife, she is free to marry Miguel, the boy she has fallen in love with . . . if you will let her stay."

A knot of tension curled in Priscilla's stomach. Everything was so different here. Nothing made sense in the way it had before. "Is my say in the matter really that important? From what I've seen so far, Stuart's word is law. What I think would mean very little."

"In most things that is true. In this, I believe he will do as you wish."

Priscilla wasn't sure if she felt better or worse. "Then of course she may stay. She's little more than a child. What happened wasn't her fault." *It was Stuart's. How could he take such unfair advantage?*

Consuela's large frame sagged with relief. A wide smile split her face, making her look a little younger. "Tonight is *fandango*. We will all celebrate your marriage. I think you will make *Señor* Egan a very fine wife."

But what kind of a husband will he make? "What's *fandango*?" Priscilla asked, picking at the now-cold food, though she felt less hungry than before.

"*Fiesta*. We roast whole bullock; there will be dancing and singing. Big celebration for your wedding to our *patrón*." She turned a sympathetic eye on Priscilla. "He is a hard man, but he looks after his people. You will be happy here."

Priscilla didn't answer.

"You are young," Consuela continued, "not much older than my daughter. You will learn to adjust to the way of things . . . besides, what does it matter? Your husband will take care of you and he will give you sons. A woman can always find happiness in her children."

"Yes . . . ," Priscilla reluctantly agreed, but she couldn't help thinking of Brendan, of the kind of warmth that could exist between a man and a woman. In his own rugged way, Brendan's power was just as imposing as Stuart's. Would he have taken advantage of a young girl's gratitude, of her need to repay her family's debt? Would he have slept with her and tossed her aside when she had served his purpose?

After the Indian attack, as they had lain beneath the oak tree, Brendan could have taken her—she wouldn't have stopped him—and both of them knew it. Instead, he had held back, protecting her from the consequences of their actions, looking after her as he had from the start. How could two strong men, so much alike in some ways, be so very different?

"Call me when you have finished eating and I will help you dress," Consuela said. "When you return from your ride with *Señor* Egan, we will prepare you for your wedding."

Priscilla nodded, and Consuela left her alone. Beyond the window beside the bed, the harsh Texas landscape seemed to ripple in the heat of the fast-approaching noonday sun. Inside the thick-walled house, it felt cool and inviting. Priscilla would have traded the comfort for the swirling dust and frying heat, the insects, and the Indians if it meant another chance to be with Brendan.

And freedom from her stone-walled prison.

"Well, my dear, what do you think of it?" Since Priscilla couldn't ride—Stuart almost seemed pleased about that—he sat beside her on the seat of a small black buggy, atop a rolling hill that overlooked the bustling compound below. Workers milled industriously between the huge two-story stone mansion, the outbuildings, corrals, and stables, none without a task, all intent upon seeing it done.

"It's like a small city, isn't it? You've created a world of your own out here on the plains."

"This is only the beginning," he said proudly. "By the time our sons are grown, I'll own three times this much land. I intend to build an empire so vast no one will be able to ignore it." Wearing buff-colored riding breeches and a white linen shirt, Stuart propped an expensive black boot on the brake, his sandy hair ruffled by the hot Texas wind.

"Why is owning that much land so important? Most people would be happy with half as much as you already own."

"I'm not 'most people,' Priscilla, though I started out that way. Like a great many men, I grew up with nothing. My father died when I was young; my mother did her best, but it wasn't much. By the time I was thirteen, I was out on my own."

"Your mother died, too?"

"Ran off with a gambler."

"Oh."

"It was a bitter existence, I'll tell you, living in the streets of Natchez, fighting for every mouthful of food. A man'll do damned near anything just to stay alive."

She thought of her bleak life with Aunt Maddie—at least she'd had a decent place to live, plenty to eat, and her schooling—far more than Stuart had had.

"Eventually I started working in the shipping trade," he continued, "loading goods aboard the steamboats going up and down the river. Later I got a job in a freighting office. I swore the day would come when people would look up to me the way they did the men I worked for. Someday they would respect me—and obey my orders without question. That day has come."

He slapped the reins lightly on the horse's rump, a lovely sorrel mare with a blaze of white on her face, and the buggy rolled off down the hill.

"I intend to be a force to be reckoned with in this state." He smiled down at her. "With a woman like you beside me, nothing can stand in my way."

Priscilla smiled with as much enthusiasm as she could muster.

"See that rise to your left?" Stuart pointed in that direction. "That's the far border of the Warton spread. It connects our eastern boundary, has good water, and brings us closer to the main trail between San Antonio and Corpus Christi. So far Warton has refused my offers to buy him out. But it's only a matter of time. Sooner or later that land will be mine."

Priscilla felt a shiver of unease at the determination in his tone. "How can you be so certain? Surely there are some men who would rather own their own land than accept your money."

Stuart pinned her with a glance, the easy smile gone from his face. "There are ways. . . ." A hard edge had crept into his voice, and Priscilla's unease grew. "When it comes to the ranch, you needn't concern yourself. Your place will be in the home."

Though she wasn't sure she liked the way he said it, she felt compelled to agree. "I suppose you're right about that. With such a large household to run, seeing to the cooking and cleaning, the mending and so forth, I'm sure I'll be busy."

"Nonsense," he said, surprising her. "Consuela will see to the house and the staff. Once you're my wife, you'll hold a position of great importance. I'll not have you working at menial labor."

"But surely there is something I can contribute. What kind of a life would I have doing nothing?"

"In a very short time you'll have sons to attend," he reminded her, and Priscilla flushed at his words. "We'll be traveling quite often. I've a trip to Washington planned. You'll need the proper clothing—I've already sent to San Antonio for some of the items you'll need. As soon as it's feasible, we'll travel to New Orleans."

His eyes slid down to the narrow span of her waist then moved upward to settle on her breasts. "In the meantime, I have plans for you of my own."

Priscilla watched the way his pupils darkened and his mouth went thin. She forced herself not to shudder. What was there about him she found so disturbing, almost repelling? Why did she sense he'd be as unyielding and demanding in the marriage bed as he was when it came to his ranch?

"Stuart . . . I know Judge Dodd has traveled quite some distance. . . . I know you've planned a celebration and all, but surely you can understand my reluctance to rush into marriage. We have only just met and I—"

"The wedding is set, Priscilla. You're under my protection and guidance from now on. I understand your shyness—you are, after all, a virgin. However, sooner or later, you'll have to do your wifely duty. The longer you postpone it, the more you'll fear it. By tomorrow, you'll know your husband and your fears will be put to rest. That is the end of it." He urged the horse into a trot, and the buggy rolled on down the road.

Priscilla said nothing more. Tears stung her eyes, but she willed them away. *Her wifely duty*. No words of affection, no caring, no gentleness. She would spread her legs for him, he would take what he believed was his, and be done with it. She would know none of the passion she had shared with Brendan, none of the joy.

None of the love.

A short time ago, she could have accepted it, would silently have endured it. Now, she'd have to steel herself, resist the urge to recoil from him, and let him have his way.

The buggy bounced along, and Priscilla forced her attention back to the land that was her new home. Besides the small cabins in the compound itself, tiny workers' houses, some of wood, some of stone, darkened the brushy landscape near its perimeter.

"With the war so close at hand," she said, determined to make conversation, "I'm surprised you haven't had trouble with the Mexicans who work for you."

"These men know little of the war. They've lived on this land for more than a century. Now that the land is mine, their loyalty is to me—and of course, to Texas. There were Mexicans who fought against General Santa Anna at the Alamo."

Priscilla arched a brow. "I never knew that."

"If it came down to it, these men would stand with me." There was pride in his tone and a toughness he hadn't shown in his letters.

"I see." Such loyalty was hard to imagine, and yet she'd glimpsed it already. As the buggy jounced along, she looked off the road to her left. Even from a distance, she could make out the shiny black skin of several Negroes, stripped to their waists in the sun, shovel in hand, bent to their tasks.

"I didn't expect to see so many Negroes this far from the South," she observed.

"Texas *is* the South, my dear. Those nigras belong to me. They're slaves."

"Slaves? You own slaves?"

"Not many, something less than thirty. When I moved here from Natchez, I brought them with me."

Why did each revelation seem so overwhelming? "I . . . didn't realize. . . . In Cincinnati, people don't believe in slavery. It seems such a harsh institution."

"Don't be absurd," Stuart snapped. "Those people are nothing like us. If I didn't provide for them, they'd probably starve. All I ask in return is a good day's labor, no different from any other man."

"Other men choose their labor," Priscilla pointed out. "Black men have no choice."

Stuart's irritation grew. "Whatever position you've held on this matter in the past, from now on your opinion will be the same as mine. I intend to enter politics. Texas is a slave state. I'll continue to uphold Southern beliefs in that institution and you, my dear, will do the same."

Priscilla's chin came up and with it a surge of anger. "Marrying you does not give you the right to control my thoughts, Stuart. We both came from

Natchez, but I've never believed in slavery, and I don't intend to start now."

Stuart started to argue, his eyes hard on hers. The woman beside him had squared her shoulders and clenched her hands into fists. *Who did the little fool think she was?* Nothing but another mouth to feed, someone to clothe and provide for. She'd pay with her body and the sons she would bear, but she would learn to obey him. A muscle ticked in his cheek but he forced himself to calm.

He smiled. "Our wedding day is hardly the time to discuss our political differences. I'm sorry if I sounded overbearing."

His smile grew broader. "It appears you aren't the only one who's nervous about getting married. I seem to have a case of bridegroom jitters myself. Why don't we go back to the house and you can rest for a while? We'll see more of the ranch in the future."

"All right." Priscilla ignored the knot in her stomach. Maybe he *was* just nervous. Across the road, one of the Mexican workers waved toward the buggy, and Stuart waved back. None of his people seemed bothered by his high-handedness. Not even Consuela. They all appeared happy and content. *Well-cared for*, Consuela had said. What more could they ask? What more could *she* ask?

"A mind of their own," she mumbled aloud.

"What did you say, my dear?"

Priscilla smiled tightly. "I said I hope you don't mind our returning home."

Stuart reached a hand to her knee and patted it solicitously. "Of course not, darling. It's obvious you've a delicate constitution. In the future, I'll be sure to remember that."

Priscilla's stomach churned.

"Your gown *es muy hermosa*—very beautiful—the prettiest dress I have ever seen." Consuela's large hand ran lovingly over the heavy silk fabric, the rich ivory color shimmering against her olive-skinned hand.

"Thank you," Priscilla said softly. "I made it my-self."

Staring at her image in the big oval looking glass, Priscilla had to admit she looked lovely. Though her face seemed pale, the skin beneath her eyes a little too dark, the gown she wore was beautiful indeed.

She touched a cluster of tiny glass beads that shimmered against the silk. They nestled here and there among layers of ivory lace festooning the voluminous skirt. The neck veed gently, framing her bosom with rows of the same delicate lace. Made of ivory peau de soie, a flat-finished satin so rich in texture it begged to be touched, the dress emphasized her tiny waist, the upturned swell of her breast. More of the ivory lace, gathered near each elbow, hung down to her wrists.

"You are a very fine seamstress," Consuela said. *"El patron's* last wife could not sew."

"You knew her?" Priscilla's head came up.

"For a while before she died. She was a fine lady. Very shy and reserved. She spent most of her time reading. *Señor* Egan bought her many beautiful books."

"Did Stuart . . . did he love her?"

"*Señor* Egan is not one to show his feelings. I think he cared for her. Mostly he was busy with his *rancho*."

"I see."

"Turn around, *señorita*. Hand me the rose, so I may pin it in your hair."

It was a single white rose from the garden below the window, the delicate petals just a shade lighter than the dress. Priscilla flinched as one of the thorns pricked her finger.

"It seems there is always a price to pay for great beauty," Consuela said, noting the small drop of blood.

"I suppose so." What price would she pay for this beautiful house, the servants, and a wardrobe of expensive clothes?

Sucking at the tiny drop of red, she handed the rose to Consuela, who plucked off the thorns and pinned it into her hair. The big Mexican woman had proved surprisingly adept, using a hot curling iron to fashion long, dark chestnut curls, then separating the heavy mass and tying a cluster of ringlets below each ear.

"There," she said as she finished. "*Señor* Egan will be very pleased."

Priscilla looked in the mirror. If only her eyes could sparkle with the same lovely lights as the gown.

On impulse she turned to the plump Mexican woman who was the closest thing she had to a friend. "Am I doing the right thing, Consuela? I mean, I hardly know him. We've been writing, of course, but he's nothing at all like his letters. Except for his

looks, that is. I mean he's handsome and all, but—"
At the look of astonishment on Consuela's face, she
broke off.

"Every bride is nervous on her wedding day," Consuela said. "But you must face the truth. You have
told me you have no family, no one to watch out for
you. You have no money, no way to find work. Unless
Señor Egan arranged it, you could not even return to
what was once your home." She cupped Priscilla's
cheek in a work-calloused palm. "It is time you grew
up, *niña*. My Dolores had no choice in this matter—
and neither do you."

At the truth of her words, tears welled in Priscilla's
eyes and slipped down her cheeks. "I don't know if I
can do this."

Consuela's voice grew stern. "You will do what all
women do. You will survive and make the best of
things. If you are lucky, and *Señor* Egan is pleased,
you may even find a way to be happy. Now end your
crying and prepare yourself to meet your husband."

Knowing Consuela spoke the truth, Priscilla swallowed the lump in her throat and wiped at her tears,
a little ashamed of her outburst.

"I'm sorry. You're right, of course." She forced
herself to smile, though it felt as if her lips would
crack. "Things will work out. I'll make Stuart a good
wife, just as I planned. We'll raise a family, and we'll
both be very happy."

"*Sí, niña*. Things will work out." Her tone was
solid and reassuring, but there was a sadness in her
eyes Priscilla didn't miss. "Come. It is time for your
wedding."

Even before Consuela opened the door, Priscilla

could hear the music, soft strains of guitar that drifted up from below, filling the room with its poignant melody.

The house rang with voices and laughter and the sound of the servants' shuffling feet. The smells of roasting meats and fresh-baked bread pervaded every corner of the house—aromas succulent and inviting.

Head held high, Priscilla walked down the hall toward the joyous sounds below, while Consuela silently slipped out of sight. At the bottom of the staircase, Noble Egan stood waiting, resplendent in his black tailcoat and smiling up at her. Beside him, a small Mexican boy clutched a bouquet of white roses that matched the one in her hair.

"You look lovely," Noble said to her, extending his arm. Needing his gentle support, she gladly accepted. "My father has chosen a very lovely bride."

"Thank you, Noble."

"For you, *señorita*." The little Mexican boy handed her the roses. He grinned, a front tooth missing, when she knelt to accept them.

"This is Ferdinand," Noble told her. "We call him Ferdy. He's one of the Juárez children."

"Juárez?" she repeated.

"Bernardo Juárez, the overseer. Besides the cattle we raise, there are gardens to attend, corn fields, vegetables—and of course the mill. Bernardo works with the men in the fields."

Priscilla smiled down at the olive-skinned boy, no more than five years old. "Thank you, Ferdy. They're beautiful."

"I helped to pick them, *con mi madre*." He held up

his thumb and Priscilla noted an ugly red dot. "The roses bite," he told her very seriously, and Priscilla's soft smile broadened.

"Yes, they do," she agreed, holding up her hand and showing him a rose bite of her own. "But they're worth it. Maybe your mother would let me help sometime."

"*Sí, señorita.* I will show you how to pick them without getting bit."

Priscilla's hand touched his cheek. Such a sweet little boy. Maybe living here wouldn't be so bad after all.

"We'd better be going." Noble took her arm once more and urged her toward the door. "My father will be waiting."

Priscilla just nodded and let him guide her through the house toward the rear. Outside the mansion, dusk had settled in, turning the sky brilliant hues of pink and purple. Cactus and mesquite in stark designs thrust up from the flatland, forming small dark sculptures. In its own harsh way, the land was beautiful, just as Brendan had said.

Brendan. The thought of him brought a rush of emotion Priscilla had to fight down. Tonight was not the time for it. The farther his memory drifted from her mind, the better her chance to find happiness.

"They're waiting over there," Noble said, and she realized Stuart stood beneath a wooden archway laced with flowers. Wearing a perfectly tailored black frock coat and breeches, with his sandy hair and fair complexion, he looked exceedingly handsome, and his hazel eyes warmed with approval at the sight of her.

Priscilla's hand tightened on the sleeve of Noble's black broadcloth coat as he led her toward the flowered awning. Rows of people dressed in their simple but finest garments lined each side of the path that had been cleared and scattered with rose petals. The effort Stuart had taken pleased her, and gave her fresh hope.

To the strum of a single guitar, Noble led her to Stuart, and placed her cold hand in his warmer one. "You look lovely, my dear. I couldn't be more pleased."

"Thank you," she said softly, barely able to form the words. Why did everything hinge on pleasing Stuart? Why did no one worry that she should be pleased? Then she thought of the huge celebration, of the trouble he had gone to for their wedding—was it just to impress the people around him?

He turned his attention to the man dressed in black who stood facing them. "You may begin, Judge Dodd."

Dear Lord, let me get through this. Priscilla felt Stuart's hand gripping hers, heard the judge's voice, but could barely make out the words for the buzzing in her ears.

She swayed on her feet, and Stuart's grip tightened in warning.

The judge said something to Stuart and she heard him respond. More words were spoken, but Priscilla heard only the drone of Dodd's raspy voice, saw only the backdrop of blackness behind his thin shoulders.

"Say 'I do,' Priscilla," Stuart urged with controlled irritation, his hold growing tighter on her hand.

"I do," she whispered with a rush of embarrassment. How could she not have heard? More words were spoken, she tried to listen this time. Then something cold slid onto her finger, a heavy jeweled ring, she saw, as its rubies and diamonds sparkled in the light of the torches.

"Since you, Priscilla, and you, Stuart, have spoken your vows in the sight of God and the presence of these witnesses, by the power vested in me by the sovereign state of Texas, I now pronounce you man and wife. You may kiss your bride."

Stuart turned her into his arms and his mouth came down hard over hers. It felt cold and unyielding, and a little bit angry. When she started to pull away, he drew her back against him, kissing her even harder. It was a show of mastery none could have missed, and all her misgivings rushed back with a vengeance.

"Drinks all around!" he ordered, and a cheer went up from the crowd. Someone struck up a guitar, a fiddle started playing, and several men joined in on homemade instruments—everything from a washboard to a mouth organ.

"It's time you met our guests," Stuart said, taking her arm and guiding her into the crowd. "You're Mrs. Stuart Egan now."

And so the round of introductions began. Stuart missed no one, from the youngest child to the oldest *vaquero*. Even the slaves were included, though they kept to themselves and declined to shake hands. All wished her well on the day of her wedding.

As the evening wore on, fresh platters of food were brought out, and dozens of casks of wine were opened and eventually emptied. When the strains of guitar settled down, the tunes much less vigorous, Stuart led her onto the dance floor.

"You do like to dance?" he asked with a smile, drawing her into his arms.

"All women like to dance." She returned the smile, but in truth she felt nearly too weary to move her feet. Only Stuart's skill and the firm way he held her kept her from stumbling. Still, he didn't relent.

"I know you're beginning to tire, but the others expect us to enjoy ourselves at least for a little while longer." He drew her indecently close. "Soon enough we'll retire to our suite, and you can allow your new husband the pleasures of the marriage bed."

Priscilla couldn't answer. Why did the thought of Stuart's hands on her body make her feel almost sick? Even now, his blunt fingers bit into her waist and she could feel their cloying warmth. His palm felt damp against hers and his breath, a mixture of tobacco and whiskey, smelled stale and slightly repugnant.

"Might I have a little more punch?" she asked him when the dance had ended. The mixture of fruit juices and sugar was heavily laced with wine, yet Priscilla's nervousness kept her from feeling the effects.

"I believe you've had enough," he said. "I don't want you drunk when I take you. I want you to know what is happening—and exactly which man has claimed you."

Dear God in heaven, there wasn't enough liquor in Texas to keep her from knowing that.

"Excuse me, boss." Hat in hand, Jaimie Walker tapped Stuart on the shoulder. "Sorry, Miss Wills—er—I mean, Mrs. Egan." His eyes, warm with approval as they had been from the first time they'd met, swept over her. He was a shy sort of man, genuine, she would call him, with a hint of gentleness that seemed somehow familiar.

"What is it, Jaimie?" Stuart asked with a trace of annoyance.

"Mace Harding just rode in. Says he's got news that won't wait."

"Who's Mace Harding?" Priscilla asked, and Stuart scowled.

"Now that Barker's gone, Mace will be foreman. I sent him to Natchez on business. Apparently he just got back." He turned his attention to Jaimie. "Tell Harding I'll speak to him now. I've got a number of things to go over." He started to leave, then turned back.

"It's getting late, darling. Why don't you go on upstairs and get ready. That'll give you some time to refresh yourself before I join you. I'll send Consuela in to help you change."

Suddenly she didn't feel tired at all. "Maybe I'll stay a little bit longer."

Stuart smiled indulgently. "Come, my dear." Taking a firm grip on her arm, he led her back toward the house.

At the foot of the stairs, Stuart turned her into his arms and kissed her. It was a kiss like the one before, with little warmth and a great deal of possession. It moved her not at all.

"I'll join you as soon as I can," he said with a

knowing glance. He squeezed her hand and then turned to leave.

Priscilla hurriedly climbed the stairs, seeking the protection of her bedroom. Once inside, she noticed the candles had been lit and the windows thrown wide to admit the evening breeze. The door adjoining the master suite had never been opened—tonight it would be. She felt as if the last barrier to the person she was inside would be broken when Stuart walked in. The last vestige of herself would be smashed when he breached her maidenhead.

And Priscilla knew she was powerless to stop him.

Chapter 10

"The nightgown is a present from your husband." Consuela lifted the edge of lace on the sheer white gown draped carefully across the pink satin counterpane. "It has come all the way from New Orleans."

"It's lovely," Priscilla said softly. And it was.

What there was of it.

"Let me help you put it on." With Consuela's help, they had already dispensed with everything but her chemise and pantalets.

With a feeling of unreality, Priscilla removed those last two garments and let Consuela pull the sheer white lace on over her head. The gown slid softly down her body and settled over the curve of her hips. The neckline opened nearly to her navel, leaving all but her nipples exposed. The dark thatch of hair at the apex of her thighs shadowed the gown a little lower, and Priscilla pinkened with embarrassment.

How could she face him in this?

"Do not forget the robe." Consuela held up the beautiful white peignoir and Priscilla slid her arms into the lacy sleeves. Though it barely covered her breasts and the curves of her body, she felt a little bit better.

The wide-girthed woman patted her cheek. "It is always hard the first time." As if sensing her need for privacy, Consuela headed toward the door. *"El pa-*

trón is still busy with his men. You will have time to prepare yourself." Walking out in the hall, she closed the door behind her.

Priscilla sank down on the low wooden stool in front of the gilded mirror on the marble-topped dressing table. Consuela had removed the pins from her hair and brushed it until it gleamed. It fell in heavy dark waves around her shoulders. Her face felt bloodless and numb, and her hand trembled on the handle of the silver-backed brush she pulled absent-mindedly through her hair.

Still, she knew she looked pretty. Her days in the sun with Brendan had pinkened her cheeks and fore-head, and the negligee enhanced the smoothness of her skin and the upward tilt of her breasts. Stuart would indeed be pleased.

She wondered what Brendan would have thought. *Brendan.* The sound of his name in the hollows of her mind made her throat close up and tears burn the back of her eyes. How could just a few short weeks with someone change her life so completely?

She thought of Stuart, of his beautiful mansion, of the security he could offer. Everything she had ever wanted. Now it all seemed unimportant.

All her dreams of husband and family she would gladly abandon just for the sight of the man she had come to love. Where was he now? What was he do-ing? Had he safely ridden on toward San Antonio, or met up again with the Indians? She wondered at the haunted look she had sometimes seen in his eyes, wondered why he was running. She wondered if he would ever settle down.

She prayed he was well and safe, and that he would someday find happiness.

Against her will, his face rose up before her, chiseled, rugged features scowling with worry, or laughing at something she had said. In the eye of her mind, light blue eyes assessed her boldly. Long brown fingers curved over her breast, teasing her nipple, sending waves of pleasure through her body. She could almost taste his warm breath, feel the silky texture of his tongue.

"Brendan," she whispered, unable to stop the tears from slipping down her cheeks. "How could you do this to me?"

Leaning over the bureau, she rested her head on her arms and quietly started to weep. It was dangerous to let herself go like this, to let down her guard and remember. Yet somehow it seemed that she must, that remembering him now, before Stuart took what was left of her, was more important than the risk. That if she didn't do it now, it would all slip away as if it had never occurred.

Stuart's touch would erase it, wipe it from her thoughts and leave only hazy memories in its place. She would never recall the passion and the tenderness, never recall the giving they had shared. Stuart's possession would destroy it. Priscilla knew it beyond a doubt.

In the silence of the room, her shoulders heaved with the force of her sobs. He would know she'd been crying and he would be angry. She wanted to stop, she had to. These final few moments of mourning were the last she would allow. A last fleeting memory of what it had felt like to love.

"Any chance some of those tears are for me?"

Priscilla whirled at the sound of the voice, afraid at first it was just another trick of the mind. Brendan stood in front of the open window, holding his broad-brimmed hat against a hard-muscled thigh, looking more handsome than her fondest remembrance.

"Brendan!" Jumping up from the stool, she raced across the room and into his arms. She cried in earnest then—sad, happy tears—she wasn't sure which. "You're here. You're really and truly here."

His hard arms tightened around her and he buried his face in her hair. "God, I've missed you. Every hour, every minute. I can't believe I was fool enough to leave you in the first place."

As the warmth in his words rushed over her, Priscilla drew back to look at him. He had recently shaved, she noticed, and his hair felt damp beneath her fingers. "How did you find me? How did you know which room I was in?"

"I saw you standing at the window the day I rode out."

"I didn't think you noticed."

"I noticed. In my mind, I've seen you standing there a thousand times since."

When she rose on tiptoe and kissed him, Brendan's fierce response staggered her. His warm lips slanted over hers, his tongue slid hotly between her teeth, and shivers of excitement raced through her, wicked heat that slid through her veins like boiling oil. Her fingers clutched his neck and her nipples grew hard where they pressed against the fabric of his shirt.

Priscilla kissed him back with all the passion she had ever felt, and Brendan's hands moved down her body, lighting a fiery trail wherever they touched. Cupping her bottom, he pressed her against the rigid length of him, and Priscilla felt the hardness of his desire.

Cold reality hit her—with such force she could barely stand up. Pushing against the muscles of his chest, she turned her face away and finally broke free.

"Y-you have to leave," she said, her voice ragged, fresh tears gathering in her eyes. "Before Stuart finds you. You've got to go before it's too late."

"Listen to me, Priscilla. I know this is not the way to do things. If I hadn't been such a damned fool—"

"Please, Brendan—"

"I know you think I'm a drifter—and I have been up until now. But I've got some money put away—quite a bit, in fact. Years ago I bought some land down on the Brazos—fine land, good soil with plenty of water. We can build a ranch of our own down there. If we run out of money, I've got a brother rich as Croesus back in Georgia. He's been wanting me to settle down for years. He and his wife have offered to back me more than once." He cupped her chin with his hand. "We'll have those kids you want—a whole parcel, if that's what makes you happy."

"Oh, God," Priscilla cried, "please don't say anymore."

"Damn it, Priscilla, you're making this even tougher than I figured—I'm askin' you to marry me."

She only shook her head. "You don't understand."

"I know I should have asked you sooner, but a man needs a little time to get used to the idea."

Priscilla clutched the front of his shirt, her knuck-

les white with tension. "I can't," she whispered bro-
kenly, "I can't marry you."

Brendan set her away from him, holding her at a
distance so he could read her face. "Is it the money?
You said money wasn't the reason, that a husband
and family were more important."

"It—It isn't the money."

"You can't mean to say you're in love with him.
You haven't known him that long."

She only shook her head. "I can't marry you—because I'm already married." She held out her trembling fingers, the blood-red rubies gleaming with
accusation in the light of the flickering candles.

Brendan's face grew taut. "When?"

"Tonight. Just a few hours ago. He'll be here any
minute to claim his husbandly rights. You've got to
leave before he finds you here."

"Why did you do it?" he breathed, beginning to get
angry. "Couldn't you have waited, at least till you got
to know him a little?"

"I wanted to wait. Stuart wouldn't hear of it. I
thought you were gone for good; I had no money, no
place to go— Oh, God, Brendan, why did this have to
happen?"

Brendan raked a hand through his hair. For the
first time he noticed her skimpy lace peignoir and
delicate white nightgown. He reached out a hand
and curled it roughly into the lace. "Egan buy you
this?"

She nodded.

"That bastard." Brendan walked to the window,
his fists balled tightly at his sides. He stared grimly
through the opening, out at the stars and the black-

ness. "The thought of him putting his hands on you makes me sick. It's all I can do not to go down those stairs and call him out."

"Please, you've got to go." He turned to face her. "He owns everything and everyone around him. You aren't safe here."

"And now he owns you."

Priscilla's eyes slid closed against a wave of pain. "Yes."

"Goddamn him."

"If I had believed for a moment you cared about me . . . that there was the slightest chance you'd come back . . ."

"How could you know?" he said harshly. "I didn't know it myself."

It was all she could do not to go to him. To let him hold her and kiss her and say those beautiful words again. Instead she stayed where she was. His life was in danger, more so every moment. "You've got to go. Time is running out."

Brendan just stared at her, as if memorizing the details of her face. "I left you before and lived to regret it."

"I'm married to Stuart," she reminded him, fighting the ache in her throat. "There's nothing we can do."

Brendan grabbed her shoulders and kissed her hard. Priscilla clutched his neck, and Brendan's hold grew tighter.

Then he broke away. Turning, he strode to the window. One long leg disappeared over the sill and he turned to look outside. For a moment he just sat there, half in and half out of the window.

Priscilla held her breath, torn between wanting him safe and desperately wanting him to stay.

Then he swung to face her one last time. "I've got to know, Priscilla . . . if I'd asked you before, would you have said yes?"

She tried to speak, but her throat had closed up and the words wouldn't come. Fresh tears trickled down her cheeks.

"Take your time, Silla. This just may be the most important question you ever answer."

Priscilla wet her lips. "I would have been proud to be your wife."

Brendan hesitated only a moment. His long leg slid over the sill and he stepped back into the room. "Grab something to wear, put on your shoes, and let's go."

"What!"

"So far this marriage is nothing but words. It hasn't been consummated and until it is, we can get it annulled. We'll ride back to Corpus, then go to Galveston. They've got lawyers there, someone who can help us. All we've got to do is get away."

While Priscilla stood gaping, Brendan threw open the door to the big rosewood armoire, tossed out her sturdy brown shoes, and one of her dresses. Opening a bureau drawer, he pulled out a handful of underthings and tossed them onto the bed.

"What about Stuart?" Priscilla asked.

"Write him a note. There's probably some paper in that desk in the corner."

"But I—"

Brendan's hard look stopped her. "It's Egan or me, Priscilla. Make up your mind."

I love you. "I want to go with you."

Brendan's stance relaxed and he broke into a grin. "Then shake your pretty little bottom, sweetness. We've got a lot of ground to cover in the next few days."

For the first time since she'd reached Rancho Reina, Priscilla really smiled. "I'd better get dressed."

"Sorry, baby, time for that later." He threw back the counterpane, pulled off a blanket, and wrapped it around her shoulders. "Just write that note, put on your shoes, and let's go."

As she hurried to the desk, grabbing her locket and sliding off the heavy ruby ring, Priscilla's smile grew wider. This was one order she didn't mind following at all.

"Are you sure you can make it?" Brendan eyed the primrose trellis he had climbed up on. "I can carry you over my shoulder."

"I can make it. The sooner we leave this place, the better I'll like it."

That made him smile. God, how he loved the sound of those words. "Just be careful. Hand me the blanket. You can put it back on once we're down."

She did as he said, and he noted the tempting sight she made in her skimpy white negligee. Long chestnut hair hung in waves that nearly touched her waist and her breasts peeped up at him, luscious dark circles beckoning through the lace. In contrast, her sturdy little shoes reminded him of the prim and proper lady she was and the contrast made him smile. He wanted just to hold her, to tell her how much he cared.

If he played his cards right, there'd be time for that later.

Checking to be sure the perimeter guards weren't near, Brendan started climbing down the trellis, keeping a watch on Priscilla, who descended above him. The way the nightgown outlined the shapely curve of her bottom, it was all he could do not to reach up and touch her.

Once he stood on the ground, he did, his hands surrounding her waist to help her down. God, how he loved the feel of her.

"Nothing to it," Priscilla said with a grin.

She looked radiant instead of pale, and Brendan's heart turned over. "Stand still," he commanded, but couldn't keep the warmth from his voice. He drew his knife from his boot, sliced a hole in the center of the blanket, and pulled it over her head. "Let's go."

Holding hands, they moved through the darkness to the wall surrounding the compound. Brendan lifted Priscilla over, then vaulted over himself. Avoiding the sentry, who had just rounded the corner out of sight, they crept along the wall until they reached a gully that carried them out of view and back to where his big black horse was tied.

He patted the animal's nose, calling him Blackie. Hell, it was as good a name as any.

He turned to Priscilla. "It'll be easier on the horse if you ride behind me." He lifted her onto a rock, mounted the horse, then swung Priscilla aboard. Her slender arms slid around his waist.

"We'll travel the ravine bottom for as long as we

can." He urged Blackie forward, and the big horse responded instantly, perking up his ears and moving off with long, sure strides.

Behind him, Priscilla's soft breasts pushed into his back, and he felt a stirring in his loins. When she rested her head on his shoulder, he could feel her trembling.

"Are you cold?"

He felt the shake of her head. "I'm just a little bit nervous. I don't mind telling you, this is the craziest thing I've ever done and I'm scared to death."

Brendan smiled into the darkness. "Sorry?" It felt good just to be near her. She smelled of lilacs, and wisps of her long dark hair grazed his cheek.

"No."

Another brief smile, this one relieved. "What did you say in the note?"

"I told him I was sorry for all the trouble I'd caused, that I would be seeking an annulment, and I asked him to try to understand."

"You don't really believe he will, do you?"

"I doubt it. What do you think?"

"I think he'll come after us with a vengeance. Probably tonight. That's why we're going to hole up till morning—right under his nose. Tomorrow we'll set out for Corpus, covering our trail, of course."

"How do we do that?"

"Backtrack, tie some brush to the saddle horn, travel in the streambeds and gullys. I've got at least a dozen tricks up my sleeve."

She snuggled against his warmth, and Brendan felt a glow of satisfaction. The stirring in his loins grew more pronounced. He'd thought of nothing but

Priscilla Mae Wills since the moment he'd ridden away from the Triple R. From the moment he'd left her, he'd felt a hollow, aching loneliness unlike anything he had experienced. It had been obvious from the start, though he had been too blind to see it, that where this woman was concerned, he was in very big trouble.

And stealing Stuart Egan's wife right from under his nose was the least of it.

Priscilla must have fallen asleep against Brendan's shoulder because she awoke when he reined up the horse.

"Where are we?" she asked as he lifted her to the ground.

"Not far from the ranch. I've circled around to a place I spotted on my way out the other day. I shot a rabbit and when I went to pick it up, I found an arroyo hidden by brush."

"We've gone north instead of south?"

"Tomorrow we'll head south. Tonight I'm going back to watch the ranch. As soon as Egan rides out, I'll be back."

Priscilla clutched the front of his shirt. "I want to go with you."

"I wish you could, but I might need to cover some ground in a hurry. I'll roll out the bedroll so you can sleep. You'll be safe here till I get back."

She thought of the last time he'd left her alone on the prairie, of the Indians and what they'd almost done. She thought of the rattlesnake and her near brush with death. She was frightened—and for the first time unsure. "I don't like being out here alone."

"And I don't like leaving you. If there was any other way I wouldn't. I'll leave you my pistol. You remember how to fire it, don't you?"

Priscilla paled. The Indian's bloody face rose up before her, half blown away by her shot. "I don't want it," she whispered, barely able to speak. Though she willed herself not to, she started to shiver.

Brendan's hard arms came around her, pulling her close. He read the look on her face and knew in a flash she was thinking about the Indians.

"It's all right, baby. We'll stay here together. If we're careful, it won't make a damn what Egan does." He tipped her chin with his hand. "Sometimes I take a little too much for granted. When we reach our place on the Brazos, there'll be time for you to learn the things you'll need to know. I'll show you how to handle a gun and—"

"Will you teach me to ride a horse?"

He smiled at that. "Sidesaddle, like a lady, or astride?"

"Both," Priscilla said staunchly, remembering the way Stuart had enjoyed her lack of independence.

"I'll teach you all about the land and the animals. I know you're going to love it here as much as I do."

I hope so, she thought. "I'll love being with you."

"God, Priscilla." Brendan buried his face in her hair. His lips found her shoulder, then moved along her throat. He nibbled an earlobe, then fastened his mouth on hers in a searing, possessive kiss that made her knees go weak.

Lord in heaven, when Brendan kissed her like that, her fears didn't matter. She knew she would follow him anywhere. His hands cupped her face, and he kissed her long and hard, then he broke away.

"If we're going to stay here, I'd better tend to Blackie and fix a place for us to sleep."

In minutes he had leveled the earth, picking up any loose rocks, and laid out a neat little place to rest. It wasn't really wide enough for two, she noted, but it was the best he could do with what little gear they had.

"I'll need your blanket," he said with a look she couldn't quite read. When she pulled it over her head and handed it to him, leaving her in just the lacy nightclothes, his pale blue eyes turned dark in the light of the moon.

He cleared his throat and looked away. Fussing with the blanket, straightening it, then turning it back so they could climb in, Brendan kept his back to her, crouching on the balls of his feet. With a burst of temper, he whirled to face her.

"Damn it, Priscilla, you have no idea how tough this is—you wearing practically nothing—me wanting you so bad I ache with it." He lifted the edge of her lacy peignoir, then released it as if it burned his fingers.

"I . . . I could sleep in my dress, if you'd rather."

One corner of his mouth curved up. "Always the lady. . . . I suppose I should be used to it." He lifted a heavy coil of hair. "I think I like you better wearing this." His hungry gaze fixed on the dark areolas of her breasts beneath her nightgown.

Priscilla slid her arms around his neck and leaned against him. Brendan clamped his jaw as he felt the familiar tightening in his groin. After so many days of wanting her, he ached with every heartbeat.

"I need you to hold me," she said softly.

Brendan released a ragged breath. "There's something we need to discuss, Priscilla." He set her away from him.

"What is it?"

He glanced from her to the bedroll, beckoning silently in the moonlight. "If I touch you again, I might not be able to stop. I want to be inside you, Priscilla. I've thought of nothing else for days. . . ." He tipped her chin with his hand. "Do you trust me?"

"I wouldn't be here if I didn't."

"Then let me make love to you."

"But I'm . . . married."

"You aren't Egan's wife. You never will be. I'm going to be your husband."

"But—"

"We'll be married as soon as we can make the arrangements. In the meantime, we'll be man and wife in the eyes of God."

Priscilla wet her suddenly dry lips. "I don't know. . . ."

"Listen to me, Priscilla. If Egan should happen to find us—"

"Don't say that—don't even think it."

"It isn't going to happen, but if it should . . . we might have a chance of convincing him to let us go, if he knew I'd claimed you—that you were no longer a virgin."

He *had* seemed overly concerned about it. She remembered him asking her about it somewhat crudely, then mentioning it again the following day.

She thought of Brendan's kisses, of his hands on her body, of the pleasures he had stirred. She wanted him to hold her, wanted to know the solid feel of his body.

She wanted to make him happy, show him how much she cared.

"Trust me, Priscilla. I promise I won't hurt you." There was tenderness in his expression, caring. There was the kind of hunger she had seen before, but more than that, she was certain she saw love.

"I trust you, Brendan. I always have."

Chapter 11

Brendan stepped away from her, allowing himself to look at her as he hadn't dared before. Moonlight touched her thick dark hair, and her soft pink mouth looked ripe and inviting.

"I'll take care of you, Priscilla. That much I promise." Leaning forward, he slid the peignoir from her shoulders, leaving her in just the lacy white nightgown. Instinctively, Priscilla's hands came up to cover her breasts.

"Don't," he said, his voice low and husky. "You look lovely."

"I . . . I don't know exactly what to do." Unconsciously her hands smoothed the front of the nightgown.

"I do." Lifting her fingers to his lips, he kissed each one gently. "We've got all night, baby. I'm not going to rush you."

She reached for him then, and Brendan pulled her against him. She felt slender and fragile, as she had that first day when he lifted her into his arms. Forcing himself to go slow, he tipped her head back and covered her mouth with his. Her breath tasted warm and sweet, and his body grew harder. This time he didn't fight it, just savored his building desire.

"God, I want you," he whispered against her soft mouth, then teased it open and slid his tongue inside.

Priscilla swayed against him. He felt the upthrusting points of her breasts, moved his hand down to cup one through the lace, and heard her soft mew of pleasure.

Brendan smiled inwardly. Beneath her prim exterior, fiery passion flowed through Priscilla's veins. He had seen it that day beneath the oak tree. This night, he'd unleash it again, and she would be his.

Once he had claimed her, she would never forget it.

Priscilla felt warm fingers curve over her breast, lifting and molding. Through the holes in the lace, Brendan teased her nipple, already hard, and warmth invaded her limbs. As they stood together in the moonlight, his mouth nipped and teased, and his hands sent hot shivers down her spine. Priscilla used her tongue as Brendan had, fencing, coaxing, sliding it over his lips. She wasn't quite sure what to do, or even what to expect, but she let him lead her, and with every passing moment, the fire in her blood burned hotter.

Brendan lowered the narrow strap of her nightgown, baring her breast, then returned to his gentle kneading. She could feel his male hardness pressing determinedly against her body as his mouth moved downward, along her jaw, along the column of her throat, then settled over her nipple. When Priscilla sagged against him, barely able to stand, Brendan slid an arm beneath her knees and lifted her up. He carried her the few short steps to their bedroll and lowered her gently.

"I'll be right back, wife-to-be," he said softly, and Priscilla felt a thrill at his words.

He left her for only a moment, long enough to strip off his shirt, pull off his boots, and unbutton his breeches. He slid them down his hard-muscled thighs, exposing his stiffened manhood, and Priscilla sucked in a breath.

A smile touched his lips as he stretched out beside her. "It's all right, baby. I'm not going to hurt you. We're going to take things nice and slow." He kissed her with gentle reassurance, then lowered the other strap on her nightgown.

His eyes ran over her, moonlight shadowing the muscles below his ribs, the hollow at the side of his neck. Incredibly wide shoulders tapered to a narrow waist and slim hips, and his legs were long, and ridged with muscle. He looked sleek and male, and she wanted nothing more than to touch him. When she did, running her fingers into his curly dark chest hair, his muscles grew taut, and Priscilla's hand stilled.

"I like you to touch me," he whispered. "I want you to." Brendan leaned over and kissed her, pressing her down on the bedroll. His mouth moved along her throat, then he took her nipple between his teeth and began to suck on it gently.

Priscilla nearly swooned. Unconsciously, her fingers laced into his wavy dark hair, the strands soft and silky. As his tongue laved her breast, she arched upward, silently begging for more. His long tanned fingers slid the gown up her thighs until it bunched at her waist, then he removed it completely and started kissing her breasts again.

Priscilla couldn't breathe. Her heart fluttered wildly, and the place between her legs throbbed and burned. As if wanting to soothe her, his hand skimmed down her stomach, a finger circled her navel, making her quiver, then he moved lower, through the dark hairs curling at the juncture of her legs.

Instinctively, Priscilla squeezed her thighs together.

"Open for me, Silla," he ordered softly, the words flowing over her like some magic incantation. It seemed her body responded with a will of its own, her legs parting, his finger sliding inside.

"That's my girl."

She flushed at the thought of the intimacy he was taking, at the wetness she couldn't explain. She wanted to pull away, but somehow she couldn't. When Brendan kissed her again, his hard body easing over her, she found herself gripping his shoulders, kneading the corded muscles that bunched beneath her hand.

"Wider, Silla, open for me wider."

A vestige of modesty told her not to, but her legs moved apart and she arched against his hand. Brendan's fingers moved skillfully in and out, stroking and teasing, setting up fiery sensations like nothing she had known. He was stretching and readying her, kissing her, his tongue hot and plunging with each determined thrust of his hand. A palm cupped her breast, urgently working her nipple, inflaming her until she moaned.

"Please," she pleaded, her voice soft and strained.

"Soon, baby. Just a little while longer."

Priscilla writhed in earnest, her stomach clenching, her nipples aching. Against Brendan's mouth she moaned and begged—for what she did not know.

"Touch me, Silla."

She reached for him with a feeling of desperation, circling his hardened shaft with her hand. "Brendan," she whispered, burning and unable to stop herself from calling out his name.

He positioned himself above her, his shaft sliding into the opening of her passage. When he reached her maidenhead, he paused. "I wish I didn't have to hurt you," he said gently, and then he plunged home.

Priscilla's cry of pain was muffled by the warmth of his mouth. Brendan stopped moving, giving her time to adjust, his body poised carefully above her. She could feel the tension in his muscles, the control it took to hold back.

"Are you all right?" he whispered.

"Yes," she said softly.

With tenderness, he kissed her lips, and instinctively Priscilla pressed against him, urging him onward, her fingers digging into the muscles of his back.

"You're a fiery little minx," he whispered, and then he began to move.

Priscilla forgot the pain of a moment before. This sweet agony was as far from pain as anything she had known. Her body felt wreathed in fire, taut and coiling and achy. As Brendan slid out and then in, slowly at first, making her quiver with heat, then moving faster, Priscilla gripped his shoulders. She kneaded the contours of his back, felt the tension in his muscles, felt the strength of his body, and something expanded inside her. The tension grew and sharpened, forcing her body upward, forcing her to take more of him, to meet each of his demanding thrusts.

"Wrap your legs around me, Silla."

They moved with a will of their own. He was driving deeper now, plunging hard against her, carrying her upward and draining the last of her will.

Priscilla's head fell back and a long fierce cry escaped. Brendan held her hips and drove into her, sending her over a great dark precipice to soar among the stars. In the eye of her mind, she saw swirling blackness, bright sparkling lights, and knew flashes of sweetness so poignant it made her want to weep.

She felt Brendan shudder and heard the husky male sound of a groan. For a moment he seemed frozen as his seed pumped hotly inside her. Then his muscles relaxed, he released the breath he'd been holding, and eased himself down on his elbows. When he settled himself on the bedroll beside her, his skin, dark against hers, gleamed with a sheen of perspiration that matched her own.

"You're mine now, Silla. Never anyone else's."

And she was. She knew that as surely as she knew the stars shone in the heavens. "I didn't know it would be like this."

Brendan chuckled softly and brushed damp hair from her cheeks. "It isn't always. Not with just anyone." *Never before for him, in fact.* "There's something special between us, Priscilla. I've never felt anything so . . ."

"Lovely?" she finished, and he smiled. "I felt as if I soared through the heavens."

His smile grew broader. "So did I." He cradled her head against his shoulder. "You've more fire in your blood than any ten women I've known."

"And you, my love, have a goodly measure of the devil." She thought of the way he'd aroused her, had forced her to lose control. "I'm not sure I like someone holding such power over me," she teased, but she wasn't sure she was teasing.

"Your body's tuned to mine, Priscilla. It understands all this, even if you don't."

"I suppose." She ran her fingers through his curly brown chest hair and surprised herself with a jolt of desire. She looked down at his shaft and saw it stir. In seconds it rose up, fierce and promising.

"Surely we can't want to do this again!"

"Can't we?" He leaned over her. "Kiss me, Silla." And just as she had before, Priscilla obeyed.

They made love two more times that night, gently, sweetly. Even at that, Brendan's hunger did not lessen. He had stopped for fear she'd be sore in the morning, and strangely enough Priscilla found herself wishing he hadn't.

In bed, she had discovered, Priscilla Mae Wills was definitely a wanton. Thankfully, the man she responded to with such fierce abandon seemed more than pleased.

"You're everything a man could want in a wife," he told her, easing her up behind him on the horse. "A lady in the parlor and a vixen in the bedroom."

"And you, Brendan Trask, are surely Satan himself."

He laughed at that and planted a quick kiss on her mouth.

They rode hard through that day and the next, stopping only long enough to rest the big horse Brendan had named Blackie, or themselves when they were too exhausted to stay in the saddle. As he had promised, they kept out of sight, going by way of streambeds and gullys, backtracking, brushing away their backtrail. They used every trick Brendan knew to disguise their travels.

At night, as tired as they were, they made love. In that sweet way, their hardships seemed worthwhile, and Priscilla was able to banish her fears. During the day, she worried and fretted and prayed God would get them safely away.

The evening before they reached Corpus Christi, they ate the last of their hardtack, and Brendan served her prickly pear for dessert, carefully peeling the spiny skin away from the ripe, red, berry-flavored core.

Priscilla ate the delicious fruit with gusto, and Brendan licked the stickiness from her fingers, his tongue sending shivers along her skin. That led to an episode of tender lovemaking that carried their weary bodies into slumber. They slept locked in each other's arms.

"Hand me that spyglass." Stuart Egan held the long brass telescope to his eye and surveyed the scene at the bottom of the hill through a curtain of pale green mesquite.

They had passed the pair sometime during the night, following a set of bogus tracks that led off toward the main trail. But Tall Wind had spotted the ruse and, more careful after his near-deadly blunder with the Comanche, correctly backtracked and found their secluded campsite below the hill.

Stuart's jaw clamped as he watched the gunman climb naked from his place beside Priscilla and pull on his breeches and boots. Curled in the bedroll beside him, Priscilla slept peacefully, her thick chestnut hair fanned out across a blanket Stuart recognized as one of his own.

His insides twisted hotly. *Ungrateful little bitch. Who the hell did she think she was?* She'd made a fool of him in front of his men, run away with her lover like some common trollop. One day she would pay and pay dearly—after he'd accomplished what he had planned.

Just then Mace Harding rode up.

"Go back and get the men," Stuart said. "Have them circle the campsite. Be ready to move in at my command."

Harding nodded and left to do his bidding. Mace was a tall, hatchet-faced, rawboned man, strong and tough as they came. He'd make a good foreman, though his loyalty couldn't match Barker Hennessey's. Mace looked out for Mace, first and foremost, and his biggest weakness was women. Where a female was concerned, he hadn't a lick of sense.

Stuart focused the lens on the man who stood towering over Priscilla. Trask was watching the way she breathed, debating, it seemed, whether to wake her or climb back into her bed.

Stuart silently seethed. Thank God only he and Tall Wind had actually seen them sleeping together—not that the others wouldn't guess. She'd already sullied her reputation beyond repair, but it really didn't matter. None of his men would whisper a word of gossip, and the ranch was so secluded no one else would ever know.

No, Priscilla's indiscretion didn't matter.

What mattered was fetching his errant wife home.

Stuart worked a muscle in his jaw. Priscilla belonged to him, not to Trask or anybody else. Half the hands on the Triple R had witnessed their marriage. That she had tried to run away was bad enough; he wasn't about to let her succeed.

She would learn her place. He would sway her with words if he could—stronger measures should they prove necessary—and have the wife he needed for his career and his future sons.

He motioned his riders silently forward. "Be ready to ride in on my signal."

Mace Harding nodded and motioned for the others to disperse. When they reached the top of the rise surrounding the camp, Stuart raised an arm, then thrust it forward. Men and horses swooped down the hill, pistols raised and firing into the air.

Trask grabbed his rifle and slammed it against his shoulder, but wisely did not pull the trigger.

Priscilla stood up, clutching the blanket around her, her wide brown eyes looking frightened in her fine-boned oval face. Through the dust that swirled around them, Stuart calmly rode forward, emerging like a specter through a storm.

"Well, if it isn't the blushing bride." He swung down from his big palomino, the horse tossing its light mane and violently pawing the earth. "And her stalwart protector— You should have been expecting me, Trask."

"I left you a note," Priscilla said to Stuart, her voice high and shaky. "I hoped you would understand."

Trask pulled Priscilla protectively behind him. "Ride out of here, Egan. The lady has made her choice." He settled his rifle against his waist, pointing it in Stuart's direction.

"I'm afraid *Mrs. Egan*"—Stuart flashed a pointed glance at his bride—"doesn't have all of the facts. I'm sure when she does, she'll be happy her husband has come to fetch her home."

"Surely you don't still want me," Priscilla said, "not after . . . what's happened."

"A good woman is hard to find, Priscilla. One as young and lovely as you is especially precious." He looked at her hard. "You're new to this country and extremely naive. What's happened out here is as much my fault as yours. I should have come for you myself, instead of trusting your care to Barker. Now you've fallen prey to an outlaw and a gunman. Thank God, Mace got word in Corpus Christi and I was able to find you in time."

Priscilla looked at Trask, whose expression had turned wary, then back to Stuart. "What do you mean outlaw? Brendan isn't an outlaw."

"I'm afraid he is, my dear. The fact is, he's wanted for the cold-blooded murder of a man in the Indian Territory—the brother of a federal marshal."

"I don't believe it." She stepped back to survey the tall, bare-chested man still gripping his rifle in front of him. "Brendan?"

"I shot him in self-defense," Trask said.

"Just like Barker Hennessey," Stuart put in with a trace of sarcasm.

"Just like Hennessey," Trask agreed.

"Just like those men at the trading post," Stuart went on.

"Yes."

"And the Comanches—how many of them did you kill?"

Trask fell silent.

Stuart's attention swung to Priscilla, whose face had turned ashen. "There's a thousand-dollar reward offered for this man's capture—dead or alive. He's killed dozens of men—some of them right in front of you. Is it so hard to believe what I'm saying is the truth?"

Priscilla studied Trask, her whole body trembling. "Is it true what he's saying . . . that . . . that you're wanted for murder?"

"I told you, I shot him—"

"Is it true!"

"I didn't think they'd come after me in Texas."

Priscilla clutched the blanket around her. She swayed toward Trask, looking as if she might faint, and his arm shot out to steady her. Priscilla pushed it away. "Why didn't you tell me?"

Trask didn't answer. His face had closed up, and his pale blue eyes looked bleak and resigned.

"Why?" Priscilla pressed.

"I'm sorry," was all he said.

"There are more than a dozen men here," Stuart said to Trask, "so you might as well lose that gun."

"What about Priscilla?"

"She goes with me."

"This isn't her fault. I don't want her hurt."

"Priscilla is my wife. She'll take her rightful place beside me." What she needed was a good and proper beating, but he had never hit a woman, and he didn't intend to start now.

"And me?" Trask ventured.

"We're a day's ride from Corpus Christi. You'll be turned over to the law just as soon as we get there."

The gunman hesitated a moment, glanced at Priscilla, who stared straight ahead as if she couldn't quite believe this was happening, then he dropped the rifle into the dirt. The moment he did, a rope whirred above him. Stuart saw the hemp burn into Trask's skin as it dropped over his head and tightened around his chest. Another rope spun and dropped, snapping tight. The two mounted men who held the ropes dallied around their saddle horns, whirled their horses, and jerked Trask into the dirt.

"Don't hurt him!" Priscilla rushed forward, tear-filled pleading eyes turned toward Stuart. She was shaking all over, her lips bloodless, her face a mask of pain.

It was exactly what he had expected, and it was the reason why he didn't hang the bastard himself. "He's an outlaw, Priscilla. He'll get a fair trial in Corpus, then odds are he'll hang. You'd better get used to the idea."

She blinked, and a flood of tears washed down her cheeks. She brushed at them with the back of her hand. "A man is innocent until proven guilty," she said with a show of courage he hadn't expected. "Surely as a man of conscience you believe that. And if you do, it's only right you treat him decently until he goes to trial." But already Mace and Sturgis had dragged the gunman away.

Stuart worked a muscle in his jaw. His eyes skimmed over Priscilla and he felt a grudging respect. Once he brought her in line, she'd make a fine addition to his empire. He turned back to his men.

At the top of the rise, Mace Harding and Kyle Sturgis dragged Trask at the end of their ropes over the rocky, brush-covered landscape. He was already bloody and battered, his hair, chest, and clothes covered with dirt.

"Hold up!" he ordered, and their animals slid to a halt. "Get him on a horse and ride out a half a mile or so ahead. Mrs. Egan and I will join you at Echo Springs."

Mace flashed him a look of comprehension. Trask would get his comeuppance, but not where the woman could see it.

"Whatever you say, boss!"

With the gunman slumped over the saddle of a wiry little mustang, the men rode off at a thundering gallop. As soon as they had dropped out of sight, Stuart turned his attention to Priscilla.

"I-I've got to go with him," she said. Fresh tears glistened on her cheeks, and it galled him that a man like Trask could move her in such a way. "He'll need someone to stand up for him at the trial."

Stuart stifled an urge to strike her. He took a steadying breath. "He's an outlaw, Priscilla. Even if he were innocent of the murder, what kind of life could he give you?"

"H-he saved my life. I have to help him." She

started toward the horizon, clutching the blanket around her, stumbling blindly after the gunman.

Stuart caught her arm and jerked her to a halt. "Get dressed, Priscilla."

For a moment she just stood there, looking dazed and forlorn, and very nearly ready to crumble. Then she glanced down at her half-clad body. She blinked back her tears and lifted her chin. "Turn around, please." Her voice sounded shaky and raw.

"I'm sorry, Priscilla, but I'm not about to. You've shown yourself to half my men and wallowed with Trask like a trollop." He set his jaw. "You're my wife, Priscilla, not his. I know you've been through a good deal and I've tried to be patient, but I'm the man you married, and it's time you faced that fact."

Priscilla dug her fingernails into her palms, working to bring herself under control. She deserved this —all of it and more.

Swallowing against the hard lump swelling in her throat, she straightened her shoulders. Letting go of the blanket she walked to where her clothes lay draped across a rock. She turned her back to Stuart and with hands that shook fiercely, began to pull on her garments.

Brendan! her mind screamed. *Why has this happened? Why didn't you tell me? What will happen to you now?* She could still see his bruised and battered face, see his look of despair and bitter resignation. What had he been thinking in those last few heart-breaking moments? What was he thinking now?

She flicked a glance at Stuart. He was angry, seething beneath his controlled surface, and hurt by what she had done. She'd expected him to be angry, and she didn't blame him. She deserved his anger and more. Yet even after all that had happened, he was willing to accept her as his wife.

Priscilla's chest constricted, the ache there nearly unbearable. Stuart would remain her husband, but it wasn't Stuart she wanted. It was a gunman named Trask. An outlaw who had deceived her and encouraged her to commit sins of the flesh.

She shouldn't have trusted him, shouldn't have loved him.

Yet in truth, she loved him still.

It was all she could do not to sink down into the dirt and let the agonizing tears wash over her. Her mind was a jumble of confusion, of questions and regrets, and dreams that could never be. She felt bewildered and lost, and incredibly alone. Since the day she had stepped off the boat in Galveston, it seemed her world had been turned upside down. From the start, she'd been frightened and out of her element, yet she had forced herself to go on. She had seen men killed, traveled over brutal, nearly uninhabitable terrain, been roughly abused, and nearly been murdered by Indians. Yet she had weathered it all and continued.

Then she had fallen in love.

Now she'd discovered that Brendan wasn't the man she'd thought he was. He was an outlaw wanted for murder. He wasn't her husband—Stuart was— yet she had given herself to him freely and completely.

It was the gravest sin she had ever committed and yet . . .

With hands that continued to tremble, Priscilla fastened her single embroidered petticoat, then pulled her dress on over her head. She fought to reach the buttons up the back, but Stuart's blunt fingers pushed her hands away.

"You're very lovely, Priscilla. I can see why a man like Trask would go to such lengths to lure you into his bed." He captured her chin and turned her to face him. "Once we're sure you're not carrying Trask's bastard, I fully intend to take up where he left off. Once that's happened, you will accept your place as my wife, and we can get on with our lives."

Priscilla said nothing. She was too upset, too uncertain to say much of anything. Besides, what choice did she have? She had no money, no friends, and no place to go. Even if she had a home to return to, she wouldn't know how to get there.

Stuart was her only answer. Just as he had always been.

Dazed and disoriented and numb clear to her bones, Priscilla let him guide her to a docile-looking sorrel tied to a tree behind Stuart's palomino. He unfastened the reins and helped her up, and she arranged her skirts to cover her legs as much as possible.

Mounted on his big palomino, Stuart led the animal off behind his in the direction the men had ridden.

"Aren't we going back to the ranch?" Priscilla asked, vaguely aware they were traveling away from the Triple R. She heard the tremor in her voice, but couldn't control it.

Stuart reined up and waited till she rode up beside him. "No. Mace brought news of a problem in

Natchez. We're nearly to Corpus Christi. We'll just go on from there."

She didn't say anything more, just let him lead the sorrel away. Her throat had closed up and more tears threatened. Blackness swirled ominously near, and the world around her narrowed until she saw only the horse and rider in front of her. The urge to sink into blissful unconsciousness was nearly over-whelming, but she willed the darkness away.

She wouldn't let him see her like that again, wouldn't let him know the terrible pain that tore through her heart. Instead she used the last of her strength to grip the saddle horn and fought to stay on the horse.

Brendan awoke to a haze of pain. His ribs ached fiercely, one of his eyes was swollen shut, and dried blood crusted over the gashes on his back and chest. His lips felt stiff and puffy, his mouth tasted like cotton, and he could barely hear for the ringing in his ears.

The bastards had really done a job on him. They'd ridden several miles from the campsite, away from Egan and Priscilla, then beat the holy hell out of him.

He shifted on the hard ground beneath him, the rough hemp rope biting into the flesh on his wrists.

"Get on your feet, Trask," a hard-jawed, rawboned man called Mace commanded. "We wanta make Corpus by nightfall."

Brendan grunted and worked to gain his feet. At least they hadn't shot him, which is what he had ex-pected. He knew when he'd taken her he was risking his life—maybe even hers. Still, the risk had been worth it. If they hanged him tomorrow, he'd go to his grave remembering the nights he'd spent in her arms. His only regret would be leaving her to face the world with a man like Egan.

He prayed the bastard hadn't hurt her. But knowing Egan's tough reputation, and seeing the anger he'd tried to disguise, Brendan feared the worst. There was a leashed quality to Egan, a subtle fury that he kept carefully controlled. What had he done to Priscilla after his men had left them alone? How would he punish her?

One thing was sure. Stuart Egan would extract justice from both of them—one way or another.

She thought she would see him. Surely, she would see him—at least one more time.

Instead, most of Stuart's men had returned to the ranch. The one called Mace and some of the others had taken Brendan on to the sheriff in Corpus Christi to await the circuit judge and stand trial, and a handful had ridden with her and Stuart, their pace a little slower in deference to her status as a woman.

Ignoring the aches and pains that had accompanied her every mile of the way, Priscilla rode in silence, her mind lost in a jumble of tortured emotions.

She had known they might be discovered—knew it, but hadn't for a moment believed they really would. While she had been with Brendan, she wouldn't allow herself to think of the consequences of what they had done, of what she—Mrs. Stuart Egan—had done. She loved Brendan and that was all that had mattered.

Now, even though she knew he was an outlaw—a

murderer—just as she'd once feared, she was terrified for him. Where was he? Who was caring for his
injuries? What would happen once Stuart's men
reached Corpus Christi? Her heart ached for him.
For what they had shared. For the plans they had
made.

*Dear Lord, don't let them hang him. Whatever he's
done, don't let him die.*

Thank God Stuart had listened to her pleas for
mercy and stopped the men's cruel treatment. She
wouldn't forget the way he had conceded to her
wishes, even after she had betrayed him.

After her brief time with Stuart at the ranch, seeing
what a hard man he could be, she'd believed he
would punish her for running away, maybe even beat
her. In a way, it might have been better. As it was,
she suffered her own brand of punishment—one that
would not soon end.

She thought of the crime Brendan had been accused of and wondered if perhaps it had happened as
he claimed. Then she remembered Barker Hennessey and the men he had killed on their journey. She
remembered the haunted expression she had seen in
his eyes. She'd known he'd been running from something—now she knew what it was.

*Lord in heaven, how could I have fallen in love with
a man like that?* Surely it was all that she had suffered, the snakebite, the shootings, being so far from
home, and often so very afraid. Maybe it was the
danger she had been in.

Priscilla wiped dust from her eyes with the back of
a hand. Whatever the reason, for the first time her
judgment had failed her, and she had made a terrible

mistake. She had fallen in love with an outlaw. She had tried to fight it, but it had happened just the same. There was nothing for it now but to put that love behind her, escape it as if it had never existed.

She sucked in a ragged breath of air, as brittle and close to breaking as a dry leaf in the wind. When Stuart had ridden into camp with his condemning words about the man she loved, something had died inside her. The determination and joy in life that had always gotten her through had gone out like a flickering flame. She cared about nothing now—especially not herself.

What does it matter? she thought. What does any of it matter?

She should have known better than to fall in love. She should have known she would wind up once more facing the unknown.

Chapter 12

 They camped for the night and rode into Corpus Christi just two hours after dawn the next morning. The streets were as vacant as she remembered, with an eerie, depressing quality that deepened her already somber mood.

Though she tried her best not to, her eyes searched the buildings for the sheriff's office, but she didn't see it. Instead they rode straight to the hotel, such as it was, where Stuart obtained a large suite of rooms.

He was cordial—always so maddeningly cordial.

What was he thinking? she wondered. She guessed she would probably never know.

"As soon as we can signal a passing ship, we'll be leaving for Galveston," he told her. "From there we'll go on to New Orleans and up the Mississippi to Natchez."

Natchez. Just the name sent a shiver down her spine.

She had once called it home, but that had been years ago, a lifetime ago, when she was only a child.

"What about . . . what about Brendan?" She had to ask, though she already knew the answer. "Maybe if I stayed for the trial—"

Stuart's shoulders grew taut. "There is nothing you can do, Priscilla. The man is being tried for a crime you know nothing about." Standing beside the sofa in their suite, his hard glance fixed on her face. "If anything, your testimony could wind up hurting him. After all, you did see him gun down Barker Hennessey."

"B-but I didn't. Not really." If only there was some way to help him. "I know it upsets you, but I owe him my life."

Stuart's fingers tightened on the back of the horse-hair sofa. "And he was more than compensated for that help by the time he spent in your bed."

Priscilla's face went hot.

"We're leaving here, Priscilla, as soon as we can find a means of transportation. The fewer people who know about you and Trask, the better off we'll both be."

Priscilla didn't argue. Once more, there was nothing she could say. Confined to her room, she found the hours passed with agonizing slowness. Her mind clouded with thoughts of Brendan but she forced the thoughts away. By nightfall of the second day, a lantern on the point had signaled a ship into the harbor. First thing the following morning, they boarded a small dinghy and made their way to where the boat stood at anchor.

All the way to the ship, Priscilla stared at the shoreline. She tried not to think of the man she was leaving behind, but his handsome face constantly intruded. Still, there was nothing she could do to help him. It appeared her life had taken another unalterable course, and if she meant to survive this new course, she would have to forget him.

While Stuart saw to their cabin accommodations and made arrangements with the captain for their passage, Priscilla stood at the rail, watching the landscape slip from view. It was nothing more than a brown speck on the horizon, smaller even than the sea gulls circling above them, when Stuart's presence beside her penetrated her gloom.

"I know this has been hard for you." He stared toward the same spot she had been watching. "If I had believed for a moment you would have been happy, I would have let you go."

He spoke to her gently today, though at times he still seemed angry. She had hurt him by her betrayal. She had treated him unfairly and she knew it.

"You'll never know how much I regret all the trouble I've caused. I wish there was some way to change things, but there isn't. After . . . what's happened . . . it's hard to believe you still want me for your wife."

Stuart's expression turned grim. "We're married, Priscilla. For better or worse, till death do us part. I accepted that fact when I spoke the vows—it's you who can't seem to believe it."

"I trusted him," she tried to explain, wishing she could make him understand what had happened— wishing she understood it herself. "I was alone, needing help, and he helped me."

"You saw him kill Barker and yet you went with him."

"He said Hennessey would have killed him if he hadn't shot him first."

"Barker was my most trusted employee and a very good friend. He was a tough man, but I assure you, he wasn't a gunman. Trask knew that. He's the kind of man who thrives on taking advantage of others . . . look what he's done to you."

Priscilla closed her eyes against a wave of pain. Her fingers grew tighter on the rail. "You're sure about him? There can be no mistake?"

"Mace Harding found out about Barker's death in Galveston, and that you had left with Trask. When he arrived in Corpus Christi, he checked with the sheriff and discovered Trask was wanted in the Indian Territory. There's no mistake, Priscilla." His eyes searched her face. "On top of that, he's got a reputation with the ladies. Apparently seduction is more to his liking than force, or he would have violated you somewhere along the trail."

Priscilla's heart squeezed tight inside her chest. Against her will, an image of the voluptuous blonde he'd left in Galveston rose up before her. She remembered one of the men on the porch of the saloon saying, "You always did have a way with the women."

I was just another conquest. He wanted me, and he took what he wanted.

She glanced down at the hands that clutched the rail. "I've been such a fool," she said softly. "Do you think you can ever forgive me?"

"I'm not a forgiving man, Priscilla. Not without reason. From now on, I'll expect your loyalty—and your fidelity. Anything less, and you may expect to receive the full measure of my wrath."

He was willing to continue with the marriage, even after all that had happened. She had nowhere else to go, no one to turn to. "Somehow I'll find a way to make this up to you."

"There are ways, my dear, I promise you. Together we'll find them." He stroked her hair, then cupped her cheek with his hand. "You're my wife, Priscilla. Once you accept that fact, things will work out."

Priscilla just nodded. A lump had risen in her throat, and she felt the sting of tears. Stuart was giving her a second chance. He had offered to set aside her scandalous behavior and continue as if nothing had happened. He was a strong, hard man, but he had been honest and, in his own way, caring.

Brendan had deceived and seduced her.

For him, she'd been willing to give up wealth, position, and security. Willing to chance losing everything she had ever wanted. And for what? An outlaw. A murderer. A man who had conned her into his bed, taken her virginity, and according to Stuart, very likely would have abandoned her.

Stuart Egan had rescued her—just as he had when Aunt Maddie had died. This time she wouldn't forget it. Somehow she would make it up to him. She would bury her love for the treacherous gunman, bury the shame she felt whenever she thought of the way he had touched her, the way she had wantonly responded.

She would be Stuart Egan's wife from now on. He'd have the sons he wanted, and she would earn his forgiveness. It was the only sane course of action.

Then she thought of Brendan, thought of the gallows he was facing. From the corner of her mind, his light eyes begged for understanding. Beautiful, gentle eyes. Loving eyes. Eyes that had won her trust and love.

Dear God, help me forget him.

Priscilla steeled herself and prayed that she could.

As the ship steamed toward Galveston, she forced herself to remember Barker Hennessey, to think of the women Brendan must have bedded and abandoned. By the time they reached the city, she had won the battle she fought with herself and had blocked Brendan from her thoughts almost completely.

She had suppressed her feelings and every tender moment they had shared. It was a matter of survival. When she had to, Priscilla was infinitely good at forgetting.

Brendan slumped on the cornhusk mattress, all that covered the wooden slats of the bunk in his cell. It was dark and hot in the thick-timbered building that served as a jail, with slits for windows and bars separating the two other cells, both of which were empty.

The small, run-down building sat off by itself behind the sheriff's office—out of sight, out of mind. The circuit judge was supposed to arrive sometime this week. In the meantime, he got one meal a day—beans and potatoes and whatever else the jailer threw in—and a couple of dippers of water. His treatment was harsh, but he'd suffered far worse.

Besides, it didn't really matter. Odds were they'd hang him.

He imagined the trial ahead of him. He had no defense, no witnesses to clear his name. Oh, there were people who had seen what happened, but they were either a damned long ways from here or not about to dispute the word of a federal marshal.

Sitting on the cornhusk mattress, Brendan closed

his eyes and leaned back against the rough timber wall, feeling the splinters bite into his bare back. He still wore no shirt. His hair, matted and dirty, clung to his neck, and a week's growth of beard roughened his jaw.

Funny, he thought, he'd never been in a tighter jam and yet his real worry was for Priscilla. Whatever happened, he prayed Egan wouldn't make her life a living hell.

He recalled the hours the two of them had spent together, of the way they'd made love. He smiled to remember her innocent passions, her fiery response to his touch. As exhausted as they'd been, he'd taken her gently, careful of her weariness and the newness of his entry to her body. But he'd hardly begun her initiation into passion—there was so much to teach her, so much they could share.

Brendan's chest tightened as he thought of Egan taking over where he had left off.

The grating of a key in the heavy plank door leading into the dingy jail drew his attention. A beam of light broke through the darkness, and the jailer, an overweight man in his forties, stepped into the thick-walled building.

"You got visitors, Trask."

Brendan looked up to see two men outlined in the light of the open door.

"Well, lookee who we got here. Ain't you a sorry-lookin' cuss?" Tom Camden walked in, shaking his graying blond head. Another man, bigger and taller, stepped into the room behind him. "Whatcha say, Badger? Think that polecat smell is coming from him?"

Badger Wallace spat onto the dirty wood-plank floor, then wiped at his mustache with the back of a meaty hand. "Must be him—ain't nobody else in here."

Brendan came to his feet and stuck his hand through the bars. Tom Camden grabbed it and gave it a hearty shake. "Damn glad to see you, Tom. You, too, Badger—that is, I think I am. You boys here as friends, or just as the law?"

"A little of both," Tom said.

"I guess you know I'm in a heap of trouble."

"You kin say that again, boy," Badger Wallace agreed.

"We found out you were wanted for murder when we landed down in Brownsville," Tom explained. "Captain Carlyle told us the story. I told him I didn't believe a word of it. I come here lookin' for ya, and I want to know the truth."

Brendan released a weary breath. "It wasn't the way they say, Tom. I was just passin' through, seein' someplace I hadn't been. I'd stopped at Fort Towson to pick up a few supplies when some young Choctaw got into a skirmish with a fellow twice his size. I stepped in when I should have minded my own business, and the man drew down on me. It was self-defense, Tom, I swear it. It should have been easy to clear up, but the man's brother turned out to be a federal marshal. He's determined I'm gonna swing for it, and so far it looks like he may be right."

"That's all I wanted to hear, Bren," Tom said. "I told Captain Carlyle I'd fought with you in Mexico, told him how you saved my life and a whole passel of others."

"Thanks, Tom," Brendan said. "You've always been a good friend."

"You got that right, boy," Badger put in.

"Carlyle said if you was half the man I said you was—and we could find you—he'd try to help."

"Go on," Brendan prodded.

"While we was talkin', I happened to mention you was squirin' that perty little filly of Egan's across the country. Seems as though Captain Carlyle don't think real highly of the man. Fact is, Carlyle thinks the great state of Texas has a rat pushin' to get in the government—and the rat's name is Egan."

"He's the bastard who put me here."

Badger lobbed a shot of tobacco into a nearby spittoon. "The cap'n's got sources say Egan's involved in a smugglin' operation in Natchez. They also say he run old Don Dominguez off'n his land."

"I'm not surprised," Brendan said. "The man's as ruthless as they come."

"Glad you feel that way. Make your job a whole lot easier."

"What job?" Brendan asked warily.

"Carlyle says he'll make you a deal," Tom said. "You get the goods on Egan—whatever it takes—and Captain Carlyle will straighten things out with the marshal. You'll come out of this a free man."

Brendan eyed his friend and felt the first subtle stirrings of hope. "Just get the goods on Egan and I'm in the clear? That's it?"

"You think it'll be easy?" Badger asked.

"I think it'll be damned near impossible. But it's a helluva lot better than sittin' here waitin' to hang."

Tom chuckled. "Word is, he's gone to Natchez."

"So I gathered." Brendan had heard Mace Harding mention some problem Egan needed to look into. He'd be gone for some time. Mace had joked about Noble being left to run the ranch, at the trouble the boy would have trying to fill his old man's shoes.

"Egan's travelin' with that perty little gal you brung him." Badger spit another gob of tobacco. "Damn shame she got herse'f involved with a man like that."

Thanks to me, she's in far more trouble than you can imagine. "If I untangle this mess, she won't be." Brendan gripped the bars of his cell, the ray of hope swelling inside his chest. "When can I get out of here?"

"Soon as this fella unlocks the door," Tom said, motioning toward the jailer. The pudgy man grumbled, inserted the key in the lock, and turned.

"You got any money?" Tom asked.

"I had some. Egan's men took it." Brendan stepped out of the cell and followed the men toward the door.

"I'll see you get enough for expenses to Natchez. That do it?"

"I've got friends I can count on in Natchez and money in Galveston. Just get me that far."

Camden clapped him on the back. "Don't know when the next ship'll be in. Meantime, looks to me like you could use a drink."

"I need a bath and a shave first."

Tom tossed him a bag of coins. "Get what you need and meet us over to Wiley's Saloon."

"You got it." Brendan stepped out in the sunshine. He took a deep breath and smelled the salt-fresh air.

The men skirted the sheriff's office and walked out into the street.

Brendan glanced toward the docks and the ocean. For the first time he allowed himself to consider that things might work out. At best, trying to uncover Egan's dirty work, he had a long, tough road ahead of him. At worst, he might wind up dead. Whatever happened, Priscilla's delicate image loomed strong.

For her he would risk all. And even if he failed, he would never be sorry.

"Not the purple silk crepe, the emerald silk with the gold tulle overskirt." Stuart leaned back in his brocade overstuffed chair, directing Madame Barrière, New Orleans's finest French seamstress, and eyeing Priscilla with such cool objectivity it made her temper flare.

Determinedly, she tamped it back down.

"*Oui, M'sieur,*" the fragile-boned seamstress agreed. "You are right, of course. Emerald suits Madame's complexion far better. Never have I seen a man with such an eye for fashion."

Stuart just smiled.

"I'm getting awfully tired, Stuart," Priscilla said, standing half-dressed atop the platform while several young women stuck her with pins. "We've been at this two days already and I—"

Stuart's sandy brow shot up, stilling her protest. "I won't have you dressed improperly. But if you really are fatigued . . . I suppose we can finish tomorrow."

She started a smile of gratitude, but Stuart's next words cut it off.

"Besides, we've a dinner engagement, and I want you back at the hotel in time for your new lady's maid to properly coif your hair." He turned to the French modiste. "I appreciate your haste in this. As you know, time is of the essence."

"I shall personally see the gown you need for this evening is finished *tout de suite*, and as many others as possible ready before your departure. The rest I will forward to your address in Natchez."

Half a dozen seamstresses had been working feverishly to clothe Priscilla in the latest silks and satins. As well as the ballgowns and dresses, Stuart had purchased cloaks, shawls, parasols, bonnets, painted and feathered fans, stockings, and expensive French lingerie.

"Thank you, *Madame*." When he dropped a bag of gold coins into the woman's thin, outstretched fingers, she sank into a feeble curtsy.

"*Merci beaucoup, M'sieur.*"

He turned to take his leave. "I'll await you in the carriage, Priscilla."

She nodded as he strode out the door.

Four hours later, standing in the elegant salon of their suite at the St. Louis Hotel, the finest in New Orleans, Stuart extended his arm and Priscilla accepted it.

"Shall we, my dear?"

Lifting her expensive peach silk skirts, perfectly fitted to her slender frame, Priscilla let him guide her down the sweeping staircases toward the lavish hotel dining room. Whenever they were in public, it was hard to believe the charming man who escorted her was the same hard man she had seen back on the

Triple R. In private, he was demanding but always solicitous, which made him even more difficult to understand.

Tonight was their second evening in New Orleans. They'd be staying four more—long enough for her to be "properly attired," then they'd be taking the steamboat, *Creole Lady*, up the Mississippi to Natchez.

"The gown looks lovely," Stuart said as they strolled through the massive marble-columned lobby toward the elegant gold-trimmed dining room. "Madame Barrière is indeed a genius."

"It's beautiful, Stuart. I know you've spent a fortune. I never expected—"

"No expense is too great for the wife of a future senator," he teased, patting her hand.

She felt like a wife, all right. Unfortunately, it was Brendan she still thought of as her husband.

They crossed the marble-floored foyer, heels clicking, echoing in the vastness of the room, Stuart's expensive black evening clothes immaculate in the light of the crystal chandeliers.

"The food here is exquisite," he was saying. "I hope you'll find the evening as enjoyable as I most certainly will."

Why did his words sound more like an order than the polite conversation they were meant for? Probably because no one, especially not herself, would dare to disagree. Even if the meal were inedible, she would smile and utter mundane pleasantries—as Stuart expected. After just weeks in his company, she was already becoming the consummate politician's wife, just as he'd planned.

"The hotel is the most elegant I've ever seen," Priscilla said, in an effort to make conversation.

"I promise you, darling, from now on you'll enjoy only the finest."

After supper, which had been as delicious as Stuart had predicted, he led her up the wide spiral staircase to their large suite of rooms. As promised, he hadn't come to her bed. He was giving her time for the arrival of her monthly flux, maybe even two. He intended to be certain she carried no child—and Priscilla couldn't have been more grateful.

She prayed that during their time together, she could arouse some sort of feeling for the man she had married. At least learn to understand him.

Why, for instance, were Jaimie Walker, Mace Harding, and two other of Stuart's henchmen staying in a hotel down the street? Why had he brought them? Were so many armed men really necessary? Or did he just enjoy the feeling of power it gave him, having such tough men at his command?

Jaimie was a little different from the other men, though. The red-haired man worshipped Stuart, but he seemed more gentle than tough. Priscilla had enjoyed a bond of friendship with him almost from the start. She could talk to Jaimie, and he would always listen. Unfortunately, they'd had very little time together.

"When we reach Natchez, things will settle down," Stuart told her, standing in the salon of their suite, just outside her chamber door. "I've a town house there—quite a nice one. You can do some more shopping; there'll be balls to attend—that sort of thing. In a few more weeks, we'll know the results of your little . . . indiscretion. If there are no . . . problems, we'll get to know each other as man and wife."

He smiled down at her with a look that might have been affection. "Once that's happened, we can put all this behind us."

"I'd like that," Priscilla said, never meaning anything more.

"Then we'll make it happen," he promised, drawing her into his arms. As he had each night since her return, he kissed her. There was reserve in his touch —and something she couldn't quite name.

Anger maybe? Or a need to possess her? Maybe a need to punish her a little. She shuddered to think so, and returned his kiss with a reserve that matched his own.

She had learned in a hurry that Stuart believed a woman's passions were unladylike. She was to submit, nothing more. Since she felt no passion, Priscilla was almost grateful. She'd allow him the "pleasures of the marriage bed," as he called it, have his children, and go on as she had planned.

Other women did it. She was determined to do the same.

Chapter 13

Natchez. How could she possibly have forgotten such a place? Standing at the rail of the hundred-seventy-two-foot *Creole Lady*, the red-and-white steamboat that had docked nearly an hour ago, Priscilla looked out at the teeming waterfront, the question taunting her again and again. Why did she have no memories of this place?

"It's really somethin', isn't it?" Jaimie Walker stood beside her at the rail. Stuart had gone ahead to see to their arrival at his town house while Priscilla completed her morning ablutions and finished the last of her packing.

"Yes . . . ," she said softly. "It is."

"Natchez-under-the-Hill. Isn't a place on this earth that's anything like it." Jaimie turned toward her. The morning breeze ruffled his thick red hair and his blue eyes sparkled as bright as the surface of the broad Mississippi. "Worse den of cutthroats, thieves, gamblers, whores, pimps—sorry ma'am— ever took a flatboat down the river." He grinned, his teeth white and even in his freckle-dusted face. "But then I guess—you bein' born here—you know all about it." He was attractive, she realized, maybe for the very first time. Boyish and a little bit shy, but fine-featured and well-proportioned.

"How did you know I lived here?" Priscilla asked.

"I . . . guess the boss must have mentioned it. How does it feel to be back home?"

"Natchez isn't home, Jaimie. I left when I was six —I really don't remember much about it." She glanced out at the ramshackle buildings that lined the steep slope.

She couldn't recall this place of squat, slab-roofed houses, the crude doggeries made from abandoned, beached flatboats. A few hastily constructed buildings of brick had been built on the narrow, winding streets, but they looked as run-down as the rest. And all of them served as home to the constant parade of drunken rivermen and their doxies who swilled the rotgut whiskey sold in the roughneck establishments at the bottom of the bluff.

"No reason you should remember a god-awful place like this." Jaimie pointed up the hill toward a row of stately mansions overlooking the river. "That's where a lady like you belongs—Natchez-on-the-Hill. Boss'll be back soon with a carriage to take you up into the city."

Jaimie had no more than said the words when Priscilla spotted a sleek black calèche with the top down, driven by a rail-thin black youth in red satin livery.

"Before he got so busy with the ranch," Jaimie explained, "the boss spent a good bit of time here in Natchez. Fact is, this is where he made his fortune. He still keeps a small staff of servants at his fancy town house; just hires extra people when he gets in."

"I see." Priscilla accepted Jaimie's arm, and they started down the gangplank toward the shore. "Will you be staying there with us?"

"There's separate guest quarters in the rear. That's where the men always stay."

She wanted to ask him why Stuart thought traveling with so many men was necessary, but a glance at the disreputable characters lining the wharf told her that maybe his caution was warranted after all.

When they reached the shore, Stuart approached, took her arm, and helped her into the carriage. "The house isn't far," he said, climbing in beside her while Jaimie climbed up next to the driver. "We'll take the long way. I'm sure you're looking forward to seeing a bit of your old hometown."

That should have been true—but indeed she felt just the opposite. Everytime the carriage rounded a corner, a prickle of dread crept up her spine. What was there about the place that made her want to run and hide?

"I've arranged for your trunks to be delivered as soon as possible. I suggest you rest this afternoon. I've several important meetings today and tomorrow, so I'm afraid you'll be left on your own. Friday evening, we're invited to a soiree at Melrose. The McMurran's—John's a very prominent lawyer—will be our hosts. The house is newly completed and reported to be one of the most beautiful in the city. All in all, it should be a lovely affair."

Priscilla forced a smile as the carriage rolled along the shady streets. When she'd agreed to become Stuart's wife, she hadn't for a moment suspected the type of life she'd be leading. She'd imagined a solitary existence on the Texas frontier, not the hustle and bustle, the glitter and social whirl of Natchez— or maybe even Washington. It wasn't what she'd bargained for—and certainly not the kind of life she really wanted. But there seemed no help for it now.

"If you're feeling up to it, why don't you have Jaimie show you around tomorrow," Stuart was saying. "I'm sure he won't mind."

"That sounds . . . fine." It was silly, this uneasy feeling she harbored. It was just the sadness of the past, the vague recollection of the pain she had felt at the loss of her mother and father. There was nothing to be afraid of—she might as well confront her childhood fears and start living in the present.

Stuart's home, situated on North Pearl Street near Franklin, was a two-story structure of fine red brick with white shuttered windows and manicured front lawns.

It was mostly Georgian in design, with parquet floors, Italian marble mantels, and lovely ornate moldings. There were English tables, French mirrors, and Aubusson carpets. Heavy red velvet draperies hung at the windows, and Chinese vases stood on rosewood pedestals near the front door. It was slightly overdone for Priscilla's taste, but impressive just the same.

"I'll join you for supper at eight," Stuart said. Having shown her through the house, he led her upstairs to the bedchamber adjoining his. It was another command, thinly veiled, but Priscilla was growing accustomed to them.

"I look forward to it," she replied, not really meaning it. It was amazing how quickly one could don the mask of banality.

Supper, a very southern affair of chicken and pork,

pokeweed, sweet potatoes, and biscuits, droned on with the same mundane pleasantries. Priscilla retired early, with only a glance toward the adjoining chamber door. She wondered if Stuart desired her, then thought of the few times she had caught him watching her when he thought she wasn't looking. He wanted her, all right. Not with the same physical hunger Brendan had, more as a means of possession, of conquering her spirit and making her his.

Brendan. For a while she'd been able to forget him. It was rare that she allowed herself thoughts of him. But on nights like these—warm, sultry evenings that marked the last of summer, with the wind blowing in from the river and the windows open to the scent of magnolias—memories of their nights together beneath the stars brought almost a physical ache.

Where was he now? she wondered. Was he alive or dead? Rotting in some stifling jail cell would be more of a death for a man like him than swinging from the gallows.

Priscilla closed her eyes against a well of tears and lay back against the soft down pillows. Above the carved wooden headboard of the big four-poster bed hung a John James Audubon portrait of snow geese winging south for winter. Brendan would have loved the painting, she had thought from the moment she'd seen it.

Go to sleep, Priscilla, her mind warned. *All of that is behind you. Keep his memory buried the way you do those from your childhood.*

And so she did. It took all of her will, but she did. And in the morning when Jaimie Walker waited in the elegant front parlor to take her on a tour of the city, she was ready. Wearing a dove-gray day dress trimmed with black embroidered brandenbourgs, she preceded him out on the porch and down the brick walkway to the carriage.

She would battle both sets of memories, fight them and defeat them—and then get on with her life.

"The hell you will!" Stuart Egan leaned over the burned and scarred top of the old wooden table. "You've got two choices, McLeary—you can stop spending money like a drunken sailor, or you can halt your operation completely. What's it going to be?"

"You've got some nerve, Egan. You live like a bloody pharaoh, and you come down here telling me to quit spending my own goddamn money."

"I'm a respected businessman. Everyone knows how I earn my living—they expect me to be a man of means. You own a stinking tavern in this armpit under the hill. Sooner or later, you keep flaunting your money, people are bound to get suspicious. If they link you to the smuggling on the river and the robberies and murders on the Trace, they'll come after you. Knowing you as I do, you'll squawk to the authorities as fast as that tongue of yours can wag. I won't have my political ambitions destroyed because you've got an itch for the gallows!"

"And I won't live like a pauper while you live like a king!" Caleb McLeary slammed a large fist against the table, but the dull thud, and the roar of his voice, were lost in the noise and laughter that filled the tavern outside the shabby back room.

"Calm down, McLeary," Stuart warned, and Mace

Harding's hand slid a little closer to the heavy Walker Colts he wore at his waist. "We're here to work out our differences—that's exactly what we're going to do."

Stuart had come into the grimy tavern through the rear so he wouldn't be seen. There was another way out of the place as well—through the honeycombed tunnels the river had conveniently carved into the soft loess soil behind the shanties and shacks—the place where the loot was stored.

"I'm not asking you to do this forever," Stuart soothed with a wave of his hand around the dusty store room. An overturned barrel with a half-burned candle on top held shot glasses filled with whiskey for the men. Beside it sat a stack of dusty crates and boxes. Flies buzzed near a crusted-over bowl of mutton stew, and a spotted brown mongrel scratched at its flea-infested hide in the corner.

"We decided going in we'd give it a five-year run," Stuart reminded him, "then you could take your share of the earnings and head off on your own. A little more discretion is all I'm asking. If that isn't agreeable, we split things up right here."

"What if I'm not ready to quit?" the burly ex-riverman asked. "What if I want to build one of them fancy houses up on the hill and stay right here in Natchez?"

Then you're a dead man. "You can't afford to take that chance. You're already living well above your means." From what Mace had discovered, Caleb had a pricey suite at the Middleton Hotel and a very expensive mistress. "Something like that would get you hung for sure."

"You're not worried about me—you're worried about your fancy reputation."

"You're damned right I am! I've worked hard to get what I have, and no sleazy, two-bit riverman is going to welsh on his agreement and ruin things."

Caleb shoved back his chair and came to his feet. He was a tall, dark-haired man in his middle thirties with a thick black mustache and unkempt muttonchop sideburns. Still, Stuart supposed he wasn't bad-looking in an uncouth, rough sort of way.

"You'd better get this, Egan, and get it good. I don't take orders from you anymore. These days, I've got my own inside information. Your man's usually a day late and a dollar short, anyhow. You want to end this partnership, that suits me just fine!"

Stuart's expression remained carefully controlled, but inside he seethed. Caleb McLeary would still be running flatboats downstream if it hadn't been for the chance Stuart had given him four years ago.

"We've made a lot of money together, you and I," Stuart reminded him. "It isn't like you to go off half-cocked." *Not much. The man had a quick, mean temper and always had.* "Why don't we both take some time to think things over. I'll be in Natchez for a while. Let's let things simmer down—you finish the Meyers job, and we'll talk again next week."

Some of the tension left McLeary's big body. "I don't want trouble, Egan. I just want what's due me."

And that's exactly what you'll get. "Since that's what we both want, there shouldn't be a problem." He extended his hand; McLeary hesitated a moment, then shook it.

"Figured you'd understand, once you saw my side a' things."

"Of course," Stuart agreed. He motioned toward Harding and started toward the low wooden back door. "I hear there's a new lady in your life," Stuart said amiably.

"She's been with me about six months." Caleb grinned. "You remember Rosie O'Conner? Pretty little gal with long dark hair and big brown eyes? Used to work over at the Painted Lady a few years back— before Ben Slocum bought her outta there. She's one high-grade filly now—and she belongs to me."

Stuart smiled. "Congratulations."

"Rose is one of the reasons I've got to get out from under the hill. She's too good for that kinda life, and I mean to see she don't ever have to live that way again."

"Very admirable, Caleb." Stuart walked toward the door. "I'm sure the lady shares your sentiment completely." He brushed past Mace, who obediently held it open. "Remember, I'll see you next week."

Little Rosie O'Conner, he repeated to himself as the door slammed closed behind him. It amused him to imagine what Priscilla would think if she ever discovered the truth about herself and the girl from Under-the-Hill.

Rose Conners, formerly Rosie O'Conner, strode purposely along Canal Street toward Briel. She'd been shopping all morning, ordering new dresses, several feather-trimmed bonnets, and a hand-painted parasol that came all the way from Paris, France. Caleb was always so generous. What did it matter if he got a little drunk and heavy-handed once in a while?

She'd suffered far worse with Ben Slocum—and him claiming to be such a gentleman! Perverted—that's what Ben was. At least he'd gotten her out from under the hill. For that she'd be eternally grateful.

Now she lived with Caleb McLeary in a fine suite of rooms at the Middleton. Not the fanciest hotel in town, but far more elegant than anyplace she'd ever been in.

It was a lonely existence, since Caleb didn't have many friends and Rose knew only the whores she had worked with and the nuns who had raised her, but that didn't matter. She dressed like a lady, she had taught herself to read and cipher—she was even learning to play the piano.

She'd come a damned long ways from the terrified little girl who'd been orphaned at five and left to survive on her own.

Rose's full silk skirts—a bright yellow overskirt above four ruffled flounces of black and yellow polka dots—rustled as she walked down the street toward the hotel. Purposely avoiding the ladies she knew would shun her, Rose usually stayed clear of crowded roadways, and even went so far as to enter the hotel by the back stairs. Someday she hoped to move away from Natchez, find a place where no one would ever guess who she was or how she had lived.

That wouldn't happen with Caleb. If necessary, Caleb intended to clash with society head on. With enough money, he vowed, he could buy his way in. Rose hoped when he tried, she'd be very far away.

* * *

"The city is lovely, Jaimie, but I think we ought to be getting back." Priscilla fidgeted on the carriage seat but forced herself to smile.

"But we've only been gone an hour. Why don't you do some shopping? The boss said I should take you over to Spencer's Millinery. Wouldn't you like a new bonnet or something?"

Before she could think up a convincing argument, Jaimie had instructed the driver to pull to the edge of the road. He jumped down lightly, rounded the carriage, and reached up to help her down.

"I really don't think—"

"It isn't very far. The walk will do you good." His freckled hand enfolded hers, and he urged her to step down.

"Oh, all right," she conceded, knowing it was Jaimie who was really enjoying the outing. It wasn't his fault the carriage ride had stirred such a hazy array of memories and unanswered questions that she felt disturbed and out of sorts. It wasn't his fault that when she wasn't struggling with the past, she was fighting thoughts of Brendan and trying her best not to cry.

Brendan. He had hurt her so badly, for a while she'd been able to forget him. Lately, his image had surfaced again and again, and only her stubborn determination had saved her from a round of bitter depression.

The ride had been Stuart's idea, and Jaimie had readily agreed. He had been pleasant and cheerful, pointing out sights he had seen on a prior trip with Stuart, lifting her mood and making her smile. He was intelligent, she confirmed, and even fairly well educated. He'd grown up in Charleston, he told her, gone to school till he was fifteen, then struck out on his own.

"Me and the boss met in Galveston," he said. "Fella was cheating him at cards. I spotted it and told him so. He hired me right on the spot."

"You like him, don't you?" Priscilla asked.

"It isn't a matter of like. It's more that I like what he stands for. He means to make Texas the greatest state in the Union. I mean to be there when he does."

Priscilla smiled at that, liking Jaimie, and thinking again what a complex man Stuart Egan was. She turned to start up the street, determined to enjoy herself no matter how difficult the task, took two steps, and bumped headlong into a woman walking the opposite way. The woman's stack of boxes went sprawling off the boardwalk and onto the cobblestones, and her pretty yellow parasol dropped from her long-fingered hands.

"Oh, I'm so sorry," the dark-haired woman apologized, stooping to pick up the boxes.

Jaimie knelt down and so did Priscilla. "It wasn't your fault," she said, "it was mine." Priscilla replaced the lid on a hatbox that had come open. "Jaimie, why don't you carry the packages home for Miss . . . ?"

"Conners," the woman said. "Rose Conners. But that isn't really necessary."

"Hello, Miss Conners, I'm Priscilla Wills." It never occurred to her she was now Priscilla Egan.

"Wills?" Rose repeated, her eyes fastened on Priscilla, and the color seemed to drain from her pretty oval face. "Priscilla Wills?"

"Why, yes. My family used to live here—Joshua and Mary Wills? Maybe you've heard of them?" Rose appeared to be just about Priscilla's age. Since they died when Priscilla was six, Rose couldn't have known them, yet her expression said that she had.

For a moment Rose just stood there, then her chin came up and she squared her slender shoulders. "I'm afraid I wouldn't know." A tight smile lifted one corner of her mouth. "Thank you for your generous offer of assistance," she said to Jaimie, lifting the boxes from his arms. "But as I told you before, it isn't necessary." In a froth of yellow polka-dot skirts, she stiffly marched away.

Priscilla stared after her, noting that Jaimie did too, his warm gaze fastened on the feminine sway of her hips.

"What was that all about?" Priscilla asked.

"I don't know, but she sure is pretty."

Priscilla didn't answer. There was something about her . . . something in her eyes . . . or maybe it was her face. Some long-dead memory stirred, tried to push its way to the surface, but another part of her mind staunchly shoved it back down.

"I'm sorry, Jaimie," Priscilla said at last. "I guess the trip up the river took more of a toll than I thought. Would you mind very much if we went to the milliner's another time?"

"Of course not, Miz Egan. I should have listened to you in the first place."

Priscilla smiled faintly and let him guide her toward the carriage, but her mind remained on the woman named Rose, on her abrupt change of manner at the mention of Priscilla's name, and the odd swirl of memories that continued to push for admittance to Priscilla's mind.

She hadn't begun to conquer her troubled thoughts of Natchez, she realized as the carriage rolled along.

When they passed the constable's office with its thick-walled, ugly-looking jail, Priscilla's heart constricted, and she conceded a second painful admission: memories of the tall, Texas gunman were no less easy to combat.

They rode in silence the rest of the way home. Only the Negro driver's, "We here, Mr. Jaimie," brought her back from wherever she had been.

"Would you mind doing me a favor, Jaimie?" she asked on impulse when he rounded the carriage to help her down.

"Sure, Miz Egan."

"Would you find out what you can about Rose Conners? I'm kind of curious about her."

Jaimie grinned as if she'd just done him a favor. "Be glad to, ma'am. I'll look into it this afternoon." He helped her down, and they walked the brick path to the house.

Chapter 14

The streets of Natchez buzzed with the elegantly dressed and socially elite. Carriages rolled past, high-stepping horses tossed their glossy manes, and long, plumed feathers danced out the windows on wide-brimmed ladies' bonnets.

Beneath a blanket of stars, Brendan strode down the far end of Main Street, turned at the corner, and headed toward the lights blazing from the mansion in the distance.

Wearing borrowed clothing—an expensive black swallowtail coat, a little snug in the shoulders but otherwise an excellent fit, and a burgundy waistcoat and black broadcloth breeches—he was dressed in fine fashion for the evening. That Christian Bannerman, a long-time friend of his brother Morgan, was just about his same size was another stroke of luck among a lengthy stream of good fortune.

Under different circumstances Brendan might have smiled.

The trip from Corpus Christi had gone off without a hitch. With the delays Egan had suffered, first in getting to Galveston, then waiting to catch a steamer, then the days Egan spent in New Orleans, he'd damn near caught up with them sooner.

Once he got to Natchez and located Chris, finding them here had been easy. Chris Bannerman was a prominent member of Natchez society, the only son of the wealthy Natchez Bannermans, and a rich man in his own right. His mansion, Evergreen, where Brendan occupied the bachelor quarters in the rear, gave splendid testimony to the money Chris had made as a cotton planter.

Two days ago, Chris's wife, Sue Alice, had discovered the Egans' name among the guests invited for the Friday night soiree at Melrose. With the man's uncanny political instincts, there was no doubt he and Priscilla would attend.

Brendan stepped up his pace, but passed the house and kept on walking. He'd go 'round the back and come in through the garden. Even if somebody saw him, dressed as he was, he doubted they would stop him. Once he got in, he'd find an out-of-the-way place where he could watch for them. As soon as he got a chance, he'd pull Priscilla aside so they could talk.

A hard knot balled in Brendan's stomach. What had happened to her in the days since they had parted? What kind of punishment had a man like Egan extracted?

He couldn't wait to see her—had thought of little else for the past long weeks. He prayed she'd be unharmed and that she'd continue to be all right until he could work things out.

The knot in his stomach grew tighter. If Egan had hurt her, so much as laid a hand on her—

It wouldn't be long before he found out.

* * *

"We'd better be going." Stuart stood in the hallway outside her bedchamber door. "We'll be fashionably late, as it is."

Dressed in immaculate black swallowtail coat, a snowy white shirt, and wide white stock, Stuart definitely looked handsome. His hazel eyes ran over her shimmering emerald gown, cut daringly low in front, veed at the waistline, and so tight she could scarcely breathe. There was warmth in his expression—and something else. Priscilla wished, not for the first time, she could feel some answering warmth.

Instead, she accepted his arm and swept down the hall, down the stairs, and into the foyer, feeling a sense of duty, nothing more.

His stylish black calèche awaited them out in front, a red-liveried servant sitting in the driver's seat. Stuart helped her aboard, and she settled against the tufted red velvet seat. Against the clip-clop of horses' hooves over the cobblestone streets, they made the same sort of small talk that had marked their relationship from the start.

With fond remembrance, Priscilla thought of the letters they had written to each other for more than two years. What had happened to Stuart's interest in her thoughts and dreams? Where was the gentleness she had sensed in him?

Fleetingly, in hopes of renewing the bond they'd once shared, she considered mentioning the woman named Conners she had met that afternoon, but Stuart's mind seemed elsewhere, and some other nebulous feeling held her back.

It wasn't long before the lights of Melrose, just off Main Street, loomed in the distance, the sounds of gaiety and laughter floating across the late September air. The house, a blend of Greek Revival and Georgian architecture, rose up among impressive manicured gardens, and a host of black-clad servants ushered an endless stream of guests inside.

"Good evening, Stuart." John McMurran greeted Stuart in the foyer. "So glad you could make it."

"It's a pleasure to be here, John." Stuart returned McMurran's firm handshake. "I'd like you to meet my wife, Priscilla."

"How do you do," she said, wondering why every time Stuart introduced her that way, something squeezed inside her chest.

McMurran's wife nodded in greeting, and the women chatted amiably for a while. A few moments later, she and Stuart drifted into the massive salon, where couples danced beneath ornate chandeliers. The mansion felt very French, with brocade draperies and carved rosewood furniture. There were fireplaces of Egyptian marble, huge mirrors framed in gold leaf, and a remarkable circular table held up by carved marble birds whose eyes gleamed with jewels.

"Shall we dance, darling?" She recognized Stuart's words for the command they were and let him lead her onto the dance floor. After several lively tunes, including a schottische and a polka, he paused to introduce her to some of the guests, and a circle of gentlemen began to ask her to dance. It was fun for a while, this freedom from Stuart's often-taxing presence. Priscilla laughed as she hadn't in weeks, enjoying the men's attention, forgetting her troubles, if just for a while.

Eventually, she began to tire.

Searching for a means of escape from the graying professor named Martin Duggan who had captured her for a second waltz, Priscilla scanned the room in search of her husband. Dozens of Negro servants scurried past carrying silver trays crowded with champagne goblets or an array of exotic foods, and beautifully dressed men and women danced or chatted, filling the room, but she saw no sign of Stuart.

"I believe this dance is mine," said a hard male voice from beside the thin professor.

"Sorry," Duggan apologized, reluctantly releasing her hand. "I suppose I *was* taking advantage."

Priscilla swayed on her feet, feeling the pressure of the tall man's grip. His menacing presence loomed like an ominous force, yet she could not move away. Not when the pale blue eyes looking down at her with such hostility held her rooted to the very spot.

"You must be insane," she whispered, forcing herself to meet his icy gaze.

A mocking smile curved his lips. "For wanting to dance with a beautiful woman? I hardly think that's crazy."

"What are you doing here? How did you get in?"

His hold grew tighter on her hand while his fingers bit into her waist. Without waiting for permission, he swept her onto the dance floor.

"Such a greeting," he taunted. "And I'd expected words of love, maybe even some weeping." He smiled, but it never reached his eyes. "Damnably disappointing."

Priscilla nearly stumbled. Only his hard grip kept

her from falling. "Why did you come here? What do you want?"

"I came to rescue you, sweetness. I was under the mistaken impression that you cared a great deal for me. I expected to find you pining away—I even feared for your safety." He scoffed. "Instead I find you dressed in silk and clinging to Egan's arm—or dancing your traitorous little heart out. You're quite the belle of the ball."

Priscilla could barely speak. "You shouldn't be here. What if someone sees you?"

"I doubt anyone is expecting me. I believe your . . . escort . . . thinks I'm dead. Obviously you did, too."

Priscilla's eyes swept him from head to foot. In his expensively tailored clothes, with his dark hair neatly trimmed and his black shoes shiny, Brendan looked every bit the gentleman. He waltzed like one, only better. With far more style and grace. He spoke like one, but recalling the men he had killed, the scandalous way he'd seduced her, she knew he was not.

Her eyes returned to his face, handsome to her still, though she knew him at last for the outlaw he truly was. Through the folds of her skirt, she could feel his muscular thigh pressing insistently between her legs, and again her steps faltered.

"You're tiring," he said with a hint of mockery and a note of false concern. "Why don't we take some air?"

"But I can't go out there with—" His hard look silenced her protest, and his grip on her waist did the rest. He had no right to be angry, she thought, reading the fury in his expression. She had been the victim—the one who'd been tricked and seduced. She was the one who should be angry!

Afraid to go with him, more afraid not to, she let him guide her out onto the terrace. He didn't stop until they'd wound their way through the garden, into a shadowy, secluded spot beneath a moss-draped oak.

"How did you escape?" She forced a note of firmness into her voice and prayed the world would stop spinning.

Brendan laughed, but it sounded bitter and harsh. "I didn't kill anyone to get out, if that's what you're thinking."

Dear God in heaven, that was exactly what she had thought.

"Did it ever occur to you that I might be innocent? Or were those words you spouted to Egan just that— a bunch of meaningless words?"

A man is innocent until proven guilty, she had said.

Priscilla glanced away, unable to look at him a moment more. There was an icy chill in his light eyes unlike anything she had seen in him before. "I know the kind of man you are. I know killing a man means nothing to you."

Brendan grabbed her chin and roughly turned her to face him. "You know only what Egan wants you to know. What kind of lies has he put into that pretty little head of yours?"

Priscilla jerked free of his grasp. "I saw you, remember? You killed Mr. Hennessey—"

"Hennessey drew down on me."

"He wasn't a gunman—you knew that!"

"No? According to whom? Egan?"

"What difference does it make?"

"A helluva lot of difference. Are you sleeping with him?"

"T-that's none of your concern."

Brendan gripped her shoulders. "I asked if you're sleeping with him."

The heat rushed into her cheeks. "We haven't reached that point in our relationship," she said with a lift of her chin. "But he is my husband. Eventually—"

"Goddamn it, Priscilla—"

"Don't you dare blaspheme!"

For the first time since his arrival, Brendan smiled. Some of the harshness left his face, and it was all she could do not to reach out and touch him.

"Damn, I'm glad to see you." He caught her wrist and before she could stop him, he hauled her into his arms. When his mouth came down over hers, scorching heat rose in her body.

Dear God in heaven! Flames roared through her, liquid fire raced through her veins and made her heart slam hard against her ribs. How had she forgotten the fiery blaze of his kisses, the feel of his long hard body? How had she forgotten the pleasure of his touch, the masculine strength of his growing arousal, the memory of his hands skimming over her flesh, heating her blood until her body begged for more?

For a moment, she gave in to it, kissing him back, longing for him, aching to press herself closer, to run her fingers down the muscles of his back, through the tight hair curling on his chest. His breath tasted warm and honeyed by the brandy he'd consumed. He smelled musky and masculine, and she had never wanted him more.

Think of Stuart, her mind screamed. *Remember the vows you have spoken.* Priscilla twisted away.

"I . . . I'm glad they didn't hang you," she said, pushing against his chest with both hands, keeping him at bay as she fought for control. "I wouldn't have wanted that, no matter what you've done. But this isn't Texas. You can't just—"

"You've got to listen, Priscilla. There are things you don't know. Things you don't understand."

"I don't want to know! Not now—not ever! I'm Stuart Egan's wife. There's nothing you can do about that, even if I wanted you to—which I don't!"

"In the eyes of God, you're *my* wife," he reminded her coldly, beginning to get angry again. "But then I didn't dress you up like a pretty little doll and parade you around in front of my high-society friends." He touched a cluster of tight, dark chestnut curls. "I wanted you for the woman you are inside, not for what you could do for an over-ambitious political career."

"Get out of here."

Brendan's jaw clamped and a muscle bunched in his cheek. "I'll get out, all right. Just as soon as I remind you the kind of woman you *really* are."

With that he pressed her up against the tree, gripped her wrists and dragged them above her head. Priscilla struggled as his mouth came down over hers, but Brendan's kiss was relentless.

He had traveled hundreds of miles, worried sick that something had happened to her, only to discover she had listened to Egan's lies and condemned him.

He wanted to punish her for the bitter betrayal he felt, wanted to lash out and hurt her as she had hurt him.

Shifting his weight against her, he captured her chin, forced her soft pink lips apart, and thrust his tongue inside. Priscilla whimpered as his hand moved down her body, sliding the gown off her shoulders, sliding inside the bodice to capture the fullness of a breast. It felt silken and warm, and the upthrusting mound perfectly filled his palm.

His body tightened, his loins growing heavy and full, the ache there becoming even more painful. He shifted again, pressing his hardened shaft against her, forcing her to remember, demanding she never forget. Beneath his mouth, he felt her soft lips tremble, felt wisps of hair brush his cheek. She tasted of champagne and smelled like magnolias.

Brendan groaned.

The hand on her breast grew gentle, kneading, caressing. His hard kiss softened, tasting her lips, coaxing them apart, giving instead of taking. Priscilla made a small sound in her throat and he felt her response in the velvety touch of her tongue.

He let go of her wrists and her arms slid around his neck.

"God, how I've missed you," he whispered against her mouth as she clung to him. Then he trailed warm kisses along her throat and down her shoulders.

"I've missed you, too," Priscilla whispered when he lowered the gown even farther. But she didn't make him stop, and he wasn't sure he could.

His tongue circled her nipple, ringing it, sucking the fullness into his mouth while his other hand worked her dress up her thighs. Long, slender legs then a softly rounded bottom filled his hands. He kneaded the fullness gently, pressing her against his hardened arousal, wondering how long he could wait before he plunged himself inside her.

Christ, how he wanted her.

"Brendan?" she whispered.

At the alarm he heard in the barely whispered word, he stilled. With his heart slamming hard inside his chest, it was difficult to catch the dim sound of voices growing nearer.

"It's all right, baby," he soothed, his breathing ragged as he forced himself under control. With a shaky hand and a skill earned from years of practice, he helped her straighten her clothes, then guided her out of the shadows and along a different pathway toward the house before the couple walking by could make out who it was.

Hurrying along beside him, Priscilla hadn't looked at him once, but he knew what she was thinking. Regret showed in the slump of her delicate shoulders, the way she clutched her elegant emerald skirts. When they reached the porch, he turned her to face him, wishing they had more time.

"I'll be back, Priscilla. Just stay away from Egan until I can get things worked out."

"Please . . . won't you just leave me alone?"

He smiled at that, hope rising at the uncertain note in her voice. "You're mine, Silla. Surely what just happened ought to prove it."

A slender hand crept to the base of her throat, and even in the torchlight of the gardens, he could see the rosy hue that tinged her cheeks.

"I didn't mean for that to happen," she said, her brown eyes dark with remorse. Then she lifted her chin. "I won't let it happen again."

Brendan arched a brow. "You're sure about that, are you?"

"Yes."

"We'll see, Priscilla. We'll just have to wait and see." With others so near, he stifled the urge to kiss her. Instead he touched her cheek, turned, and faded silently into the shadows of the garden.

Priscilla watched him until he disappeared, her heart thudding painfully inside her chest. *God in heaven, Brendan had come!* He had been there with her in the garden. Just the memory of his handsome face made her throat close up and her body tremble with longing. Brendan had escaped from Texas, escaped the gallows!

She thanked the Lord for his infinite mercy, all the way up the back stairs. The tightness in her chest seemed to ease, and for the first time in weeks, she felt she could breathe.

But why had he come to Natchez? It was impossible—incredible—and yet he was here. Surely a woman's seduction couldn't mean that much to him. Did she dare to believe she meant something to him after all?

Priscilla reached the landing, passing only a matronly woman along the way. She closed the door to one of the chambers and rested her head against the smooth paneled wood.

Brendan had come for her in Natchez. Part of her wanted to sing with it—to revel in the knowledge that he really did care. The other, more practical part asked, *What difference does it make?* Brendan was an outlaw and a gunman, not a man of conscience and reputation like Stuart. He was wanted by the law, might yet face the gallows, or would at least go to prison should he be captured. And even if he weren't, even if he wanted to change, what were the chances he actually could succeed?

She thought of the promises she had made to herself, her vows to forget Brendan Trask, to be a wife to Stuart and get on with her life.

It had been hard enough when Brendan had been in Texas, hundreds of miles away. How could she possibly forget him knowing he was here in Natchez —knowing he wanted her just as much as she wanted him.

Stuart Egan is your husband, she told herself firmly. He's the man you have married, the man you've promised your life and loyalty—nothing else matters.

It was easy to say, and very hard to accept.

Still feeling shaky, Priscilla crossed the bedchamber to the gilded cheval glass mirror. As she adjusted the pins in her hair with an unsteady hand, smoothed and straightened her gown, she prayed Stuart hadn't missed her. She prayed even more fervently that God would forgive her for what she had almost done.

Brendan watched the mansion from the darkness behind the carriage house. It was late in the evening when Priscilla and Egan finally left Melrose. He followed them from a distance, as he intended to do from now on.

When the carriage reached the house on North

Pearl, Egan and Priscilla went inside. Brendan's chest tightened as he watched the second story from the darkness, waiting to see where Priscilla spent the night. A lamp began to glow, and he saw her silhouetted in the window beside a woman he guessed to be her maid.

He held his breath as a second lamp came on, outlining Egan's sturdy frame in the room next door. Eventually both lamps went out, and Brendan breathed a sigh of relief. Priscilla appeared to have been telling the truth. At least for tonight Egan hadn't gone to her room—to her bed.

He wasn't sure what he would have done if he had.

Brendan spent most of the following day the same way he had spent the night before—watching Egan's every move. Sooner or later, if his luck held out, Egan would provide some sort of lead, some connection to the smuggling that plagued the Mississippi as well as the Natchez Trace, the main route of travel inland.

Chris Bannerman had been more help than he could have dreamed. His friend had been able to fill him in on the problem and how it had mushroomed over the last few years. Chris had even spoken to the constable about current investigations. As a prominent citizen of the community, his concern didn't seem out of place.

Though Brendan's efforts were progressing—at least he hoped they were—he ached to see Priscilla. He wanted a chance to explain things, to make her understand. But every time Egan left the house, providing the opportunity he needed, he had no choice but to follow. Clearing his name came first. There

would be no chance for them to find happiness with
the gallows still over his head.

"Damn it, Chris," he said to his friend one afternoon, his frustrations growing every day. "I've got to
see her. What the hell am I going to do?"

"That's easy." Chris clamped Brendan's shoulder
with his one good arm. The other had been lost above
the elbow in a wagon accident on his plantation a
few miles out of town. "You'll need to go in after
dark, so the next time Egan leaves the house by himself in the evening, you follow him till he settles
somewhere, then come get me. I'll take over while
you go see Priscilla."

An attractive blond man in his middle thirties,
Chris and his wife, Sue Alice, along with their three
towheaded children, had welcomed him into their
home as if he were a member of the family.

"Too dangerous," Brendan said. "Egan's a ruthless bastard. If he caught you spying on him, he'd
very likely kill you."

"Natchez is my home," Chris countered. "I can
come up with a dozen good reasons to be anyplace I
choose."

Brendan shook his head. "I don't want you getting
hurt."

"A man with one arm is still a man," Chris said
with conviction. "My daddy wasn't always rich and
pampered, and neither was I." He grinned. "I'm a
whole lot tougher than you think I am." They were
sitting in Chris's walnut-paneled, book-lined study,
his favorite part of the house.

"I don't know, Chris. This isn't really your concern."

"Look, Bren, your brother has helped me out of a jam or two. Let me help you."

Brendan searched his friend's intelligent face. He didn't doubt Chris Bannerman's abilities—handicap or no. "All right. If Egan settles in someplace that doesn't look too risky, I'll come after you." Brendan smiled his thanks.

That had been two days ago. Four days in all since he'd been with Priscilla in the garden at Melrose. Four days of worrying about her, wanting her, and needing her as he never had another woman.

Now, as dusk purpled the horizon and he stood outside the mayor's office where Egan was engaged in a meeting—all very civic, of course—Brendan figured this might be his chance.

Traveling the crowded streets on a rented saddle horse—Blackie was liveried back in Galveston—it didn't take long to reach Evergreen. In minutes, Chris rode a tall bay gelding toward the mayor's office to take up his promised vigil, and Brendan made his way to the house on North Pearl.

From his place in the shadows, he could see Priscilla up in her room, bustling about with the help of her lady's maid. He remembered the way she had looked at the party, dressed in her beautiful emerald ballgown, dancing with one man after another. She'd seemed different, more sophisticated—more Egan's—and Brendan hadn't liked it one damned bit.

With a glance around to be sure he wouldn't be seen, he climbed the back stairs, slipped down the hall, then hid in a linen closet, where he could watch her door. When it opened, he saw her dressed in a turquoise gown trimmed with silver, getting ready for another evening out. It galled him that Egan had bought her such beautiful clothes.

Hell, he wasn't rich by any means, but he could buy her nice dresses and, if things turned out the way he planned, eventually just about anything she wanted. He cursed Stuart Egan and the situation he found himself in.

As soon as the maid had been dismissed, he moved into the hall, opened her bedchamber door, and stepped inside.

Priscilla stood before the mirror, her bosom near to spilling from her gown, her hair perfectly coifed, dabbing expensive French perfume behind an ear. He thought of her drab, high-necked dresses and, as beautiful as she looked right now, found himself yearning for the unpretentious woman she had been.

"Goin' out?" he drawled, unable to disguise the mocking note in his voice.

Priscilla whirled to face him, a hand unconsciously rising to the base of her throat. "What . . . what are you doing here?"

"I thought we went through that before."

"You've got to get out of here. I told you I don't want to see you."

Brendan moved closer. He had worn his black breeches and a clean white shirt that stood open at the throat. Priscilla must have approved, for her eyes ran over his body and unconsciously she wet her lips. *Just as fiery as ever*, he thought with a jolt of desire.

"I came to talk, Priscilla. I want you to know the truth about what happened to that man I killed in the Indian Territory. It wasn't murder, I swear it."

"You shouldn't have come here."

"I want you to know the truth." *I want things to be the way they were.*

Priscilla fought to maintain her control. Just the sight of him, standing there so tall and proud, made her heart ache unbearably. She watched his eyes, the stormy array of emotions they revealed. Anger, regret, determination . . . tenderness.

"It . . . it doesn't matter," she said, beginning to falter. "Things are different than they were before. I'm Stuart's wife now—"

"Are you?"

"Yes."

"It's only a piece of paper, Priscilla."

"N-not any more." She had to convince him. She didn't believe him and even if she did, it wouldn't change things.

"Are you trying to tell me he came to your room last night?" Brendan's hands balled into fists. "If he forced you—"

"He didn't. It was what we both wanted." Dear God, she had to get him out of there. Just watching the shadows cross his handsome face made her dizzy inside and hot all over.

"I don't believe you. Not after what happened in the garden."

She hated to lie. She had to.

"That's exactly why I did it. Stuart didn't come to me—I went to him. I wanted the past laid to rest. I wanted whatever there was between us over and done with." She forced herself to look at him and not glance away. "I wanted you out of my life once and for all."

Long, angry strides carried him across the room. He gripped her arms and hauled her against him. "You're lying."

"I'm not."

For a moment he just stood there. "You don't love him. You probably don't even like him. How could you do it?"

"I . . . I care for him. A great deal, in fact. You wouldn't understand."

The line of his mouth grew thin and grim. "You're right, Priscilla, I don't understand." He ran a finger along her cheek and she trembled. "If you belong to Egan, I don't understand how you could kiss me the way you did in the garden. I don't understand how you could want me to touch you—the way you do right now."

Priscilla wet her lips. "You're wrong."

"Am I?" His eyes fastened on her mouth, his hold on her arms grew tighter, then he kissed her—not a punishing, brutal kiss, but a hungry, aching kiss that stole her breath and maybe her very soul. In seconds, she was kissing him back, opening her mouth to him, her tongue sliding over his, her body arching against him.

Dear God, where did he get this power he held over her?

"Silla," he whispered against her ear. Slipping the gown from her shoulder, he bared a breast, cupped it with his hand, and teased her nipple until it hardened. Priscilla sagged against him.

"S-Stuart might come," she warned, her voice ragged, "he could be here any moment."

Brendan looked at her with a mixture of anger,

desire, and pain. "Then we'd better hurry," was all he said. Turning her toward the mirror, he placed her palms on the top of the dresser and lifted the hem of her turquoise gown.

"W-what are you doing?"

His hands cradled her breasts, squeezing them harder now, molding them, lifting them. "We've had so little time," he whispered, his hardness pressing against her bottom while his teeth nipped the side of her neck. "You've only begun to know the pleasures a man can give a woman."

One hand worked the buttons at the front of his breeches while the other bunched her gown and petticoats above her waist. She started to straighten, but Brendan pressed her back down. His hands skimmed over her thighs, covered only by her thin pantalets, moving inward, upward until he cupped her softness. "Spread your legs for me, Sill."

Priscilla swallowed. His fingers found the opening in her undergarments, slid inside, and began to stroke the damp folds of her sex.

"You know you like this," he whispered. "Open for me."

Flames licked her body. She couldn't move, could very scarcely breathe. His fingers worked the slickness building inside her, the rhythm matching that of his hand on her breast. Priscilla moaned.

Brendan untied the cord of her cotton pantalets, pulled the string, then slid them over her buttocks and down her thighs.

"Do it, Sill. You know you want to."

Priscilla made a mew in her throat and her legs moved apart with a will of their own. His hands stroked the curves of her bottom while he kissed her neck and shoulders, his mouth trailing slick damp heat, his dark hands skillfully readying her. He cupped her bottom, kneaded it, then slid a second finger inside her. A wave of pleasure broke over her, making her shiver with longing. They were magical, those hands. Priscilla's stomach clenched, and ripples of heat swirled through her body.

"You're mine," Brendan whispered, his voice low and rough as he stroked her heated flesh again and again. Then he moved closer, probing for entrance until his rock hard length slid inside her.

Priscilla nearly swooned. A rush of heat invaded her body, making her breasts throb and her flesh burn. Holding her hips immobile, Brendan thrust into her, stirring the fires, making her cry out his name. Out and then in. Harder and harder. With each driving stroke, her need for him grew and strengthened.

He was pounding against her now, long, seductive, demanding strokes that left her weak and quivering all over. Unconsciously her back arched, forcing her hips toward his, meeting each of his long hard thrusts. Priscilla's palms pressed into the bureau. Her nails dug into the wood, and her body grew slick with perspiration. Caught up in the passion and pleasure, she bit her lip to keep from crying out, then her head fell back, the world careened into blackness, then burst into a thousand colored stars.

Sweetness. So much sweetness and such impossible pleasure.

Brendan followed her over the edge, shuddering with his release then holding her against him. For a moment, he just stood there, his arm enfolding her waist, his breathing labored and his body still tense. Then he buttoned the front of his breeches, adjusted Priscilla's undergarments, and carefully lowered her skirts.

When Priscilla turned toward him, she tried to read his face, but the hard planes fell into shadow.

"Can Egan make you feel like that?" he asked, his voice rough and husky.

Priscilla didn't answer. Stuart would never be able to move her as Brendan did, never make her feel the passion and love—yes love, she couldn't deny it—that made her want to hold him and never let him go. She felt the warning of tears but willed them away.

"Thanks for the . . . distraction," he said, with more than a trace of bitterness. "Good-bye . . . Mrs. Egan."

It was all she could do not to go to him, to abandon her dreams as she had before and beg him to take her with him. Instead she stared at his broad back and narrow waist as he strode across the floor, walked out, and closed the door.

Instead of following her heart, she sank down on the bed, feeling a mixture of anguish and despair. For the first time since her return to Natchez, she gave in to her tears and wept for the man she had lost, and with him her dreams.

Dear Lord, I love him so. Her chest felt leaden and her hands trembled. She sat there for long, achingly empty moments, her throat burning, hot tears spilling down her cheeks. If only she could believe in his innocence, believe he could solve his problems with the law, could give up his outlaw ways and make a life for them.

But she didn't.

Stuart had told her the truth about what happened with Hennessey, and she had seen Brendan kill more than once. Besides, if he were innocent, why had he been running? And he very definitely had been—she had seen it in his eyes almost from the start. Brendan was an outlaw and a gunman. Men like that didn't change.

And there was Stuart to think of. There was the debt she owed him, the family she'd always wanted and the vows she had made.

God in heaven, what kind of a woman am I? By making love to Brendan, she had done the very thing she had sworn not to. How could she live with herself? How could she face Stuart?

With a numbness that came very close to grief, Priscilla washed herself, then straightened her hair and clothing. From the moment of Brendan's appearance in Natchez, she had tried to dissuade him. Tonight she had lied to him, hoping he would leave. Now he was gone—out of her life forever—but not before he'd proven his mastery of her in the most insensitive way.

Brendan Trask was her weakness—like a craving for the opiates smoked by some of the rivermen under the hill.

Priscilla's nails bit into her palms. *Think!* she demanded. *Don't let this man—this fugitive from the law—destroy you. You can't run away this time, you can't weep and beg God's forgiveness. You've got to look out for yourself!*

She forced herself under control. Brendan wouldn't be back—of that she was sure. Not when he believed she had given herself to Stuart—not after the way he had treated her. No, Brendan would not be back.

Priscilla's throat closed up, and fresh tears threatened, but she wouldn't let them fall. She had betrayed Stuart, just as she had before, but with Brendan gone from her life, it wouldn't happen again.

Priscilla's resolve strengthened. She wouldn't let her attraction to the handsome outlaw ruin the rest of her life. She wouldn't let her desire for him, her wantonness—her weakness—destroy her chance for family and home.

She ignored the sad little voice that said a home without love wasn't really a home at all.

Chapter 15

Raking a hand through his wavy dark brown hair, Brendan sank down on the tapestry sofa in the parlor of Evergreen's bachelor quarters. The ornate cherrywood clock ticked loudly, matching the slow, dull beating of his heart.

After he'd left Priscilla, angry at himself as much as her, he had gone back to the mayor's office, only to discover Egan's meeting had adjourned. Egan was gone—and so was Christian Bannerman.

His worry for Chris overrode his bitterness and disappointment with Priscilla. Since Egan hadn't shown up at the house on Pearl Street while Brendan was still there, he could be anywhere. And Chris might very well be in trouble. Still, without the vaguest notion where to look, he had no choice but to sit and wait.

An hour passed with agonizing slowness. Brendan paced the floor and looked outside a dozen times. He had almost decided to go back to Egan's and wait for his return when Chris rapped lightly on the door and walked in.

"Chris! Thank God you're all right." Feeling a rush of relief, Brendan rose to his feet.

"You look like hell," Chris said without preamble, noting the smudges beneath his friend's eyes and the tension that lined his forehead. "Worry about me? Or trouble with your lady?"

"Both, I'm afraid. It appears my efforts with Priscilla came too late. She'd made up her mind to believe the worst, but even if I hadn't already lost her, the way I treated her tonight would have been the crowning blow."

"Sorry to hear it, my friend. I had hoped things might work out."

Brendan just nodded. "What about Egan?"

"His meeting with the mayor ended about five minutes after I got there. From there, he headed straight for the Iron Butterfly."

"Iron Butterfly? What the hell is that?"

Chris chuckled softly. "Fanciest whorehouse in Natchez. Caters only to the wealthy, and it's all kept very hush-hush. Even Egan, as careful as he is, wouldn't have to worry about a place like that."

"How long was he in there?"

"Long enough to take his pleasure. He patted one of the girls on the bottom as he left, and there wasn't much doubt about what they'd been doing. I followed him home, and that's where I left him. Figured I'd better get back and check in."

Brendan paced the Aubusson carpet. "It doesn't make sense, Chris. Why would Egan go to a whorehouse? With a woman like Priscilla to warm his bed, why would he want to?"

"Obviously, it's just as you thought—he isn't sleeping with her yet. The way things stand between you two, she probably hasn't invited him."

"A man like Egan doesn't need permission. Besides, I was wrong. Priscilla said that last night she . . ."

Chris cocked a brow. "Priscilla said what?" he asked, but Brendan didn't answer.

Instead, he mentally replayed their angry conversation, trying to recall her every word, every expression—then he grinned.

"She's lying. She told me the marriage has been consummated, but it hasn't. If I hadn't been so damned mad, I would have seen it on her face. She could never win a hand at poker."

"Are you sure, Bren? Maybe that's just what you want to believe."

Brendan shook his head. "From what Priscilla has told me, Egan wants sons. That's the reason he married her in the first place. He hasn't been to her bed because he wants to be sure she's not carrying my child. A man like Egan would want to be damned certain the baby was his—not somebody else's."

Chris's hand came up to his shoulder. "If she told you that, even if it isn't the truth, maybe it's what she wants. If it is, you've got to resign yourself."

Brendan remained unconvinced. "You don't know her like I do. She's confused right now. Egan's got her convinced I'm some kind of monster. She's got no money, no friends, nobody to turn to. . . . She's so damned inexperienced, she doesn't even understand what happens between us whenever we're together. She's ashamed of the way she feels, of the things we've done. She feels guilty for betraying Egan when it's Egan who's betraying her—and has been all along."

"What you're telling me is that she loves you, whether she knows it or not."

Brendan flashed a second grin. "Exactly."

"Then I'd suggest you get her out of there. Before she does something she really will regret—or Egan does."

"But where would I take her? I sure can't bring her here."

"Why not? It's private; no one in the world would look for her at Evergreen. You'll have time to get things worked out."

Brendan searched his friend's face. "She can't stay in the main house. Too many visitors, too many people going in and out each day."

"She can stay here with you. If it weren't for all this trouble, she'd be your wife already. Besides, she may need your protection."

The thought of having her there made his heartbeat quicken. "I don't know, Chris. It might be dangerous, and you've done so much already."

"Just get her here. Sue Alice and I will make sure she's taken care of until you get the evidence you need on Egan. In the meantime, I'd suggest you get some sleep. If you're going to convince her what a prize you are, you'll need all that rugged masculine charm the ladies can't seem to resist."

Brendan laughed aloud. He'd get her there, all right. And once he did, he'd make her listen. One way or another!

Priscilla survived the dinner party they attended at Auburn, a lovely mansion owned by one of the city's most prominent families.

She was getting very good at hiding her emotions, and even better at playing the role of dutiful spouse. All she had to do was sit quietly, listen to Stuart's practiced political banter, and nod whenever it seemed appropriate. He appeared more relaxed this evening, but she wasn't quite sure why. Afterward they had come home and said their usual good-nights in the hallway. Priscilla had tossed and turned for hours, then finally fallen into an exhausted sleep.

Now, with the morning sun pressing down on her in waves of yellow heat, her eyelids still refused to open.

"It is time you woke up, *Madame* Egan." Charmaine Tremoulet, her gangly French maid, shook Priscilla's shoulder. "The day passes and you are still sleeping."

What business is it of yours? Priscilla thought nastily, then remembered she'd told the tall graying woman not to let her sleep past ten.

"All right, Charmaine, I'm getting up." Her strained evening of socializing had certainly taken its toll. That, and her shamefully wicked encounter with Brendan.

Priscilla tossed back the pale blue silk coverlet. "I'd like a bath," she instructed, "a nice hot one." Maybe it would help. She forced a smile and slipped into the mauve silk wrapper the tall woman held.

"*M'sieur* Egan has already left. You should have gotten up sooner."

"I'm sorry you don't approve." The woman grated on her nerves something awful. Stuart had hired her, and like the others in his employ, Charmaine bowed and scraped at his every command. She saw only his charming manners and the coins that crossed her palm.

Charmaine called for the upstairs maid and arranged for the bath, then turned to the bureau and began to choose Priscilla's undergarments, which she laid atop the bed. The bedchamber, lavishly furnished with Oriental carpets and gilded mirrors, blue-tasseled floor lamps, and silver doorknobs, seemed every bit as overwhelming as the rest of the house. Priscilla preferred a more simple design.

"You will be going out?" Charmaine asked, opening the ornate cherrywood armoire.

"I'm not sure yet. For now, I'll just wear the blue muslin." Summer had just about ended, except for the hot spell they'd been having for the past few days.

"The apricot dimity would be more—"

"The muslin is cooler."

"*Oui, Madame.* After your bath, we will dry and curl your hair."

"Fine," Priscilla said, with growing irritation, "but none of those tight little curls Stuart likes. I want it softer, more natural."

"But the curls are very stylish. Your husband wishes—"

"I don't care what Stuart wishes. He's got meetings all day, so I won't have to worry about it." Lord in heaven, she got sick of pleasing Stuart—of taking orders in general.

"*Oui, Madame.* Whatever you say." There was censure in the lift of the woman's thin gray brows, but Priscilla ignored it.

The upstairs maid, a short, brown-haired girl named Betty June, arrived a few minutes later. "Mr.

Jaimie has come to see you. He wants to know when you'll be down."

"Tell him I'll be ready in half an hour."

Unlike Charmaine, who grumbled from dusk till dawn, Betty June was a cheerful girl. She willingly left to deliver Priscilla's message. At least she'd have Jaimie for company. Stuart didn't seem to mind their friendship. It was almost as though he expected Jaimie to look after her. Of course, Jaimie had little else to occupy his time. It was Mace Harding who usually went with Stuart, unless he left the house alone.

Half an hour later, as promised, Priscilla descended the curving staircase in her simple blue muslin dress, her hair arranged in soft brown curls at the shoulders.

Jaimie waited in the front parlor. "Mornin', Miz Egan."

"Good morning, Jaimie." She wished he would call her Priscilla, but Stuart wouldn't like it, and both of them knew it. "Would you care to join me for breakfast?"

"No thanks, ma'am, I've already eaten. I just stopped by to tell you I'd found out some about Miss Conners, just like you asked."

In the dining room, with its gold-flocked wallpaper and gold silk draperies, Priscilla sat down in a carved mahogany chair and motioned for Jaimie to do the same. Negro servants brought them coffee in gold-trimmed porcelain cups, along with ham and biscuits for Priscilla. The succulent aroma made her mouth water, though she hadn't thought she was hungry.

"So what did you find out?" she finally asked, after a few tentative bites.

"She lives with a fella named Caleb McLeary, over at the Middleton Hotel."

"Is he some sort of relative?"

Jaimie cleared his throat. "No, ma'am, not exactly."

Priscilla's eyes went wide. "You mean she's his mistress?"

"Caleb says she's his niece, but everybody knows the truth." Jaimie's gentle features grew taut. "Word is he mistreats her some. Gets drunk and beats her."

"That's terrible. Why does she put up with it? She's a beautiful woman. Surely she doesn't have to stand for that kind of behavior."

"Seems she hasn't got much choice. You see, she comes from under the hill. Worked at a place called the Painted Lady."

"A saloon?" Priscilla asked.

Jaimie reddened. "Sort of."

"Oh my."

"Don't get me wrong, Priscilla—I mean, Miz Egan. From what I gather, Miss Conners has had a rough life. She lost her ma and pa when she was five—"

Priscilla's chest tightened.

"There was some kind of scandal involved, but her pa's relatives kept things quiet. Besides, that's been nearly twenty years ago. Nobody seemed to remember."

Priscilla set her coffee cup down and it clattered noisily against the saucer.

"Her real name's Rosie O'Conner," Jaimie finished. "That's all I know."

Not Conners—O'Conner. Irish. It had an oddly familiar ring. The pressure in her chest grew tighter, making it hard to breathe. "I know this is a little crazy, but I was wondering . . . if it wouldn't be too much trouble . . . maybe you could do a little more digging."

"Do you mind my askin' why?"

"If I knew, I'd tell you. It's just a feeling. Something about her. . . ."

"She takes a walk every mornin' about ten. Maybe I could talk to her, get to know her a little."

"Don't tell her I put you up to it."

"To tell you the truth, I was planning to talk to her anyway." Jaimie grinned, stretching the freckles on his face.

"Caleb McLeary might not like it."

He shrugged his shoulders. "He's not her husband. And until he is, she doesn't have to answer to him."

Priscilla fell silent. Rose wasn't married to McLeary. A few simple words that changed a woman's life completely. If she had it to do over, would she marry Stuart again? In her heart she knew that she would not.

"The Meyers job went off without a hitch, just like I said." Caleb McLeary sprawled in a rickety wooden chair in the store room. "You worry too much, Egan. Why don't you relax and enjoy life a little?"

"Went off without a hitch?" Stuart repeated, incredulous. He stood several feet from McLeary, every muscle tense. "For God's sake, man, there were bodies all over the river! This whole operation is getting way out of hand."

Caleb just laughed. "So someone got spooked and started shooting. It wasn't our fault. What the hell were we supposed to do?"

"The problem is you just don't care anymore. You've got the meanest gang of cutthroat river rats under the hill, and you don't think anyone can stop you. Well, I'm telling you, Caleb, the mayor's forming a vigilante committee. They're going to crack down on all this smuggling and murder, and they're going to crack down hard. I suggest we cut bait and drift for a while. Let things cool down. You get rid of some of those no-goods who work for you, send the rest out of town, and when things get quiet, we can start back up again. Ease into it gently, no murder, no mayhem, just a little flatboat robbery here and there, a wagon load of goods stolen along the Trace."

McLeary just scoffed. "You got your money, you don't have to worry. I need a bigger stake."

Unconsciously, Stuart's hands fisted, but he forced himself under control. Outside the door, a burst of raucous laughter filled the silence in the room. Mace Harding shifted his eyes from McLeary to Stuart and back again. Jake Dobbs, McLeary's man, eased back against the wall.

"So how do you plan to keep the vigilantes off your back?" Stuart finally managed to ask.

McLeary came out of his chair, wearing a look very near excitement. "I plan to make one last haul— the biggest cache of plunder ever taken on the river. Your man at the shipping office sent word just this morning. The *St. Louis* will be moving downstream loaded with bales of fur, barrels of flour, whiskey, and hardwood—and a big shipment of gold to the federal troops in New Orleans. We take the *St. Louis*," he said, pronouncing it *St. Louie*. "I'll retire, your precious reputation'll stay intact, and we'll all wind up rich men. What do you say?"

It was tempting. More than tempting. His problem with McLeary would be solved—one stray bullet among a barrage certainly wouldn't be noticed. The robberies and murders would end—or at least his connection to them. And his fortune would swell considerably, since his usual percentage for providing the information would increase by Caleb's share.

"Taking a steamboat that size won't be easy. What have you got in mind?"

McLeary walked over to the scarred wooden table and unrolled a map of the river. "She's been shifting real bad lately. Big sandbar building at the 370 mile marker."

That was ten miles north of Natchez as measured from the Head of Passes, the spot one hundred miles south of New Orleans where the river diffused to make its entry to the Gulf of Mexico.

"We move the markers, figure some way to run the boat aground, then board her and blow the boilers. The passengers and crew'll be too damn busy runnin' for their lives to worry about what we're doin'."

Not a bad plan. Once in a while, McLeary flashed sparks of brilliance from an otherwise dullard brain. "When?" Stuart asked.

"Ten days. You keep the mayor and his vigilantes busy in the wrong direction until then, and a little more'n a week from now, we'll all be sittin' pretty."

"You'll store the stuff in the cave, as usual?" Stuart asked.

McLeary nodded. "I've got buyers lined up for all the goods we can deliver—no questions asked."

"And the operation folds afterward?" Stuart pressed the issue because McLeary would expect it. Once his long-time partner was out of the way, along with Jake Dobbs, the only other man in McLeary's employ who knew about Stuart's involvement, it really didn't matter what the other men did.

"We'll close up shop and fade into the sunset," McLeary promised.

Stuart smiled and extended a hand. "Let me know what other information you're going to need and I'll make sure that you get it." Caleb met Stuart's out-stretched hand with his own, and the men shook.

McLeary! The door stood open at the rear of the Keel-boat Tavern on narrow winding Royal Street only for a moment. But it was just long enough for Brendan to make out the big brawny Irishman that Christian Bannerman had told him was the sheriff's prime sus-pect in the smuggling operation on the river and the murders on the Trace.

McLeary owned the Keelboat Tavern, a pit of dere-liction if ever there had been one. Though Caleb ran the place and worked there most of the time, he lived well above the income a dingy hole like that could earn, and it was common knowledge he kept an ex-pensive mistress. Little else had been discovered, and living high certainly wasn't cause to arrest a man, or half of Natchez would be in jail.

Brendan watched Egan make his way to a sleek bay saddle horse, his dark brown slouch hat pulled low, his plain twill pants and cotton shirt not much different from the clothing of any of the other men under the hill. In itself, Egan's meeting with Caleb McLeary wasn't much to go on, but now at least Brendan knew for sure where to look for the evidence he so desperately needed.

According to Chris, another robbery had occurred on the river last night, dry goods, whiskey, and a small cache of gold stolen from six men on a flatboat coming down from Memphis. Four of the dead men's bodies had been dragged from the water. The others were probably fish food by now.

Brendan headed up the hill toward Evergreen. He'd gotten what he wanted from Egan. Now he needed the time and place of the next attack on the river. The Keelboat Tavern held the answer. Unlike the sheriff or any of the other men who lived in town, Brendan could go to the tavern unnoticed, blend in with the hard-drinking rivermen without arousing suspicion.

He could move among them, talk to them freely— unless Mace Harding or some of Egan's men were drinking there, too. He'd have to be careful. With a man like Egan, there'd be no second chance.

Brendan thought of Priscilla, living in Egan's house, trusting him and never once suspecting the truth. He had to get her out of there.

As soon as he got the chance, that was exactly what he planned to do.

"Mornin' Miss Conners."

The dark-haired woman turned at the sound of Jaimie's voice and recognized his red hair and gently masculine features though she'd only seen him once. "Hello."

"Nice day, isn't it?" Jaimie sauntered up beside her, matching his long steps to her shorter ones. In her pale green dimity day dress, she looked just as pretty as she had before.

"Lovely. It's been so hot and muggy, it's nice to see a few clouds coming in." She looked as though she expected him to take his leave, but he just kept on walking.

"Might mean a thunderstorm," he amiably continued.

"Might. But then I kinda like it when it rains."

Jaimie smiled at that. "So do I."

They walked along in silence for a while. "Is there something you wanted, Mr. . . . ?"

"Walker. Jaimie Walker. Not really. I was just enjoying your company. Do you mind?"

She appraised him, looking for some motive to his kindness. Finding none, she shook her head, her dark brown hair swinging loose around her shoulders. "I don't mind, but I have a friend who might."

"McLeary?"

Rose stopped walking. "If you know him, then you know who I am, what I am, and you had better be on your way." She started up again, stiff-backed, shoulders squared, but Jaimie caught her arm.

"What I know, Miss Conners, is that you're a fine lookin' woman who's very nice company. You aren't married to McLeary, so you can do whatever you want. If you like my company, too, then we'll just keep on walkin'."

Brown eyes looked into blue. Rose searched his

face, saw nothing there but gentleness and warm masculine interest. She smiled. "Aren't you afraid of him? Everyone else is."

"Including you?"

"A little. He isn't as bad as some of the men I've known."

"He's a whole lot worse than some, too." He meant himself, and he let her know it by the look in his eyes.

"Funny," she said, with a steady regard that seemed to be sizing him up, "sometimes it's the one you never expect turns out to be your champion. Buy me something to eat, Jaimie Walker?"

Jaimie grinned. "It'd be my pleasure, Miss Rose."

Brendan stood in the darkness out behind the house on Pearl Street. In the servants' quarters to the rear, Egan's henchmen played cards; he could hear their occasional laughter between intermittent claps of thunder. A light rain had started. It wouldn't be long before the city fell prey to a full-fledged autumn storm.

Which, considering his intentions, suited Brendan just fine.

Egan had gone out for the evening, dressed in a fancy frock coat and breeches, hopefully to see his pretty little whore. Priscilla sat upstairs reading. He could see her silhouette in the glow of a whale-oil lantern.

As he had done before, Brendan climbed the back stairs to a door on the second floor. This time the door was locked, but using the knife he carried in his boot, it didn't take him long to get it open and step inside. Finding no one around, he moved down the hall to Priscilla's room, turned the doorknob, and walked in, closing the door behind him.

Priscilla dropped the small leather-bound volume she'd been reading, which landed with a heavy thud as she bolted to her feet.

"Brendan! What are . . . why are . . . I can't believe you'd come back here."

"I've got to talk to you."

"There's nothing to talk about, I told you that before." She was wearing a prim little white cotton nightgown, her chestnut hair loose around her shoulders, as yet unbraided for the night. Her cheeks were flushed and her lips looked full and inviting. He felt his body stir and smiled at how easily she could arouse him.

"There's plenty to talk about," he told her, "but we can't do it in Egan's house. I want you to come with me."

"You're crazy." Brendan started toward her, but Priscilla backed away. "Stay where you are, or I promise you I'll scream."

He just grinned. "If you do, Egan's men will come running. They'll shoot me this time—is that what you want?"

Priscilla swallowed so hard he could hear it. "Of . . . of course not. But you can't just come in here and . . . and . . ."

"And what, Priscilla? Make love to you again?"

She wet her soft pink lips. "Please don't say that."

"Why not? It's what you were thinking. It's what you want—" His eyes raked her, taking in the peaks of her breasts, growing stiff at his words beneath the soft cotton nightgown. "It's what I want, too," he admitted, his voice husky, "but it isn't what I'm here for."

"Then why *are* you here?"

He noticed her tone had softened as her eyes ran over his face. He thought how sweet she looked, how fragile, how desirable. The Priscilla he had wanted to marry—not the untouchable woman Egan had created.

"I'm here to take you away. I've got a place for us to go. Someplace safe where we can work things out." He moved closer, but Priscilla backed away.

"I'm not going with you. I thought you understood. Stuart and I—we're going to be a family. Everything's settled."

Brendan scoffed. "Nothing's settled, and we both know it." *Little fool.* Damn, if only he could tell her the truth about Egan. But what if something happened to him? What if Egan got away with it? Priscilla wouldn't be safe for a minute.

He moved closer, his jaw set with determination. "You're coming with me, Priscilla—we're going to have this chance—we both deserve it, and I mean to see we get it."

Brendan's arm snaked out, he caught her around the waist, and jerked her against him. His hand clamped over her mouth, and he held her while she struggled, working to get her arms behind her back, careful not to hurt her.

"You can make this easy or hard, sweetness. Either way, you're coming with me."

He'd been prepared for this. Pulling a length of rope from his pocket, he bound her wrists, then stuffed a handkerchief into her mouth and tied it around her head with another. He didn't really think she'd scream—then again, looking at the flecks of fury in her wide dark eyes, he wasn't so sure.

Brendan eased her down on the floor, tied her flailing legs, then went to the bed and pulled off the ice-blue counterpane. She raged at him through the gag as he rolled her in the bedspread, hauled her up, and tossed her over his shoulder. He'd have his hands full when he got her to his quarters at Evergreen.

He could hardly wait.

Chapter 16

 How dare he ruin my life again! And this time there'd be no reprieve. Priscilla kicked her feet and shouted muffled words, but it did no good, bound as she was and rolled in the bedspread.

She felt every jarring step Trask took down the back stairs, every jolt along the path through the garden. It was raining steadily now, and she could hear thunder, though she couldn't feel the heavy drops of rain. The air smelled of damp earth and leaves.

Not far from the house, Brendan settled her into the back of a small flatbed wagon, climbed up on the seat, and clucked the horse into a trot. The wagon rolled away, and the next thing she knew, he was lifting her out, carrying her inside a building, then with a motion that made her stomach turn over, he plopped her down on a soft feather mattress and rolled her out on the bed.

When he knelt to untie her feet and the rope fell free, she jammed one bare foot in the middle of his chest and shoved just as hard as she could. Brendan sprawled on the floor on his backside, knocking over a flower vase, which crashed to the floor. If the gag had been removed, Priscilla would have shouted with glee.

"You little minx," he said, getting his feet back under him, "you're gonna pay for that." But he was grinning, and even wet from their trip through the rain, he looked so handsome it took her breath away.

Brendan untied the gag and pulled it away from her mouth.

"Damn you!" It was the first swear word she had ever uttered and it made her feel unbelievably good. "You're the vilest, most despicable—"

"You shouldn't curse, Priscilla. It isn't ladylike." She tried to kick him again, but he stepped away. "Why don't you just take it easy? We're gonna have this talk if it takes the rest of the night."

"I've got nothing to say, you—you—abductor!"

"All you have to do is listen."

Priscilla just glared at him.

"If you'll behave yourself, I'll untie your hands."

She set her jaw, trying not to notice the way a lock of his dark hair had fallen over his brow, or the way the lamplight glistened on his smooth tan skin. When his light blue eyes settled on her mouth, soft heat curled in the pit of her stomach.

And the fact that it did only made her madder.

With feigned indifference, she nodded her agreement, but when Brendan untied the rope around her wrists, Priscilla jerked free and swung at him. Brendan caught her arm, his expression no longer warm.

"You're gonna listen, Priscilla, if I have to tie you to the bedposts." He smiled then, as if he might enjoy it. She tried to pull away, but he wouldn't let go. "Not until you hear what I have to say."

It seemed she had no choice. "All right, talk. But it isn't going to do a lick of good."

"First, let's talk about the murder I'm accused of."

As briefly as possible, Brendan relayed the events leading up to the shooting at Fort Towson, pointing out that he had only shot the man in self-defense. Then he explained that in Corpus he had spoken to Tom Camden and Badger Wallace, and that together they had worked out a way to help him clear his name. He didn't go into detail, just mentioned he was gathering information on a gang of smugglers here in Natchez in exchange for the charges being dropped.

She looked at him for several long moments. "That's really why you're here, isn't it? My being in Natchez had nothing to do with it. You didn't come after me—you just found out I was here, decided you hadn't quite had your fill of me, and helped yourself. You're even worse than I thought!"

She jerked free and swung again—and this time the blow connected, the resounding slap echoing across the room. She sprang off the bed and raced to the door, but Brendan caught her in two long strides.

Cursing beneath his breath, he turned her into his arms as he pressed her against the door. "You're wrong, Priscilla. I would have come after you, no matter where you were. You've been mine since the night we made love on the prairie—Egan isn't the only man who keeps what belongs to him."

With that his mouth came down over hers. Priscilla struggled against him, felt the hard strength of his body, felt the yearning in his touch, the hunger, and the passion. She also felt his need for her. It was there in the way he held her, securing her tightly, yet not hurting her. He had never hurt her, she recalled. Never.

His long-fingered hands moved down her body, gentling her, willing her to respond. How could she not when she loved him so? Brendan let go of her arms and she settled them around his neck. When her tongue slid into his mouth, he groaned. He kissed her again, so thoroughly her knees went weak, and then he pulled away.

"You trusted me once, Priscilla. In a grubby seaport town on the Texas Gulf where trusting a man was the craziest thing you could do. You looked into my eyes and you believed in me. I'm asking you to believe in me now."

Priscilla didn't answer. Her throat had closed up and her eyes filled with tears. "If you were innocent, why were you running? I knew you were—I could see it in your face."

"But you don't see it there now, do you?"

Her gaze searched his, looking for the truth. "No."

Brendan raked a hand through his hair. "I was running, Priscilla, but not from a murder charge. I killed that man because he tried to shoot me. I was innocent of anything but defending myself, and I never really believed the law would follow me to Texas. What I was running from—hiding from—was the war. There were things that happened in Mexico . . . things I didn't want to face up to."

She let the words sink in, remembering the way he had withdrawn whenever someone mentioned his involvement in the war. "And now you can?" she asked softly.

"In Texas—after I left you at the Triple R with Egan—I realized I'd found something worth living for. A reason to put the past behind me and make something of myself. I want us to build a life, Priscilla, have the children we talked about. I need you, Sill, and I want you for my wife."

She reached out to him then, touched his face with trembling hands, and knew without doubt his words were true. His strong arms went around her. It felt so right to be held by him, as if she were finally where she belonged.

Tears trickled gently down her cheeks. "Make love to me," she whispered. It was madness, she knew, for anything might yet happen. But the moment Brendan had carried her out of the house on Pearl Street, she had known the chance for a life with Stuart was past. She loved Brendan Trask, and no amount of denial could change that.

It wasn't fair to Stuart, hadn't been since the night she had married him. Whatever happened now, she intended to set things right between them. In the meantime, Brendan was here and she loved him. She wanted to show him how much.

Brendan stepped back to look at her and his heart swelled with love. His wet shirt and breeches had dampened the front of her nightgown, making it cling to her willowy curves. The tips of her breasts thrust upward with every soft breath, and tendrils of shiny dark hair fanned out at her temples. His body, already hard, throbbed with an ache he knew only too well. God it felt good just to look at her.

Sliding an arm beneath her knees, he lifted her up, carried her across the room, and laid her gently on the bed.

"You're wet," Priscilla said softly, running a finger through the dampness on his neck. Drops of water clung to his chest hair and glistened in the glow of the lamp. "You'd better get out of those clothes."

Brendan smiled slowly. "Exactly what I had in mind." He tugged his shirt from the waistband of his breeches and stripped it off, then sat down on the edge of the bed to pull off his boots. Priscilla ran her fingers along the muscles of his back, and they tensed beneath her hand.

"I love the way you feel," she said, trailing small soft kisses where her hands had just been, making his loins grow thick and heavy.

Turning toward her, he lifted away a lock of her hair and kissed her shoulder, then stood up to unfasten his pants. Priscilla's hands came up to work the buttons.

"Just this once," she said, "I'm not going to think about what we're doing, whether it's right or wrong. Tonight I'm going to touch you the way I've always wanted, be just as wicked as the other women you've known." She popped the first button free, but Brendan stilled her hand at the second.

"I know this is all still new to you. I wish we were married, that you didn't have to worry about the problems we still have to solve. But I want you to understand that no matter what happens, making love isn't wicked." He tipped her chin with his fingers. "It's beautiful. It's sharing and joy, giving and receiving. At times it can be playful, sometimes passionate, but nothing has ever been more right than what we're doing here now."

She blinked back a fresh mist of tears. Brendan picked up her hand, kissed it, then returned it to the hardness at the front of his breeches. "I believe you were helping me undress," he said with an edge of roughness.

Priscilla's mouth went dry. With fingers a little less steady, she unfastened the buttons that closed up his breeches, then started in surprise at discovering he wore nothing underneath.

"Need some help?" he teased, his blue eyes warm with amusement. There was hunger there, too, and bold masculine power.

She shook her head. "No." The word came out on a soft breath of air as she slid his breeches down his hard-muscled thighs. Brendan stood naked in front of her. Priscilla stared at his rigid manhood, thick and virile and demanding. On the prairie, their love-making had come between rounds of exhaustion and their fear of being pursued. There'd been no time for exploration, only time to ease their need.

Now, in the glow of the lantern, Priscilla let her eyes drift over him, taking in the width of his shoulders, his narrow waist, and smooth dark skin. A thatch of springy brown hair covered his muscular chest, then arrowed down his flat belly to surround his manhood.

"Touch me, Silla."

It was what she wanted, what she ached to do. Reaching for him, she encircled his hardened length with her hand and Brendan groaned.

She'd only begun to discover his secrets when he pulled her to her feet in front of him and drew the nightgown over her head. They stood naked before the big bed, touching, caressing, getting to know each other's bodies.

Brendan cupped a breast, expertly teased a nipple,

and Priscilla felt the heat of it all the way to her toes. He pulled her closer, bending to place his mouth where his hand had just been. Flames licked her body; gooseflesh danced up her spine. Her breasts felt heavy and achy, and the place between her legs grew damp and throbbing.

He hadn't kissed her yet, and she thought she might die if he didn't. Reading her as always, he fitted her against him and captured her mouth with his. His tongue felt like satin and his breath held the clean scent of rain. When Brendan deepened the kiss, his hands sliding down to her bottom, cupping it to bring her closer, Priscilla swayed against him, clutching his neck for support.

"I want you," she whispered against his ear. Brendan groaned and lifted her into his arms. She thought he would take her then, but he only set her down on the edge of the tall four-poster bed. Kissing her all the while, he eased her legs apart, and settled himself between them.

"Remember what I told you, baby. Nothing we do is wicked." Trailing kisses along her throat and down her shoulders, he nipped a breast, kissed the flat spot below her navel, then moved lower. Priscilla stiffened, tightening her legs against his intrusion when she realized where he was headed.

"Open for me, Silla," he whispered, urging her legs apart. "Let me love you."

Priscilla relaxed, accepting the fingers he slid inside her, feeling his lips moving hotly along her thigh. He pressed her down on the mattress as his mouth touched her most intimate parts and he began to nip and tease, sending a wave of heat through her body.

Priscilla couldn't think, couldn't move, in fact she could barely breathe. Fire engulfed her, waves of liquid heat and mounting pleasure. In seconds, the fiery sensations had built until she was thrashing against him, begging him for more.

"I need you inside me," she told him when the ecstasy rose to a pleasure she couldn't quite bear. "Please, Brendan."

He kissed her breasts as he rose above her. She felt his thick shaft pressing against her, and then he slid inside.

"Brendan. . . ." she whispered, feeling the heavy length, absorbing the heat it created, the waves of spiraling passion. He paused for a moment, gathering his control, and Priscilla squirmed in frustration. "More . . . I need more, Brendan. Please. . . ."

He plunged hard inside her. "All you want, baby," he promised, filling her completely. "All you can take."

Priscilla moaned at his words. When she gripped his shoulders and arched against him, Brendan began to move, slowly at first, easing in and out, setting up a rhythm that drove all other thoughts from her mind. With each of his strokes, he grew bolder, demanding a little more, driving a little deeper. Priscilla met each of his demands and begged for more.

She wasn't disappointed. Brendan drove hard and deep, staking his claim, forcing her to accept it. Their bodies pounded together in an age-old rhythm, hurling them higher and higher. They reached their peak together, bright stars bursting in Priscilla's mind among a backdrop of rich dark sweetness so poignant she could taste it. Brendan shuddered, his muscles grew rigid, and his warm seed spilled inside her. He rode the crest of the wave, the sheen of his perspiration mingling with her own.

Several heartbeats later, he moved to a place beside her and snugly fitted her against him. "Everything's going to be all right," he said with conviction. But something in the way he said it made it seem even harder to believe.

I love you, she wanted to say, but didn't. There were too many things unfinished, too much still unresolved.

Instead she lay awake beside him, watching the movement of his wide chest, thinking about what they had done, about how she felt. He was right, she decided. Nothing that wonderful could ever be wrong.

With a little more confidence, she let her fingers trail over the hairs on his chest and down his stomach. One slim finger ringed his nipple, making it pucker and grow hard. It wasn't the only thing to harden, she discovered, as his maleness began to rise up.

"Minx," he whispered into the darkness. "I suppose this means you want more."

Priscilla laughed softly. "You said I could have all I wanted."

Brendan chuckled, a husky masculine sound. "I've got a surprise for you, sweetness—that works both ways. I mean to take all you can give."

* * *

They made love three more times that night. Content and satisfied as they'd never been before, they slept until late in the morning. Priscilla awoke first, happy just to lie there watching the rise and fall of his powerful chest.

When his eyes opened a few minutes later and he felt her gaze on him, he rolled her beneath him and took her gently one more time.

In the silence that followed, Priscilla curled against him. "I lied to you about Stuart," she said softly. "I've never been with any man but you."

Brendan smiled gently. "I figured that out for myself. You're not a very good liar."

She braced a hand on his chest and drew back to look at him. "I'm frightened, Bren. What are we going to do?"

"First we'll get that annulment, just like we planned. The man who owns this place is a friend of mine, a cotton planter named Bannerman. He knows a lawyer who can help us. Barton Stevens. He's already been to see him. Stevens will talk to us whenever we're ready."

"Do you really think it'll work? That Stuart will let me go?"

"With the Bannerman family's support, the social pressure they can bring to bear, I don't think he'll have much choice."

She released an uncertain sigh. "I hope you're right."

Brendan lifted dark chestnut hair away from her throat and kissed her ear. "Does that mean you'll marry me?"

Priscilla smiled, feeling a rush of warmth. "You're still an outlaw. There's that to consider."

"I'm working on it," he assured her. "Just give me a little more time."

They lay quiet for a while longer, enjoying the closeness they hadn't had time for until now.

"I supposed we'd better get up," Brendan finally said. "Though God knows, I could stay with you like this all day." Tossing back the sheet, he swung his long legs to the floor.

"Easy for you to say," Priscilla countered, "thanks to you, all I have to wear is my nightgown."

Brendan grinned lazily. "Maybe if we get lucky, something will happen to that."

"Very funny." He handed her the nightgown, which Priscilla pulled over her head.

"I'll go up to the main house, see what I can do to solve the problem." He pulled on his breeches and boots. His shirt was too wrinkled to wear, so he found another and shrugged it on, then started for the door. He stopped midway there.

"You wouldn't leave, would you? I mean, you're not going to run back to Egan?"

Priscilla shook her head, a flush creeping into her cheeks. "Not after . . . what happened last night. It wouldn't be fair to Stuart."

Brendan's jaw grew taut. "You just worry about what's fair to Priscilla. The rest will take care of itself." Turning, he strode out the door.

She heard him coming long before she saw him through the window, trailed by a bevy of Negro servants, one of whom carried a copper bathing tub. Two more carried steaming pails of water, a short black woman carried a sewing basket, and Brendan lugged an armful of lady's clothes.

Priscilla dove back beneath the covers as the entire entourage came barging into the bedchamber. "What in the world—"

"The lady of the house insisted," Brendan said with a grin and a flash of white teeth. "From now on this place will have a butler and a maid. The dresses will be too big, but Jewel is here to alter them for you." Brendan spread the clothes out on the bed.

"But I can't stay here—what will people say?"

"The Bannermans know the truth—all of it—and they've agreed to help us. The servants think you're my wife, and nobody else knows you're here."

At this point, what choice did she have? She looked at the clothes and counted several muslins, a gingham, and a calico among the pile, a russet silk day dress, a deep rose moire, a midnight-blue silk, and a forest-green evening gown. "I can't accept someone else's clothes—they're far too costly. How would I ever repay them?"

Brendan turned to face her with pale blue eyes that looked grim. "I told you before, Priscilla. I'm hardly a pauper. I can afford to pay for the clothes. I can afford to take care of you. When will you start believing me?"

She glanced down nervously. "I'm sorry. I keep thinking of you as a rugged frontiersman. Finding you here . . . playing the part of a gentleman . . . well, it takes a little getting used to."

"You're going to get all of the "gentleman" you can take, remember? Or the rugged frontiersman—

whichever it is you prefer." Priscilla blushed crimson. "We've got a lifetime ahead of us, Sill."

She prayed he was right, but she wasn't really sure. There was still so much to sort out, so many problems they still had to solve.

"Can we speak to Mr. Stevens today?" she asked, hoping the subject of her annulment would placate him some.

"The sooner the better," was all he said.

After they'd both had a bath, and Priscilla spent some time with Jewel, getting her borrowed wardrobe fitted, she and Brendan went up to the main house so she could meet their host and hostess.

"Lord knows what they're going to think of me," she mumbled as they approached the back door.

"They'll think you're beautiful and sweet, and that we're madly in love. And you'll think they're a delightful family, which they are."

He was right about that, she discovered. Susan Alice—Sue Alice, she preferred—was a ripe-figured blonde with a cherub face and cupid-bow mouth. Gracious and warm, she never once made Priscilla feel uncomfortable.

"Brendan has told us so much about you," she said with a soft southern burr as the two of them sipped jasmine tea. "I just know it'll all work out."

"I hope so, Mrs. Bannerman."

"I'd be pleased if you'd call me Sue Alice. I feel like we're already friends." She arranged her full silk skirts on the sofa in front of the marble-manteled fireplace. A Queen Anne table sat atop the Aubusson carpet, topped by a bouquet of beautiful yellow roses.

Priscilla smiled, liking the woman already. "I'd like that very much—if you'll call me Priscilla."

"How 'bout a brandy, Bren?" Chris Bannerman asked. "Give the ladies a chance to talk."

She liked Chris, too. He worked hard, she could see by the dusty clothes he'd just ridden up in, and his loss of an arm seemed to bother him not at all.

"Good idea," Brendan said. He winked at Priscilla and followed Chris out of the richly furnished salon. A few moments later, a noisy whirlwind of activity made up of the Bannerman's three towheaded children stormed into the room.

"Lawd, you children behave yourselves," Sue Alice scolded, "we have guests in the house."

The children, a boy of eight or nine and a matched set of twin girls, looked not the least bit daunted.

"Matthew won't let me ride his rocking horse," one of the little girls said, "but Charity got to—so I want to, too."

"Matthew, I've told you before, just because you're the oldest doesn't mean you don't have t' share." Sue Alice tried to look stern, then smiled and reached out a hand to him. His small white fingers were dirty, but she didn't hesitate to grasp them. "Children, I want you t' meet Miss Wills." She pronounced it more like *Wheels*. "She's a friend of Mr. Trask's—and now she's a friend a' ours, too."

Priscilla felt a rush of gratitude at the way the older woman had handled things.

"This is Matthew, Patience, and Charity," Sue Alice said. "Matt is eight, and the twins are six."

"Why, they look so grown up—" Priscilla pulled

her rose silk skirt aside to kneel down beside them, "—I would have sworn they were much older."

All three children beamed at that. Matt was tall for his age, thin but not skinny, with soft blue eyes and a bright, inquisitive face. The girls would both be beauties: peach complexions, big green eyes, and the feminine cupid-bow lips of their mother.

Just looking at them made some warm, womanly instinct blossom in Priscilla's chest. "They're beautiful," she said to Sue Alice. "I've always wanted children of my own."

Her hostess looked pleased. "If that man a' yours has anythin' to do with it, I'm sure you will." She turned to her towheaded brood. "All right now, you've all met our guest; go on outside and play."

"Can't we stay and talk to Miss Wills?" Matt asked.

"Miss Wills will be joinin' us for suppa'. Afterward, Matt can recite the poem he's just learned, and each of you girls can play a song for us on the pianoforte. How does that sound?"

"Couldn't she come outside just for a minute?" Charity pleaded. "I want to show her my rabbit."

Sue Alice started to say no, but Priscilla interrupted. "I'd love to see your rabbit, Charity." She turned to her hostess. "As long as it's all right with your mother."

"Lawd, they can be tryin' at times," Sue Alice said, but a warm light shone in her pretty green eyes as she looked at her three children.

"Do you like rabbits?" Patience asked, taking Priscilla's hand.

"I love rabbits. I used to have one of my own." For

a moment, the forgotten knowledge stunned her. Where in the world had it come from?

"The cages are out in back," Matt said, taking charge in a manly way.

Priscilla nodded and followed him toward the door. Being in Natchez had certainly stirred up the past, but in a way she was glad. It felt good to know she had done some of the same things every other child had. She took Charity's hand. "What did you name your rabbit?" she asked.

"Herbert."

Priscilla laughed aloud.

The next four days were the most joyous Priscilla had known. She and Brendan spent long, lazy hours making love, went for walks in secluded spots down by the river, and talked far into the night. Brendan spoke often of Texas, of the home they would build on the rugged frontier.

He talked of the land and its beauty, and how he was sure she would love it. And when he held her and kissed her, she was certain she would.

They spoke to Barton Stevens, the lawyer Chris Bannerman suggested that first day. Though she didn't love Stuart, she knew he would be frantic at her disappearance, and she wanted to cause him as little grief as possible. By the evening of the first day after her disappearance, he'd been served the annulment papers, making her intentions clear.

Brendan continued his investigation of the smuggling ring whose capture would mean his freedom. Several nights he'd gone out, unwilling to tell her where he was going.

"The less you know about this, the better," he said. "I don't want you putting yourself in danger."

"But how could I be in danger? When you're out there alone, I worry about you. I just want to know what's going on."

"You'll just have to trust me, Sill." He captured her mouth in a searing bone-melting kiss. Then he turned and strode out the door.

Every afternoon he was gone for several hours, again refusing to tell her where. She spent the time with Sue Alice and the children. She read the girls stories, and played toy soldier with Matthew. They went for long walks, and had tea parties, and she helped the girls dress up their dolls. Miss Wills seemed too distant a name, so they'd decided to call her Aunt Silla, which pleased Priscilla no end.

Sometimes Brendan joined them, surprising her by how good he was with them.

"It's easy," he said. "I just remember the things I used to do, the way I wanted to be treated."

"They think a lot of you," she said.

"They've fallen completely in love with you," he countered, "but then I don't blame them."

Priscilla smiled. For the first time in her life, she knew a little what it felt like to be a wife and mother. It was what she wanted, she realized, more than anything else in the world.

Though they spent most of their time together, on several occasions, Brendan awoke with the sun and accompanied Chris to the cotton fields.

"We'll be planting cotton of our own," he said. "Chris is an expert. I couldn't learn from anyone better."

"Will we have . . . slaves?" Priscilla asked.

He shook his head. "Lots of people pouring into Texas. Germans, French, Irish—immigrants from all over the world. They'll all be lookin' for work. We'll have all the help we need."

Priscilla just smiled.

On Thursday, she and Brendan took a picnic lunch to the country—a secluded spot on Chris's plantation where they wouldn't accidentally be found.

After a meal that included cold fried chicken, fresh strawberries, and bread pudding for dessert, they settled against the trunk of an oak tree. It was a quiet, reflective time—until Priscilla asked the question she knew he had been dreading.

Chapter 17

 Cicadas buzzed in the leaves overhead and the Mississippi sprawled majestically in front of them. Priscilla's head nestled in Brendan's lap and he used a curl to tease her cheek.

She sat up and turned to face him, loving the way he looked in his open-necked white linen shirt and black breeches, his back propped up against the tree. He'd gone hatless today, his dark hair ruffled by the breeze.

"We've talked about so much," she said to him, "about Texas, about our future, our hopes and dreams. We've talked about friends and family, but there's a subject we always avoid." She felt him tense, his fingers growing taut beneath her own. "I know it's painful for you, but just this once, won't you tell me what happened in Mexico? What happened during the war?"

He let go of her hand and raked his fingers through his hair. "I've wanted to. A couple of times I tried, but, I don't know . . . something always seemed to hold me back."

"Maybe once you've told me, you'll be able to let it go."

Brendan nodded, but his eyes shifted away, and his face took on a harder, more distant expression. He looked out at the river, but didn't really seem to see it.

"It was like Tom Camden said," he began. "We were fighting the Mexicans on the Yucatán, taking cannon fire something awful. I destroyed the cannon, but took a musket ball in the arm. I ran into a nest of Mexicans in the process. It was terrible, Sill. For three of the longest days of my life they marched us—about half the Texas forces—through the jungle. There were bugs as big as your hand, crawlin' all over us, stinging and biting. It was hot and steamy—like a Georgia swamp in the summer, only ten times worse. We had nothing to eat and only enough water to keep us on our feet.

"At the prison, things got worse. They kept us in a Mayan ruin a couple days' march from Campeche. Half the men got dysentery within the first week. I'd lost a lot of blood, and my wound got infected. I was scared to death I'd lose my damned arm. . . . Then I met a man named Alejandro Mendez."

"Go on," Priscilla urged softly, when Brendan seemed reluctant to continue.

"Mendez was a Federalist, one of the rebels the Texians"—he pronounced it the Texas way, with an extra "i"—"were there to support. The Centralists were opposing the Texas Republic—had been since Santa Anna and the battle of the Alamo. The Texians hoped the Federalists, with Texas's support, would overthrow the Centralist government and be more amenable to a peace that accepted Texas boundaries."

"So this man, Mendez, was also a prisoner."

Brendan nodded. "Mendez was wounded and very

clearly dying. But the man was a born leader. You should have seen him, Sill. He had more courage and determination than any man I've ever known. He rallied his people and kept them going no matter how tough things got. He was good with doctoring, too. Knew every herb in the jungle, and exactly what it could do. As long as he was able, he treated the injured. He doctored the wound in my arm and stopped the infection. After that we became friends—closer than most, because of the circumstances. He was the oldest man in the prison and like a father to most of us."

Brendan stared off across the river, watching a flatboat drift downstream, no more than a speck in the distance. A steamboat whistle echoed toward the shore.

"We'd been in prison several months when the Centralists discovered the Texians had sent a rescue party—led by my brother—which, fortunately for me, none of them knew at the time. The Mexicans were furious. They wanted information, and they were determined to get it. They tortured a bunch of us. . . ."

She could see he'd been one of them by his flash of remembered pain. Unconsciously her hand covered his, and she felt it tremble.

"No matter what they did, how badly they beat us, no one talked, so they started killing people." His voice cracked, then turned flat, lifeless. "A man a day, they said, until one of us broke."

"Dear God in heaven."

"We drew straws. They'd killed fifteen men by the time I drew the short one—" He looked up at her, his eyes dull with anguish. "You know, I almost welcomed it. Anything to stop the hurting I felt inside. Seeing men tortured and starving, the wounded screaming for help. . . . They came for me at dawn, but . . ." Brendan swallowed and glanced away.

"You don't have to go on," Priscilla said softly. "It doesn't matter. All of that's in the past." Her heart wrenched at the agony written on his face.

"No," he said. "I want you to know what happened. I just pray it doesn't make a difference. . . ."

Dear Lord, what demons had she unleashed? "Brendan—"

"Alejandro crawled over to me—on his hands and knees because he could no longer stand up. 'Let me go in your place'—that's what he said. He said I had my whole life ahead of me, that he was just an old man days away from the grave.

"At first I wouldn't consider it—at least I was that much of a man."

"Don't! For God's sake, Brendan, it isn't worth it."

"I told him he was crazy. I walked away, but he kept calling out to me. I should have kept going, met my fate like the other fifteen men, but he kept talking, begging me to do as he asked. I could hear his raspy breathing across that filthy, lice-infested room—and I began to listen."

"You must let me do this thing. I ask it as a favor."

"If you die for me today, Alejandro, I'll only have to die tomorrow. It's only fair to the others."

"Each day is worth living. You will have one more day of life, and I will go to my grave a soldier, instead of a withered old man. Besides . . . a man never knows what fate may bring."

"He told me I'd be doing him a favor, letting him die like a man. At the time . . . I don't know . . . I guess I wanted to believe him . . . I wanted to go on living." Brendan turned to face her, and trails of wetness marked his cheeks. "I did it, Sill. I let him take my place. They carried him out into the sunshine and shot him in front of a firing squad. I'll never forget the sound of those muskets—I felt every bullet as if it had entered my own heart."

Priscilla touched his cheek, but Brendan pulled away.

"What kind of a man would do that, Sill? What kind?"

"You mustn't do this to yourself. At the time you did what you thought—"

"The next day my brother fought his way into the prison, and those of us still alive broke out of there. That old man might have lived. A man of such greatness—and he might have lived if hadn't been for me."

She reached for him then, slid her arms around his neck and pulled his head down to her shoulder, pressing her face against his cheek. She could feel the wetness of his tears as they mingled with her own.

"Nothing happens without a purpose." Priscilla stroked his hair. "God had a reason for wanting you to live. Alejandro Mendez believed that. He gave his life so you could go on. It isn't your place to question God's will."

The tension in his body seeped into hers. She wished she could absorb it, along with some of his pain.

He pulled away to look at her. "Do you really believe that?"

"Your friend got to choose the time and place of his death. He got to die with dignity. It was God's gift to him. Yours was to go on living."

"It's been a long time since I've thought about God."

"God forgave you a long time ago, Brendan. It's time you forgave yourself."

Something eased inside him; she could feel the tension leave his body. He cupped her face with his hands. "Mendez would have loved you, Priscilla. But no one could ever love you like I do." His mouth moved over hers in a gentle kiss that spoke more poignantly than his words.

Priscilla returned it, hoping with every touch, every caress, she could help to ease the sadness he had carried for so long. She kissed his eyes, the dampness on his cheeks, then returned to his mouth. When he urged her lips apart and his tongue touched hers, something flamed between them.

Brendan's kiss, no longer gentle, stirred the fires inside her body. With an urgency she hadn't expected, he opened the front of her dress and he slid his hands inside to cup a breast. As he pebbled her nipple, fiery kisses scorched her neck.

"I need you, Sill," he whispered. "You'll never know how much." Pulling her down on the blanket, hidden from the river by a thin line of rushes, he shoved up her skirts, unbuttoned the front of his breeches and found the split in her pantalets.

In a frenzy of need, he jerked them open, positioned himself above her, and with one determined thrust, buried himself inside her.

Priscilla moaned.

Coupling with an urgency that shook them both, they made wild, passionate love. As Brendan drove into her, Priscilla met each of his demanding strokes, arching her body, needing him as badly as he needed her. She reached her peak in minutes, her body tightening around his shaft, urging him to join her. Stars burst and the heavens seemed to open, lifting the burden from Priscilla that she had taken from him.

Afterward they lay sated, closer than they'd ever been before. For Brendan it seemed the past had at last been put to rest. For Priscilla, the future was all that mattered. God had spared Brendan's life and given him another chance.

Priscilla prayed God would grant that same fate to her.

They returned to their quarters late in the afternoon to find the children awaiting them outside the door. Priscilla looked down at her slightly rumpled dress and flushed. She fiddled with loose strands of her hair.

Brendan just grinned. When he bent down, the children gathered around him, and Priscilla thought again what a wonderful father he would make.

"Do you children think you can keep Aunt Silla entertained while I'm gone?" he asked.

"Sure, Uncle Brendan," Matt said. "We'll let her play soldier with us. Mama bought me some new dragoons. Would you like to see them?"

"I don't have time right now, son, but I will when I

get back. I'll show you how the Texians took the battle of San Jacinto.''

Matt bobbed his head with such enthusiasm his pale blond hair tumbled forward into his eyes.

"I won't be long," Brendan said to Priscilla. They went inside, and Brendan headed straight for the gun cabinet, where he kept his rifle and both his pistols locked away.

While the children talked to Priscilla, he opened the desk drawer and took out the key, then unlocked the cabinet and withdrew his .36 caliber. Stuffing the gun into his breeches behind his back, he went into the bedchamber and came out wearing a soft black leather vest that camouflaged the weapon a little.

Priscilla glanced up from her place on the brocade sofa. "How long will you be gone?"

"Not long. Maybe an hour or two." He strode toward her, leaned down and kissed her, then walked away.

"Be careful," she called after him.

"You can count on that." With a look that could only be called hungry, he strode out and closed the door.

The man had an appetite—that much was clear. Priscilla smiled. She'd discovered, to her astonishment, she had one, too.

Brendan strode along Silver Street toward the Keelboat Tavern on Royal. He had never felt better, more certain things would work out. Thanks to Priscilla, he'd dealt with the past and laid it to rest. And now that he could look at that awful day with some sense of objectivity, he knew that the decision he had made that morning was the right one at the time.

There'd been his men to consider, and Alejandro's men, and his old friend never would have survived the escape, weakened as he'd been. The burden of the old man's death, which had haunted him so long had finally been put to rest by Priscilla's words.

Brendan reached the tavern and pushed open the swinging double doors that led into the low-roofed, wood-framed building set into the hillside. It was noisy in the dimly lit room, rowdy with the sound of men's laughter and the strum of a guitar played by a scantily dressed woman in bright orange satin. Brendan searched the throng of men, some seated at tables playing cards, others standing at the long rough-plank bar, but saw no one he needed to avoid.

Shouldering his way through the crowd, he crossed the room to the bar beside a beefy, thick-chested man with a heavy, gray-black beard and shaggy salt-and-pepper hair.

"I'll have a whiskey, barkeep." Brendan looked at the man's empty shot glass. "And bring my friend here one, too."

"Thanks, mister."

"Name's Avery," Brendan lied, "Jack Avery." He extended a hand, and the beefy man shook it.

"Marlin's mine—Boots Marlin. You from up-river?"

Wearing his ruffle-fronted white linen shirt, black pants, black leather vest, and flat-brimmed hat, Brendan looked the part of the gambler he had been more than once. "New Orleans of late. You?"

"Been here nigh on two years. Used to flatboat

downriver, then take the Trace back home. Helluva life, I'll tell ya." Boots stroked his heavy graying beard.

"So you wound up stayin' here?"

Boots grinned, exposing a missing eyetooth. "Got a better proposition."

Brendan took a drink of his whiskey. "What kind of proposition?"

Boots's grin faded. "Nothin' a tinhorn like you'd be interested in."

"That so?"

Boots just grunted.

"Why not?"

The riverman reached a brawny arm behind his back and came up with the longest "Arkansas tooth-pick" Brendan had ever seen. "Ever use one a' these?" He stuck the wicked, gleaming blade into the bar, so close to Brendan's hand it almost cost him a finger.

Brendan smiled thinly. Easing his hand away, he reached behind his back, jerked his pistol, and jammed it beneath the big man's chin before he had a chance to move or even breathe. "You don't need one of those when you can use one of these."

Boots grinned again, this time a little nervously. "I take yer point. No offense intended."

Brendan pulled the knife from the bar, handed it to Boots, who slowly resheathed it, then he stuck the gun into the back of his breeches beneath his leather vest. "None taken."

"Buy my friend here a drink," Boots ordered, beginning to relax again. The barkeep brought them both a round, and Brendan tossed the balance of his first shot back in one gulp, the liquid burning a path down his throat.

"I'm gettin' damned tired of running up and down this river," Brendan said. "Gambling isn't the most reliable profession a man can pick. You need any help with that *proposition* you got, you let me know."

Boots eyed him a moment, then slugged back his whiskey. "Just supposin' that might be—how would I find you?"

Brendan polished off his second shot and set the glass back down on the rough-hewn bar. "You won't have to. I'll find you." Touching the brim of his hat in farewell, Brendan turned and strode to the door.

Outside, he ignored the smell of dead fish and rotting wood and headed back up the hill. Things were coming to a head—he could feel it in his bones. Now if his luck just held a little longer. . . .

Brendan's bright mood faded. His gambler's instinct said every lucky streak ended sooner or later, and his had already gone on far too long.

"If you children will give me a moment to get my shawl, we can take a walk. How does that sound?" When all three young Bannermans nodded enthusiastically, Priscilla left the parlor and went into the bedchamber, where she found the blue woolen shawl Sue Alice had loaned her.

She joined them out on the porch and thought how like his father Matt looked, how adorable the two little girls were standing there in their identical lace-trimmed pink pinafores. Patience stood a little taller, or Priscilla would have had trouble telling them apart.

"Where shall we go first?" she asked.

"Let's go see Herbert," Charity suggested.

"First I want to show you my new toy soldiers," Matt said. "They're guarding some enemy troops out in the garden."

How early they learn, Priscilla thought, wishing little boys didn't have to play war. But Patience took one hand, and Charity took the other, urging her along. Together the three of them strolled into the garden, helped Matt rearrange his troops, then checked on Herbert and several other of the family's animals. All the while, Priscilla listened to their tales of adventure.

Though she nodded with enthusiasm, she found it hard to concentrate, her mind turning instead to thoughts of Brendan. She wondered where he was and what he was doing.

If only he would confide in her.

Then she remembered the scene at the river, the way he had opened his heart and soul. In time, she believed, he would tell her what she wanted to know.

But as the afternoon wore on, she watched the sun make its way toward the horizon, and her worry increased. She hardly noticed when the twins got fidgety and asked to run ahead to the house. It wasn't that far away, so she nodded and they raced off while she walked back with Matthew, who held on to her hand.

They had just rounded the corner of the main house when she heard the shot—a loud echoing blast that vibrated the air around her. It took only a moment for Priscilla to realize it had come from the bachelor quarters. When she did, her heart nearly slammed through her chest. Grabbing up her skirts, she started running.

Heart pounding, terrified of what she might find, she raced toward the sound, opened the heavy front door that led into the parlor, and stopped dead in her tracks.

The desk drawer stood open; the key to the gun cabinet still rested in the lock of the open cabinet door. Brendan's spare pistol lay on the carpet at Patience's feet, and Charity's small body sprawled on the floor just a few feet away.

Dear God in heaven. Charity's pinafore ran red with blood, the carpet beneath her pooled with it, and it had splattered on the curtains. Priscilla gripped the doorjamb.

"Dear God. . . ." She looked at the lifeless little body and swayed on her feet. *Do something!* her mind screamed, but the walls moved in on her, squeezing her breath, and the room grew dim and narrow. Her vision blurred and the focus shifted until all she could see was the blood-drenched little body in front of her.

"What the hell . . . ?" Brendan stood behind her, but only for an instant. "Sweet Jesus!" Then he was moving, racing toward the stricken child. "Get me something to stop the bleeding," he commanded, but Priscilla didn't move.

He turned to Patience, who stood trembling, her face so pale it appeared almost translucent. "Go get your mother. Tell her Charity has been hurt and she's to get a doctor." The child spun and raced out of the room. Priscilla could hear her terrible sobs, but still she didn't move.

"I need bandages, Priscilla!" Brendan shouted, but the room had changed, grown distant and distorted, and the circle of blood seeped toward her. The walls of the room were red now, the curtains, and the carpets. They were closing in on her—just like they had before.

"Goddamn it, Priscilla!"

She should move, she knew, do whatever it was he wanted, but the blood was running toward her, and his voice sounded very far away. She heard the sound of running feet, looked across at Brendan, saw his mouth moving, but couldn't hear his words. When she looked again, it wasn't Brendan she saw but her father. Wounded and dying. Lying in the big brass bed, a woman she had never seen lying naked and silent beside him covered with blood.

No, Mama! No Mama! Mama, I'm so scared!

Go away, Priscilla. Go away from this place and never come back. Her mother walked back into the bloody bedchamber, the pistol still gripped in her hand. Her eyes looked bleak and lifeless. She closed the door in Priscilla's face as if she weren't there.

Mama? Priscilla jumped when her mother fired the gun. She heard a heavy thud, then nothing but silence. With trembling fingers, she turned the brass doorknob and pushed open the heavy wooden door. Her mother lay at the foot of the bed, as bloody as her father and the woman who lay beside him. Priscilla turned and ran.

Just as she did now.

She thought she heard someone calling out to her, but she couldn't be sure. It didn't really matter—she had to get away.

Just like before.

She would run until the hurting stopped, until her blood-red vision cleared. She would run until she couldn't remember the way her father had looked with his chest blown open, the way the woman had looked on the blood-soaked sheets beside him. The way her mother had looked in the crimson pool on the floor.

Priscilla ran until her sides ached and her legs burned. Her hair had come loose from its pins and hung wildly around her shoulders. Branches scratched her cheeks and tore her dress. Still she ran on. Twice she fell, but hardly noticed the mud that coated her skirts, just got up and kept going.

When she couldn't take another weary step, when her legs refused to hold her up, she sank down on the ground beneath a moss-hung oak, her heavy breathing broken only by her sobs.

How long she sat there, she didn't know, but only a half dome of orange flamed the horizon and the evening had started to chill. Priscilla leaned back against the trunk of the oak. She felt burned out. And empty clear to her soul. She'd stopped crying; she had no more tears.

Another hour passed before she had emptied her mind completely, had drained her heart of all emotion, and recovered herself enough to start back toward the house.

Back to poor little Charity, lying there dead on the floor.

Dear God in heaven.

Her stomach rolled and the bile rose up in her throat. Brendan's pistol had killed her, taken Sue

Alice's precious little girl just as a gun had killed her mother and father. She thought of the Indian she had shot in the back of the wagon, saw his bloody face, and closed her eyes against the terrible image. She felt sick inside and nearly as dead as the child on the floor.

As darkness surrounded her and the chill seeped into her bones, Priscilla walked back the way she had come. The numbness she felt stayed with her, blotting some of the pain and allowing her to function. She made a couple of wrong turns, but corrected her path until the lights of Evergreen blazed ahead of her. She didn't want to go back at all, but she had nowhere else to go.

She started for the front door, looked down at her ragged and muddy appearance, turned and walked to the house in the rear. It took all her resolve to go into the bloody parlor. But she fixed her eyes on the door to the bedchamber, walked in and closed the door. In minutes, she had straightened her hair, pulling it back into a severe knot at the back of her neck, and put on a clean brown gingham dress.

Back through the parlor, staring straight ahead, she walked out of the house toward the lights of the main house glowing across the garden. Until tonight she had never noticed how dark and cold it was on the path in between.

Pausing at the back door, Priscilla drew in a shaky breath, pulled it open and walked inside. Servants she knew but now couldn't seem to recall worked silently in the drawing room, but no one else was downstairs.

"Where are they?" she asked remotely.

"Upstairs, ma'am."

She climbed the stairs on weary legs that would barely hold her up, but finally she made it. Spotting Brendan's tall frame in the cluster of people outside a chamber door, she moved in that direction.

"Priscilla!" He broke away from the others and strode toward her, taking her cold hands in his warm ones. "Where in God's name have you been?" His eyes assessed her red and puffy eyes, the grayish hue of her skin. "You'd better sit down." He tried to guide her toward a chair in the hallway, but she pulled away.

"I've got to go to Sue Alice. Where is she?"

"She's in the room with Charity."

Priscilla nodded and started in that direction, but Brendan stopped her.

"You can't go in, the doctor's working over her. He wants as little disturbance as he can get."

That cut through her shell. "Working over her? I don't understand. Charity's dead."

Brendan shook his head. "The bullet went into her chest. She's in critical condition, but—"

Priscilla whimpered and sagged against him. His hard arm went around her, the only thing holding her up. "She's still alive?"

"Yes. You'd better sit down, Sill."

She shook her head, pulled away, and started for the door.

Brendan caught both her arms and forced her to face him. "You can't go in, Sill. The doctor says we have to wait."

It took a moment for his words to sink in. She raised her eyes from his chest to his face. "This is all your fault—you and your arsenal of weapons. The gun was yours. If you hadn't—"

Chris Bannerman cut off her words. "You're wrong, Priscilla. "My guns were in that case, too. It could just as easily have been one of mine."

She swallowed hard. "Then the fault is mine. I should have stayed with them, kept a closer watch."

"The children are old enough to play in their own home. You were only a little ways behind. You couldn't have known they'd seen Brendan put away the key."

He cleared his throat, but his voice still came out gruff. "If you're determined to place the blame on someone's shoulders, place it on mine. I've spent hours teaching my son to value and respect firearms, but never once have I spoken to the twins. I thought, because they were girls, it wasn't necessary. If I had seen to their education as I did Matthew's, Charity wouldn't be lying in there now." He looked older than he had just hours ago, but there was strength in his expression, and a determined force of will.

Priscilla didn't know what to say. "How . . . how is she?" she finally asked.

"Too soon to tell." Chris glanced toward the closed bedchamber door. On the opposite side, a man's and a woman's voice, speaking in hushed tones, seeped out into the hallway. "We'll know more in the morning. In the meantime, all we can do is pray."

And so they did.

Brendan had grown silent at Priscilla's accusation, and she remained in a state of exhausted numbness. But each of them prayed throughout the endless hours of the night. In the morning when the door swung open and the short balding doctor stepped into the passage, they roused their weary bones and went to meet him.

"The prognosis is good," the doctor said. "She's a strong little girl, and we've taken every precaution to prevent infection. I've given her laudanum; given a dose to Sue Alice as well, and one to poor little Patience. They'll sleep for a while." He looked Priscilla up and down. "It appears you could use a draught yourself, my dear."

"That's a good idea," Brendan agreed.

"No. I'm fine, really I am. I just need a little rest."

"Then I suggest you get it," the doctor said.

"Chris has moved your things into the guest room," Brendan told her. "I'll be staying in the room next door."

Priscilla felt a wave of relief. She dreaded returning to the guest house. And she needed some time alone, needed a chance to think things through. Excusing herself, she made her way down the hall, entered her bedchamber, and silently closed the door.

"Priscilla is taking this nearly as hard as Sue Alice," Chris said, staring after her.

"She loves children. She feels very close to yours."

"I think it's more than that. Something's not right, Bren. If I were you, I'd keep an eye on her."

Brendan released a weary breath. "She wants to be alone, she's made that perfectly clear." He hadn't missed her look of relief that they would be sleeping apart. He hadn't missed her scathing accusation that he was to blame, either.

Chris glanced at Priscilla's door, then back to

Brendan, whose face looked tense and strained. "I meant what I said about the gun. This wasn't your fault, Bren, any more than it was Patience's or Priscilla's. It was an accident, one which—with God's help—we'll all survive. Years ago, when my father turned over that wagon and it cut off my arm, he hated himself. Nearly drank himself to death before it was through. That was an accident, just like this. God's will, Brendan, nothing more."

Brendan mustered a tired, faint smile. "Thanks, Chris."

Chapter 18

 "How is she, Doctor Seely?" Priscilla stood outside the bedchamber door as she had off and on throughout the day, anxiously awaiting the balding doctor's words.

He removed the pince-nez spectacles from the end of his blunt nose, looked up at her, and smiled. "She's over the worst of it." Chris and Sue Alice had gone in over an hour ago, but Brendan and Priscilla waited outside in the hall. "Starting tomorrow she can have visitors—not so many as to tire her, but enough to keep up her spirits."

"Thank God," Priscilla said softly.

"Thanks, Doctor Seely." Brendan shook the doctor's thin hand.

"You'd best be saving your thanks for the good Lord. He had more to do with it than I did."

Brendan smiled. "We'll do that."

They both went in and stood by the bed, looking down at Charity's sleeping figure. "Why don't you let me sit with her a while?" Priscilla asked Sue Alice.

"I want to be here in case she wakes up," Sue Alice said, but she looked tired and badly in need of sleep.

"I promise I'll wake you the moment she stirs."

"She's out of the woods," Chris said. "It's you we've got to worry about now."

His wife smiled wanly. "I suppose you're right."

"Come on." Chris took her hand. "I think a little rest would do us both a world of good." He led her from the room and closed the door behind them.

"Would you like me to sit with you?" Brendan asked.

"No."

"Are you sure?"

"I'll be just fine."

"If you get tired, I'll be right down the hall." Brendan watched her a moment, then quietly left the room.

After that, Priscilla spent hours by the little girl's side, spelling Sue Alice and telling Charity stories. Patience often sat with them, holding onto her sister's hand. Priscilla worried about the other twin as much as she did Charity, who was recovering remarkably well.

Priscilla spent a great deal of time with both of the girls, but to Brendan she said little. He had moved back into the bachelor quarters but she had remained in the house.

"I don't like it, Priscilla. What if someone discovers who you are and tells Egan?"

"I'll stay in my room whenever someone comes. I-I'm just not ready to go back out there."

She wasn't ready. In fact, he thought, Priscilla seemed glad for the distance it put between them.

Several times he had tried to start conversations, but she had found one excuse after another to end them before they got started. Then one night after supper, he stopped her on the way up the stairs.

"It's a lovely evening, Priscilla. Why don't we go for a walk in the garden?"

"I need to check on Charity."

"Sue Alice is up there, and we need to talk."

Brendan thought she might refuse, then with a look of resignation, she nodded.

Outside the full moon glistened on the leaves of a spreading magnolia as they strolled along a path in the garden. Brendan laced Priscilla's arm through his but it rested there limply, and her eyes looked cloudy and far away.

"I know this has been hard on you," he said, drawing her into the shadows beneath the tree. "But Charity is going to be fine, and it's time things got back to normal."

Priscilla looked up at him. "Normal? What makes you think things will ever be normal again?"

"What are you talking about?"

"You saw what happened to me. When I saw Charity lying there in all of that blood, I panicked. I couldn't even move. What would have happened if that child had been ours? What would have happened if we were living in some wilderness in Texas and you hadn't been there? I couldn't handle it, Brendan. If it hadn't been for you, God knows what might have happened."

"Listen to me, Priscilla—"

"No, Brendan. When I listen to you, I believe I can do the things you say. I believe we'll be happy and everything will be all right. After what's happened, I'm just not sure anymore."

"You're tired, is all. Once you're feeling better—"

Priscilla shook her head. "My parents brought me into a gentle life. Aunt Maddie taught me to be a proper lady. I don't know how to be a frontier woman."

Her face looked pale, her eyes distant. He had never seen her look quite that way.

"Stuart saw the truth," she was saying. "With his money, he could have protected me, sheltered me. What you're asking me to do is accept this horrible violence that seems to surround you and learn to live with it. Well, I don't know if I can."

Brendan's expression turned hard. Who was this woman who looked like Priscilla but sounded nothing like her? Where was the courageous woman who had followed him across the plains?

"I believe you can do whatever it is you want to. But you're the one who has to choose." His eyes searched her face, hoping to reach her, hoping to rouse some emotion. "You can be your long-dead parents' little girl, your aunt's too-proper niece, or Stuart Egan's possession. Or you can be your own woman—live your life as you see fit. It's up to you, Priscilla."

She didn't answer. Brendan watched her a moment more, trying to read her expression. He had never seen her so remote, so guarded. He wouldn't have believed this was the same woman who had fought her way across the Texas frontier, determined to make a life for herself.

When Priscilla still said nothing, Brendan turned and walked away. She didn't return to the house for several hours more. By the time she did, he had gone.

* * *

"You can't be serious."

"I assure you, Chris, I'm deadly serious." Brendan sat beside Chris Bannerman at a small wooden table in a corner of the Main Street Tavern. It was a quiet little place, a well-run establishment frequented by the more successful local planters. "She doesn't think she's cut out for a life on the Texas frontier."

At the dismal expression Brendan had worn back into the house, Chris had suggested they go out for a brandy. Brendan had gratefully agreed. Afterward, he would make his rounds, searching for information in the gaudy saloons of Natchez-under-the-Hill.

"But she loves you," Chris said. "It's written all over her face every time she looks at you."

"Not lately. Ever since the accident, she hardly knows I'm alive. I guess she blames me. . . . Or maybe . . . ah, hell, Chris, I just don't know."

"Give her some time, Bren. Surely, she'll snap out of it."

"Maybe. . . . Then again, maybe she won't. I owe her one helluva debt for helping me deal with the past, but I'm not willing to give up the rest of my life in repayment. If she doesn't want me, I sure as hell don't want her."

"With a little patience, maybe you can bring her around, make her see things more clearly."

"A dozen people tried that with me, and it didn't do a lick of good. Only one person can put things right for Priscilla—and that's Priscilla. There's not a damn thing I can say or do. It has to be her choice."

He took a sip of his brandy. "To tell you the truth, Chris, I'm beginning to think she may be right. In fact, when I met her, I did everything in my power to convince her she wasn't cut out for a life on the plains. Now, well . . ." He picked up his glass and shot the amber contents to the back of his throat. He grimaced as the burning liquid trickled down to his stomach.

"I don't suppose you'd consider returning to Savannah? Your brother could help you make a fresh start there."

Brendan twirled the empty glass in his hand. "If I thought it could work, I might consider it, but it isn't where I belong. The truth is, a life on the Texas frontier is only part of the problem." He set the glass down hard on the table.

"I've got to get going," he told Chris, dropping several coins beside the glass. "I've been talkin' to a fella who may be involved with McLeary. Every time I see him, he opens up a little more. Another friendly nudge and a little more free whiskey just might do the trick."

"If you can find out when the next raid is planned, we'll bring in the sheriff, arrest McLeary in the act, and press him to incriminate Egan."

"That happens, I'll be in the clear and on my way back to Texas." *With or without Priscilla*, he thought, but didn't say.

Priscilla tied her wide-brimmed bonnet beneath her chin, picked up her reticule, looping it over a gloved hand, descended the servants' stairs, and went out the back door. At the rear of the house, she found Zachary, the huge black servant who handled the livery, and asked him to bring one of the smaller carriages around.

She felt a little guilty, not having asked permission, but Chris was out and Sue Alice was upstairs reading to Charity. Besides, if she told them where she was headed, they might not let her go.

Since the hour was late, Zachary drove the carriage himself. She figured he'd decided to act as her protector. If so, she felt grateful.

"Where we goin', ma'am?"

"The Middleton Hotel."

He didn't say more, just clucked the horses into a trot. They traveled through the quieting streets and finally rounded a corner onto Washington. Near the corner of Wall sat the Middleton Hotel. Zachary pulled the animals to a halt.

"I be waitin' right here," he said, and his dark eyes seemed to assess her.

She knew what he was thinking—why was an unescorted female traveling in the evening to a hotel alone?

Fortunately, she didn't have to tell him. Priscilla lifted her rust silk faille skirts, stepped down from the carriage, and crossed the boardwalk, entering the green-shuttered, solid-looking building. Inside the lobby, done in a heavy Spanish motif with thick wooden beams and red-tiled floors, she approached the front desk and spoke to a thin, sallow-skinned man in a dark gray tailcoat who leaned back in his chair, reading a book.

"Excuse me," Priscilla said, "I'm looking for a woman named Rose Conners. Could you tell me which room she's in?" When the clerk didn't answer quickly enough, she added, "She's Mr. McLeary's . . . niece."

He arched a thin gray brow. "McLeary's suite's on the second floor, down at the end of the hall. You want I should tell 'em you're here?"

"Are . . . are both of them in this evening?" *Please, God, let McLeary be working."*

"Only Miss Rose. McLeary's down at the tavern."

Thank you, Lord. "Then I'll just go on up." She wanted this meeting in private, not in the hotel lobby. It would be hard enough without an audience.

"Suit yourself," the clerk said, burying his nose back in his book, Richard Henry Dana's *Two Years Before the Mast.*

Priscilla climbed the stairs with determination, and an eerie sense of fatalism. Since she'd run into Rose Conners that day on the boardwalk, this meeting seemed destined to occur.

Priscilla knocked on the heavy oak door. She could hear feminine footfalls and the sound of rustling skirts, then the lock turned, and the door swung open.

"Hello," Priscilla said softly. "May I come in?"

Rose Conners surveyed her from head to foot. "Why not? I expected you to show up sooner or later."

Priscilla followed her into the well-appointed parlor. "Then I gather you know who I am?"

"I know."

"Then you must know why I've come."

"I haven't the vaguest idea," Rose said, "but I figured you'd piece things together sooner or later. When you did, I assumed you'd come here to gloat."

"Gloat?" Priscilla repeated. "Why on earth would I do that?"

Rose motioned for her to take a seat on the brown horsehair sofa and Priscilla sat down, then busied herself arranging her rust silk skirts. The room smelled pleasantly of the bayberry tapers sitting on the table. It was furnished in a heavy but comfortable Spanish motif, and looked immaculately clean.

"How 'bout a brandy? Sorry, I'm fresh outta tea." There was an edge to every word, a bitterness that hadn't been there at their first meeting.

"I believe I could use a drink," Priscilla said, refusing to be intimidated, though she had certainly never tried alcohol of any sort before.

Rose poured brandy from a cut-crystal decanter into two crystal snifters, crossed the room and handed Priscilla a glass. She wore an expensive turquoise quilted silk wrapper, ruffled at the wrists, high-necked, and buttoned up the front. Long dark brown hair, the same shade as Priscilla's own, hung nearly to her waist, and her skin looked smooth and clear.

She was more robust than Priscilla, slender, yet more amply endowed, her features a little less refined. But the resemblance was there—Priscilla could see it in the curve of her soft pink lips, the arch of her fine dark brows. For the first time she noticed the slight bruise beside the woman's left eye.

"Admiring Caleb's handiwork, are you?" Rose sat down on a wing-backed chair across from her and took a drink of her brandy.

More violence. Dear God, how she hated it! "Why . . . why did he do it?"

"Apparently one of his cutthroats mentioned my

untimely luncheon with your friend, Jaimie Walker. Caleb doesn't like me talking to other men."

"Why don't you just leave?"

She scoffed. "Where would I go? How would I support myself?"

"You're obviously intelligent. Surely you could get a job, find some way to take care of yourself."

"Look, Priscilla—that is your name as I recall? What I do is none of your concern. It wasn't eighteen years ago, it isn't now."

"I was only six years old. I didn't even remember what happened until a few nights ago."

"You didn't remember?" Rose came out of her chair. "Your mother killed my parents, and for all those years you didn't remember? Well, I sure as hell remember. Every day of my life I cursed that woman for what she did. Every day I cursed you for having a family to take you in while I went hungry and slept on a cornhusk mattress down at the whorehouse. You didn't remember—and I could never forget!"

Priscilla just sat there. The clock on the mantel ticked loudly. "I'm sorry," she finally said. "My aunt never told me what happened. My memory . . . lapsed. If I hadn't come back to Natchez, I might never have remembered. But there was an accident —a shooting—and I put the pieces together. I recalled things my aunt said, when she didn't know I was around. I remember my mother crying, talking about you and your mother. Saying how Megan O'Conner had stolen my father's love."

"He was married to your mother, but he was in love with mine. We were a family."

Priscilla felt a lump swell up in her throat. "I loved him, too."

"You didn't even remember him."

What could she say? In a way it was the truth. "So much violence," she finally said. "Why does it have to be this way?"

"That's just life, Priscilla. You might as well get used to it."

"I can't. I know that now. As soon as I can get the money, I'm leaving for Cincinnati. I'll find a job, a way to support myself."

"What about your fancy husband? Looks to me like he's taking care of you just fine."

"I left Stuart several days ago. I don't love him—I never did." Brendan's face rose up, but she blotted it out. "I'm getting an annulment, and I'm going back home." *Where I belong.* "Why don't you come with me?"

Rose laughed aloud. "I've spent the better part of my life working my way out of the gutter. I'm not about to return to it now."

"You'd rather stay with a man who beats you?"

"Maybe. And maybe . . . someone . . . will come along who doesn't beat me." She straightened in her chair. "Until then, I'll stay right here. If you were smart, you'd do the same."

Priscilla almost wished she could. It would be so simple to let Stuart take care of her as he'd wanted to from the start. But she didn't love him, and she had continued to betray him with Brendan. She could never go back to him now.

Priscilla set the brandy snifter aside and stood up. "Thank you for seeing me. After all that's happened,

I know you have every reason to hate me, but I hope
you'll think about what I've told you and try to understand. Whether you like it or not, we're sisters—"

"Half sisters," Rose corrected.

"Like it or not, we're the only family we've got."

Rose set her own glass down and strode past Priscilla to the door. "It's too late for family. I've got
myself—it's always been enough."

Priscilla studied her sister's pretty face and something stirred inside her. She felt a flutter of warmth,
but it wasn't enough to melt the icy shell she had
built around her heart. "Maybe if we had more
time. . . ."

"Maybe. . . ."

But they didn't. Priscilla walked out the door.

In the morning she spoke to Sue Alice. Though Priscilla hadn't seen him, Brendan had come home
sometime during the night. The servants mentioned
his appearance for breakfast, and that he'd left for
the cotton fields with Chris.

Priscilla felt nothing but relief. She talked to Sue
Alice, explaining her decision to go back to Cincinnati. As she had expected, Sue Alice tried to dissuade
her, but when she saw the extent of Priscilla's determination, agreed to give her the money she would
need.

"I won't accept your charity," Priscilla said. "But
if you and Chris will make me a loan, I'll pay it back
just as soon as I'm able. I don't need much, just
enough for a steamboat ticket and a place to live until
I can get a job."

"Are you sure about this? Until Charity's accident,

you and Brendan seemed so happy. Why don't you
wait a while, let things settle down?"

Priscilla staunchly refused. "I just want to go
home. I want to live where things are normal. I don't
want to face unpleasant memories or try to be something I'm not."

"When are you plannin' to leave?"

"Tomorrow. If that's all right with you."

"What about Brendan?"

"I'll speak to him tonight. I'm sure that once he
thinks things over, he'll see that I'm right."

Sue Alice took her hand. "Life's never easy, Priscilla. Sometimes what seems to be the simplest path
turns out to be the hardest. At times it's better t' face
up t' things than let them lie."

"Not this time."

Sue Alice sighed. "I hope for both a' your sakes
you're right."

The meal that night was strained and a little too
silent. Everyone seemed to sense the coming con-
frontation. When Priscilla declined a sherry in the
drawing room with her hostess and asked for a moment with Brendan, the others politely melted away.

She took his arm and let him lead her out the
French doors to the garden. The moon had begun to
wane, but it still lit their way. Whale-oil lanterns
along the oyster-shell path helped a little more.

"I hope your investigation is proceeding as you
wished," Priscilla said, breaking the awkward silence.

Brendan drew a small cigar from the pocket of his
shirt, struck a match against the trunk of a magnolia,
and lit up, blowing a puff of pungent tobacco smoke

into the air. "As a matter of fact, I think we're very close to a solution."

"I'm glad to hear it."

"As soon as things are cleared up, I'll be going back to Texas." Light blue eyes searched her face. "Will you be going with me, Silla?"

An ache rippled through her, then it was gone. "I'm afraid that's not possible. I've given this a lot of thought, Brendan. It just isn't going to work between us. I'm not cut out for the sort of life you want me to lead. I'm going back to Cincinnati, back where I belong."

A muscle in his jaw grew taut. "Now who's running?"

Priscilla glanced away. "Maybe I am. It doesn't really matter. My decision is made. I'm leaving sometime tomorrow."

"I hear your voice, Priscilla. I hear you speaking, but I don't recognize the woman who's saying the words. I wish I understood what's happened. If I've done something . . . if you still feel I'm responsible for Charity's accident—"

"It isn't that. Chris was right. What happened was an accident."

"If there's anything I can do, anything I can say to put things back the way they were, just tell me." She only shook her head. "We had something special, Priscilla. Whenever we were together, whenever we made love—"

"What happened between us was a mistake. I hope you'll try to understand."

He took a long draw on his cigar, exhaled slowly, the smoke curling into the cool night sky, then he dropped it on the ground and crushed it out with the heel of his boot.

"There was a time, Priscilla, when I admired you. I watched you cross that prairie and nothing seemed able to stop you. You knew nothing of the country, nothing of that way of life, and yet you kept on. You had more grit, more determination than any ten women I'd ever known. Now, I look at you and I wonder whatever gave me the idea you could help me conquer that land of mine—whatever made me think you could even survive."

He caught her chin and roughly forced her to look at him. "I guess I was right about you in the first place. Tomorrow you get on that boat and you go back to wherever it was you came from. I don't want you. I don't need you. And I don't love you—maybe I never did."

Brendan let her go. With a look that told her exactly what he thought of her, he turned his back and strode toward the house. She watched the angry set to his broad shoulders, the movement of his narrow hips, she watched the way the muscles bunched beneath his shirt, the moonlight on his thick dark hair.

I don't want you. I don't need you. And I don't love you—maybe I never did.

He disappeared inside the house, and Priscilla felt the solitude like a weight across her shoulders. She stared at the door he'd closed between them—the door she had closed—and wondered for the first time if she had done the right thing.

In minutes the door opened again and Brendan strode out, heading toward the stables in the rear.

For the first time in days, her heart did more than thud dully against her ribs. It beat with an intensity that frightened her. Her chest felt tight, tears filled her eyes and began to slip down her cheeks.

I don't want you. I don't need you. And I don't love you—maybe I never did.

Priscilla sat there trembling, hurting inside and not understanding. This was what she wanted, wasn't it? It had seemed so right when she'd made her decision. In the glow of the moon she saw Brendan's tall silhouette atop one of Chris Bannerman's big bay horses. He pulled his hat brim down and rode off without a backward glance.

For the very first time it occurred to her just exactly what she was giving up. Brendan was the man she loved, the only man she would ever love. He was strong and loving, giving and caring, passionate and protective. For her there would never be a man who could take his place.

She had wanted home and family above all else— but she also wanted love.

Brendan had offered her those things and more, yet she had turned him away.

The lump in her throat grew so big it threatened to choke her. She *had* to go back. She wasn't cut out for his kind of life.

I don't want you. I don't need you. And I don't love you—maybe I never did.

She had meant to end their relationship in the gentlest possible way. It had never occurred to her that Brendan might be wanting an end to it, too.

Priscilla forced her feet to move ahead, forced herself to walk the lonely pathway through the garden.

As long she had thought he loved her, she'd been able to maintain control, keep her tight, protective wall around her. In a perverse way, she suddenly realized, it was the strength of Brendan's love that made her able to give him up. Without it, she saw the truth of how lonely and bleak her life would be.

I don't want you. I don't need you. And I don't love you—maybe I never did.

Never had so few words hurt so much. It should have made things easier, knowing this was what he wanted, too. Instead, a new pain lanced her heart, burning, twisting, hurting more with every step. There was no numbness now, no emptiness to shield her. During the days after the accident, she had lost him, her coldness had driven him away. It was what she had wanted—what she'd had to do in order to survive.

Now that she had achieved her goal, she wanted nothing more than a merciful end to her agony.

You've got to go through with this, Priscilla. You can't live the way he does. The voice inside her strengthened her resolve. She thought of little Charity, lying on the floor in a pool of blood, of the way she had panicked and run. She remembered the Indian she had killed, how sick and empty she had felt. She was doing the right thing.

Besides, Brendan didn't want her—she really had no choice.

Placing one unsteady step in front of another, she had almost reached the porch when the snap of a twig underfoot drew her attention.

"Matthew?" She prayed the disturbing sound was

just the boy, playing some childish game. Instead Mace Harding stepped from the cover of a tree, his black eyes glinting with triumph. "Evenin', Miz Egan. Time to go home."

Chapter 19

Merciful heavens, when will this night-mare end? Priscilla tried to scream, but Harding's hand clamped over her mouth.

Dave Reeves and Kyle Sturgis, two of Stuart's henchman, stepped up beside Mace to help him still her movements, stuff a gag into her mouth, and bind her hands and feet. They dropped a canvas bag over her head, then one of them lifted her onto his shoulder.

"I've got an errand to run," Mace said, dumping her roughly on the floor of a carriage. "You two can take it from here."

"Don't worry, we'll get her home," one of them said. Mace's footfalls receded, she heard the sound of horse's hooves riding away, then the carriage started up.

How had they found her? Only the Bannermans and Brendan knew she was staying at Evergreen. And, of course, Barton Stevens, the attorney whose name would have appeared on the annulment papers.

Now that she thought about it, Stuart would have very little trouble forcing a demure little man like Stevens to talk. But why bother? She had shown Stuart clearly this time that she didn't want to be his wife. Why didn't he just let her go?

The carriage rolled over the cobblestones, jolting

her with every rock and pothole, but eventually came to a halt. Someone carried her into the house, which she recognized as Stuart's when Kyle pulled the sack off her head, tearing the last of the pins from her hair. It tumbled in a riot of long dark curls around her shoulders.

"Welcome home, my dear." Stuart stood in the foyer, looking as handsome and imposing as ever. He wore an expensive dark gray frock coat, brocade silver waistcoat, and light gray trousers, his sandy hair perfectly groomed. "Take her upstairs to her room, untie her, and lock her in."

Sturgis lifted her into his arms, climbed the stairs, and carried her into the room she had occupied before. Using a knife he took from the sheath at his waist, he cut the ropes that bound her wrists and ankles, then untied the gag in her mouth.

"As the boss says, 'Welcome home, ma'am.'" He gave her a look that clearly spoke disapproval, then went out and locked the door.

Priscilla sank down on the bed. "Dear Lord, what will happen to me now?"

Brendan might not be home for hours and even when he got there, considering his problems with the law and the way things stood between them, she wasn't sure he'd involve himself in her life again. Even when Chris and Sue Alice discovered her missing, with her sporadic comings and goings of late, they wouldn't start looking for her right away. In the meantime, what would Stuart do?

As the thought occurred, footsteps echoed in the hallway. Two men. The heavier footfalls she recognized as Stuart's. Outside the room, a key grated in the lock, the door swung open, and Stuart walked in. He held a brandy snifter in one hand and a glass of sherry in the other. While Priscilla stood staring, he crossed the room and extended the sherry.

"I'm not thirsty."

"Take it."

"I don't want it."

Stuart set his snifter on the bureau, carried the sherry to where she stood, clasped the back of her neck, and forced the glass against her lips. Priscilla tried to twist away, but his hold grew tighter and he held her easily. She finally gulped down a burning swallow, and he took the glass away.

"That's better," he said.

"I want an annulment, Stuart." Her voice sounded shaky; she prayed he wouldn't notice. "Surely, Mr. Stevens has made that perfectly clear."

"Mr. Stevens has been out of town," he said with an iron control that was only too apparent. "Or I would have located your whereabouts sooner."

"Why are you doing this? You don't love me, and I don't love you. I want to go back to Cincinnati." *No you don't. You want to be with Brendan.* The unbidden thought rocked her almost as much as Stuart's presence. "I . . . I want to go home." *Liar.*

"Your home is with me, my dear. You're my wife, though you seem unable to accept that." He took a sip of his brandy, set the glass down, and pulled off his frock coat, hanging it neatly over the back of a brocade satin chair.

"I'm partly to blame for that," he said. "If I had done my duty by you that first night, none of this would have happened." He unfastened a diamond stickpin, untied his black silk stock, and laid them over the chair.

"What . . . what are you doing?"

"What I should have done before—ending any grounds you might have for an annulment. Take off your dress, Priscilla. It isn't up to the quality I had purchased for you, but I'm sure you don't want to see it in shreds." He started unbuttoning his shirt.

"But . . . but what about the time I spent with Brendan . . . your concern for legitimate heirs?"

He tugged the shirt from the waistband of his breeches, unbuttoned the cuffs, shrugged it off and tossed it away. The sandy hair on his chest glistened in the lamplight. His face and neck were tanned, his hands and wrists, but the rest of his skin looked pale.

"Are you carrying Trask's child?" he asked.

"It's . . . possible." She hadn't thought about it before—now that she did, a surge of joy welled up inside her.

"You monthly time has come and gone—either you are or you aren't. Either way, it doesn't matter."

He doesn't know Brendan's in Natchez. Mace Harding hadn't seen them together! At least Brendan was safe. Stuart started toward her, but Priscilla backed away.

"Stuart, please. It's never going to work out between us. I don't want to be your wife."

Stuart's eyes turned hard. "I intend to have you, Priscilla. Whether you believe it or not, I've discovered I'm quite fond of you. Now you may remove that dress, get in that bed, and do your wifely duty—or you may fight me. In which case, I will call Kyle Sturgis in here to hold you down and strip you naked. If it takes all four of my men, I intend to lay claim to you this evening, my dear. I would suggest you make up your mind to it."

Priscilla just stood there. "No."

In two angry strides, Stuart reached her, grabbed the front of her dark green silk dress, and ripped it to her waist. The sound of rending fabric echoed in the silence of the room. Her heart lodged somewhere in her throat, Priscilla tried to fight him, but he was stronger than she ever would have guessed.

Dragging her over to the big four-poster bed, he pressed her down on the soft feather mattress, grabbed her chemise and ripped it open, leaving her breasts bare above the top of her corset. Priscilla raked her nails down his cheek.

Stuart hissed at the stinging sensation. His mouth went thin, and he slapped her hard across the face. Several more stunning blows had her ears ringing and tears burning her eyes.

"It's a shame I've had to hurt you, but you've left me no choice. I want you, Priscilla. You have thwarted me at every turn, but it has only made me want you more." He shoved up her skirts, his damp palm sliding along her thigh as he fumbled with the buttons at the front of his trousers.

Priscilla tried to twist free, but her mass of hair had been caught beneath her, and it pulled her scalp painfully. She tried to kick him, tried to bite—and barely heard the pounding at the door.

At first she thought it was just her heart, slamming against the walls of her chest.

"What the blazes do you want?" Stuart called out, breathing heavily, keeping Priscilla's wrists pinned.

"Sorry to bother you, boss, but there's a message from Harding—he says it can't wait."

Stuart worked to control his temper. "It better damned well be important, Sturgis, or you'll both be out of a job." He let go of her arms, and Priscilla covered her breasts with them.

"Take these moments to resign yourself, Priscilla. The next time I step across that threshold, you will be my wife in every way."

Priscilla bit back the sob in her throat. Stuart climbed off her, pulled on his shirt and tucked it in, then fastened his trousers. Grabbing his frock coat from the back of the chair, he strode toward the door.

When he slammed it behind him and turned the key in the lock, Priscilla started to cry.

"It's him all right, the bastard." Stuart peered through the crack in the door to the storeroom and fought to control his anger.

Through the smoke in the roomful of grimy, boisterous rivermen, he saw Brendan Trask leaning against the bar, sipping a whiskey. He was dressed like a gambler, ruffle-fronted white shirt, leather vest, and black breeches. A flatboat man named Boots Marlin, one of McLeary's men, stood beside him, flapping his jaws.

Stuart turned toward Mace, fists balled tightly at his sides. "You did right in sending for me. We need to know why he's here."

"You want us to take him? I'll make him talk—I promise you."

Stuart glanced toward the door. "I'd rather have

you follow him, see what he's up to, but with the raid coming off tomorrow, I'm afraid we don't have that much time. Take a couple of McLeary's men and wait for him outside the tavern. Once you've got him, tie him up in the cave. Do what you can to make him talk, but don't kill him—I want that pleasure my-self."

Stuart turned away and started toward the back door. "I've got plans for the evening," he finished. "I'll be back tomorrow. When we're through with him, we'll take him out to the sandbar and get rid of him along with McLeary and Dobbs. We'll take their cut of the profits from the *St. Louis* and be on our way back home."

Harding smiled, his face looking gaunt and mean. "All neat and tidy." A raspy chuckle escaped from his throat.

"Exactly," Stuart agreed. *In the meantime I'll deal with that lying little whore I married.* "It's getting late," he said, "I've got to be getting back."

Mace smiled thinly. "Have a good time, boss."

A little over an hour had passed before Priscilla could rouse herself enough to move off the bed. When she did, it was to the rasp of metal scraping against metal—someone was twisting the lock on her door!

Priscilla glanced around the room for something to use to defend herself, spotted nothing but the heavy, ornate Chinese vase on the pedestal near the door, and started toward it.

With a gasp, she realized the bodice of her dress hung open, exposing her breasts. Priscilla caught the

ends of the shredded green fabric, tied them together
in a crude knot that at least gave her some semblance
of modesty, and hurried to pick up the vase. She
stepped behind the door just as it swung open.

Gripping the vase above her head with trembling
hands, Priscilla held her breath.

"Priscilla?" came the whispered word. "It's me,
Jaimie."

The air she'd been holding rushed from her lungs.
Lowering the vase, she stepped from behind the
door. "Jaimie—thank God."

He closed the door behind them. "I picked the
lock," he explained. "I had to see if you were all
right." His eyes ran over her face, noting the bruise
that already darkened her cheek, the one along her
jaw. He saw her torn dress and the scratches on her
neck and shoulders. "Good Lord, Priscilla—I can't
believe the boss would do such a thing."

"He's planning to finish what he started, Jaimie.
You've got to help me."

"If I'd had any idea . . . if I'd thought for a minute he'd hurt you, I wouldn't have told him where
you were."

"*You* told him? How did you find out?"

"I talked to Stevens. Threatened him a little. It
wasn't too hard." He touched her cheek and unconsciously she flinched. "Damn him. We've got to get
you out of here."

Priscilla nodded, feeling a rush of hope. She
should have known she could count on Jaimie. "I
can't go back to Evergreen." That would lead Egan
straight to Brendan. "I've got to find someplace else
to go until I can get out of town."

Jaimie crossed the room and threw open the door to her armoire. He pulled a satchel from the bottom and tossed it onto the bed. "We'll go to your sister's. You'll be safe there."

"How . . . how did you know about Rose?"

"She told me about you, after you went to see her." He motioned toward the satchel. "You'd better hurry, Priscilla."

Priscilla threw open her bureau drawers, pulled out a few undergarments and as many dresses as she could fit into the satchel. She wanted nothing from Stuart Egan, but she figured the bruises on her face and the trouble he'd caused were payment enough.

"What about McLeary?" She closed up the satchel.

"He's out of town for a couple of days. Rose is alone."

"How do you know she'll help me?"

Jaimie smiled. "She's a good woman, Priscilla. She's tough on the outside, but her heart is pure gold. She'll help you, all right."

Jaimie crossed the room to the desk and pulled open the top drawer.

"What are you looking for?"

"This." He held up a silver-handled letter opener, went to the door and jimmied the lock, then tossed the opener onto the floor. "He'll think you got out by yourself." Hoisting her bag onto a shoulder, he motioned her toward the door, and they moved silently into the hallway.

After listening for a moment to be certain no one was near, they crept toward the stairs in the back. Outside, they walked a goodly distance from the house, hailed a hack, and climbed aboard.

It didn't take long to reach the Middleton Hotel. Pulling her shawl a little closer around her, covering the rips and tears in her dress, they entered the lobby and climbed the stairs.

Jaimie knocked on the door. "It's me, Rose," he called through the heavy plank door.

Priscilla didn't miss the warmth in his words. A few minutes later, the door swung open, and Rose stood framed in the entry. She took in Priscilla's battered appearance in an instant.

"My God, what's happened?"

"Egan's gone crazy," Jaimie said. "I had to get her outta there."

Rose hesitated only a moment. Wearing her pretty turquoise wrapper, her hair hanging down to her waist, she motioned them in and closed the door.

"I know this is a great deal to ask," Priscilla said, "but I've got nowhere else to go."

Rose eyed her a moment, then shrugged. "What's one more stray cat?" She indicated Priscilla should sit down on the horsehair sofa.

Jaimie carried the satchel into one of the bedchambers, and Rose followed him in. Priscilla heard them speaking in low tones, heard her dresses being pulled from the satchel and hung up, then they walked back into the room.

"I can't stay," Jaimie said.

"Egan's going to be furious," Rose said.

"He won't know I had any part in it." He went to the door, and Rose followed. "He's planning to leave for Texas within the week. He's got to get back to the Triple R. If he doesn't find her by the time his boat is ready to leave, I suspect he'll let her go. I'll let you know what's going on."

Rose looked at him, a softness creeping into her face. Jaimie saw it and touched her cheek. "I'll be back, Rose. I won't leave you here with McLeary. I won't let him hurt you again."

Rose's pretty brown eyes went wide. She started to speak, but didn't.

"I'll be back," he repeated, bent down and kissed her, a gentle, possessive kiss that seemed to surprise them both.

"Be careful." Rose sounded a little bit breathless.

Jaimie grinned. He looked handsome and much more in charge than Priscilla had ever seen him. "I will." He went out and closed the door.

Rose crossed the room, looking a little bit dazed. She flushed beneath Priscilla's regard, then straightened her shoulders and regained her taut control. "Why don't I ring for some tea?"

Priscilla smiled wearily. "I'd rather have a brandy."

Rose glanced at her in surprise, saw nothing but her sister's grateful regard, and returned the smile.

"Good idea." She poured two crystal snifters, handed one to Priscilla, and sat down in the chair across from her.

Priscilla sipped the brandy, which felt warm and relaxing. "Jaimie's a wonderful man," she said.

"A very good man." Rose glanced away, toying with the snifter, running a long slim finger around the rim. "Too good for someone like me."

Priscilla leaned forward, feeling a surge of protectiveness she wouldn't have expected. Her eyes went from her sister's dark chestnut hair so like her own, to the full pink lips and big brown eyes. Their features were similar, but Rose's face held a guardedness, almost an agedness that Priscilla's didn't. Her heart went out to the woman who had suffered so much.

"Jaimie doesn't believe that. He obviously thinks a great deal of you. It seems you think something of him as well."

"We haven't spent much time together," Rose said. "You know him far better than I."

Priscilla arched a brow, wondering at the tone of her sister's words. "Jaimie and I are friends, nothing more. I only met him when I reached the Triple R."

Rose seemed relieved, though she did her best to hide it. "I thought maybe . . . you see it was Jaimie who wrote you the letters."

Priscilla's own dark eyes went wide. "Jaimie wrote the letters? But they were from Stuart."

"Egan told him a few things he wanted you to know, Jaimie filled in the rest. Egan didn't want to be bothered."

Priscilla's hand gripped the folds of her skirt. "I should have known! I knew something about him wasn't right. The man in the letters was so honest, so gentle. I thought Stuart had somehow buried those qualities, that they were someplace deep inside him. It gave me hope that things might work out between us."

She looked across at Rose. "The truth is he's exactly the brutal, self-serving—bastard—he seems."

Rose watched her closely, as if there was more she ought to say, but didn't. "Jaimie said there was a man . . . someone you fell in love with . . . a gun-man back in Texas."

Priscilla felt a lump rise up in her throat. "His name is Brendan." A pain knifed through her chest just to think of him. "I fell in love with him almost the moment I saw him."

"Jaimie said Egan had him arrested for murder. Do you know if he's . . . if he's . . . ?"

Priscilla smiled. She couldn't help it. She remembered the feel of his hands on her body, of his warm lips covering her mouth. She remembered the feel of his hard body over hers, of his maleness thrusting inside her. She shifted on the sofa, and a blush tinged her cheeks.

"Oh, he's alive—very much so." Could she tell her sister the truth? She sighed. "It's rather complicated, I'm afraid."

Taking a sip of her brandy, Rose leaned back in her chair. She studied Priscilla with a calm regard that seemed to be sizing her up. "Caleb's out of town. I'm used to late hours—and you're not going anywhere. The way I see it, you could use someone to talk to."

"I thought you hated me for what happened to your parents."

Rose released a long, weary breath. "As you said, you were only six years old. The truth is, life's nothing but a roll of the dice. Your roll came up sevens, mine came up craps. What happened to me wasn't your fault any more than it was mine."

Priscilla looked at Rose. Though her sister was a year younger, she seemed far older and a whole lot wiser. "I'd like someone to talk to. I'd like it very much."

* * *

"Everything went just like you planned." Mace Harding crossed the book-lined study to pour himself a shot of whiskey from the decanter on the heavy mahogany sideboard. Stuart sat rigidly behind his ornate walnut desk, smoking a thick cigar.

"Not exactly." Unconsciously he clenched a fist. "My little bitch of a wife is gone."

"What?" Mace whirled to face him. "How did she get away?"

Stuart fingered the silver-handled letter opener he had taken from the floor of her room. "It appears she picked the lock." Once again, he had underestimated her.

"Son of a bitch. Think she's gone back to Evergreen?"

Stuart had been contemplating that possibility—and several others—ever since his return. "Maybe. If that's where she thinks Trask is. But she doesn't know we've got him, so she'll probably try to protect him, go into hiding someplace else. Either way, she'll want to get word to him. I need you to hire a couple of men to watch the place. Anybody comes calling, have them checked out. Sooner or later, somebody will lead us to her."

"What about the Triple R?" Mace asked. "Shouldn't we be getting back?" *Getting the hell out of Natchez*, he was thinking.

"Just as soon as we find her—which shouldn't take long. In the meantime, we'll deal with Trask and the others."

"Tonight?"

Stuart shook his head. "Tonight we rest up, get

plenty of sleep. We need to be ready for tomorrow." He ground out his cigar. "I find myself looking forward to the . . . festivities."

"Do you really think there's a chance he still wants me?" Hours had passed, yet still they sat conversing. Since Priscilla had started talking, holding nothing back, confiding in her as if they were sisters in truth, Rose's attitude had softened.

It was hard to hate your own sister, especially when she had never really had one. And Priscilla *had* offered to help her, even tried to persuade her to go to Cincinnati.

"Of course he still wants you," she said. "A man doesn't follow a woman all the way from Texas unless he's in love with her. He's just hurt and angry—and more than a little disappointed."

Priscilla brushed a tear from her cheek. She hadn't meant to cry, hadn't really meant to tell her sister so much, but once she'd gotten started, she couldn't seem to stop herself.

"Even if he wants me, I don't know if I can be the kind of woman he needs. I don't know the first thing about frontier living."

"Neither do I," Rose said, "but if I loved a man the way you love Brendan, there isn't a place I wouldn't go to be with him."

There was a time when she would have agreed.

"You told me you went to Texas to marry Stuart and raise a family," Rose continued, "to make a home for the two of you, no matter what it took. But you met Brendan and discovered that without love, that wasn't enough."

Priscilla smiled forlornly. "When I'm with him, I feel like there's nothing I can't do."

Rose left her chair and sat down on the sofa. "You've got a chance for happiness, Priscilla—the kind few people ever get. If you don't take it, you'll be sorry for the rest of your life."

"What if he doesn't want me?"

"You won't know that for sure until you ask him."

"What if I go with him and can't make it? What if I fail?"

"At least you will have tried. That's all anyone can do."

Priscilla mulled over her sister's words. In the hours just before dawn, she had told Rose Conners more about herself than any other person in the world—more even than she had told Brendan. "Jaimie was right," she said softly. "You do have a heart of gold."

Rose's head came up. She looked at Priscilla as if seeing her for the very first time, then she glanced away. "Jaimie said that?"

Priscilla nodded. "If he asks you, will you go with him?"

Rose released a slow breath. "I'm not sure."

"Why not?"

"Because I'm not sure it would be fair to Jaimie. I've done things . . . the life I've led has been pretty seedy at times."

"Do you think that matters to Jaimie?"

"It should."

"You worry for Jaimie . . . I worry for Brendan. How fair would it be if I went with him to Texas and then let him down? If I can't be the woman he needs —how fair is that?''

This time Rose didn't answer.

Neither of them spoke for a very long time. "Why don't we get some sleep?" Rose finally said. "Tomorrow we'll need to get word to Evergreen, let them know you're safe."

On impulse, Priscilla leaned over and hugged her. "I'm glad I got this chance to know you."

Rose squeezed her hand. "So am I."

Together they made their way to the bedchamber to try to get some sleep. Both seemed to know it would be a long time in coming.

Chapter 20

Jaimie pounded hard on the door. "Rose! It's me—let me in!"

Wearing a simple blue cotton dress, Rose hurried to the door and pulled it open. "Jaimie! Come in." She closed the door behind him.

The late afternoon sun streaked through the open window, throwing a shaft of light on the tall red-haired man's worried face. One glance at the tension in his features and Priscilla's chest grew taut.

"What is it, Jaimie? What's happened?" Having fallen asleep just before dawn, battered and exhausted from Stuart's harsh treatment, she had slept away most of the day, then bathed, and dressed. Her freshly washed hair, still damp, fanned out around her shoulders.

She clutched Jaimie's arm. "Tell me what's happened."

"It's Trask. Egan's got him—he's planning to kill him."

Priscilla choked back a sob. "Dear God, no."

"You should have told me he was here, Priscilla."

"I wanted to. I just had to be sure I could trust you."

"How did you find out?" Rose asked.

"I overheard Egan and Mace in the study. I would

have come sooner, but this is the first chance I've had to get away."

"What are we going to do?" Priscilla asked, her hands beginning to shake.

Rose released a weary breath. "Before we do anything, you might as well hear the rest of it."

"What rest?" Jaimie's gaze swung to her face.

"Egan and Caleb are partners—they have been for years. McLeary's the man behind the piracy on the river. Egan's connections in the freighting business gave him access to inside information which one of his men passed on to McLeary." She gestured to their plush surroundings. "How do you think he pays for all this?"

"You knew about his involvement and yet you stayed with him?" Priscilla asked.

For an instant Rose looked hurt, then she lifted her chin. "I never expected you to understand."

Jaimie slid an arm around her waist. "It's all right, honey. None of that matters now. What matters is that Egan isn't the man I thought he was—" He glanced to Priscilla. "—the man any of us thought he was. He's got to be stopped."

Priscilla's mind flashed with understanding. "Brendan must have found out before he came here. He said he had made a deal with the Texas Rangers. He said he'd come to Natchez to help stop the smuggling on the river. They must have known Stuart was involved."

"Somebody probably recognized Trask and tipped Egan off," Jaimie said.

"Dear God . . . we've got to find a way to help him."

"I know it's happening tonight," Jaimie said, "but I don't know exactly when or where."

"Ten miles north of town," Rose said flatly. "There's a sandbar building up—they plan to scuttle the *St. Louis.* I overheard Caleb talking to Jake Dobbs about it."

"The *St. Louis*," Jaimie repeated, incredulous. "My God, that's one of the biggest steamboats on the Mississippi."

"Nothing's too much for McLeary," Rose said with a trace of bitterness. "He thinks he's the king of the river."

"Yeah, well, His Highness is about to get dethroned." Jaimie turned to the door. "It'll be dark soon—I've got to hurry. I'm going after the sheriff. It'll take him some time to gather enough men."

"Chris Bannerman will help," Priscilla told him. "I know you can count on him. Just tell Chris they've got Brendan and that you've spoken to me."

Jaimie nodded. "If that's the case, I'll go there first. I might need someone who will back up my story."

Rose caught his arm. "Be careful, Jaimie."

He bent down and kissed her, not gently, but hard. Rose slid her arms around his neck and kissed him back.

"I'll come back for you," Jaimie promised. "You just stay right here." He gave her a last quick kiss and then he was gone.

Priscilla studied her sister, who stared straight ahead, her emotions carefully concealed.

She wished they could talk, as they had before, but this was not the time. "I wish there was something I could do." Priscilla started pacing. "But if they've taken Brendan out to the river . . ."

Rose seemed lost in thought. "I don't think they have," she finally said.

"What?"

"If someone recognized him, it was probably down at the Keelboat Tavern. Even if they caught him someplace else, that'd be the best place to keep him locked up until they could find a way to . . ."

"To what?" Priscilla asked, eyes wide.

"You won't like what I'm going to say."

"Just say it."

Rose stiffened her spine. "If they haven't killed him already, they'll probably do it tonight—take him out to the sandbar, make it look like he's one of the raiders. That way there'd be no connection to Egan or McLeary and the Keelboat Tavern. Just another dead body floating downstream."

Priscilla felt the bile rise up in her throat. *Dear Lord, no!* Then another feeling assailed her—a surge of determination so strong that for a moment it staggered her. "So you think he might still be at the tavern?"

"They won't chance moving him till dark."

Priscilla's resolve strengthened. "I need a weapon. Does McLeary keep a gun here?"

"A gun?" Rose repeated.

"If they're keeping Brendan at the Keelboat Tavern, I've got to get him out of there before it's too late."

Rose stared at her in astonishment. Then a slow smile curved her lips. "Maybe you really are my sister." She crossed the room and went into the chamber she shared with Caleb. In minutes she came out with a rifle draped over one arm, the barrel pointing downward.

"Brand new eight-shot revolving-breech Colt's," Rose proudly announced. "The latest thing in weaponry, according to Caleb. Mr. Timmons, the storekeep, brought it over yesterday, but Caleb had already left. He ordered it months ago—he was madder than a hornet 'cause it hadn't gotten here sooner."

Priscilla took the heavy weapon from her sister's slender hand. "Is it loaded?"

"Yes. Mr. Timmons told me it was loaded and ready to fire, just like Caleb asked." She threw Priscilla a sidelong glance. "I've had a hard life, Priscilla, but in truth, I'm a city girl. I don't have the slightest idea how to use the damned thing."

Priscilla fingered the heavy weapon, trying not to think about Charity, about the Indian brave she had killed. "It's exactly like the one Brendan has. He never showed me, but I watched him several times. You just aim it and pull the trigger. When you want to shoot again, you pull this metal ring and it rotates the cylinder for another shot."

"Are you sure you want to go through with this?"

Priscilla thought of Brendan, alone and facing death. "I've never been more sure of anything in my life."

"Then I'm coming with you."

Priscilla's head came up in astonishment. "Why would you do that?"

"Without me, you'd probably never even find him. Besides . . . we're sisters, aren't we?"

Priscilla smiled, feeling something warm touch her heart. "Yes, we are."

"Caleb's got a carriage next door at the livery. I can have them hitch up the team, but I don't know how to drive them."

Priscilla shot her a glance that said more than words. "I do."

"So you cheated the hangman after all?" Stuart circled the chair Brendan sat strapped to, his head slumped forward on his chest.

It took all of his will just to raise himself up and meet his enemy's triumphant gaze. "Sorry to disappoint you," he rasped, between swollen lips.

He cocked his head to the side, trying to focus through eyes he could barely hold open. One was blacked and puffed, the other ached from the crushing blows he had taken to the side of his face.

"No trouble. We'll be happy to finish the job." Stuart motioned with a nod of his head, and Mace Harding's fist exploded into his stomach. His nose had been bloodied, his ribs ached unbearably from Harding's ruthless kicks, and blood oozed steadily from the corner of his mouth.

"What were you doing at the Keelboat Tavern?" Stuart asked as Brendan worked to make the walls of the cave stop spinning. It smelled dank and musty, and rats skittered by at his feet.

"Having a drink," he said. It was the answer he'd given to Harding more than a dozen times already. Egan had just arrived.

"And when you weren't at the tavern, you were at Evergreen screwing my wife."

That brought his head up. Brendan felt a tightness in his chest. "I don't know what you're talking about."

"Don't you? She's a hot little thing—you've taught her well."

Within his rope cocoon, Brendan's hands balled into fists. "If you've hurt her . . . if you've touched her, I'll kill you." He strained against his bonds, tortured at the thought of Egan's blunt fingers on Priscilla's slender curves.

Egan just laughed, the sound echoing harshly off the walls of the cavern. "Just imagine, Trask, while you were . . . occupied . . . with my friend Mace, I was pounding into Priscilla. She has the loveliest breasts, don't you think? Just enough to fill a man's hands. I like the way they point upward—"

Brendan growled low in his throat. He lunged toward Egan, but succeeded only in toppling his chair and landing in the dirt on the cavern floor. Around them, crates of hemp and bales of cotton sat beside casks of whiskey and hogsheads of sugar.

Mace reached down and righted Brendan's chair, then punched him hard in the ribs.

Brendan hissed with pain.

"I need a drink," Stuart said, walking toward McLeary's storeroom, taking the whale-oil lantern with him. "We'll be back, Trask. In the meantime, just relax and enjoy yourself."

He could hear their laughter echoing off the walls of the cave.

Priscilla surprised herself by how well she handled the team. Though dusk had fallen, disguising her a little, she had received several questioning glances as she sat atop the driver's seat, since it was unusual to see a woman driving alone at that hour. Rose sat tensely in the back.

"If they've got him, they'll have him in the caves behind the tavern."

"How do we get in?"

"There's a way through the rear, but I don't know it. We'll have to go in through the back of the tavern. There's an abandoned building next door—what's left of a building, really more like a shed. We can hide the carriage there."

Priscilla did as Rose suggested, and in minutes they were tying up the horses, climbing over the heavy fallen timbers of the abandoned building and walking toward the rear of the Keelboat Tavern.

"I'm scared to death," Rose whispered as they hurried along.

Priscilla smiled. "So am I." It was all right to be afraid, she was learning, as long as you did what you had to. They reached the back door and stood outside listening for voices.

"Stuart," Priscilla whispered, recognizing the heavy cadence. "The other one's Mace Harding. I don't know the third one."

"That's Jake Dobbs, he's Caleb's right-hand man." The voices grew distant and finally faded away. "They're going into the cavern."

Priscilla's heart speeded. It was dark outside. Time to finish whatever Egan had planned. "We've got to stop them." She listened for a moment more, heard nothing, and pulled open the door.

"We'll need a lamp," Rose said. "I know where

Caleb keeps them." She ran to a chest and pulled out
a small whale-oil lantern. Striking a match against
the rough wooden wall, she lit the wick, then slid the
chimney down. "When we get close enough to see
them, we'll snuff our light and go the rest of the way
guided by theirs."

Priscilla nodded. *Please God, let him be alive.* She
prayed, too, that she recalled correctly how to use
the rifle. "Let's go." She'd tied back her thick, dark
hair with only a ribbon, and now it bobbed against
her back as they hurried along in the darkness.

Priscilla's stomach rolled at the dankness and the
rotting smell of mold and decay. When something
furry touched her foot, she bit back a scream and
kept on. The cave wasn't as deep as she had imagined. The first turn showed a beam of yellow light up
ahead.

It wasn't moving.

Priscilla snuffed the lamp and rounded the corner
into the darkness of the passage. She couldn't see
where she was walking, but the circle of light ahead
gave her direction, and they wouldn't be able to see
her. She heard Rose stumble over a rock, the sound
echoing, and both of them froze.

"What was that?" Mace Harding asked.

"Probably just a rat." They listened for a moment,
heard nothing more, and went on with whatever it
was they were doing.

"Throw some of that water on him," Stuart di-
rected. "I want him to know exactly what's going
on."

Priscilla heard a splash and then a low, agonized
moan. She knew in an instant it was Brendan. Her

heart turned over. *God in heaven, what have they done to him?*

Priscilla edged her way to the rim of the circle of light. Bound tightly to a chair, Brendan slumped forward against the ropes that bit into his flesh. Harding grabbed him by the hair and jerked his head up. Priscilla sucked in a breath at the sight of his bruised and battered face.

Feelings of love overwhelmed her. And a jolt of protectiveness so fierce it took iron control to keep from rushing to his side. Priscilla's hold tightened on the rifle. Brendan's life depended on these next few crucial moments—she wouldn't let him down.

With hands far steadier than she would have imagined, Priscilla lifted the rifle and pointed it toward the three men.

"Hold it right where you are," she warned from the darkness. "Step away from him—very slowly—and put your hands in the air."

Brendan swiveled his head toward the sound of the voice. Stuart's eyes snapped forward, searching the blackness. Mace Harding reached for his gun.

"Don't do it," Priscilla warned, stepping into the circle of light, pointing the gun directly at Harding's chest.

"Priscilla!" There was anguish in the hoarsely spoken word. Brendan strained against the ropes that bound him.

"So my treacherous little wife has decided to join us." Stuart chuckled, the sound echoing eerily. "You've saved me the trouble of finding you again. Thank you, my dear."

"Untie him," Priscilla commanded, steeling herself against Stuart's taunting words and the terror she held at bay.

"I'll get their guns." Rose stepped out of the dark and started toward the men.

"I wouldn't try that," Harding warned, a dangerous edge to his voice. Rose stopped walking. Mace inched forward, ignoring the gun Priscilla still pointed at his chest.

"You shouldn't have come here, Priscilla." Brendan's words sounded more like a plea.

"I'll shoot," she warned Harding.

"I don't believe you," he said. "You haven't got what it takes to shoot a man in cold blood." He took another step forward.

"I'll do it, I promise you." He smiled and eased forward. Priscilla's finger tightened on the trigger. "Don't make me kill you."

Harding moved again. He didn't believe her. He wouldn't stop until he reached her side and wrenched the gun from her hands. He wouldn't stop until Brendan was dead, maybe she and Rose, too.

"Run, Priscilla," Brendan urged. "Get out while you still have a chance."

Mace inched forward, closing in, watching for any sign of weakness.

"I'll shoot you. I'll do it if I have to."

Mace just laughed. "You're not a killer." He took another step, bringing him little more than an arm's length from the end of the barrel.

"Get out of here, Priscilla!"

She glanced from Brendan's dear, sweet battered face, saw the smile of triumph on Harding's, angled the barrel a little bit lower—and pulled the trigger.

Harding went down with a shriek of agony that vibrated the walls of the cave. Priscilla worked the ring, rotating the cylinder, and aimed the rifle at Stuart. "Tell Dobbs to back away."

Stuart motioned with his head and the heavyset man backed up a step.

"You bitch!" Mace roared, holding his shattered knee and writhing in the dirt on the cavern floor.

"Throw down your gun, Stuart." Very carefully, he did as he was told. "Now you," she said to Dobbs, "nice and easy."

He pulled his pistol from its holster using the tips of his fingers and dropped it onto the ground. Rose moved quickly, picking them up and tossing them into the darkness of the tunnel outside the light.

Rose had just started toward Mace, intending to take his weapon, when he spun and rolled, pulling his pistol at the same instant. Priscilla swung the rifle and fired. Mace flew backwards with a second shriek of pain, blood erupting on his chest. She worked the ring on the rifle, pointing it at Stuart's heart.

"I didn't think you had it in you," he said with what sounded strangely like pride. Rose moved to Brendan's side and starting untying the ropes.

"Some things are worth fighting for," Priscilla said, realizing for the first time how much she meant it.

"We would have made a good pair, you and I."

"I hardly think so."

Rose finished loosening the ropes, and Brendan staggered to his feet, leaning on her heavily for support.

"Can you make it?" Priscilla called to him, her

heart aching for what he'd been through. Their eyes met, locked, hers fiercely protective, his searching, questioning, filled with gratitude and something she couldn't quite read.

"I'll make it." He took a step forward, propping himself against Rose, and together they crossed unsteadily to where Priscilla stood. He took the gun from her hand, their fingers brushed, and love welled up in her heart.

"We're going to the sheriff," Brendan told Egan, his voice sounding stronger. "Move out ahead of us. You, too, Dobbs." The heavyset man walked past them.

As casually as if he were going out for a night on the town, Stuart started down the dimly lit corridor. Rose picked up the lantern, leaving Brendan to lean against Priscilla. Stuart followed Dobbs, but just as he walked past Brendan, he spun, grabbed the rifle, and shoved as hard as he could. Brendan held onto the gun, but went down, dragging Priscilla with him, the rifle firing into the air.

Brendan swore as Dobbs raced one way and Egan raced past them the other way, his feet pounding hard against the floor of the cave. He disappeared into the darkness behind them.

"There's another way out," Rose cried. "He must know where it is."

"It's all right," Brendan said, "let them go. I know where both of them are headed. Let's get the hell out of here."

Brendan draped an arm over Priscilla's shoulder, trapping the hair that had come loose from the ribbon. She could feel the tension in his muscles, but his

steps had grown steady, some of his strength had
returned. They reached the back room inside the tavern, saw no one, crossed the room, and walked out
the rear door.

"We've got a carriage hidden in the empty building
next door," Priscilla said.

Brendan just nodded. With every step she felt him
gaining strength. By the time they'd reached the carriage, he was walking by himself.

He looked around for the driver, but saw no one.

"I drove the team," Priscilla said from behind him.
She wanted him to know she had done it—wanted
him to believe she could make it in Texas. She knew it
now, more clearly than she had ever known anything
in her life.

*I don't need you. I don't want you. And I don't love
you—maybe I never did.*

Dear God, don't let it be true.

Inside the abandoned building, Brendan helped
her climb into the carriage, helped Rose, then
climbed to the driver's seat above. He snapped the
reins against the horses' rumps, urging them out
onto Royal Street and on up the hill.

"Where are we going?" Priscilla asked.

"Evergreen. You'll be safe there."

"But what about you?"

"I've got to get Egan."

"And I've got to go back to the hotel," Rose interrupted determinedly. "Jaimie may be looking for
me."

Brendan pulled the carriage to a halt beneath a
spreading oak at the top of the hill. He climbed down

from the driver's seat, wincing a little with each movement, and joined them in the carriage.

"Before we go any farther, I think it's time you two did a little explaining." He looked at Priscilla, his expression inscrutable. "You can start by telling me who the lady is."

"Rose is my sister. She's also a friend of McLeary's."

"Rose Conners," Brendan said. He'd been following Caleb. Of course he would know who she was. He flicked a glance at Priscilla. "I didn't know you had a sister."

"Neither did I—at least I didn't remember." He seemed so nonchalant. Just an acquaintance, nothing more. A hard lump swelled in Priscilla's throat, and she blinked back a film of tears. "It's kind of a long story."

"How did you get away from Egan?"

"Jaimie Walker helped me escape. He took me to Rose's. When she told him about Egan's connection to McLeary and the robbery they were planning, he went after the sheriff. I told him to get Chris Bannerman's help."

Brendan just nodded. "I owe you a debt of thanks," he said to Rose, but to Priscilla he said nothing. She had to look away.

"You ought to thank Priscilla," Rose prodded. "I just went along for the ride."

"If I take you to your hotel," he said instead, "will you be safe from McLeary?"

"He won't be back before dawn. If Jaimie hasn't come by then, I'll pack my things and join Priscilla at Evergreen . . . if that's all right with her."

Priscilla took her sister's hand. "I wish you would come with me now, but I understand why you can't."

Rose looked at Priscilla, saw her sadness, glanced at Brendan but couldn't read his face. She squeezed Priscilla's hand. "I know you do."

Brendan returned to the driver's seat and climbed aboard. In minutes they reached the Middleton Hotel. Priscilla hugged her sister and she went inside.

Silence broken only by the clip-clop of horses' hooves accompanied them to Evergreen. Brendan pulled the animals to a halt in front of the house, and a groom took the reins. Brendan rounded the carriage and helped Priscilla down. She felt his hands at her waist, his hold a little firmer than it should have been, but still he said nothing. Taking her hand, he led her to the bachelor quarters in the rear, Priscilla fighting tears all the way.

I don't want you. I don't need you. And I don't love you—maybe I never did.

Dear God, he had meant every word.

Once inside, he closed the door and turned to face her. "Well?" There was censure in the single word— and something else she couldn't quite name.

Priscilla didn't understand. "Well, what?"

"Well, what do you have to say for yourself?"

Priscilla's head came up. "What are you talking about?"

"You're supposed to be on a steamboat back to Cincinnati. Instead you're sneaking around the Keelboat Tavern, determined to get yourself killed."

Priscilla's dark brows shot up. "Have you lost your mind? I just risked my life for you."

"My point exactly. What the hell did you think you were doing? You almost wound up dead."

"What the hell did I think I was doing?" she repeated, incredulous. Anger pulsed through her veins. "I thought I was saving your stubborn, arrogant neck! I thought I was proving how much I loved you. I thought maybe . . . if we got out of that horrible place alive . . . you might decide you needed me after all—that you still loved me—that you wanted me with you in Texas."

She lifted her chin, but tears burned the back of her eyes.

"I do," he said, the word rough and husky.

"You do what?" None of this made sense. Priscilla wanted to weep.

"I've never known anyone who showed more courage than you did, standing in that dirty cave, facing three armed men. I've never seen so much love in anyone's eyes as I saw in yours when you looked at me. I've never needed anyone as much as I needed you in that moment . . . as much as I need you right now. I've never loved anyone the way I love you, Silla. I've never wanted anything more than to marry you and take you with me."

The tears she'd been fighting trickled slowly down her cheeks.

"I discovered out on the prairie the kind of woman you are," he said gently. "It was you who didn't understand."

A soft sob caught in her throat. She started toward him, and he caught her up in his arms. Priscilla clung to him, her cheek against his, her fingers laced in his hair.

"You didn't mean what you said in the garden?"

"I was desperate. I had to make you see."

"I love you," she whispered, "more than anything else in the world. I've been such a fool."

"It doesn't matter. All that matters is that we're together."

"It does matter. So much has happened . . . there's so much I haven't told you."

He pulled back to look at her, surveyed the bruise on her cheek. Something flickered in his eyes, then it was gone. "When I get back, we'll have plenty of time to talk. Right now, I just want to kiss you."

He cupped her face with his hands, and his mouth came down over hers, gently at first, then with longing. He kissed her fiercely, savagely, claiming her, showing his love so boldly she could only return it with equal measure.

"I want you," he said roughly. "It's all I can do not to take you right here."

"I want you, too."

He kissed her again, his hand cupping her bottom to hold her more solidly against him. She could feel his solid arousal through the folds of her dress—then he pulled away.

"We haven't got time for this," he said, his voice a little ragged. "I've got to get Egan. I'll be back as soon as I can."

"I'm going with you."

He smiled at that, white teeth flashing against his battered face. "After what I saw in that cavern, I probably ought to take you." He bent over and kissed her, quick and hard. "You just be here when I get back. I've got plans for you that don't include sleep."

She clutched the front of his shirt. "Be careful, Bren. Promise me you'll be careful."

"I'll be careful. I've got every reason in the world to live. I'm not about to let that bastard win now."

Brendan strode to the gun cabinet, unlocked it, and pulled out his heavy leather holster. He shoved in his .36 caliber Patterson, buckled the holster around his waist, and tied the leather thong. He stuffed one of Chris's small derringers into a pocket, unsheathed a slender stiletto, similar to one Mace Harding had taken, and tucked it into his boot.

"You've done more than your share, Silla. Now, it's my turn." A last brief kiss and then he was gone.

Chapter 21

Brendan went straight to the stables, saddled one of Chris's best horses, and rode out toward the spot on the river where McLeary's men awaited the unsuspecting *St. Louis.*

As battered and beaten as he was, he felt exhilarated, hopeful, as he hadn't been in days. He'd been right about Priscilla—she was every inch the woman he'd believed she was. When he'd seen her standing in that cavern, pointing a rifle at Egan, he had never been more terrified—or more fiercely proud.

If it hadn't been for her courage, he knew without doubt he'd be dead. The moment his ropes had come loose, he'd wanted to crush her against him, tell her how much he loved her. Instead he had waited.

He'd had to know for sure that she wanted him as much as he wanted her.

He had to know that she loved him.

Brendan grinned as he remembered her fiery burst of outrage. She'd be a handful—but she'd make one helluva wife.

That thought sobered him. Until he dealt with Egan, she still wasn't free, and neither was he. He thought of Egan's words in the cavern, thought of him thrusting into Priscilla, touching her, hurting her.

His stomach knotted and his mouth went dry. He

wanted to kill the bastard for what he had done, but he would not. Killing Egan would leave no way to prove the man's involvement in the smuggling and thus clear his name. McLeary was the key, and if Brendan's guess was right, Egan was on his way to the river to take care of the threat Caleb posed.

Brendan traveled the road along the river, moving fast, pressing hard. Egan wouldn't be far ahead of him. In the cavern, he had heard enough bits and pieces of conversation to know what McLeary had planned. He just hoped to hell Chris and the sheriff hadn't sprung their trap too soon and scared the raiders away.

He needn't have worried.

When he reached the spot near the sandbar ten miles north of town, all hell had broken loose. In the light of a waning moon, the *St. Louis*, all hundred and seventy-five feet of her, sat aground near the far side of the river, her steam whistle hooting into the cool night air. But the boilers had not been blown, and the passengers stood at the rails, safe for the present, the craft in no danger of sinking. The sheriff had stopped the attack before it had been completed.

Now the banks on this side of the river echoed with rifle shots, a firefight between the sheriff and his deputies, and McLeary's cutthroat river rats. Brendan tied his horse some distance away from the gunfire and cautiously made his way toward the sound of the fighting.

Staying low and moving silently, he crept forward, taking up a position behind a rotting stump. In the trees off to his left, three men he recognized from the Keelboat Tavern fired blindly toward their attackers, two others slumped over a rock, covered in blood, and several more sprawled on the ground some distance away.

He searched the trees to his left. Two men fired sporadically, while Jake Dobbs balanced a rifle in the crotch of a tree and squeezed the trigger. Beside him, a brawny man in a red-checkered shirt fired round after round at the sheriff and his deputies. Caleb McLeary. Brendan crept silently in that direction, but stopped when he caught a flash of movement coming up from the rear. Stuart Egan leveled a rifle toward the group of men and fired. Dobbs went down in a heap, and McLeary and the others spun to face the threat.

They saw no one.

Damn! If Egan succeeded in killing McLeary, his involvement with the smugglers would come down to Brendan's word against his—an outlaw against a powerful businessman and respectable politician. Jaimie Walker might testify, but how much did Walker really know? Rose would, but her reputation was less than shining. Priscilla? A wife couldn't testify against her husband.

McLeary changed position, dodging a hail of bullets, and took cover near the edge of the river. Brendan spotted a small boat nearby, bobbing at the end of a rope. If Caleb could reach the boat, he might just make it. Brendan couldn't take the chance. Moving closer, pistol in one hand, rifle in the other, he skirted the clearing and moved silently in through the trees.

Across the open space, he spotted Chris Bannerman's blond head, and a man he figured must be the sheriff. He remembered meeting red-haired Walker at the Triple R and saw him now beside Chris. Three more men crouched beside them. McLeary started moving. So did the sheriff.

"Hold it, McLeary!" Brendan stepped into the open, his rifle trained on Caleb. The brawny Irishman spun and fired, Brendan fired, bringing him down. A shoulder wound. He'd been damned careful not to kill him.

A twig snapped behind him. Brendan whirled and crouched behind a fallen log. Egan fired at McLeary just as the sheriff fired at Egan. He slammed back against the trunk of a tree. Wounded, but still standing, he started running. Brendan raced after him, so did Chris, Walker, and the sheriff. Egan ran toward the boat, shoved it out from shore and got in. He fired a last shot at Brendan, then one at the sheriff, who aimed his rifle and pulled the trigger.

The bullet slammed Egan over backward, and he tumbled into the river. Brendan raced toward him, but the water eddied near the shore and the current was swift in this narrow spot between the two banks. Egan flailed frantically, then went under.

Brendan reached the water the same instant as the sheriff and his men. They all stood tensely, waiting for Egan to surface, trying to figure exactly where he had gone down.

Nothing.

They watched the banks, anyplace he might be able to swim to, though odds were the shot had been mortal. There were brambles and overgrowth, so the men waded along the perimeter, using the barrels of their rifles and muskets to check the foliage.

Nothing.

"You all right?" Chris Bannerman walked to his side, surveying his bruises, his cut and swollen face.

"Thanks to Priscilla."

"Priscilla?"

"It's a long story."

Chris nodded.

"Still no sign of him." Jaimie Walker came up beside Chris. "Glad to see you're all right," he said to Brendan.

"Maybe a little the worse for wear, but I'll be fine." He extended a hand, and the two men shook. "Thanks for what you did for Priscilla. We're both in your debt."

"I'm glad I could help." They watched the men following the shoreline, searching but finding nothing.

"I wish they'd find the bastard." Brendan still gazed at the water. "I don't like loose ends."

"He was dead by the time he went under," Chris told him.

"He's right," Jaimie agreed. "There's no way he could have lived through a shot like that." He released a weary breath, lines of regret creasing his forehead. "I can hardly believe he's the same man I worked for."

"A lot of people will feel the same way," Chris said.

"What about Sturgis and Reeves?" Brendan asked. "The men who took Priscilla from Evergreen." Jaimie seemed surprised he knew about them.

"They've never been a part of this. They were just Egan's hired muscle."

"The sheriff will take care of them," Chris said. "If

they weren't involved in the smuggling, they shouldn't be hard to find."

Jaimie nodded and turned away. "I've got business in town," he said. "I'm headin' back." With a last wave at Brendan, he walked off the way he had come.

Brendan stared out across the path of moonlight, watching the river flow past. "I still don't like it."

"Ol' Miss doesn't give up her victims without a struggle." Chris clapped Brendan on the shoulder. "Egan's dead. McLeary's already singing like a bird. Let's go home."

For the first time, Brendan smiled. "That's the best idea I've heard all night."

"I don't suppose you want to come in for a brandy?" A sly smile played on Chris Bannerman's face. Evergreen loomed ahead as they walked their weary horses through the tall iron gates and down the oyster-shell drive.

Brendan just smiled. "I've got something else to attend."

"That's what I figured. Tell her I'm glad she's all right."

They passed the house and rode around back to the stable. It was late, but Zachary had waited up. The two men dismounted and handed their reins to the big black groom.

"You take care a' dat river scum, suh?"

"Not singlehandedly"—Chris grinned—"but I think you could safely say they're out of commission—permanently, I hope."

With a smile of approval, Zach led the horses away.

"Thanks, Chris—for everything." Brendan extended a hand, and Chris shook it. "I couldn't have done it without you."

They parted company on the path that separated the bachelor quarters from the main house, Chris heading in to Sue Alice, Brendan coming home to Priscilla. He couldn't wait to see her; his long strides covered the ground almost at a run.

She threw open the door even before he reached it, love and relief in her eyes.

"Bren!" She raced toward him, and he swept her into his arms, tightening them possessively around her.

"It's over," he said against her ear. "Stuart is dead."

In a lace-trimmed nightshirt she had borrowed from Sue Alice, her shiny, dark chestnut hair hanging loose around her shoulders, her slender body went tense. She pulled back to look at him. "Did you . . . ?"

"No. Sheriff Harley shot him. There was no other choice."

She pressed her cheek against his and clung to him. "I wish none of this had happened. It's still hard to believe."

"I know. In time, you'll forget it."

"Not completely. And I don't really want to."

Brendan smiled faintly. Sliding an arm beneath her knees, he lifted her up and carried her through the parlor into the bedchamber, where he settled her gently on the bed.

"There are things I need to tell you," she said, "things—"

"Later." His mouth came down over hers. He could feel her trembling, her lips parting, her fingers kneading the muscles of his shoulders. Her tongue felt warm and silky; she smelled of violets and tasted like honey.

His hand moved to cup and lift a breast, he hefted it, used his thumb to stroke her nipple, felt it grow hard beneath his fingers. Her tongue touched his, firing his blood, his shaft growing thicker, harder, beginning to throb where it pressed against her skin.

He drove his tongue inside her mouth, claiming her, possessing her, making her his. He felt her fingers in his hair, then down along his neck until they gripped his shoulders.

His hands grew more urgent, sliding down her body, lifting the nightgown, cupping her bare bottom, forcing her against his hardened length. He heard Priscilla's low moan as he started on the buttons at the front of her nightgown, but his hands were unsteady. He fumbled, swore, wrapped his fingers in the light cotton fabric and ripped it to her waist. Her lush cone-shaped breasts pointed upward, heaving with her rapid breathing, urging him to touch her.

He recalled Egan's words in the cave, knew he had used her, imagined what the bastard had done, and anger infused his passions. He would take her as he never had before, show her his love, cleanse her of Egan's touch. From this day forward, she belonged to him and no other.

Priscilla felt Brendan's urgency, felt his fiery passion, and matched it with a passion of her own. How she wanted him! While he slid the torn nightgown from her shoulders and eased it down her body, she frantically worked the buttons on his shirt. Her hands skimmed over his chest, feeling the muscular ridges, testing the valleys beneath each rib, her finger skimming over a flat copper nipple.

She lowered her head and took one into her mouth, laving it, kissing and tugging. The muscles in his chest bunched, and the hand that cupped her breast grew tense, kneading its weight with renewed demand. She jerked his shirt free and worked the buttons on his breeches, pulling them open, her hand reaching inside to free his straining flesh.

"God, Priscilla." Brendan kissed her hard, then his mouth burned a path along her neck and shoulders. She stroked his thick length, velvety smooth beneath her hand, felt his muscles tighten, and then he pulled away.

"Easy, baby." With a look that spoke his hunger, he sat down on the bed, and tugged off his boots, then slid off his breeches.

Both of them naked at last, he pressed her down on the mattress, his body coming to rest between her legs. He kissed her fiercely, suckled her breasts, then nipped and tasted her all the way to her damp woman's flesh. When his mouth settled over her, Priscilla moaned and writhed against him, white heat engulfing her body.

In seconds he had her shivering with pleasure, begging to feel him inside her. She needed him as she never had before. She needed him to claim her, possess her. She needed to feel every hard-driving inch of his body.

There were no more uncertainties, no more fears. She was his woman—all he could handle and more. She knew without doubt she could give him what he needed, match him passion for passion, fire for fire.

As if reading her thoughts, Brendan moved above her, his solid length hot and bold. He found her soft passage, kissed her long and thoroughly, and buried himself fully inside.

He felt huge and burning, thrilling in a way he hadn't before. She arched her back, and he thrust into her hard and deep. His hands slid down her body, cupped her buttocks, and lifted her to meet each driving thrust.

"Such fire," he whispered, his voice no more than a husky rasp.

Such beauty, Priscilla thought as the heat of each stroke rolled over her, pushing her skyward, higher and higher with each pounding movement. She clawed his back and arched upward, straining against him. A soft cry of pleasure escaped as she swirled into a void of sweetness, a bright spinning pit of pleasure and oneness more powerful than any she had ever known.

"You're mine," he whispered, soft and low, then his muscles grew rigid, and he reached his release. Priscilla felt his warm seed spilling inside her and knew a joy so poignant her eyes filled with tears.

"I love you," she whispered as they began to spiral down, holding each other in the afterglow of their passion.

"I love you, Silla. More than you'll ever know." He

thought of what Egan had done to her and a knot coiled hotly inside him. Was Egan really dead, or had the bastard managed to slip away?

He stared out into the darkness. *It's over*, he told himself. *She's safe now, and even if she isn't, she's got you to protect her.*

But the little voice reminded him that he had failed to protect her before.

Still dressed in the clothes she had worn the day before, Rose awakened with the first rays of dawn. Jaimie lay beside her on the horsehair sofa, shirtless, cuddling her against him, already awake.

"Sleep well?" he asked, the words a soft caress against her ear.

She smiled. "With you here, yes."

"I like waking up with you, Rose."

She didn't answer. When he'd come to her last night, she'd been so happy to see him safe she had started to cry. Now, hearing the kindness in his words made her want to cry again.

Brushing sleep-tangled hair from her face, she sat up and turned to face him. "There are things I need you to know, Jaimie. I want you to understand about Caleb." She had wanted to explain last night, but couldn't seem to find the words.

"You don't have to say anything."

"Please, Jaimie. . . ."

He took her hand in his. "All right."

Rose steeled herself. "Once I found out what he was doing, that he was involved in the robberies on the river, I knew I should leave him. I knew it was wrong to stay, but . . . well, this was the first decent place I'd ever lived . . . and I couldn't stand the thought of going back to the Painted Lady."

His hold tightened protectively.

"I kept telling myself it was just for a little while longer. I'd been saving money, bits here and there from what Caleb gave me. I figured pretty soon I'd have enough to go away, make a respectable life someplace else." She stared down at her hand, trembling beneath his against the folds of her skirt. "I know it was wrong, I should have—"

"You did what you had to. I can't fault you, and unless they've worn your shoes, neither should anyone else."

Did he really mean that? She prayed that he did.

"I don't care what happened before we met," Jaimie said with conviction. "I want you to marry me."

"Marry you?" Though he'd mentioned taking her with him, she never dreamed he intended marriage. A woman with a past like hers became a man's mistress, nothing more.

"Why not? I know this is all happening pretty fast —I know you're not in love with me, but I've got enough love for both of us."

Rose just stared at him. "You can't be serious."

Jaimie's blue eyes darkened. He let go of her hand. Swinging his legs to the floor, he reached for his shirt. "I figured you'd probably say no; I didn't expect you to take it as some kind of joke."

He grabbed his boots, pulled one on and then the other. He started to get up, but Rose caught his arm.

"You really mean this, don't you?"

"Of course, I mean it." His eyes searched her face.

"I'm in love with you, Rose. I believe . . . if we had enough time . . . you might come to feel something for me, too. I'd be good to you, give you time to get used to things. When you were ready, we could start living as man and wife."

Every other man she'd ever known had wanted only one thing. Jaimie was willing to wait. He'd marry her, even without taking what would be his lawful right. "You would do that for me?"

"We could go to Texas. Noble Egan's been running the Triple R. He's a good boy, but he's got a helluva lot to learn. He could use a man like me."

I could use a man like you.

"Of course, bein' a wife, there'd be kids to consider. Do you like children, Rose?"

A lump swelled in her throat. All her life she'd done everything in her power not to have them. Bastard children of men she didn't even know. Now the thought of a family seemed like a dream she'd kept bottled up inside her. Unattainable. She had never dared to think of it.

"I love children," she said softly.

"Marry me, Rose."

"What about Caleb? What about the things I've done?"

"None of that matters."

"You're sure about this? Sure you want to marry me?"

"I'd be proud to call you my wife."

She couldn't do it to him. He deserved so much more. "I'll go with you, Jaimie," she said softly. "You don't have to marry me. I'll warm your bed and stay with you just as long as you want me."

He tipped her chin with his hand, saw the haze of tears, lifted one away with the tip of his fingers. "I love you, Rose. I *want* to marry you. Say you'll be my wife."

"Oh, Jaimie." The truth of his words was there in his eyes. "I love you. I have almost from the start."

"Rose. . . ." The single word spoken with so much love. "Does that mean yes?"

She nodded. Jaimie pulled her against his chest, and her arms went around his neck. "You'll never be sorry, Jaimie, never."

"I know that, Rose." Cupping her face with his hands, Jaimie kissed her.

Rose kissed him back with all the love in her heart. She was going to Texas. Making a fresh start. But instead of being alone, instead of fighting every moment just to survive, she had Jaimie.

The dreams she had never dared to dream were going to come true.

Sunlight beaming through an open window awoke them late the next morning. Brendan took Priscilla carefully, aware of the bruises she carried, wanting to show her his love. Afterward, she curled against him.

"It feels different this time," she said softly, "being here with you like this. Before I was always uncertain. As if I would wake up and this would all be a dream."

"Everything's going to be all right now." He rolled onto his side to face her, one hand brushing back tangles of her thick dark hair. "We'll be married just as soon as we can make the arrangements."

Priscilla's gaze met his. "I never felt like Stuart's wife. No matter how many times he called me that, it's been you I thought of as my husband since the first time we made love."

"I wish I could have told you the truth about him, but it was just too dangerous." *I wish they would have found the bastard's body.* "If I had failed, your life would have been in danger."

"I should have believed in you, trusted you. Stuart was so convincing . . . and I knew you were running. . . . I was just so confused."

"It's all right, baby." He brushed her lips with a kiss. "It's all over now."

"There's one thing more you should know—"

He turned away from her and sat up in bed. "If you're going to tell me what happened with Egan—don't." There was an edge to his voice and his fingers unconsciously gripped the sheet. "He'll never touch you . . . never hurt you again."

"Did he tell you what happened?"

Brendan glanced away. "You're safe now, whatever he did makes no difference."

Priscilla laid a hand against his cheek, his jaw roughened by several days' growth of beard. "I don't know what you think happened, but thanks to Jaimie, whatever might have, didn't."

Probing blue eyes swung to hers, searching, intense. "Egan didn't . . . force you?" He touched the bruise on her face.

"He tried to. He would have succeeded, but Mace Harding sent for him, and while he was gone Jaimie helped me escape."

"God, Priscilla." Brendan's hand laced into her

hair. He pulled her head against his chest, then tipped her face up and kissed her. Priscilla kissed him back, showing him how much she cared. It felt so good just to be near him, so much a part of him.

They lay quiet for a while, sharing the closeness, enjoying just being together. Still, there were things that needed to be said.

"There's something else I need to tell you . . . something I wanted to say last night."

He smiled lazily. "Last night we got . . . side-tracked." A long brown finger trailed warmly down her cheek. "Why don't you tell me now?"

Priscilla captured his hand and kissed the palm. When she made no attempt to continue, he didn't hurry her, just let her take her time. Then,

"Sill?"

It was now or never. "I want to explain what happened to me the day little Charity got hurt . . . why I acted the way I did. I should have told you then but . . . somehow I just couldn't."

She shook her head, recalling the unpleasant memory. "It was like a nightmare, Bren, only I couldn't wake up. When I saw that little girl lying on the floor . . . when I saw all that blood . . . it was as if a window in my mind opened into the past." She raised her eyes to his face and saw the concern etched there. "I remembered what happened when I was a child here in Natchez eighteen years ago. I remembered—and it was so ugly that I couldn't face it."

For the next half hour she told him about her family, about her mother and father, about Megan O'Conner, her father's mistress, about her half sister

Rose. She told him of her mother's jealousy and how it had ended in three terrible needless deaths. When she finished she was crying.

"It's all right, baby." Brendan turned her into his arms. "Sometimes things like that make us stronger. You proved that by coming after me in that cave."

Priscilla knew it was the truth. Facing up to it had made her stronger. "I know you're right. I feel like I've finally been set free."

He rested her head against his shoulder and smoothed back her hair. "You have been, baby. Free to be with me."

He held her a moment, letting her cry against him, letting the past drift away. Then he handed her the edge of the sheet to dry her eyes. "All right?"

She nodded.

As she lay back against him, he toyed with a length of her hair. Priscilla said nothing for the longest time, enjoying the closeness, feeling completely unburdened.

It was Brendan who broke the silence. "What'll we do about the wedding?"

Priscilla turned to face him. "To tell you the truth, I haven't given it much thought. Until last night, I never really believed it would happen."

"We could go to my brother's in Savannah," he said. "You could have the fancy gown and the bridesmaids—the whole damned thing, if that's what you want."

She smiled and shook her head. "None of that matters. I just want to say the words so it will finally be legal. As far as I'm concerned we've been married since that night on the prairie."

Brendan smiled with so much pleasure Priscilla's heart turned over. "Since legally you're a widow, we can do it today—if we can make the arrangements that fast. We'll get married here in the garden."

"I'd like my sister and Jaimie to be here. Without their help, we wouldn't be together."

He nodded. "I'd still like to go to Savannah—afterward, I mean. It's beautiful in the fall and . . . well, I haven't seen my brother in years. I've got a terrific sister-in-law and two little nephews I've never even met." He grinned, white teeth gleaming. "Besides, I'd like a chance to show off my new bride."

Priscilla's heart expanded even more. "I'd love it, Bren. I just hope they like me."

"Like you? Are you kidding? The woman who brought the wayward brother in line? They'll think you walk on water."

"Just imagine," she said, leaning back against his chest, "by tonight I'll be Mrs. Brendan Trask."

His eyes alight with approval, Brendan bent down and kissed her. As always, the touch of his lips started a warming in her limbs, and soon their breathing turned ragged. Her hands moved from his incredibly narrow, hard-muscled hips to his wide, furred chest, then upward till her arms locked around his neck.

Brendan chuckled softly. "You little minx, you're determined to wear me out, aren't you."

"I intend to make that my greatest challenge."

"Then we might as well get started." He kissed her again and slid himself inside her, practicing for the wedding night ahead.

Chapter 22

 In the end, Brendan and Priscilla had to wait another day. Sue Alice was determined Priscilla should have a wedding, no matter how small. There were flowers to arrange, foodstuffs to prepare—to say nothing of a wedding gown.

"I wish we had time to have a proper dress made," Sue Alice said, bustling into the main salon, "something special, just for you. Since we don't, I hope you won't mind wearin' mine."

Priscilla started in surprise. She set aside her mending with an unsteady hand and turned to find Sue Alice holding up the loveliest white lace gown Priscilla had ever seen. The sleeves were sheer above the elbow and so was the bodice above the bustline. The skirt was voluminous, flounced with row upon row of delicate white lace. Clusters of seed pearls glistened in the sunlight reflecting off the crystal chandelier.

"It's beautiful, Sue Alice, but I couldn't possibly— The dress must mean a great deal to you."

"I want you to wear it."

"But what about your daughters?" Priscilla reached out to touch the fine white lace. "Shouldn't you save it for them?"

"Lawd, those two mischief-makers may never find a man! Besides there's two of them. They'd probably just wind up fightin' over it. Anyway, your wearin' it won't hurt it a bit.'' She sized Priscilla up from head to foot. "With a nip here and a tuck there, it'll fit just right, and I know you're gonna look lovely."

The gown was a pure, snowy white. Priscilla flushed to admit she was hardly a virginal bride. But the man she would marry was already her true and proper husband. In the eyes of God, they had never sinned.

"Can we be bridesmaids, Aunt Silla?" Charity asked, tugging at her skirts.

"You aren't old enough yet for that," her mother said, "but you can be flower girls."

"What do flower girls do?" Patience asked.

"They walk in front of the bride dropping rose petals," Priscilla said.

"And then they're very, very quiet until the ceremony is ova'." Sue Alice patted her daughter's hand, and Priscilla fought a smile.

As the hour drew near, Priscilla grew more and more nervous. Sue Alice had insisted it was bad luck for a bride to see her groom before the wedding, so Priscilla had moved back into the main house for the night. Brendan had grumbled, but finally agreed. She hadn't seen him since.

Rose had consented to be her maid of honor. Priscilla hadn't seen her, but Sue Alice had spoken to her, and the two women had been working to get things ready.

Now, standing at the window of her bedchamber in the lovely lace gown, Priscilla looked down at the white-painted arbor the men had set up in the garden. Magnolias decorated the arch, and a runner of white cloth marked the path she would follow. A black-garbed preacher stood with Bible in hand, talking to Jaimie. Little towheaded Matthew stood beside his equally towheaded father, Chris wearing a black frock coat, forest-green waistcoat, and tan trousers, his son in knee breeches and a short brown jacket.

A soft rap sounded that Priscilla hoped was Rose.

"I'll get it," Sue Alice said. "Then I'd better go see to the girls." She opened the door and Rose walked in. "I'm glad you're here. You can help your sister with her veil." She flashed a last approving glance at Priscilla and dashed out into the hallway.

"You look beautiful," Rose said, walking toward her.

"Thank you."

"I'm happy for you."

Priscilla smiled. "Sue Alice said she saw you with Jaimie. Does that mean things have worked out?"

Rose smiled and held out her hand. A simple gold ring on her third left finger gleamed in the sunlight. "We're married."

"Oh, Rose!" Priscilla leaned over and hugged her. Rose still seemed a little uncertain of their newly discovered kinship, but Priscilla was determined their sisterhood would flourish. "I'm so happy for you."

"I almost didn't do it. I was afraid that later . . . after he'd thought things over . . . he'd be sorry."

"Jaimie isn't like that. If you had read his letters, you would know."

"I figured if he was willing to take a chance on me, I could surely take a chance on him. We got married by the justice of the peace yesterday afternoon. Jaimie is taking me with him to Texas."

"He's going back to the Triple R?"

"He says Noble will need him."

"And Jaimie needs you. I saw it in his eyes whenever he looked at you."

Rose smiled again, and Priscilla took her hand. "I owe you an apology, Rose."

"An apology? What in God's name for?"

"When you told me about Stuart and McLeary, about Caleb's involvement in the smuggling on the river, I didn't understand how you could have stayed with him."

"You were right. I should have—"

"I wasn't right. You did what you had to. If I'd been through what you had, been abandoned and left to fend for myself the way you were, I don't know if I could have made it. You not only survived, but did everything in your power to better yourself. Look how much you've accomplished—" Priscilla surveyed her sister's blue silk crepe dress, the height of fashion and good taste. "You've taught yourself to be a lady. Now, as Jaimie's wife, you'll be a lady in every respect."

"Do you really believe that?"

"Absolutely." Priscilla held up her sister's hand, admiring the ring on her finger. "This is the best wedding present you ever could have given me."

Rose smiled. Then her fine dark brows drew together as she caught a flash of gold above the bodice of Priscilla's gown. She reached for the locket nestled in the hollow of her sister's throat.

"Papa gave it to me," Priscilla said. "I've kept it with me always."

Rose's hand shook as she studied the locket. She let it fall away, then reached into the neck of her gown, and pulled her own small gold locket from where it dangled at the end of its chain. The two were identical.

Priscilla's throat closed up.

"He must have loved us both," Rose said softly. She stared at Priscilla, blinked, then discreetly brushed a tear from her cheek. "The best present anyone has ever given me is you, Priscilla," Rose said. "I never thought of you as a sister. I hated you for so many years. . . . I blamed you—and I envied you. But once I met you, I realized you were nothing like I'd imagined. You were warm and kind, and you cared about me. I want you to know how glad I am to know you, how happy I am that you're my sister."

Warm tears slipped down Priscilla's cheeks. "I'm just so glad I found you."

Rose blew her nose on a lace-trimmed hanky she pulled from her reticule. "I think it's time we stopped all this fussing and got ready for your wedding. I have a hunch your groom is more than a little impatient."

Priscilla dabbed the last of the tears from her eyes. "You're probably right," she agreed straight-faced. "He's taking this marriage very seriously. Why, the last time we were together, he kept me up half the night—practicing his husbandly duties."

She tried not to grin, but the look on her sister's face was just too priceless. They both went off into gales of laughter.

* * *

"Where the devil is she?" Brendan stood at the altar, shifting impatiently from one shiny black shoe to the other. Wearing a frock coat of fine black broadcloth, a silver waistcoat, and dove-gray trousers, he looked toward the house for the fifteenth time since his arrival.

"Relax, my boy. It's a woman's perogative to keep her groom waiting at the altar." The preacher smoothed the ribbon that marked his place in the Bible.

"Better here than in bed," Brendan grumbled.

"What?"

He cleared his throat. "I said, she'd better have a darned good reason." Then he saw the twins in their best blue taffeta dresses, their hair clustered in blond ringlets that bobbed over their small shoulders, and smiled. Flower petals fell in great wads from their baskets as they walked along to the music of a harp that had been set up in the garden.

Rose followed the twins. From the corner of his eye Brendan saw Jaimie's chest expand at the sight of her. She wore a gown of blue silk crepe, and her dark hair glistened like polished wood in the sunlight. The smile on her face reflected her happiness.

The harpist strummed the bridal march, and Priscilla stepped onto the long white runner. Looking as beautiful as Brendan had ever seen her, she clung to Chris Bannerman's arm.

God I love her. How it had happened, he couldn't quite say. He never would have believed the fragile young woman who had passed out cold on the dusty Galveston streets would one day be his wife. That she would be the one to free him from the past. That she would prove to be a woman of courage and determination, a woman who would show him the way to love.

He never would have believed he could be that lucky.

Chris placed Priscilla's hand in Brendan's, and his long fingers curved over her delicate ones. He felt a fierce pride and an undeniable longing.

"Dearly beloved," the preacher began, "we are gathered together in the sight of God and these witnesses to join together this man and woman in the bonds of holy matrimony."

Brendan hardly heard the words. His gaze remained fixed on the woman who would be his wife—had belonged to him in his heart since the moment he'd gone back to the Triple R to claim her.

There were the usual phrases; he heard them, but none of it mattered except that she would soon be his. From the corner of his eye he saw Sue Alice in her pretty pink silk dress, standing next to Chris, their fingers interwoven. She sniffed back a tear, and her husband squeezed her hand. Standing next to Priscilla, Rose pressed a hanky to the corner of her eye.

The preacher's attention swung to him. "Do you, Brendan, take Priscilla, to be your lawful wedded wife? Do you promise to love her, comfort her, honor and keep her, for better, for worse, for richer, for poorer, in sickness and in health, forsaking all others, for as long as you both shall live?"

He had thought the words wouldn't matter. Now

he felt an ache in his throat. He would cherish her always. "I do."

"Do you, Priscilla, take Brendan, to be your lawful wedded husband? Do you promise to love him, comfort him, honor and keep him, for better, for worse, for richer, for poorer, in sickness and in health, forsaking all others, for as long as you both shall live?"

Priscilla heard the catch in her voice. "I do." In a few more minutes she would be Brendan's wife. He had come to her from a place deep inside him, crossed hundreds of miles, buried a dozen bitter memories. She vowed he would never regret it.

"You may place the ring on her finger."

Chris handed him the simple gold band, and Brendan slid it onto her third left finger. Her hand shook a little and he glanced down at her. She prayed he could read the happiness and love in her eyes.

"With this ring, I thee wed," Brendan repeated. There was so much pride in his voice, such fierce possession, Priscilla's heart turned over.

"Having consented together in wedlock and having pledged your troth in sight of God and these witnesses, in the name of Almighty God, I now pronounce you man and wife. You may kiss your bride."

Priscilla smiled at Brendan with all the joy she felt inside. As he lifted the veil from her face and pulled her into his arms, tears of happiness clung to her lashes. He kissed her thoroughly, pressing her against him, ignoring the minister, who began to clear his throat. Finally he broke away.

"I love you, Sill," he said and then he grinned. "God, I'm glad that's over."

Priscilla gave him a dazzling smile. "Me too."

Chris hugged her and kissed her chastely, and so did Jaimie. Then the small party adjourned to a corner of the garden where a table had been laid with foodstuffs, and crystal champagne glasses sat beside a silver ice bucket. Chris did the honors, toasting the couple and wishing them well through the years. Brendan toasted Jaimie and Rose.

It was a wonderful, loving celebration that went on for several hours, then she and Brendan left in Chris's carriage. A suite at the Natchez hotel awaited them for the evening, a present from Chris and Sue Alice.

After a sumptuous dinner in their elegant suite of rooms, they retired to the huge four-poster bed to officially consummate their marriage. It was several hours later that Priscilla stirred, coming awake slowly, smiling with contentment as she propped herself against Brendan's bare chest.

"This is the happiest day of my life," she said.

He smiled down at her and tugged playfully on one of her curls. "For me, this is the luckiest. In fact, I can't remember having such a streak of good fortune. If I were a gambling man—which I no longer am—I'd be rich. Then again, I guess I already am."

Brendan kissed Priscilla lightly, holding her against him. He felt happy as he never had before, and yet with his words about good fortune, something continued to disturb him. Some loose end he couldn't quite name.

It was crazy and he knew it, yet that same, uneasy, prickling up his spine had saved his skin more than once.

Priscilla pulled back to look at him. "Is something the matter?"

He shook his head. "I've got a beautiful naked woman in my bed. I love her and she loves me. I'm about to make mad passionate love to her for the third time since we got here—what could possibly be the matter?"

Priscilla smiled. "You're right. The only thing that could possibly be wrong is that you might not be up to the challenge."

Brendan just grinned. His hard length slid inside her. "Why don't we try it and see?"

They left the hotel two days later, returning to Evergreen just long enough to say a misty farewell to the Bannermans and their three children.

"I hope you won't be stayin' away too long," Sue Alice said. "The children will miss you somethin' awful."

"We're going to miss them, too," Priscilla agreed. She had said her tearful good-byes to Matthew, Charity, and Patience a little earlier. Leaving them behind had been harder for her than she had imagined.

"At least you'll have Rose and Jaimie for company as far as New Orleans," Chris said.

"Walker's a good man." Brendan was damned glad to have him along. He couldn't seem to shake this nagging suspicion that all their well-laid plans were about to go wrong. "But I doubt we'll see much of each other." He flashed a heated look at Priscilla. "I think we'll all be spending a good deal of time in our cabins."

Everyone laughed at that. Hugs were exchanged,

and their baggage loaded into the carriage. Jaimie and Rose would be waiting at the docks.

"I can't thank you enough," Priscilla said, with a last tearful glance at Sue Alice. "Write often."

"I will, I promise." She dabbed a handkerchief against her eyes.

"Tell your brother we're hoping he'll bring Silver and the children and come for a visit," Chris said. "We'd dearly love to see them."

"I'll tell him." Brendan extended a hand and Chris shook it, then he threw an arm around his friend's shoulders in a brief masculine hug. "I'll never forget what you've done for us, Chris."

"My pleasure," Chris said.

The trip to New Orleans went just as Brendan had said. They had dinner aboard ship with Jaimie and Rose, but for the most part, the couples spent their time alone. Nothing untoward happened, so Brendan's worry began to ease.

In New Orleans, the Walkers stayed only one day, determined to catch the first steamboat to Galveston. Jaimie promised to contact Badger Wallace and Tom Camden, though both Sheriff Harley and Chris Bannerman had written to the head of the Texas Rangers with a detailed explanation of Egan's involvement in the smuggling on the river and Brendan's role in putting an end to the crimes.

Brendan and Priscilla accompanied the newly-weds down to the docks.

"Jaimie says as soon as Noble gets things worked out at the Triple R we can come for a visit," Rose said.

"We're going to build a house right away,"

Brendan told them. "I want a place big enough for guests." He grinned roguishly. "And of course we'll be needing a nursery."

Rose's big dark eyes went wide. "You're going to have a baby?"

Priscilla's face flushed crimson. "Not that I know of. But we hope to in the future."

"Just think," Rose said, "someday I'll be an aunt."

"You've been wonderful, Rose," Priscilla put in. "If it hadn't been for you and Jaimie—"

"If it hadn't been for you," Jaimie said, "Rose and I never would have met."

The steam whistle blew, the girls embraced, and the men shook hands. Priscilla watched with teary eyes as Jaimie and her sister walked hand in hand up the gangway.

"Come on, baby." Brendan slid an arm around her waist. "We'd better get going." He tipped a glance back over his shoulder, surveying the dock and the myriad people who swarmed along the quay.

The feeling was back with a vengeance. Someone was following them—Brendan was almost sure.

"How many times have you been to New Orleans?" Priscilla asked. They were standing at the window of their hotel room, an intimate little inn in the French Quarter with delicate rosewood furniture and a view of the Cabildo, the old Spanish statehouse.

"I was here for several weeks with the military in eighteen forty, a couple of times before that, and maybe a couple of times since."

"This is my third trip here, and I've yet to see more

than a few city blocks. How about showing me around?"

He seemed a little bit hesitant. "I was kinda hoping you'd stay here while I ran a couple of errands."

She laced her arms around his neck. "This is our honeymoon. You're supposed to ply me with attention."

Brendan arched a brow. "And I haven't been? I believe, Mrs. Trask, you've received about all the attention you can handle."

She flushed at that. "That's not what I meant and you know it."

"All right. I'll run my errands while you get dressed. When I get back we'll see some of the city, then have lunch at Café St. Marie. It's a quaint little French bistro down on Chartres Street."

"That sounds wonderful."

He kissed her until she clutched his shoulders, then he grinned and backed away. "Just so you won't forget me while I'm gone."

How could she ever forget him? In the days since their wedding, her love for him had mushroomed tenfold. She knew it was because she finally felt able to trust him, to know without doubt he was there for her, and that she belonged to him.

"I couldn't forget you in the next hundred years."

Brendan's look turned serious. "I hope not." His lips brushed hers gently, then firmly. "Lock the door when I go out. I'll be back as quick as I can."

"Where are you going?" she started to ask, but he was out the door before she got the chance.

Still, true to his word, he wasn't gone long.

"I had some ranch business to take care of," he

told her on his return. "I want everything in order when we get there."

That afternoon he took her shopping, walking at her side down the streets of the Vieux Carré, then he hired a carriage and had the driver take them along the river. Afterward they lunched at Café St. Marie as he promised.

"You're going to love our place, Priscilla. It sits right down on the river. And there's a perfect little spot up on a knoll for us to build a house." He talked about the future, and Priscilla found herself looking forward to the challenge of forging a life from their own piece of land.

"We'll build the place strong and solid," he said, "with an eye to adding on as our family expands." He smiled at her softly. "I'd like to name one of the boys after Chris, if that would be all right with you."

Priscilla's heart expanded. "I never dreamed I could be so happy."

"I won't lie to you, Silla. It isn't going to be easy. There'll be dangers to face, sickness, hardships . . . but every family faces those kinds of things. It'll be tough going at first, but we'll have each other. The land is rich, and with time and effort, we can build ourselves a future we'll be proud of."

"I'm not afraid any more. I know we can do it. As long as you're with me, I can do anything."

Brendan took her hand. "I love you, Sill."

And because he did, he was worried. He hadn't uncovered any clues as to who might be out there, but he felt certain someone was. Damn, he just knew things were going too well.

Chapter 23

 Brendan brushed sleep-tangled hair from Priscilla's cheek, leaned over, and kissed her. She stirred on the deep feather mattress and opened her eyes.

"Go back to sleep," he urged softly. "You didn't get much rest last night."

"Neither did you," she whispered, blushing faintly, her voice still thick with sleep. "Where are you going so early?"

"I've got a few loose ends to tie up before we leave, and I need to go down to the dock and pick up our steamship tickets."

They'd be leaving for Savannah first thing tomorrow morning aboard the *H. J. Lawrence*. "Why don't I go with you?" She stretched and yawned and started to sit up, but Brendan pressed her back down.

"Why don't you stay here and wait for me?" His hungry look warmed her, heated her blood as it always did. "I won't be gone long. I'll lock the door when I leave."

It did feel good to snuggle underneath the fluffy down comforter. It was October-brisk outside, the mornings cool and clear. "I'll wait, if you promise to hurry."

Brendan traced a long brown finger along her shoulder, used it to ease the blanket away, then the strap of her sheer silk nightgown, a present he had bought her in the French Quarter just yesterday. He ringed her nipple, making it grow hard and distended.

"You can count on that," he said with a lazy grin.

Walking to the tiny fireplace against the wall, he stirred the coals to life and added another small log. The fire blazed cheerily, and Priscilla sank lower beneath the covers.

He walked to her bedside. "Pleasant dreams," he said with a last brief kiss, and then he was gone.

As the room slowly warmed, Priscilla drifted into a pleasant state of drowsiness. This was her honeymoon, after all. She deserved to pamper herself. In minutes she slept soundly, immersed in images of her wedding, of Brendan, and the warm, loving nights they had shared.

In her dream-state she imagined the feel of his hands on her body, of him lowering the strap of her sheer silk nightgown. She could almost feel the brush of his fingers, his hand splaying over her stomach, the roughness of his thumb against her nipple.

Priscilla stirred, the dream growing stronger, the sensations becoming more real. His hand cupped her breast, lifted it, molded it, his fingers moving over her skin. The pressure became less gentle, more urgent, less a caress than a squeeze. There was a roughness in his movements that hadn't been there before, and in her mind the dream altered.

It was no longer Brendan but Stuart who bent over her, his hands skimming her flesh. It was Stuart not Brendan who lifted her breasts and stroked her skin, Stuart's impatient urgings that pulled the covers to her waist, slipped the gown from her shoulders and bent to cover her nipple with his mouth.

Priscilla tried to rouse herself, wishing she could awaken from the dream that had somehow turned ugly. Her fingers slipped into his hair. She tried to tug his head away, tried to end his hurtful kneading. She began to thrash on the bed, willing herself to awaken. It's only a dream—a nightmare—she told herself firmly. Oh, but it seemed so real!

Priscilla whimpered as Stuart's hand gripped her chin and his mouth came down hard over hers. She tasted whiskey and tobacco, and the metallic taste of her own blood.

Priscilla's eyes snapped open.

Her heart thundered wildly as she tried to pull away, but her hands were pinned against his chest.

Dear God, this can't be real!

But it was.

With an effort born of terror, she wrenched away from his mouth and tried to jerk free.

For the first time, she saw him, and her eyes went wide. "Harding!" she breathed.

His mouth twisted up in what might have been a smile, but his eyes, black as midnight, looked as cold as she remembered.

"Expecting your husband, were you? Well, you can forget it. The bastard's as dead as you both thought I was."

"You're lying!" She tried to break loose, but he held her wrists and squeezed until she flinched. "I don't believe you."

"I don't give a damn what you believe, you little

whore. Nobody shoots Mace Harding and lives to tell about it."

"Get away from me!" She tossed her head, bucked and struggled, trying to work her legs free of the confining blanket.

Harding yanked it back for her. Her nightgown rode at her hips, nearly exposing her and baring her long slender legs.

"Nice," he said. "No wonder the boss fell so hard."

"That just shows what a fool you are. Stuart never loved anyone but himself." She had to stall for time, find something she could use as a weapon.

"Egan was the fool. He let himself get tangled up with you and look what it got him. Nothing but a watery grave. I intend to take my pleasure and be done with it."

Harding's words unnerved her. Maybe he really had shot Brendan. Why else would he so boldly come into their room?

"How did you get in here?"

His mouth curved into a vicious smile. "Desk clerks are notoriously underpaid."

Priscilla strained against him, and he grunted at the pressure it put on his injured knee. She had shot him there. She wished she had aimed a little higher.

"You'd better behave yourself. You got a lotta paybacks comin'. You can make it hard or easy."

"And you had better start worrying about my husband." She willed her voice not to falter. "He's due back any minute—he'll kill you when he finds out what you've done."

He jerked her wrists above her head and shifted her position on the bed. He pried her legs apart with his good leg, then settled himself between them, his heavy weight pressing her down in the mattress.

"I told you, he's dead. You just resign yourself to giving me a little a' what you been givin' him, and the two of us will get along fine."

Dear Lord, don't let it be true! Deep inside, something told her it wasn't. She took heart from that, willed it to be so, and forced herself under control.

"You know, Mace, you may be right. I'm a practical sort of girl. If what you say is true, then I'm all alone. I could use a man's protection."

Mace drew back warily, his eyes running over her face, down her body, then returning to the peaks of her breasts. She felt a shudder of revulsion but suppressed it.

"I'll give it some thought. You show me you're talking straight, maybe we can do business."

He shifted both of her wrists to his one hand, then his other hand cupped a breast. Priscilla felt the bile rise up in her throat, and such a blinding rage, it nearly overwhelmed her. She worked to control it, seductively wet her lips and lowered her lashes.

"You keep looking at me that way," he said, "things might just work out." As he fumbled with the buttons at the front of his breeches, Mace leaned down and kissed her. Priscilla ignored his foul breath and kissed him back. When Mace let go of her wrists, she slid her arms around his neck.

His breathing increased and so did his frustrations. Fighting to get his pants undone, he cursed and drew back to finish the task.

Priscilla's hand crept forward, inch by inch. She jerked his gun from its holster, thumbed back the hammer, but Harding grabbed her wrist. Priscilla twisted the weapon as far as she could and fired. The shot went wild, missing him completely. Harding jerked it from her fingers, shoved it back in his holster, and slapped her hard across the face.

"You little bitch."

Priscilla cried out as he wrenched her arms behind her back and pain shot through her body.

"Get off her, Harding." Brendan's voice, as cold as a Texas frost, cut through the room. "Let go of her—now."

Harding spun toward the voice that dripped with icy rage. "You bastard, I killed you!"

Straining to look over Mace's shoulder, Priscilla could barely see him, but she didn't miss the patch of red that blossomed on his shirt.

"I thought it was Egan," Brendan said. "If I'd known it was you, you wouldn't have even come close. Now back away, before I pull this trigger."

Mace eased himself off Priscilla, and she drew her nightgown back into place with a trembling hand.

"Step clear of her."

"I'm not hangin'," Mace said. "One of us is goin' down—I'm bettin' it's you." Mace jerked his gun. Brendan fired, Mace fired, and Priscilla screamed. Black eyes wild with disbelief, his chest erupting with blood, Mace turned and slowly sank down to the floor. The gun clattered to the ground beside him, and Brendan kicked it away. Mace's body twitched once before his eyes slid closed and he lay dead.

"Brendan!" Priscilla scrambled off the bed and raced across the room into his arms. He tightened them protectively around her.

"H-how bad are you hurt?" She pulled away to look at him, a knot of worry in her chest.

"Shoulder wound. I've survived a whole lot worse."

"He said you were dead. He said—"

"I heard what he said. I also saw what *you* did. God, Priscilla, you are really something." There was such pride in his eyes, Priscilla blinked back a well of tears.

A loud rap sounded at the door, and Brendan walked over and pulled it open. The hotel manager stood in the hallway.

"I thought I heard shooting," the little man said. "What's going on?"

You'd better call a constable," Brendan told him. The man peered into the room and saw Mace Harding's body covered in blood. Behind his spectacles, his face grew pale. He turned and ran for the stairs.

"We'd better get you to a doctor," Priscilla said.

Brendan nodded. "It isn't as bad as it looks. The bullet went all the way through. I'll be fine by the time we reach Savannah."

With hands a little unsteady, Priscilla wrapped a linen towel around his shoulder to slow the bleeding, and they made their way down the stairs to the tiny hotel lobby.

"At least this time it's really over," Priscilla said.

"I knew we were being followed. I was trying to catch the bastard. I didn't want you to worry."

He waved down a hansom cab, and Priscilla helped him climb in. "The next time something like this happens," she scolded, "you had damned well better tell me."

"Damned?" Brendan repeated, incredulous.

Priscilla flushed. "Well, you'd better."

"What a bossy little wife you've become." But his look was warm on her face. "I'm sorry he put you through that. I wish I'd gotten there sooner."

"You got there soon enough," she said softly. "That's all that counts."

That night they lay in a canopied bed in another small hotel room down the hall. A fire crackled pleasantly in the fireplace, and Priscilla nestled in the crook of Brendan's arm. He'd been sleeping off and on, the effects of a dose of laudanum the doctor had ordered. As Brendan had predicted, the wound looked worse than it really was, but the doctor had insisted he rest.

The constable had come to the hotel to see them, but since Brendan had paid him a visit several days earlier, explaining what happened in Natchez, and voicing his suspicions, the matter of Mace Harding's death didn't take long to clear up. Afterward Priscilla had firmly ordered him to bed.

Now he stirred, and his light blue eyes came open. When he saw Priscilla watching him, an easy smile lifted one corner of his mouth.

"What's the matter, sweetness, can't sleep?" He ran a finger along her jaw.

He was so handsome, so totally and utterly male. Her eyes strayed to the dark brown hair on his chest, the bands of muscle across it, the shadowy indentations beneath his ribs. She wanted to reach out and touch him, to show him how much she cared.

"I was just worried about you."

He grinned. "I'm fine. Well . . . almost fine. Actually, I'm feeling kind of hungry."

"Would you like me to go down and get you something from the kitchen?"

"No."

"It wouldn't be any trouble. It'll just take a minute for me to get dressed." She started to get up, but Brendan pulled her back down. "What on earth are you doing? You've got to be careful of your shoulder."

"You're right, baby, I've got to get plenty of rest, but I can't seem to fall asleep."

"What's the matter?"

He took her hand, drew it along his chest, down his flat stomach until she touched his hardened arousal.

Priscilla sucked in a breath. "You are without doubt the most—"

"Tell me that has nothing to do with what you were thinking."

How could she deny it? "But your shoulder—we can't just . . . just . . . "

"Just what, Silla?" There was a roughness to his voice she knew only too well. "What is it we can't do?"

She swallowed hard, trying to ignore her pounding heart. "We can't make love."

With a sigh of resignation, he thrust his hands behind his head. "I suppose you're right. I'm far too weak. I'll just have to suffer. Of course I won't be able to sleep, so I'll probably feel worse in the morning. Too weak to make love, so I'll get no rest, and I'll feel worse, and then—"

Priscilla's laughter cut him off. "Well, I suppose . . . if you promised not to overdo things . . . I could just sort of—" Priscilla leaned over and kissed him.

"What a lusty little wench you are," he teased against her ear as he moved to lift her astride him.

"I love you, Sill," he said, surprising her.

"I love you, too, Bren."

Content as she had once only dreamed, she let him work his magic.

Epilogue

Brazos River, Texas
April 3, 1852

"I'll get the kids in the wagon. You about ready?"

Clutching to her breast the bright yellow wildflowers she had gathered just that morning, Priscilla glanced up at her handsome husband.

"I'll just be a minute. I picked these for Chris. They used to be his favorite."

He nodded solemnly. They were driving into Waco, going to church as they did at least once each month. It was a goodly distance, but they played games and picnicked along the way, and in Waco picked up letters from family and friends. Last time Rose and Jaimie had written of the new addition to their family, a little red-haired boy, and Silver and Morgan had mentioned an upcoming visit.

"Tell the children not to get impatient," Priscilla said, "this won't take long."

"Want me to go with you?" Brendan asked, his blue eyes filled with compassion, lending her his strength.

"No. I'll be fine." She touched his cheek with the palm of her hand. "I kind of like going alone."

He understood, as always. "Take all the time you need."

She nodded and turned away, walking out toward the huge old oak that shaded the grassy knoll down by the river. The Brazos rolled by, lazy this time of year, though it could run in torrents in the winter.

She picked up her simple brown calico skirts and made her way along the path beside the garden. Squash, melon, corn, beans—all of it grew in abundance from the rich black soil that belonged to them. In the distance, spring cotton had been planted, and cattle grazed contentedly on the range that ran for miles in several directions.

Her gaze swung up to the knoll. A gentle breeze blew the soft grass that covered the small mound marked by a carved chunk of granite. Approaching silently, reverently, she sank down on the grass and touched the cold gray stone with loving hands.

> Christopher Thomas Trask
> Born December 15, 1848
> Died January 8, 1850
> Loved by his parents.
> Now in God's loving hands.

Ignoring the tightness in her chest, she traced the words chiseled into the hard rock surface and laid the flowers atop the tiny grave. More than two years had passed, but still she ached for him. She guessed she always would.

She reached down and plucked a weed that seemed to have sprung up overnight. Chris had died of a fever that had ravaged the country, but God had been merciful and none of the others had fallen sick. With Brendan's tireless help, she had tended the child for hours, sitting by his bedside, willing him to live.

With a wisdom few mortals understand and certainly not Priscilla, God had chosen to take him.

As she thought of him now, her lips curved up in a bittersweet smile. She had been fortunate to know him, even for a while, yet she wished she could have known him longer. Christopher Thomas, their second son, had been the image of his handsome father, but then, so were they all.

Priscilla stood up from the grave and brushed the dirt from her palms. Once the thought of losing a beloved child had nearly cost her her happiness. She had run from the only man she had ever loved.

Her gaze swung back toward the house, a big rambling structure he had built for her, just as he had conquered his land. She saw him standing beside the wagon, next to their firstborn son, the child she had given him the summer after their wedding. A beautiful boy they had named Morgan.

Already he looked like Brendan, carrying himself tall and proud. He held his little sister Sarah's hand, ever watchful of her, waiting patiently for his mother's return.

Her heart constricted just to look at them, the family she loved so much. She had lost a child, as crushing a blow as any she could have imagined. But she had gained a gift more precious than any she could have dreamed. The love of a husband and family.

They had given her the strength she needed.

Just as Brendan had said, they'd shared hardships —devastating ones—but they had also shared a joy so profound that words could never describe it.

She left the grave and walked along the path back toward the wagon.

Brendan's eyes found hers as she approached. "All right?"

She smiled softly. "As long as I have you and the children, I'll always be all right."

Brendan pulled her into his arms, and his cheek felt warm and solid against her own. "We've got lots to look forward to, Silla, years of happiness ahead of us."

She nodded into his shoulder, knowing it was the truth.

"Let's go, Papa," Morgan said. "We're gonna be late."

"Just like his mama," Brendan said. "Always steady and reliable."

"Just like his father," Priscilla teased. "Sinfully handsome and utterly charming. He's probably planning a rendezvous with one of the little Porter girls."

They both laughed at that and climbed aboard the wagon. The sun warmed the prairie, and wildflowers of every color dotted the landscape.

"It's just as beautiful as you said it would be." Priscilla smiled softly. She had fallen in love with the rough Texas landscape, the freedom and open space, the animals and birds. The courageous frontier people.

"That's because you've made this land your home," he said gently.

Priscilla knew that she had.